The Master of the Forge

Also by Harold Courlander

Novels and Novellas
The African
The Mesa of Flowers
The Big Old World of Richard Creeks
The Son of the Leopard
The Caballero

Nonfiction
A Treasury of African Folklore
A Treasury of Afro-American Folklore
Tales of Yoruba Gods and Heroes
The Heart of the Ngoni, Heroes of the African Kingdom of
      Segu (with Ousmane Sako)
The Drum and the Hoe, Life and Lore of the Haitian People
Negro Folk Music, U.S.A.
Haiti Singing
Big Falling Snow (with Albert Yava)
Hopi Voices: Recollections, Traditions and Narratives of the
      Hopi Indians
Negro Songs from Alabama
The Fourth World of the Hopis

Folklore and Folk Tales
The Hat-Shaking Dance and Other Ashanti Tales from Ghana
Olode the Hunter and Other Tales from Nigeria
The King's Drum and Other African Stories
The Crest and the Hide and Other African Stories of Heroes,
      Chiefs, Bards, Hunters, Sorcerers and Common People
The Cow-Tail Switch and Other West African Stories (with
      George Herzog)
The Fire on the Mountain and Other Ethiopian Stories (with
      Wolf Leslau)
People of the Short Blue Corn: Tales and Legends of the Hopi
      Indians
The Tiger's Whisker and Other Tales from Asia and the Pacific
Terrapin's Pot of Sense
The Piece of Fire and Other Haitian Tales
Kantchil's Lime Pit and Other Stories from Indonesia
Uncle Bouqui of Haiti
Ride with the Sun

The Master of the Forge

of the Forge

A West African Odyssey

HAROLD COURLANDER

MARLOWE & COMPANY
NEW YORK

First Marlowe Edition

Published by
Marlowe & Company
632 Broadway, Seventh Floor
New York, NY 10012
http://www.marlowepub.com

Library of Congress Catalog Card Number: 96-78329

ISBN 1-56924-789-7

Manufatured in the United States of America

To the Reader

THROUGHOUT THE WESTERN SUDAN, IN THE lands of the Malinke, the Bambara, the Manding, the Fula and other peoples, bard-historians known as djeli preserve and recite stories of important families and epic heroes. Some of the accounts go back to the time when the great Empire of Mali was still flourishing, some speak of the Empire of Ghana, and some are of more ancient days when history and legend were virtually inseparable.

The djeli refer in their songs to memorable battles, wars between city-states, the accomplishments of warriors, acts of generosity and chivalry, and a seemingly endless pursuit of honor. Chivalry and fate are vibrant threads out of which the narratives are woven, as are questions about the natural and supernatural worlds and about man's place in the scheme of the universe.

Though its themes are familiar to them, this story about Numukeba, the iron forger of Naradugu, is not in the repertoire of the Sudanic bards. It is an epic drawing on the cultural traditions of West Africans during those days, several hundred years ago, when the Bambara had their own kingdoms along the western bend of the Niger River, which they called Joliba. It draws its substance not only from their way of life, but also from the questions that occupied their minds, such as the eternal conflict between fate and accident.

When I began to write Numukeba's story, he soon took form almost without regard for my intention to define him and plot his course, seeming to know better than I the nature of his epic journey. Perhaps that was because he is a kind of epitome of the Sudanic heroes of his times. As he went out to confront the destiny that had been written for him in golden ink, I felt more spectator than creator, and I followed and became his chronicler. It might be said that I became the djeli of Numukeba of Naradugu.

Harold Courlander

For three friends:
Virginia, Roger, Mary

The Master of the Forge

I

The Cow
of Heroes

NUMUKEBA, THE BLACKSMITH, FORGED AT HIS forge, completing the last iron link for his vest of chain mail. He heated it to a white glow and tempered it in millet water. When it was done he fastened it in place and hung the vest over his shoulders testing its fit. His slave said to him, "Master, the armor becomes you." Numukeba answered, "Iron does not turn away weapons because it 'becomes,' but because it contains the life force of the sun." And the slave answered, "Yes, Master, it is so."

Numukeba removed the armored vest and handed it to his slave. He said, "Now I will eat, now I will sleep. When the dawn comes, have my horse ready. I will go to the place where the brave men of Naradugu share the Cow of Heroes." His wife, Baniaba, brought him a calabash of water so that he could wash. After that she brought him a dinner of cooked millet and goat meat. While he ate he spoke to Baniaba, saying, "Tomorrow I will share the Cow of Heroes," and she answered, "My husband, how will you do it? The Cow of Heroes is only for the bravest among nobles, not the bravest among blacksmiths."

Numukeba said, "My wife, there are only two kinds of men, those who were born slave and those who were born free. I was not born a slave. I am free to claim my portion of the cow." His wife answered, "My husband, I am only a woman, not a man. Yet my father was a man, my brothers were men, and my husband is a man, so I know something about how it is in the world of men. It is true that you were not born a slave. But it is also true that you were not born a noble, and only nobles may share the Cow of Heroes."

Numukeba said, "My wife, listen. A young noble comes to me, saying, 'Great Blacksmith, I am going on an expedition against such and such a town. Forge spirit into my sword for me so that it will cut through the toughest leather. Put the life force of the sun into my spearpoint so that it will pierce iron mail. Give my gun the power to propel my bullet mightily, and give my bullet irresistible flight. Give me these things and I will be an invincible hero against the enemy.' I say to him, 'Yes, bring me three kolas, bring me a chicken, bring me a gourdful of cowries. I will do what you ask, because that is the art of the blacksmith.' He brings me what I ask. I give his weapons force. He goes to battle. He is victorious over his enemies. He returns. He says, 'Now I am a hero. I claim a share of the Cow of Heroes.' But is it he who has defeated the enemy? Or is it the fiery forces that I forged into his weapons? Without the blacksmith no man would have a spear, a knife or a gun. He would be as helpless as a child. I have thought about these things, and now I will go to the terrace where the heroes gather."

Numukeba slept. When the dawn came, he arose. His wife gave him bassi to eat. He dressed and put his leather-covered amulets and talismans on his arms. He put on his vest of mail and hung his cutlass across his chest. His slave brought his horse for him to mount. The horse wore a leather breast protector and many beautiful trappings. Strips of red and blue cloth were woven into its mane and tail, and tinkling brass bells hung from the saddle. Numukeba placed his sandaled foot in the iron stirrup and mounted. His slave gave him his gun, which he slung over his shoulder, and he took his spear in his right hand. He said to his wife, "If you see me again on my horse I will be alive. If I am not on my horse, the light will have faded for me."

Numukeba rode away, his slave following on foot. Numukeba rode into the center of Naradugu and passed through the streets. When the people saw him they said, "Aaah! Something is happening today!" Numukeba came to the terrace where the great heroes gathered every fifth day of the week. The heroes were already there, some on their horses, some sitting on the ground. When they saw Numukeba they said to one another, "Why is the blacksmith here?" But they did not address him directly. He sat silently in his saddle. At last one of the heroes said to Numukeba, "Blacksmith, why are you on the terrace of heroes? There is no forging to be done here." He said, "I have come for the thing for which I have come." The heroes became uneasy. They turned away and ignored him, sipping at their millet beer and recalling heroic achievements.

Slaves came leading the Cow of Heroes. They slaughtered it

and cut it into portions. And after a while the heroes began to claim their portions. The right foreleg was claimed by one, the head by another, the neck by another. Numukeba spoke, saying, "Wait. You ask me why I have come. I have come for my portion." The heroes laughed. They said, "What are you saying? Yesterday you were a blacksmith. Did you become a noble overnight? You should not even be here at the terrace of heroes, but we did not make an issue of it. Now you have allowed yourself to go too far. Return to your forge and do not intrude on us any more."

Numukeba said, "You valiant fighters of Naradugu, I did not come to intrude, only to receive my share of the Cow of Heroes. Give it to me peaceably and I will go away." They said to him angrily, "Blacksmith, how can you claim a portion of the cow? Was your father a noble? Was your grandfather a noble? Did you ever achieve valor against the enemy? Have you ever conquered a town or brought back the head of a king? No, my friend, your tree is a tree of blacksmiths. You fare well because we are liberal with cowries for your work. But do not dream impossible dreams. Go home and put away your weapons and your vest of iron. When we need your services we will come to your forge."

Numukeba said from where he sat in his saddle, "You heroes are indeed valiant fighters, and indeed you have brought back the heads of kings. But let us consider things. Do you go into battle without a cutlass or a spear? Do you go to fight without a gun or powder? No, you come to me, saying, 'Great Blacksmith, make for me a cutlass with the power to cut through armor at a single stroke. Make for me a spear that can penetrate five men at a single throw. Make bullets for me that can overpower the amulets of the enemy.' I give you these things. You go to war. You fight, you conquer. But who are you when you are on the battlefield? Are you men who perform miraculous deeds? Or are you merely men who carry weapons, talismans and amulets that perform miraculous deeds? As your horses are beasts of burden that carry you on your expeditions, perhaps you are men of burden who carry the mystic weaponry of my forge. Is it you who deserve the honors? Or is it the weapons into which I have infused the force of the sun and the universe? Let us not argue this thing too long. Acknowledge my right to a portion of the meat and I will go away."

One of the heroes, named Nkassa, he who was foremost among them and therefore claimed the breast of the cow, stood up angrily, saying, "Who are you, a blacksmith, to question our valor? Your impudence is beyond belief. Turn at once and go to the place you came from." Numukeba answered, "Only when I have taken my portion." Nkassa drew his cutlass and approached him. Numukeba dismounted and drew his cutlass. He said, "You, Nkassa, challenge my right with your weapon. Therefore, strike the first blow." Nkassa struck, but Numukeba's amulets and armored vest protected him from harm. Nkassa struck three times, but his cutlass could not penetrate Numukeba's skin. Numukeba said, "Try your gun." Nkassa picked up his gun, aimed and fired, but the powder fizzled and the bullet rolled from the barrel. He tried three times, and each time it was the same.

Numukeba said, "Now it is my turn. Stand like a hero and take my blows." He pressed his spear into the earth and left it standing there. He put aside the gun from his back. He took up his magic garan, the leather rope used for hobbling horses. The links of metal that covered his chest glistened in the sunlight. The heroes saw luminescence around each of the talismans on his arms. Numukeba struck Nkassa with the garan, and Nkassa fell to the earth as if he had felt the weight of a heavy iron bar. Nkassa arose, and again Numukeba felled him with the garan. Once more Nkassa arose, and when Numukeba felled him a third time he did not arise again.

Numukeba said, "If there are others who contest my right to a portion of the Cow of Heroes, tell me now." No one answered. Numukeba put away his garan. He took up his gun and spear and mounted his horse. He said, "My portion will be the heart of the cow, for the blacksmith is the heart of everything." They said, "Yes, take the heart." Numukeba said to his slave, "Take it." The slave took the heart and departed. Numukeba said, "He who understands the mysteries of iron is the greatest of heroes. Henceforth, do not say to a blacksmith, 'Why are you here?' Give him the heart of the cow." He turned his horse and rode away, passing once more through the streets of Naradugu. The people crowded to one side to make a path for him. He arrived at his house. His wife was at the gate to greet him. He said, "You see me again on my horse, therefore I am alive."

He went into his house, put down his weapons and took off the vest of mail, saying, "Now the kolas have been cast. The heroes will not leave it where it is." He went to his forge and shaped iron. The sunlight was a rain of force from the sky, and he drew it together in his mind and infused it into his glowing metal. When the hoe was shaped it had within it the living spirit of iron. When the spearpoint was shaped it had within it the living spirit of iron. And when he made the handle for the hoe and the shaft for the spear they had within them the invisible fluid that made trees emerge from dry earth where no trees had grown before.

In the late afternoon when the sun was sliding toward its place of rest, Numukeba saw the twelve heroes of Naradugu coming on their horses. The heroes wore their cutlasses across their chests and their guns on their backs, and held their spears upright pointing toward the sky. They arrived at the place of the forge. They saw Numukeba standing in the red afternoon light, his beard dusted with grey and his face smeared with charcoal. Numukeba said to them, "Welcome," and they replied, "We bring you good will." Numukeba said, "Dismount and refresh yourselves." They answered, "Thank you, but we will defer it." Numukeba asked, "Why then are you here?"

One of the men said, "This morning you defiled the heroes' terrace. You took the heart of the cow, claiming that you are the heart of Naradugu. You killed Nkassa not with your iron weapons but with a rope meant for hobbling horses. You demeaned what is noble and called our valor into question. We cannot leave it where it is." Numukeba said, "That is good. You speak like a blacksmith who understands that work must be brought to a conclusion. He digs ore from the earth, but that is not the end. He smelts it in his furnace, but that is not the end. He forges it, but that is not the end. He shapes it into a blade, but that is not yet the end. The end is only when the blade cuts down the enemy." They said to him again, "We cannot leave it where it is. Otherwise it would be said that the heroes of Naradugu are women."

Numukeba said, "I hear you. How is it to be done?" One of them replied, "The heroes in our group have fought side by side. We are equal. Choose any one of us. Give your challenge. He who does not die will live. Whatever the outcome, there the matter will rest." Numukeba pondered. He said, "I agree. But how can I choose among so many? Let each of you insult me, and whoever speaks the worst insult, him I will fight." So each of the heroes in turn insulted Numukeba.

The first said, "Your smell offends all men. When you walk through the streets the women have to close the doors of their houses. You are dirty and do not know how to bathe. You defecate on your sleeping mat."

The second said, "You are not the son of your father. Your mother availed herself of any man, and he who planted your seed is not known."

The third said, "You are a slave in disguise and ugly beyond description. Your beard is made of goat's hair. Only the hyena compares with you."

The fourth said, "You are only a woman in man's clothing. You do not defend the city with other men. You do not go out to raid for cattle with other men. You do not go with other men to punish towns and cities. You hide behind your forge hammering metal bars."

Each of them insulted Numukeba. And when the turn of Nkala, the twelfth man, came, he said, "Numukeba, you have no substance. Wherever you walk, you leave no footprints. When the sun shines on you, you cast no shadow. If you were to fall into an animal pit, a child could lift you out with one finger. If you were in the bush, a hungry lion would pass you by and chase a rodent.

Without the cowries men give you in charity, you would be living in a hovel and your family would have nothing but rags to wear. The points of your spears are soft, they do not have the spirit to pierce anything. The fluid of life you claim to fuse into your iron is only urine. The weapons you make have no heart within them. When you beat the hot iron it laughs."

Numukeba said, "You, Nkala the Eloquent, I choose you. Let us meet outside the city gate tomorrow as the sun comes up." Nkala said, "I agree," and the twelve heroes rode back to their place on the terrace. There they drank millet beer and boasted of their accomplishments.

When the cocks crowed, signalling that the sun would soon rise from its sleeping mat in the east, the heroes mounted their horses and rode outside the city, and after the last one passed through the wall, the city guards closed and bolted the gate. The people of Naradugu climbed to the roofs of their houses to see the battle between Numukeba and Nkala.

Numukeba was already in position, sitting astride his horse on a high knoll. His vest of mail was obscured by a hundred and one leather-covered talismans. Fastened around his upper arms were more talismans, and a necklace of mirrors and bells hung around his neck. A cloth of banded red and blue bound his chin and hung down his back. Shining brass serpents spiralled around his forearms. The sun rose fiery red behind Numukeba's back and transformed him into a tall, shimmering evanescence.

When the heroes saw him they said, "Surely this is not an ordinary man who sits there." Now, Nkala was a great and valorous fighter who had ridden against the Fula, the Manding and the Soninke. Wherever the battles had been most fierce, there he had been, in the vortex of the fighting. His defeated enemies had carpeted the earth around him. Yet when Nkala looked at the blacksmith it seemed as if Numukeba were floating in the air, and as if red light were emanating from his body. For the first time in his life Nkala felt himself in the presence of his own death. And he had to remind himself that valor was to be found not in killing but in dying.

So he rode toward the knoll, calling out, "You, Numukeba, the overnight noble, do not sit there like a housepost with its foot in the ground. You who claim to be the sharp edge of all weapon blades and the soul of every hero's achievements, come forward now and prepare to die. Your impudence is great, but because you demand the right to be tested I will fight you."

Numukeba rode down slowly from the knoll, and it could be seen that there was no spear in his hand, no cutlass on his chest, and no gun behind his back. He halted facing Nkala and said, "You, Nkala, have earned much honor. We are here only because your honor told you you must provoke me with insults, and because my honor forced me to reply with a challenge. Before we fight, let us think about the meaning of honor. Honor makes orphans and widows. Honor cuts down the city's defenders. When we have fought and one of us has died, there will remain behind a riderless horse whose tail is braided with red and blue cloth. Your children will look at your horse and say, 'Here is our father's honor.' But a horse is mortal. It has a short life. When the horse dies, what then remains of honor? Perhaps honor will survive in a praise song sung by a bard. The song will say, 'Nkala did this,' or 'Numukeba did that,' but when the bard dies, Nkala and Numukeba will be forgotten. Let us fight to protect our families. Let us fight to protect Naradugu. Let us fight to defend our wells. Let us fight to preserve our fields. In this way Naradugu will live in the minds of men. But let us not struggle to the death over honor. Instead, let us each go his own way."

Nkala said, "Blacksmith, it was you who came and took the heart of the cow, saying, 'I am the source of everything.' It is a hero's right to boast. If he says, 'I did this, I did that,' it is acceptable unless he lies. But if he says to someone else, 'I am the author of your achievement,' or proclaims himself the living spirit in the steel of the other man's sword, then he is saying that the other man is nothing. You say, 'Let us each go his own way.' Yet on the terrace you said, 'The heart belongs to me.' Perhaps we did not hear your true words. Tell us again in the Bambara way so that we may believe it. Say to us three times what you meant to say." And Numukeba answered, "The heart is mine. The heart is mine. The heart is mine."

Nkala said, "We have all heard it. Now prepare to defend yourself. Whoever wins shall take the other's head and throw it over the city wall." Numukeba answered, "Let it be that way. Let it also be that whoever wins shall leave Naradugu and go from one place to another proving his worth. After four years have passed he may return and speak of his accomplishments." Nkala said, "Yes, I agree. Pick up your gun, your spear and your cutlass." Numukeba replied, "Spear, gun and cutlass, I do not need them. I myself am the weapon. I am my own talisman. I am my own amulet. The garan with which I hobble my horse is sufficient, for through it passes the strength of iron and fire that is stored in the forge."

Nkala took the gun from his back, charged it with powder and placed his bullet in the barrel. He aimed it and fired. The bullet sped toward Numukeba, but the blacksmith waved his garan and the bullet passed him by. Twice more Nkala charged and fired his gun, and twice more Numukeba turned the bullet aside with his garan. Nkala rode closer and thrust a mighty thrust with his spear, but Numukeba's garan bent the point and splintered the shaft. The two men dismounted and stood face to face. Nkala drew the cutlass from the scabbard on his chest and struck a fierce blow, but it was turned away by the amulets covering Numukeba's body. Then Numukeba struck Nkala three times with his garan, and Nkala lay lifeless on the ground. Numukeba took the cutlass from Nkala's hand and severed the head from the body. He mounted, rode slowly to the wall of Naradugu and threw the head into the town. After that he returned to his home and his forge.

The next morning Numukeba arose at dawn. His wife gave him bassi and goat's milk to eat. When he was finished he said, "Now I am leaving, because it was agreed that the winner of the fight between Nkala and me must go away for four years. This will prevent more killing of young men and the weakening of Naradugu. My fields are fertile and I have many cattle. In the covered calabash by my sleeping mat are cowries. If they are used up, there is gold dust buried beneath my floor. If the gold is used up, sell crops from the fields. You need not be short of anything. Let my two sons grow into manhood at the forge. They will learn the art of shaping metal, and from the heat of annealing iron they will absorb the strength given by the warmth of the sun. On the last day of the fourth year, stand on the roof of the house and look toward the bush. He whom you see coming will be alive. He whom you do not see coming will be dead."

He went out and mounted his horse. His slave handed him the cutlass to hang across his chest, the gun for his back and the spear for his hand. The slave mounted his donkey. Then Numukeba went out of Naradugu, his slave riding behind. His wife went to the rooftop. She saw him moving into the bush. He became smaller to her eyes. He disappeared.

2
Malike of
Massina

NUMUKEBA RODE MANY DAYS, KNOWING ONLY
the companionship of his slave, Malike. One
night at the fire the slave said, "Master, why am I your slave?"
And Numukeba answered, "Why, because that is the story
within you. It was written in golden ink by the Architect." Malike asked, "Master, where is the writing? I would like to see it."
Numukeba replied, "Where it is written is a mystery, yet it is
your story, just as it is my story to be Numukeba of Naradugu."

The slave pondered, then he said, "Master, perhaps what is
called destiny is not written anywhere. Perhaps it merely de-
scribes what happens. When you bought me as a slave I said to
myself, 'I was a noble, but because I was captured in war I was
sold to you and became your servant. But am I not the same person who was born to my mother?' When the diviner read my future he did not tell my father, 'Your son, Malike, will be a slave to
a blacksmith.' He said, 'Your son will grow strong and prosper.'"
Numukeba said, "Aaah, perhaps he read the divining seeds
wrong."

Malike answered, "What you say must be true, because you are
the master and I am the slave. The story written into a man by
the Architect is as strong as the steel of your cutlass. May I hold it
for a moment?" Numukeba said, "Yes, surely, Malike, hold my
cutlass." Malike took the cutlass from its scabbard and held it
pointing upward. Then with one finger he pressed the blade to
one side and released it. The blade sprang back, vibrating rapidly
from side to side, until at last it came to rest. Malike said, "Master,
let us say that your cutlass is the story written for a man. Yet it is

_____9

not immovable. It points where it points. But another story meets it and causes it to spring one way and another. For a time it does not point in its own true direction, yet in the end it points where it is destined to go. Is it not possible that this is the way with a man's life? Perhaps a man's story is like a river. The river flows its course, but one day there is a landslide and the water cannot pass. It turns and flows into the bush, but in time it returns to the riverbed and goes on as before." Numukeba answered, "Yes, Malike, what you say is true. The story of a river is written in its riverbed."

They slept, they arose, they rode again. And in the evening at the fire once more, Malike resumed his questioning of Numukeba. He said, "Master, does the writing in golden ink deal with the smallest things in life, or only with heroes, battles and catastrophies?" Numukeba answered, "Why, a person's story is his story, and everything in that story is part of the story." Malike said, "Aaah, does the story say, 'Today you will find no game and be hungry'? Does it say 'Tonight when you lie on your mat you will be disturbed by lice'? Does it say, 'Tomorrow the wind from the bush will blow dust in your eyes'? I do not believe the Architect had time for all these writings." Numukeba answered, "My slave, your thoughts come out of a deep well. Perhaps what you say is true."

Malike said, "My master, Great Blacksmith of Naradugu, perhaps it is the same with my story. Its flow was deflected from the riverbed, but surely it will return and follow its course to the end. In Massina I was a noble. My father, my grandfather and all my ancestors back to the beginning performed valiant deeds. They secured water holes for their cattle, built cities, and ruled cities. They governed justly and made the people prosperous. Traders came to my city from Timbuktu. There was peace and I was young. In my family only I had not performed a valorous deed. I thought, 'I will go on a journey and find honor.' I armed myself and went out into the world. I joined a war party going on an expedition against a large army of Fula warriors. I was struck down and taken captive. The Fula sold me as a slave, and he who bought me sold me again. Finally I came to be the slave of Numukeba of Naradugu. You have been a good master. You never struck me with a stick or spoke harshly to me. Yet the story I am living is surely not the story that was written for me. My heart lives with my family and friends in Massina. My story begins there and must end there. That is what my heart tells me." Numukeba answered, "Aaaah, Malike, I hear you."

When morning came again, Numukeba and his slave mounted and continued their journey. They travelled twenty days and on the twentieth day they saw smoke from village fires rising in the distance. Numukeba said, "Wait, let us pause." The slave said,

"Yes, Master." Numukeba said, "Let us exchange clothes." Numukeba dressed himself in the slave's clothes made of hide. Malike put on Numukeba's armored vest and his talismans. Numukeba said, "Take my gun, my spear and my cutlass. Mount my horse." The slave did as he was told, and Numukeba mounted the donkey. Numukeba said, "Ride on ahead. I will follow as your slave." In this manner they approached the village.

Ahead of them they heard a voice. They heard the sound of an ngoni being played. They saw a djeli coming toward them on a black horse. The djeli was singing:

> "From Segu to Kiban
> From Kiban to Badugu
> From Badugu to Kerwani
> From Kerwani to Timbuktu
> There is no hero greater than Famoli.
> Famoli, the lion, named Diara;
> Famoli, the lion, named Waraba;
> Famoli, the lion, named Kunkotiti;
> Famoli, the lion, named Nianga.
> He is the brightest star of morning
> He is the brightest star of evening
> The sun reflects his light
> The moon reflects his light.
> If you are a hero who wants to die,
> Come forward.
> If you are a hero who wants to live,
> Turn away."

Malike said to the djeli, "You are a mouthful of greatness. But I do not see the Famoli whom you praise. I have not called you from the underworld to sing to me. So why are you here?" The djeli replied, "My master, Famoli, waits on the trail. No one may enter the village without fighting him. Therefore, no one enters the village." And Malike said, "Your village, I do not know its name, and it has no interest for me. It is only an insignificant place in the bush. Yet if your master forbids me to enter, I will enter. Let me hear it from his own mouth."

The djeli turned and led them along the trail. And at a bend of the trail Famoli sat waiting on a tall white horse. Malike said to him, "Are you the great Famoli? I thought you would be more fearsome. I thought your face would cause trees to fall and rivers to run uphill." Famoli moved his arms, and the thousand and one talismans that covered his body rustled like leaves in the wind. He said, "You who hides inside the vest of mail, who are you and why do you want to enter my village?" Malike said, "I am Malike of Massina. I did not wish to enter your worthless village, but now I will come in because you wish to prevent me. You, Famoli, what kind of man are you? A true noble would say, 'Stranger, come and rest, come and be fed, come and make conversation.' Therefore, I know you are nothing worth anything."

Famoli answered, "No one enters here without giving himself up as a slave. Throw down your weapons, your cowries and your gold. Give me your horse and its trappings. Give me your meek slave and his donkey. After that you may come and serve me in my house and fields." When Numukeba heard these words, anger seized him. Yet he thought, "This is the affair of Malike. He has put the chaff in his mouth, so it is he who must swallow it."

Malike answered Famoli, "Oh, you shapeless heap of talismans, is it you who is speaking, or is it your horse? If you are a jinn or the son of a jinn I could not care less. I am coming now. Remove yourself from my trail." He placed his right hand on the handle of the cutlass that hung across his chest and went forward. Famoli raised his iron-spiked war club and rode toward him. Malike moved to one side and struck with his cutlass. Though his blade did not touch Famoli's body, it slashed through a hundred talismans that hung on his chest and they fell and scattered on the ground. Famoli struck with his war club, but it did not touch Malike. Twisting and turning, striking back and forth, they stirred up a great cloud of dust. Each time Malike slashed with his cutlass, more talismans fell from Famoli, whose spiked war club was turned aside by the magic force of Numukeba's vest of mail. At last, stripped of talismans, Famoli fell from his horse.

Malike said, "You are finished. Let me hear it from your mouth. Otherwise I will not stop until I have taken your head." Famoli said, "Yes, yes, I acknowledge it." Malike said, "Go back and tell your people that although you once were great, now you are nothing." Famoli said, "Very well. Let me mount my horse." Malike said, "No. Tell your people that although you once were a noble and rode a tall white horse, now you will always go on foot like the humblest of men." Famoli turned and walked toward the village, passing into a dense grove of trees.

Malike said to Numukeba, "I will rest, then we will follow and enter the village." He rested, and after a time he said, "Now let us go." They rode, Malike on the horse, Numukeba behind him on the donkey. And when their trail took them into the grove they saw that Famoli had hanged himself from the limb of a high tree.

In the village they were greeted with enthusiasm by the people, and the chief's djeli sang praise songs for Malike of Massina. They gave him a guest house and feasted him, while Numukeba stayed outside with the slaves. And when the festivities were nearly ended, Malike astonished the chief and his people by saying, "You, djeli who keeps the history and praises heroes, I ask you to compose a new song so that this day will always be remembered. I who conquered Famoli am the slave of Numukeba, who fraternizes outside with the slaves of your village. Bring in my master to sit with you, and I will go outside and take care of my donkey."

They sent for Numukeba, who confirmed what Malike had said. He said to the chief and his counsellors, "What is real and what is not real? Malike put on my vest of mail, took my weapons and mounted my horse. I put on his clothing made of hide, and sat upon his donkey. He became a hero at once, and I became his slave. He said, 'Do this and do that,' and I did it. When he challenged Famoli, Famoli took him to be a great hero. When I heard Malike speak, I did not recognize his voice. When I saw him maneuvering his horse in battle, I did not know him. When he wielded his cutlass, it seemed that he was another man. Because of his generosity of spirit he did not kill Famoli and bring his head to you as a trophy. It was Famoli, the noble hero, who behaved as a slave. He did not say, 'Kill me and take my head.' He said, 'I will go back to the village and tell the people I am nothing.' But he failed to do even that. A man who has lived as a hero needs courage to announce that he has lost his honor. Famoli had no courage, and he hanged himself in the grove." The chief and his counsellors exclaimed, "Aaaah! It is true!"

Numukeba went on, saying, "What is the meaning of 'slave' and what is the meaning of 'hero'? Because a man wears elegant cloth and boasts of his deeds, do we believe we know him? Because a man covers himself with skins and works in our fields, do we believe we know him?" The chief and his counsellors replied, "Numukeba of Naradugu, we hear what you are saying." Numukeba said, "The true hero is a person who has the spirit of a hero, not he who has taken a head. Therefore I cannot keep Malike as a slave any longer. Though I did not know it, he was never a slave. I renounce him as a slave. He has no choice but to live as a noble hero. I give him my vest of mail and my weapons. I give him Famoli's tall white horse. I will forge new weapons for myself. He will go his way seeking honor and I will go mine."

Now he addressed Malike, saying, "The chief and all the people of this village are witnesses. You are free. Henceforth call no man by the name of Master." Malike replied, "Aaaah, was I not right in saying that destiny can be bent?" Numukeba said, "No, you were wrong. What you are now, that is the story that was written for you. When you were still young and the filelikela divined your future, did he not tell your father, 'Your son will be strong and prosper'? You are strong. You will prosper."

So the bards of the village composed a song and sang it, playing on their ngonis:

"Naradugu Numukeba
Numukeba of Naradugu
Forger of weapons,
Son and grandson of a great family.
Not to a king did he give his slave,
He gave his slave to himself
Numukeba, the lion, Diara;
Numukeba, the lion, Waraba;
Numukeba, the lion, Kunkotiti;
Numukeba, the lion, Nianga.

Massina Malike
Malike of Massina
He who humiliated Famoli
And now rides Famoli's horse.
He received himself from Numukeba.
Son of the lion, Diara;
Son of the lion, Waraba;
Son of the lion, Kunkotiti;
Son of the lion, Nianga."

They slept the night, and when it was dawn Numukeba went
to the village forge and began to make new weapons and a new
vest of mail for himself. He forged for eight days, until he was
finished. Then he put on the vest of mail, took up his weapons,
mounted his horse and rode away southward along the great river
called Joliba. Malike also took up his weapons, mounted, and rode
away northward along the river. The people stood on their rooftops to watch them go, saying, "When have such heroes ever before appeared in our village?" As Numukeba grew smaller in the
distance they said, "A red glow surrounds him. What is the
meaning of it?" As Malike grew smaller in the distance they said,
"A blue glow surrounds him. What is the meaning of it?" But
they did not know the answer.

3
Etchuba of the
Red Powder

NUMUKEBA TRAVELLED, HE HUNTED, HE TRAV-
elled again. Sometimes he thought, "Why am I
here? Why do I seek deeds to perform? Deed after deed, do they
change the world?" But he put the thought away in the vault of
his mind and went on. For many days he saw no humans, and he
wondered if he was still in the land of the Soninke, the Bambara
and the Bobo. Then one morning he came to a lone house sitting
in the bush. A woman was pounding her mortar in the shade of a
tree, and Numukeba greeted her, saying, "Good health to all in
your house. I do not know the name of the country I am in. Have
I left the Soninke, the Bambara and the Bobo behind me?" She
answered, "No, in one direction or another those people are living." He said, "You do not speak as if you were one of them." She
answered, "No, we are Yoruba. My husband is Ekun, a famous
diviner from Esie." Numukeba said, "I am Numukeba of Naradugu. Give him my greetings."

The woman went into the house, and after a while Ekun of
Esie came out. He said, "Welcome to this point in the bush. All
those who go and all those who return must pass my doorway.
What is it you want from me?" Numukeba answered, "Why,
until this moment I wanted nothing, only to greet you. But since
you are a famous diviner from Esie, read the kola seeds for me so
that I can know where my trail goes." Ekun of Esie looked intently at Numukeba's weapons, his armored vest, his talismans
and his horse. He said, "Yes, you are a man who needs to know
what lies ahead. But kola seeds have to be fed or they will not

speak." Numukeba said, "I hear you, Ekun of Esie. Here are ten cowries to feed them."

So the diviner sat on the ground with his divining tray and cast his seeds. The first time he cast he made a mark in the dust with his finger. He cast again and made another mark, on and on until he had made twenty marks. Then he said to Numukeba, "There is a long journey for you. You are going wherever you are going, and you return when you return. What goes well goes well, yet there is danger where there is danger." Numukeba said, "Aaaah, it tells me nothing. Surely there is a meaning behind it?" The diviner answered, "Restrain your impatience, for things that seem to have no meaning have meaning behind them. I have cast only the first series."

He cast again, twenty times, and after that he cast yet another twenty times. At last he put his divining tray aside and said, "The kolas speak to us of only one thing. They speak of Etchuba, whom you will meet on the trail." Numukeba said, "Famous diviner of Esie, who is Etchuba, and what is he to me?" The diviner answered, "He is the Owner of the Red Powder. He speaks all languages. He travels every trail. He frequents every market-place. He is old, yet he never grows more old. His eyes are dim, yet he sees everything."

Numukeba said, "I hear you, but I understand nothing. What is the character of Etchuba? Is he a hero? A trader? A farmer? A chief, or perhaps a slave?" The diviner answered, "Etchuba's substance is the force of uncertainty and disorder. What is straight he makes crooked. What is sure he makes uncertain. If an arrow is launched, he may deflect it. If rain falls toward a certain field, Etchuba causes it to move away and fall elsewhere. Let us say that a certain man asks his filelikela to cast kola seeds for him. The kolas say the man will arrive safely at his destination, so he travels. But Etchuba places a stone on the trail and the man kicks it with his foot. It rolls into the bush and creates a noise. A buffalo hiding in the bush is startled. It comes out and kills the man. The man does not arrive safely at his destination."

Numukeba exclaimed, "Aaaah! Then he is an evil force." The diviner answered, "No, he is neither good nor evil. He simply exists. He has no purpose. He does not care one way or another. Whatever he does is merely whim." Numukeba said, "Can it be true that such a person lives among us?" The diviner said, "Did I call him a person? No. Did I call him a jinn? No. I called him a force. If you doubt what the kola seeds have told us, take back your ten cowries and go wherever you are going." Numukeba said, "Great Ekun of Esie, forgive me. I doubt nothing that came from your mouth. As the measure of its worth, here are ten more cowries." He put the cowries next to the divining tray, mounted his horse and rode away.

He came one day to where an aged blind man sat at the edge of the road. Numukeba dismounted from his horse and greeted him. The old man said, "You, Numukeba of Naradugu, let us sit and talk." Numukeba answered, "Grandfather, you must have mystic powers. You must be a filelikela, otherwise how could you know my name?" The old man answered, "Though my eyes are shaded with darkness, I have inner sight. I saw you riding on the trail. I heard you conversing with your slave, Malike." Numukeba asked, "Grandfather, do not be offended if I ask who you are and where you come from." The old man answered, "I am Etchuba, the Owner of the Red Powder. What does it matter?"

They talked for a long time. And when they had explored the world with talking, at last Numukeba said, "Grandfather, Etchuba of the Red Powder, your many years have brought you much knowledge. Tell me, if you can, who it is who writes in golden ink when a person is born what his story will be." The old man laughed. He said, "Why, did you hear that it is written?" Numukeba said, "Yes, it is told to us that a man's story is within him from the moment of his birth. It is the thing within that guides him. It judges for him what he will do and not do."

Etchuba said, "Aaaah, you do not understand. It is not a story that is in him but perceptions. He hears things telling him what to do, and therefore he does this or that. The shade of a tree says to a person, 'Come and sit here so you may be cool,' and so he sits. You, Numukeba, the battles you had in your town told you, 'Go and make a journey,' and so you journeyed." Numukeba answered, "No, Grandfather, I cannot grasp it. I believe there is a story inside every person when he is born. Two men go to war side by side. One is heroic, one is fearful. Is it not the story in each of them that is speaking?" Etchuba replied, "No, it is only that one man hears his spear saying, 'I am powerful and deadly,' while the other man hears the spear of his enemy saying the same words. Everything that matters is outside of us. Things do not care anything for a man's story. They do what it is their nature to do."

Numukeba said, "Grandfather, you are old and you are a filelikela. I respect what you tell me. Yet I believe every man has his story in him from the beginning of life." The old man answered, "No, his story is known only at the end. Then people say, 'This is what happened.' A man goes through his days hearing the voices of wind, rain, trees, sand and other men, and those voices turn him one way or another." Numukeba said, "Grandfather, I cannot be turned by such things." The old man laughed. He opened a small pouch and took some red powder from it. He threw the powder on Numukeba, saying, "Blacksmith of Naradugu, let us see." He arose from where he sat and went away without any more words.

Numukeba also continued on his way. He could see from the numbers of people travelling on the road that he was approaching a city. He asked a woman, "What is the name of the city ahead?" And she answered, "Have you never heard of Massiba?" Massiba meant Catastrophy, and he thought, "What city would call itself by such a name?" He camped for the night on a knoll beside the road, and just as dawn was breaking he heard the sound of many cattle running. He stood up and saw a herd approaching from the direction of the city, and driving them from behind were three mounted men. Because the men were shouting and the cattle were running, Numukeba thought, "Surely these men are stealing a herd. I will stop them." He mounted his horse and rode out to meet them, saying, "Stop. I know these cows are not yours because you are running them so hard." They answered, "Stand aside or we will kill you." Numukeba drew his cutlass from its scabbard and went forward. At first they positioned themselves to fight him, but when they saw his vest of mail, the talismans covering his chest and a red glow that appeared to emanate from his body they faltered, then turned and fled.

Numukeba said to himself, "These are fine cattle. They must belong to an eminent personage in Massiba." And so he drove the cattle back toward Massiba from where they had come. Before he was within sight of the city, however, he saw a large party of warriors coming to meet him. When they arrived they surrounded him, and their leader said, "Here is the thief who killed the Fula herdsmen and took the cattle of the chief." Numukeba answered, "It is true that I am driving the cattle, but I am only bringing them back to the city. I took them away from the thieves who fled into the bush. I myself need no cattle, because I have hundreds of my own." The warriors shouted, "Haaaa! Haaaa!" in derision. Numukeba said, "If I were guilty of stealing the cattle I would not be sitting on my horse speaking in a quiet voice. I would fight you. But I am innocent. Therefore, take me to your chief and we will talk together, one freeborn man to another. But do not put a hand on the bridle of my horse, and do not draw a weapon of any kind. If you do, I will have to kill you all." The warriors all exclaimed again, "Haaaa! Haaaa!" But no one drew a weapon and no one placed a hand on the bridle of Numukeba's horse.

They rode together, driving the cattle into Massiba. And when they arrived in the city, the warriors escorted Numukeba to a stone building near the chief's compound. They said, "Wait in here, and we will tell the chief you want to have a discussion with him." Numukeba dismounted, put his bridle in the hands of a small boy and entered, whereupon the chief's warriors quickly closed the heavy wooden door and bolted it. Numukeba now perceived that he was not in a guest house but a prison without windows or furnishings. He sat on the earthen floor and waited. No one came. In the darkness of the room he could hardly tell if it was day or night. At last he said, "Yes, Massiba is well named." After much time passed, he saw a small stone being removed from the top of the wall, and through the hole a beam of sunlight entered. He heard a voice from the outside calling to him, "You, stealer of cattle, how is your life in there?" Numukeba answered, "I wish to talk to the chief of the city." The voice called back, "Yes, that is why you are here. If you had not asked for a discussion with the chief you would not be here. We would have killed you on the road. So now you can wait. Perhaps when our chief returns from his journey in several months, he will talk to you, perhaps not. But because you refused to be killed on the road, now you must wait, and your head will be cut off later."

He sat many days and nights in the prison. A little water and a little millet soup was brought to him once a day and passed through the hole at the top of the wall. In the darkness he recalled the old filelikela, Etchuba, throwing red powder on him. He seemed to hear, once again, the old man saying, "It is not what is within, but what is outside that turns a man one way or another." Numukeba comprehended that it was the old man's magic that had caused the cattle to be stolen and that had brought him to indignity in Massiba.

A week passed. He thought, "Very well. It was Etchuba's red powder that caused this indignity, but I will not suffer it any more." So that day when someone handed him his millet soup through the hole in the wall he said, "You, out there, I cannot see whether you are a slave or a noble. But go back to those who sent you and say that tomorrow morning Numukeba of Naradugu is coming out. Tell them I am angry. Tell them they have abused a stranger. Tell them that Massiba is not a city but a wretched village. Tell them I challenge their greatest hero to fight me by the rules of noble combat. And if they do not have a hero with valor enough to fight, I will fight all those men who brought me here and placed me in this dungeon."

The next morning Numukeba heard voices on the other side of the wall. He heard many people talking. He heard the sound of weapons. He took his magic garan from his belt. He struck the heavy wooden door with it. He struck again. Four times he struck, and the door fell from its hinges. He stepped outside, and saw a crowd waiting for him. He spoke in a loud voice, saying, "You people of Massiba, now we will see if you are worth anything at all. Who is the hero who will defend your honor?"

A rider whose face was veiled beneath his eyes with a black scarf came forward on a tall black horse. He said, "I am known as Chekele. I do not like you. You are a thief. You are a stealer of cattle. You skulk into our city like a hyena searching for carrion.

Son of slaves, we should cut you to pieces and scatter your bones. But you claim the right to fight by rules of noble combat. Therefore you will fight me. When I strike you, do not cry out in pain like a child. Do not turn and flee, because the chief's soldiers will catch you and hang you. Do not ask for time to invoke your protective spirits. There is no time. Here, the boy brings your horse. Mount at once and let us begin."

Numukeba mounted his horse. He said, "You who are known as Chekele, you speak coarsely like a man from the bush. Your boasting is nothing more than the frothing of a mad boar. If you are the first of the heroes in this city, how wretched are those who are last. Say no more, because the people will remember your words and the djeli will ridicule you in their songs. Let us begin."

Chekele took an arrow from his quiver and launched it, but Numukeba waved it aside with his magic garan. Chekele launched another arrow, and again Numukeba's garan turned it away. Chekele launched a third arrow, and when Numukeba motioned with his garan the arrow passed him harmlessly. By the rules of noble combat, it was now Numukeba's turn. But Chekele did not give him his turn. Instead, he drew his cutlass and rode against Numukeba to slay him. Numukeba drew his own cutlass, and moving his horse to one side, he cut the bridle lines Chekele held in his left hand. Chekele now could not guide his horse. He dismounted. Numukeba dismounted. The two men fought body against body. Chekele's cutlass could not penetrate Numukeba's vest of mail. At last Numukeba seized his opponent and threw him to the ground and placed one foot on his neck. People shouted, "Now Chekele will lose his head!" But Numukeba did not kill Chekele. Instead he cut off both of his ears.

After that he said to the crowd, "Is there another hero who wants to prove his valor?" No one came forward. Numukeba said, "Very well. Let your bards remember this man's boasting. Let your chief see him without ears, and he will say, 'Where are his ears?' Then you will tell the chief how your city mistreated me. If this man has a son, let him grow into a great warrior, and if this son has the courage, let him come and find me and claim his father's ears. Chekele already has lost nobility because he did not fight honorably. If the son does not come to avenge his father, his family will be disgraced forever. And now, you great warriors and heroes, stand away so that I may pass." Numukeba moved forward. The crowd parted in the middle, and Numukeba rode out of the city into the bush.

The trail he followed meandered. It did not seem to go one way or another. At a certain place it branched into three trails, and he paused, wondering which of them to follow. At last he thought, "Why does it matter? My journey is not to one place or another. Where the trail goes, I also go." So he took the left trail, and after a while it also branched three ways. This time he took the middle trail, and when he came to a place where it branched three ways he took the right-hand trail, thinking aloud, "What is behind me remains behind, what is ahead remains ahead." After a while he observed that all the trails he had avoided returned and joined the trail on which he was riding. He thought, "The trails are meaningless."

He saw a man sitting in the shade of a tree, and as he came closer he saw that it was the filelikela Etchuba, Owner of the Red Powder. Etchuba said, "Dismount, Blacksmith of Naradugu. Let us talk to one another." Numukeba dismounted and sat near the old man. He said, "You, Grandfather, caused me a great indignity with your red powder." Etchuba answered, "Aaaah! Then it was not destiny that was responsible?" Numukeba said, "My destiny was to survive, and I survived. But it was you who caused the stolen cattle to come my way. Because I am a man of honor, I had to bring the cattle to Massiba. Because I did so I was treated as a thief. What was your purpose in all this?"

Etchuba said, "There was no purpose." Numukeba persisted, saying, "If there was no purpose, why was it done?" And the old man replied, "Chance and accident have no purpose. They merely exist. They are an invisible force in the world. They surround us. They touch us or they pass us by. A man supposes, 'If I do such and such a thing, such and such a thing will happen.' But does it happen? It happens or it does not happen, depending on the wind of chance." Numukeba said, "Grandfather, you have had many years in your life, and you are a master of the mystic sciences. How can you believe that chance is more powerful than the fate written for each person? If it were true, life would have no meaning." Etchuba answered, "You speak wisely, blacksmith, because there is no meaning. Did you not perceive it in the trails you followed? Was there a good trail and a bad trail? They branched from one another, going this way and that, yet in the end whatever trail you chose brought you here where I have been waiting for you. The trails are meaningless."

Numukeba pondered. He said, "Learned Grandfather, it was my destiny to be here talking to you, and therefore I am here. Destiny says, 'No matter how confusing the road, it has a beginning and an end.' Etchuba became angry. He said, "Blacksmith of Naradugu, you are stubborn." He took out his small pouch and threw more red powder on Numukeba. Then he arose and went away. Numukeba thought, "Aaaah! Etchuba has more bad things in mind for me!" He travelled till darkness, after which he put his camel-hair blanket on the ground and slept.

Morning came. Numukeba hobbled his horse and turned it loose to graze, after which he went hunting for antelope. He went far without finding any game. He continued his search, going deeper and deeper into the wild bush. He thought, "Nothing seems to be living here. There are no antelope, no buffalo and no birds in the air. If I find even a bush rat I will take it and be satisfied." Night came again and he slept, and with the coming of daylight he went on searching for game. His mouth was dry, but there were no water holes. He thought, "There are no creatures here because there is nothing to drink. I am in lifeless country." Again he slept through the darkness of night. On the third day he arose and licked dew from the rocks, and once more he searched but could not find any meat.

Just as discouragement was beginning to overtake him he saw a large bush rat. He pursued the animal but could not overtake it. So he loaded his gun, and when the bush rat paused and raised his head to look back, Numukeba fired. But a strange thing happened. The powder burned but it did not explode, and the bullet fell without force from the end of the barrel. Again Numukeba loaded, again he fired, but again the bullet merely fell from the end of the barrel. He thought, "Aaaah, Etchuba's magic has followed me into the bush!" He loaded again, this time with a double charge of powder and two bullets. When he fired the third time, the bullets again fell to the ground. So he placed his gun in the fork of a tree and went on with his spear in his throwing hand. Twice he threw his spear without hitting the bush rat. The third time the spear struck the animal a glancing blow. Though it was wounded, it went on running. Numukeba was coming closer, but suddenly the bush rat disappeared under a large termite mound.

Numukeba arrived there. He saw a hole under the mound. He enlarged it with the point of his spear until he was able to crawl inside, and he discovered that the hole led to a large tunnel. The tunnel became wider and higher, and soon he was able to stand up and walk naturally. Emerging from the tunnel at the other end, he found himself on a road. He went where the road went, and came to a village. He saw people working in the fields and cattle grazing. He heard human voices and the sound of pestles pounding in mortars. People greeted him, saying, "Stranger, you have had a long journey in the bush." Women came out of their houses and offered him food. They led him to a spring where he could drink. After he had rested a while he said, "I do not know the name of your village. I was hungry and went hunting. I could not find an antelope, but I discovered a bush rat and pursued it. It entered a hole beneath a termite mound, and I followed. I went through a tunnel and found a road, and so I arrived here."

People answered, "Aaaah!" Then they fell silent. Numukeba said, "I am from a place called Naradugu. It is proper for me to announce myself to your chief." Again the people said, "Aaaah!" They took him to the chief's house. The chief's wife came out. She said, "Then it was you." Numukeba answered, "I do not understand." She took him into the house. The chief was lying on his mat, and a young girl was holding a blood-soaked cloth to his side. The chief's wife said, "He was struck by a hunter's spear while he was out searching for roots for us." Numukeba asked, "Why would one hunter injure another this way?" They did not answer. Then Numukeba understood. He said, "I did not know. I merely pursued a bush rat because I could not find an antelope."

He took medicine from a small leather pouch and gave it to the chief's wife, saying "Put this on the wound to heal it." And he took one of the talismans from around his neck and placed it around the neck of the chief. He sat for a long time beside the mat, until at last the chief spoke, saying, "Thank you for the medicine and the talisman. I will recover soon." Numukeba said, "What happened, I regret it. It was because of the old filelikela, Etchuba. We spoke of destiny and chance, and he became impatient and threw his red powder on me. When I pursued you I did not know what I know now." The chief said, "You who come from Naradugu, what happened was because of a powerful force in the world. Magic is great, Destiny is great, Chance is great, Knowledge is great, but the strongest force of all is the Wind of Not Knowing. Because of this wind, men become lost in the bush, heroes die, cities are conquered, kings are beheaded, wives become widows, and children become orphans."

Numukeba answered, "Yes, Older Brother, but is there no medicine to counteract the Wind of Not Knowing?" The chief said, "The medicine is to look beyond the appearance of things. Perceive if you can the spirit that lives within a stone, the force within a falling leaf, the inner meaning of fire and water. That is the only magic to counter Not Knowing. Now I must rest and recover from my wound, so that tomorrow I may again hunt for roots." The chief closed his eyes. Numukeba went out, and people took him to the guest house to sleep. He lay on a freshly woven mat and reflected on things. He slept.

When he awoke he was again in the bush, lying under the tree in whose fork he had left his gun. He thought, "If I followed the bush rat into a tunnel under the earth, why am I here? No, it did not happen. Etchuba's red powder caused me to fall asleep, and what I remember is only dreaming." But he examined his talismans and found that one of them was missing. He thought, "No, in all certainty I went through the tunnel and found the place where the bush rat lived, only he was not a bush rat but a man like myself, the chief of a village. And I gave the chief the talisman and he spoke to me of the Wind of Not Knowing. Yet because he spoke those words, does that make them true? And because Etchuba said that things have no meaning, must I believe it? The force of the sun, I know it, for through me and my forge it transforms earth into iron. And I know that fate is written by the

Architect of life, also called the Composer because he writes every person's story in golden ink. Still, it is said that knowledge is strength, so knowledge too must be a force. If this is true perhaps it is in eternal combat with the Wind of Not Knowing. Perhaps the world is a weaving, and all these things are like the reeds that are intertwined to make a basket."

Finally Numukeba arose, took his gun from the tree and found his horse grazing in a grassy place. He mounted and went searching for a road to follow.

4

Bassa of Kassala

HE NOW RODE TOWARD THE EDGE WHERE THE Sun Sleeps, and on the fourth day he again saw Etchuba sitting by the trail. He dismounted, saying, "You, venerable filelikela with a passion for sprinkling red powder, you who have no purpose in life but to make men's plans miscarry, I am here again." Etchuba answered, "Numukeba of Naradugu, is it not chance that brought you here?" Numukeba said, "No, Grandfather, we meet again because it is my fate. What you willed to happen to me through chance did not come about. I nearly killed a man unjustly, but it was not my destiny and therefore the man did not die. Your red powder cannot undo what the Architect has inscribed in golden ink."

Etchuba laughed, saying, "There is no Architect and there is no golden ink." Numukeba said, "What you caused to happen to me brought me new knowledge about the nature of things. Knowledge is strength. Therefore I am stronger than before." Etchuba replied, "Your words are mere vanity. A man is no more than a thistle seed floating here and there in the wind." He threw more red powder on Numukeba.

Numukeba mounted again and continued riding till he came to a river. He turned his horse loose to graze, and he removed his armored vest and his clothing and went into the water to bathe. While he was there, a party of brigands came along the bank and saw Numukeba's clothes, his talismans, his iron vest and his weapons, and they quickly gathered up these things and went off with them. They also took the horse, so that Numukeba could not pursue them.

Numukeba saw from the river what was happening, but he could not do anything to stop the brigandage. He came out of the water. Everything he owned was gone. He sat on a rock and reflected on his situation. He thought, "How can I hunt without weapons? How can I defend myself without a gun and a vest of mail? What am I without my talismans and my magic garan? How will I journey from one part of the bush to another without a horse? How will I present myself to other people without any clothing?" He thought of Etchuba. He said to himself, "Etchuba wishes to give me a lesson. He says, 'Everything that matters is outside of us.' My clothing, my iron vest, my weapons, my talismans, all these things are outside of me. Without them am I still Numukeba of Naradugu?"

He pondered these questions, and at last he thought, "Yes, I am Numukeba. I have the character that I had before. I have honor. I have the knowledge that comes with the working of iron. I have the story that was written for me at the time of my birth. You, Etchuba, Owner of the Red Powder, are wrong." And while he was still reflecting this way on his condition, a young girl came carrying a load of firewood. Her clothing was ragged, showing her skin through its rents. Her arms and legs were covered with sores. She stopped and looked at Numukeba. He said to her, "Small Sister, do not be afraid of me. You see me as I am because brigands ran away with my clothes while I was bathing." She did not say anything, but unwrapped the headcloth that she wore and gave it to him. Numukeba put it around him as a waistcloth. He said, "Thank you, Small Sister. Is there a village nearby?" She motioned for Numukeba to follow her, and he did so. They arrived at a small hut on the outskirts of a large town.

A woman was pounding grain in a mortar. The girl put down her firewood and said nothing, and Numukeba understood that she could not speak. He said to the woman, "Mother, Small Sister here led me to your house. She found me on the riverbank, where brigands had stolen my clothes and my possessions, and she loaned me her headcloth. I can see that you do not have any food to spare, so I will go on to the town."

The woman answered, "No, those people there will not give you anything." She put down a mat for him to sit on, and she brought him a gourd of boiled millet flavored with fish. After he had eaten, she brought him a waistcloth to replace the headcloth that the girl had given him. Numukeba said, "Mother, your hospitality is greater than that of wealthy merchants. If the chief of your town gave me a handful of gold, it would be nothing at all compared to this gourd of food, because I can see that your granary jar is nearly empty." The woman answered, "I was taught that when a hungry stranger comes to your door you should feed him. It was never said, 'Look in the grain jar first to see if it is full.' "

Numukeba asked, "Are there no men here to hunt for you?" The woman answered, "My house is empty of men. There are only my grandchild and myself." Numukeba asked, "Are there no people in the town to bring you meat sometimes?" The old woman replied, "In the old days it happened now and then, but now they have put us out of their minds. Sometimes my grandchild catches small game in a snare. We exist." Numukeba said, "Are you a stranger who came from a far-off place to settle here?" The woman said, "No, I was the wife of one of the chief's favorite heroes. My husband's name was Djalan. He performed deeds of valor for the town. When there was war, he went out ahead of the others to meet the enemy. When there was peace, he was generous to the people, giving them cowries and cattle. Sometimes people whispered, 'It is Djalan who should be our chief. He would look after us.' When the chief, whose name is Bassa, heard of these whisperings he became angry. He instructed his counsellors to spy on Djalan and to provoke him some way into performing an act of treason.

"There was a night when the heroes were together drinking and telling each other of their accomplishments. One of the chief's counsellors asked Djalan, 'It is said that when our town fought against the Fula, you were surrounded by twenty of the enemy but killed them all. Had Chief Bassa been there, would he have performed such a heroic deed?' And Djalan answered, 'Why, yes, had Bassa been there, he would surely have done such a thing.' The counsellor said, 'When the Maraka attacked us, you went single-handed against them and drove them off. Do you think Bassa would have done the same?' Djalan answered, 'Yes, there is no doubt, had he been there.' The counsellor asked, 'And when you fought against one hundred brigands who had stolen the chief's cattle you cut them all down and brought the cattle home. Could the chief himself have performed this deed had he been there?' Djalan replied, 'Why do you ask these silly questions? The chief is a lion among men. But Bassa was not there.'

"The counsellor went to the chief and said, 'The rumors are true. Djalan speaks against you to the other heroes.' The chief asked, 'What does he say?' The counsellor replied, 'Why, whatever the question, he always answers that the chief is a coward. Referring to this battle and that, he implies that you were never with the heroes but, instead, hiding in your house.' The chief sent his soldiers to bring Djalan to him. He asked Djalan about his treasonous words, and Djalan replied that he had never spoken treason. The chief said, 'When we fought the Maraka, according to your words, I was not there. When you fought the brigands,

according to your words, I was not there. And when we fought
the Fula, according to your words, I was not there. You say over
and over again, "The chief was not there." Your meaning is clear.
You are conspiring against me, Djalan, and for that you will die.'
He instructed that Djalan be killed. It was done, and they cut off
his head and gave it as an offering to the chief's guardian spirit."

Numukeba exclaimed, "Aaaaah! What kind of chief is this?"
The woman said, "Then the chief ordered my house burned
down and told me to go and live in the bush. That is why I am
here. Once there were people in the town who had loved Djalan,
and they sent me little gifts of food or cowries. But after a while
they forgot that I was alive." Numukeba asked, "But you have a
grandchild living with you. Surely, therefore, you have a son or a
daughter somewhere?" The woman said, "This girl whom I call
my granddaughter is only a child who cannot speak and who has
no family. She was starving in the town, so I took her to live with
me."

Numukeba exclaimed, "Aaaaah! What kind of town is this?"
The woman answered, "The name of the town is Kassala. What
kind of town it is you will discover for yourself." Numukeba said,
"Mother, the story is not finished. You will see me again." He
arose and went into Kassala. He walked through the marketplace
where people were trading their goods, and on the far side of the
town he came to a shed where a blacksmith was forging hoes and
knives. He said to the blacksmith, "Do you need a helper to carry
for you?" The blacksmith said to him, "Whose slave are you, and
where do you come from?" Numukeba answered, "My name is
Did-Djalan-Never-Live. I come from a village in the north. My
master was a blacksmith, and I carried for him and helped him
forge hoes and knives."

The blacksmith said, "Very well. I will feed you and let you
sleep in the shed. Now begin your work by carrying. Take these
hoe blades to the house of the chief and give them to his senior
slave." Numukeba took the hoe blades to the chief's house and
asked for the senior slave. The senior slave came out. He asked,
"Whose slave are you and where do you come from?" Numukeba
answered, "I am Did-Djalan-Never-Live, and I bring these blades
from the blacksmith." The chief's senior slave said, "I have never
before seen you in Kassala." Numukeba replied, "No, I used to
live in a place called Naradugu, but my master sent me on a journey for him." The chief's senior slave asked, "What is the name
of your master?" And Numukeba replied, "His name is Numukeba." The chief's senior slave accepted the hoe blades, saying,
"You who are called Did-Djalan-Never-Live, you have an unfor-
tunate name. Be careful. You are far from home with no master to
speak for you. Some noble of Kassala may decide to seize you for
his own." Numukeba said, "Yes, thank you. I will be careful."

He returned to the forge and did other work for the blacksmith. He was given food each day and he slept at night in the shed. Whenever he was sent somewhere on an errand he was asked, "Whose slave are you and what is your name?" And he always answered, "I am Did-Djalan-Never-Live." One day the blacksmith had to attend to a funeral in another town, and he said to Numukeba, "There is much to be done. When I return I will have to work all night. Therefore, keep the fire going for me." Numukeba said, "Yes, I will do it." When the blacksmith departed, Numukeba went to the forge and did the work. He made twenty hoes, twenty spears and twenty knives. Then he let the fire subside. He lay down on his mat and slept.

The blacksmith returned in the middle of the night. He saw that the fire had gone down. But when he lighted a torch he also saw all the hoes, spears and knives that Did-Djalan-Never-Live had forged in a single day, and he saw a red glow around the mat where his helper was sleeping. Because he himself was a blacksmith he understood that Did-Djalan-Never-Live was no one's slave, but a great master of forging.

He went into his house, and in the morning he said to Numukeba, "My blacksmith brother, let us speak together. I now know you for what you are. Why did you say you are someone's slave?" Numukeba answered, "I did not say it. It was you who asked, 'Whose slave are you?'" The blacksmith said, "Yet you call yourself Did-Djalan-Never-Live. What is the meaning of it?" Numukeba said, "It is a question for the people of Kassala. Let them answer it if they can."

Numukeba did more work for the blacksmith, who one day said to him, "You, my fellow blacksmith, I do not know your real name, but from now on I will think of you as Elder Brother, because I see that your knowledge of forging is greater than my own. It is not fitting for you to be seen merely as the poorest of slaves. I must go to Massina for forty days. Take over my forge and make for yourself all the things you need. Also make things to sell, so that you can buy cloth to cover yourself."

And so it was that for forty days Numukeba again worked at the forge. He made a cutlass for himself, then a vest of mail, then a spear, then a gun, then gunpowder. After that he made knives and hoes and sold them in the market, and with some of the cowries he received he bought elegant cloth. He took the cloth to Djalan's wife in the bush and asked her to make clothes for him, and for this work he gave her cowries. He went to the foremost leatherworker in Kassala and asked him to make three things for him—sandals, a scabbard for his cutlass and a new garan to replace the one that had been stolen. He went to a filelikela and had him make new talismans, and the filelikela, whose name was Namaba, also endowed the garan with magical power. Namaba divined with kola nuts for Numukeba, and then he said, "You who call yourself Did-Djalan-Never-Live, you are no slave, but a great master of the forge. The kolas tell me how you came to be here in Kassala. They also say there will be fighting in the town. They also say that the djeli will compose songs for you."

Numukeba still lacked an important thing, a horse. One morning he dressed in his new clothing and put on his sandals. He put on his vest of mail and hung his cutlass across his chest. He put on his talismans. He took up his spear and his gun and went through the village to the heroes' terrace where the foremost warriors of Kassala gathered every day. One of the warriors said, "Aaaaah! You who arrive, are you a hero of some kind? We have never seen you before." Numukeba answered, "What is a hero? A hero is a blade that cuts, and the force of the sun that has been forged into it." Someone said, "He speaks mystically. Can such a man be a hero? A hero says, 'I am so-and-so from such-and-such a city.' "

Numukeba said again, "Who can ever say 'I have conquered an army and taken a city'? It is his talismans that protect him from death, and the strength of his iron weapons that wounds the enemy. Is it not more honest for a man to say, 'My talismans and weapons are heroes, and I am merely the donkey that carries them?' "

One of the warriors said, "Does he not insult us, calling us donkeys?" Another said to Numukeba, "You who walk on the ground like a slave instead of riding, why are you here?" Numukeba replied, "You have said the words. Because I now have to walk upon the ground, I am here to get a horse." Someone said, "Go to the marketplace then, and buy a dog to ride on." Numukeba answered, "You men of Kassala, I do not know who among you is great and who is small. I do not know who has performed good deeds and who has not. But I must challenge one of you to combat. We will fight on foot. If I win, I win a horse. If you win, take what you want." Someone said, "Aaaaah, he offers us his head." Numukeba said, "If that is what you want, then take it if you can. But it is understood that we will fight according to the code of heroes. All who are here will judge what is right." One of the warriors said, "Yes, it is agreed. I will accept your challenge." Another said, "I am the one to challenge, because you were looking at me when you said, 'You are donkeys, only your weapons are heroes.' "

But Numukeba said, "Do not be too offended by words. Words are only shadows. It is easy to say 'war,' but war itself is harsh. It is easy to say 'die,' but dying makes wives into widows. Therefore, what men may say back and forth in making a challenge is only fleeting. What I have come for is a horse, and I have no wish to kill any of you for the sake of valor. Therefore, give me a horse of my choice, and in time I will pay for it with forty cattle. Thus we need not fight." But the warriors of Kassala were angry. They answered, "You, who never announced your name, came with a challenge and insults. Now, like a woman, you tell us, 'I came meaning to beg for a horse, not fight for it.' " Numukeba said, "Yes, what you say is true. If you insist, we will fight."

He went to where the warriors' horses were grazing. He examined each horse, and when he came to one that was white, tall and strong he said, "This is the one I want. He who owns this horse is the one I challenge." One of the warriors came forward, saying, "I am Massina Da. The horse is mine. Therefore, the combat is mine." Numukeba said, "Good. Let us begin." Massina Da said, "First, announce your name. I am a noble. I cannot fight anyone but a freeborn man." Numukeba said, "My true name I will reveal later. For now, I call myself Did-Djalan-Never-Live. I swear to you as one hero to another that I am freeborn." Massina Da said, "Good. I accept your oath."

They went outside the walls of the town, followed by many persons who wanted to see the combat. The two men faced each other at a distance. Numukeba said, "Massina Da, strike the first blows." Massina Da balanced his spear in his hand. He came running toward Numukeba, and when he was only a few steps away he hurled the spear. It struck Numukeba's vest of mail, and its force was so great that Numukeba staggered back. But the point did not penetrate anything. Massina Da retrieved the spear from the ground, and he saw that the point was scorched and dulled as if it had been in a blacksmith's fire. He launched his spear a second time and a third, and each time the point of the blade became more dulled and scorched. Now the people began to perceive a red glow around Numukeba. They said, "His magic is powerful."

It was Numukeba's turn. Massina Da waited for him to attack. Numukeba went forward with his cutlass in his right hand and his magic garan in his left. When Massina Da saw the garan he said, "Stop. You want to strike me with a hobble for horses? The insult is too great." Numukeba answered, "Aaaaah, it is no insult, Massina Da. This is not an ordinary garan. It has great force within it. If you were not a person of valor I would not use it at all." Massina Da said, "No, we finished the insults before we began to fight. Now there must be respect." Numukeba answered, "There is nothing but respect. But let me show you something." He went to a large tree and struck it a hard blow with the garan. The tree trembled, its roots came out of the ground. Numukeba struck three times with his garan, and on the third blow the tree fell.

Massina Da contemplated the fallen tree. He said to Numukeba, "Such force I have never seen in any weapon. The insult is

_____*31*

gone. But you, Did-Djalan-Never-Live, are not an ordinary man. How can I fight against a jinn?" He threw down his weapons, saying, "I do not fear death. Kill me and take my head." Numukeba answered, "Massina Da, I do not doubt your valor. It was I who provoked the fight. Yet we cannot stop now because there are ill-thinking people in Kassala who would say you have lost your honor. Therefore, let us continue without weapons, merely one body aganst another." Massina Da said, "Yes, I agree." Both men removed their clothes, and they came together and wrestled. First one gained the advantage, then the other. Drummers played to accompany their movements, and people sang praise songs to encourage the fighting. They wrestled until the sun was overhead. They wrestled until the sun began to slide down toward the hills in the west. Finally, with one more mighty effort, Numukeba seized Massina Da around the middle, raised him in the air and thew him on his back.

Massina Da said, "It is finished. Take my head." Numukeba said, "No, my valorous brother, I did not come for a head." Massina Da said, "Then take my right hand," and he held it out so that Numukeba could sever it. Numukeba replied, "No, I did not come for your right hand. It is only a horse that I need. Since I have won the horse, let us go back to the heroes' terrace and talk." They went back to the heroes' terrace, the crowd behind them. Numukeba and Massina Da sat together and drank palm wine. They told each other their thoughts. They became friends.

Massina Da said, "Now we have fought and become companions. So tell me your true name." Numukeba answered, "I am Numukeba of Naradugu. I came to the house of a woman in the bush. She was once the wife of a hero of Kassala called Djalan." Massina Da said, "Aaaaah! I knew Djalan." Numukeba said, "Was not your chief jealous of Djalan and did he not conspire against him and have him killed?" Massina Da said, "Yes, it was like that." Numukeba said, "And did he not burn down Djalan's house and send his wife to live in the bush and be forgotten?" Massina Da said, "Yes, it was like that." Numukeba said, "Had the people of Kassala remembered Djalan's wife living in the bush, there would have been honor for them. But they put Djalan out of their minds, thinking, 'What is the use of remembering?' Therefore, by taking the name Did-Djalan-Never-Live I cause people to remember." Massina Da said, "I understand you, Numukeba. But be careful, or the chief will hear of it. He is a ruthless man." Numukeba answered, "My friend, when the chief hears of it, it will not be in the whisperings of servants and slaves."

Numukeba returned to the blacksmith's shed where he lived, taking his horse with him. He put on his work clothes and rested a while from his exertions. Then he made a bush knife, for there was a saying among blacksmiths that a fire must not be allowed to consume itself without bringing a weapon or a tool into the world. When the sky was dark he looked upward at the stars, saying, "Small suns, tell your older brother that I have used the force he has sent to me to smelt the sand. I have taken pure iron from the slag and shaped a bush knife that will fell trees and clear land for planting. The fire cools and now I sleep."

When he arose in the early morning, Numukeba filled a calabash with water and bathed. He put on his new clothing, his vest of mail and his talismans. He took up his weapons and rode into town to the place where the chief held his morning court under a large tree in front of his house. Numukeba sat with others who had come to hear Bassa issue edicts and settle disputes. In time, the chief came out and sat on his leopard skin. A djeli sang:

> "Bassa of the family of Dukunu,
> You are the brightness of our days
> And the comfort of our nights.
> When you tell us what is wise,
> We accept because it is wise.
> When you tell us what is just,
> We accept because it is just.
> Bassa, our cattle are yours,
> Our cowries are yours,
> Our fields are yours,
> Our labor is yours
> Because you know what justice is."

When he finished singing, he said, "You men of Kassala, any of you who is freeborn may speak what is on his mind." Men petitioned for this or that, and Bassa made rulings. After each ruling, everyone applauded, even those who had been ruled against. When the freeborn had spoken, the djeli said, "If there is a slave who wishes to petition for something, he may speak." There were no slaves among them, and so the hearings were at an end.

Now Numukeba addressed the djeli, for that was the proper way to speak to a great chief. He said, "I am a stranger here in Kassala, and I wish to announce my arrival." The djeli relayed the words to Bassa, who indicated that he had heard. Numukeba said, "My name is Did-Djalan-Never-Live." When the chief heard what Numukeba said, he called his counsellors and they whispered together. Then he instructed his djeli to ask the meaning of the name. Numukeba answered, "You, Bassa, are great. You hold the lives of many people in your hand. You tell them what is right and what is wrong. But first they must ask the question. If questions are not asked, who knows what is on people's minds? My name, Did-Djalan-Never-Live, is a question." Bassa

_____ *33*

frowned, and through his djeli he replied, "A man named Djalan lived. What is your purpose?" Numukeba said, "Great chief, if a man lived he should be remembered. His deeds should be preserved by the djeli. His family should be comforted." Bassa replied, "Yes, I hear. What is your purpose?"

Numukeba said, "Great Bassa of Kassala, it is said that there was once a conspiracy against Djalan because of jealousy, and that Djalan was killed and his wife sent out into the bush. If this is not the truth, I wish to know." Again the chief frowned and consulted with his counsellors. He replied, "I hear from my advisors that such a thing may have happened." Numukeba said, "Great chief, dispenser of justice for all who live under your fatherly rule, my petition is this—that he who is guilty of killing Djalan should be punished, and that Djalan's wife be brought from the bush and given a home in the town so that she may live decently." The chief exclaimed, "Aaaaah!" He spoke to the djeli and the djeli said, "Chief Bassa will consider what you have said. Come back tomorrow."

So Numukeba left the assembly and returned to the shed where he lived. Word went through the town that a stranger had demanded justice for Djalan's death. And soon people were speaking of it in the marketplace, saying, "Yes, Djalan really lived, and he was executed to get him out of the way." When Massina Da heard the news he came to find Numukeba. He said, "My friend, do not go back to the chief's court tomorrow. He will have no answer for you but to have you killed." Numukeba replied, "No, I must go back." Massina Da said, "Then I will go with you." Numukeba said, "I cannot ask it." Massina Da answered, "The matter is decided."

And so the next morning when Numukeba arrived at the chief's court, Massina Da was there waiting for him, and they sat together. The chief came out and sat on his leopard skin. When he saw Numukeba he said, "You, stranger, you asked a question reflecting on the character of Kassala. Kassala is a just town. Retract everything you said, and say it three times. If you do so I will spare your life. Otherwise you will die." Numukeba answered, "Great chief, when you say Kassala is a just town it means that you, Bassa, are just. And when I petitioned you yesterday I was appealing to the justness of your rule. The people of Kassala are my witnesses. You said, 'Yes, Djalan lived.' You said, 'Yes, Djalan was killed because of jealousy.' These were your words. I did not speak the name of the person who killed Djalan, because I am a stranger here. I asked questions and I petitioned for justice. You are father of Kassala. You have the responsibility for justice. Are you saying now that whoever asks you to perform a just action must die?"

The chief ordered his guards to seize Numukeba. Numukeba and Massina Da arose from where they were sitting and stood back to back. The chief's guards surrounded them but hesitated to approach. The chief threatened his guards, saying, "Kill them both. If you do not do it, it is you who will die." So the guards rushed forward slashing with their weapons, and Numukeba and Massina Da fought them. Numukeba and Massina Da, standing together, killed many of the chief's guards, and finally the others fled, calling to each other, "Either these two heroes will kill us or Bassa will kill us." They ran from the town and found sanctuary in the bush.

Numukeba said to the chief, "Is it over, or do you have more guards for us to kill?" Now, eighteen of the guards had been slain, and those who had run away numbered more than thirty. The chief exclaimed, "Aaaaah!" but he did not answer Numukeba. He looked to his counsellors to give him advice, but they were silent. Then Massina Da spoke. He said, "Bassa, you know me because I am a citizen of Kassala. It is no longer a matter between you and Did-Djalan-Never-Live. I stand with him, and other heroes of Kassala will stand with me, because now we have remembered what we never should have forgotten. Djalan lived, and you killed him because his name grew too great. A chief must be the father of justice, but you are not just. How can we trust you in days to come?"

The chief said, "What is it you want?" Massina Da said, "We will have a meeting of heroes and decide." The chief said, "Yes, come back tomorrow." Massina Da said, "No, remain there on your leopard skin. We will decide now." And he sent for the other heroes of the town to come to the court. When they arrived, they discussed everything. Then Massina Da said, "Bassa, you are no longer chief in Kassala. Gather your family together. Gather your counsellors together. Gather your slaves together. Take some grain from your storage places and leave the town behind. Go somewhere in the bush and establish a new town if you want, or find another town that will take you. Live in a new place, and may Kassala never see you again. If some stranger with the name Did-Bassa-Never-Live ever comes to Kassala, we will answer him, 'No, Bassa never lived.' Go now and be forgotten."

Bassa of the family of Dukunu arose from his leopard skin and went into his house. He gathered his family, his counsellors and his slaves. He took grain from his granary and departed from Kassala. After the chief was gone, Massina Da ordered a new house to be built for Djalan's wife. When it was finished, the people brought her and the mute girl from the bush and installed them in the house. They gave the woman gifts of meat, grain and firewood. The heroes of Kassala gave her goats and cattle. There was a festival with music and dancing. Many djeli came from other places and composed songs in honor of Numukeba and Massina Da. The djeli who had belonged to Chief Bassa sang:

"Where is the town to equal Kassala?
    What town has heroes like Numukeba and Massina
        Da?
    Numukeba remembered what had been forgotten.
    Massina Da stood with him against the chief's guards.
    They scattered Bassa's protectors into the bush.
    They restored the honor of Kassala.
    And now once more Djalan's name may be mentioned.
    They are two bright stars in the night sky.
    If the king of Kaarta has not heard of them, he will.
    If the king of Segu has not heard of them, he will.
    If the king of the Fula has not heard of them, he will.
    If the Manding have not heard of them, they will.
    If the Soninke have not heard of them, they will.
    Numukeba and Massina Da are lions among heroes.
    This is Kassala's song to you, Numukeba and Massina
        Da."

But Numukeba was not yet finished in Kassala. He took the mute girl to the filelikela named Namaba, and Namaba divined with kolas. He made medicine to cure the sores that covered the girl's body. In twenty-one days the sores were gone, and her skin shone like polished brass. Though she still could not speak, she was one of the most beautiful girls in Kassala. Massina Da fell in love with her and took her as his wife.

After that, when everything had been done, Numukeba rode again into the bush. The name Did-Djalan-Never-Live became a proverb in the town. It was spoken whenever what should have been remembered was forgotten.

5

The River Jinns

NUMUKEBA RODE ON, CAMPING AT NIGHT
wherever he found himself, lighting his fire
with a lodestone. For seven days he ate sparingly, and on the
eighth day he killed a gazelle with a single shot and dried the
meat to carry behind his saddle. On the twentieth day he hunted
again and killed a boar with a single shot, dried his meat and rode
again. In time he came to a village. He entered, his cutlass across
his chest, his gun behind his back, his spear in his hand, talismans
on his arms, and colored cloth braided into the tail of his horse.
The people said, "There is a glow of red around him. Such a man
must have great mystical powers." They asked him, "You who
are radiant, what is the reason for the glow around your body?"
Numukeba answered, "I am the Blacksmith of Naradugu. The
glow is a reflection of the force of iron." They said, "Aaah! A
blacksmith. A blacksmith has knowledge of mystical sciences."
He answered, "What you see, that you will know. What you do
not see, that you will not know."

The chief of the village came forward, saying, "Can you bring
back my oldest son, who was taken by the water jinns living in
the river?" Numukeba answered, "I arrive from the bush, I am
dusty, I am hungry, my horse is weary, and you do not ask, 'How
is your health, how is your village, how is your family?' You say,
'Go and fight the water jinns for us.' " They were ashamed. They
gave him a guest house next to that of the chief. They killed a goat
and fed him. He slept.

In the morning the people assembled outside his door. He said
to them, "Build me a forge at the edge of the river." They built

his forge, fueled it and bellowed the fire until it was hot. He said, "Bring me a bar of iron." They brought it and he placed it in the fire. He said, "Bring me a large hard rock for an anvil." They brought it and set it next to the fire. When the iron was hot, Numukeba removed it from the coals and beat it into the shape of a paddle and made mystic marks on its surface. He said, "When you see me coming, I will be here." And holding the iron paddle in his hand he walked into the water. The river rose to his knees. It rose to his hips. It rose to his shoulders. After that, Numukeba disappeared and they could not see him any more.

Darkness came and the people saw a red glow below the water, nothing more. Day came. People said, "Look! The water does not flow!" The river did not move. They threw leaves on the surface, and they rested there without motion as if on a small pond. Night came again, and once more they saw the red glow. When day came they saw that the river had reversed itself and was flowing toward the hills. Another day and night passed. The sun rose again, and once more the water was motionless, flowing neither one way nor the other. In the darkness that came in its turn, they saw the red glow. On the fifth morning the river was moving in its usual direction. The water rippled as if something were moving toward them. Numukeba's head appeared, then his shoulders, and they saw that he was holding the hand of the chief's son. The two of them came from the river. The boy was grasped by his parents. They asked him, "Are you well?" But the boy could not talk. He had lost the power of speech. They asked Numukeba, "How did you conquer the jinns?" He answered, "Let the boy tell you. If his voice comes back you will know. If he speaks no more, only he will have the knowledge of it."

The chief said to Numukeba, "How can I reward you for what you have done?" Numukeba said, "It is nothing." The chief answered, "Do not say my son is not worth something. Let me give you a gift of your choice." Numukeba answered, "I already have the knowledge of iron. I need nothing more." The chief said, "Then stay in my village. The people will build your house. I will give you land and cattle. I will give you slaves to work your fields. Our families will give you wives." But Numukeba replied, "No, this village is only the beginning of my journey." They asked him, "Which way, then, are you travelling?" He answered, "The bush is endless, and beyond one village is another. If I come to a place where no creature of the bush has ever left a footprint, I will go no farther. If I come to a place where the sun does not rise, I will turn back. I will not go beyond the edge of things, for I must return in four years to Naradugu." He went into the guest house and slept. The chief ordered that the women should not pound their mortars. He ordered hoods placed over the heads of the village fowl so that they would not crow. He ordered the men

to stay in their fields all day. He ordered the children to go outside the village to play. He ordered no gun to be fired. He ordered
these things to be done so that Numukeba could sleep without
being disturbed.

The day melted into night, and the next morning Numukeba
came out of the guest house fully dressed in his armor. His talismans covered his arms and his chest. The chief said to him, "Give
us something to protect our village against the evil forces of the
river and anyone who might wish to harm us." Numukeba answered, "At the gate of your village you have an amulet of feathers and beads hanging from a cottonwood tree. It is worthless.
Take it down, and instead build a shrine of lodestones there. It
will radiate the breath of iron, the strongest force in the universe.
Call it the Shrine of Iron." The chief answered, "Yes, we will do
it."

Numukeba mounted his horse. As he rode away into the bush,
the village musicians played drums, the chief's djeli plucked the
strings of his ngoni, and the women sang a song of praise. Numukeba disappeared, first in the morning haze that rose from the
ground, then beyond the horizon.

The chief called his filelikela and ordered him to construct a
shrine of lodestones at the gate of the village. The filelikela sent
his slaves to gather lodestones, and when they had done so he
made a shrine at the place Numukeba had indicated. When the
light of day faded and darkness enshrouded the village, the people
saw the lodestones glowing in the night.

6

The Expedition
Against Chief Monza

As Numukeba expected, he again met Et-chuba on the trail. This time he did not dismount, but said, "Filelikela of the Red Powder, you told me, 'No man has a story inside him, he merely floats like a thistle seed. Everything that matters is outside.' Then you had my clothes, my armor, my weapons and my talismans taken away to prove your words. You imagined I would be helpless in the world. You were wrong. My destiny was to perform a deed in Kassala, and this I did. I am still who I was. As for you, how are you different from Chief Bassa of Kassala? Bassa did not like the story inside Djalan so he had him killed. You do not like order in the universe and so you try to make things fall apart."

Etchuba answered, "Aaaah, deny as you wish. I thought, 'Numukeba of Naradugu will be my student. I will teach him that everything in the world is chance. Then he will be wise.' Destiny is only a wish invented by humans so they can deny accident. There is no story in a man. Chaos governs all." Numukeba said, "No, old man, order governs. You see me here because it was written. Your red powder is worthless. Sprinkle it on a river and the river continues to flow. Sprinkle it on a mountain, and the mountain is still a mountain. Sprinkle it on a man, and he is still a man with his story within. If I die on my journey, it is because that is my story, not because you haunt the roadsides. I leave you now for the last time." And Numukeba rode away without looking back.

He came in time to the town of Wassiri, and because darkness was falling, the people saw a red glow emanating from his body.

They knew Numukeba was a hero, yet no one addressed him. He rode from one end of Wassiri to the other, then back again. Finally a bearded man stepped into the street, saying, "You, man of worth, accept my greeting. Where do you come from, how are your wives and children, and do your fields prosper?" Numukeba answered, "You, man of hospitality, I am Numukeba of Naradugu. When I left Naradugu my family was well and my grain thrived. But I have travelled far and I cannot say how things are going now in my town." The bearded man said, "Dismount, Numukeba, come into my house to rest. I am Kamanike, the senior djeli of Wassiri."

Numukeba dismounted. He went into Kamanike's house and sat on a fresh woven mat. Kamanike's wife brought food, and Numukeba ate. Kamanike said to him, "The distance from Naradugu to Wassiri is far, yet I see you are not a trader." Numukeba answered, "No, but still I trade for something. I look for honor, because that is my work. I trade blow for blow, generosity for generosity, and learning for learning. Wherever good is given I trade good in return." Kamanike said, "Yes, I know these things from your armor and your weapons, and I know them also from your face. I know from the way you ride that somewhere there are djeli who sing praise songs about you and your deeds." Numukeba said, "How can you know it? Perhaps I am only a brigand masquerading as a hero." Kamanike said, "Aaah, no. While my eyes can be deceived, my heart tells me only the truth. I know that when the time comes, I, like other djeli, will compose praise songs about Numukeba of Naradugu." Numukeba replied, "Yes, a djeli lives by heaping praise on praise, but what can you praise me for? I am only a traveller coming from one place and going to another. If I have ever performed a noble deed, the song has already been sung. Tell me about your town of Wassiri."

The djeli answered, "The story is too much to tell. Wassiri is sick, and how it will recover no one can say. Our chief was Wakanai. He was challenged by the town of Mpeba to come and fight, but he replied, 'To speak the word war is simple, but I have no grievance against the people of Mpeba.' Mpeba questioned his valor, but he did not accept the challenge. Then Mpeba sent raiding parties to steal the cattle of Wassiri. They also captured young women and girls. So Wakanai organized an expedition against Mpeba.

"There was a great battle. Many men on both sides fell. In the late afternoon when the fighters of Wassiri were preparing to withdraw to their camping site, Wakanai's horse stepped into a hole and he was thrown to the ground. He lost consciousness and did not get up. The warriors of Mpeba seized him and dragged him within the town walls, where they stripped him of his clothes and talismans, then dragged him to the house of Monza, their chief. Monza was pleased. He gave the men gold for their deed. When Wakanai regained consciousness he was lying on the ground. He saw Monza standing there, and he said, 'You, Monza, have overcome me because of a small hole in the ground. We have a proverb that says, "A small hole can send a man to a large hole." Because my horse stepped in the small hole, now I will be killed and buried in a large hole. Do not delay things. I have nothing to which I may look forward. Kill me now.'

"Monza only laughed. He said, 'Wakanai, you once seemed great and handsome, but now you resemble only a pitiful beggar covered with dust. No, why should I kill you now? I can do it whenever I wish. Meanwhile you can be my slave, and whenever I see you I will remember, "Aaaah! That man was once chief of Wassiri, and now he serves me."' Wakanai said, 'Monza, I respected you. I had no reason to fight you. But you provoked me until I had no choice, so I came. Now fate has put me in your hands. Therefore, take my head and the matter will be finished.' But Monza said, 'No, you will be my slave and a slave to my slaves. I give you the name Djondjonou, Slave of Slaves.' Wakanai is a slave in Mpeba to this day. We have no real chief any more. Wakanai's twelve-year-old son Toto pretends to rule, but he understands nothing. When he holds court, thieves are rewarded and their victims are punished. When taxes are collected, he does not say, 'Good, may the people prosper.' He says, 'This is not enough, bring me more.' If a chicken pecks a grain of corn in the marketplace, Toto says, 'The chicken has stolen my corn. Kill it.' As you can see, Wassiri has a great sickness." Numukeba exclaimed, "Aaaaah! Great indeed, too great to be cured by a filelikela."

He slept that night in the house of the djeli. In the morning he bathed in water brought to him by the djeli's wife. He ate. He sat for a long while saying nothing. Finally he asked, "Are there no heroes in Wassiri?" Kamanike said, "Yes, there are heroes, but nothing moves them. They sit on the heroes' terrace and recount their accomplishments. They are like a forge whose fire has gone out." Again Numukeba pondered silently. Kamanike spoke first, saying, "Is there not a saying, 'If iron is to be shaped, the blacksmith must smelt the ore'?" Numukeba answered, "You speak as if you know something." Kamanike said, "I perceived a red glow around you while you slept. And I observed iron filings clinging to your skin as if you were a lodestone."

In the afternoon Numukeba went to the terrace where ten heroes of Wassiri were drinking palm wine. They saw from his manner of dress, his talismans and his noble bearing that he also was a hero, and they greeted him. He sat with them and they offered him a gourd of wine. They asked, "You, stranger in Wassiri, from where do you come and where are going?" He answered, "I am Numukeba of Naradugu. I go from one place to another, looking for whatever is there. Yesterday I arrived in Wassiri and received the hospitality of your djeli, Kamanike. I heard of the misfortunes of your town." They said, "Yes, whatever Kamanike told you is true, for he is a great djeli." Numukeba asked, "Is there no remedy?" They said, "We have reflected. There is no remedy but to destroy Chief Monza and his town. But Mpeba is strong, and it has many allies. We have sometimes said to one another, 'Let us go and bring our chief back.' But our filelikelas have divined with kolas, and they have told us, 'Only the power of the sun can overcome Mpeba.' Therefore we wait for the sun to melt Mpeba away."

Numukeba said, "I have some of the mystic power about which your filelikelas speak. I will go with you on an expedition against Chief Monza and his town." The heroes looked at Numukeba in silence, not believing what they heard. One of them said, "Numukeba, we receive you with the honor due to a hero. But who contains the magic of the sun within him? If we had such a person among us we would follow him to Mpeba without further words. Prove to us what you say." Numukeba said, "Yes, let us do it that way. First, take note of my name, meaning Master of Blacksmiths. Masters of the forge receive their power to smelt and shape iron through the fluid that flows from the sun." They said, "Aaaah, then why don't we ask our own blacksmith to lead us?" Numukeba answered, "There are ordinary blacksmiths and there are those who possess the power." The heroes said, "Show us then, Numukeba, so we can see for ourselves."

Numukeba answered, "Though you do not believe, still you have not questioned my honor. Therefore I will do what you ask. Bring me a large stone, the hardest you can find." They brought it and put it before him. He drew his cutlass from the scabbard on his chest and struck the stone with it, cleaving it in two. They exclaimed, but some said, "It is a noble blow, Numukeba, but other men also have cleaved stones." Numukeba said, "Very well, give me one of your spears." They gave him a spear, and he took it in his hands, not by the shaft but by the long sharp blade. He held it firmly, closing his eyes. His lips moved silently. The blade began to glow red, faintly at first, then brightly. Numukeba bent the blade so that its point was turned backward. He placed the spear on the ground, and they saw that the metal was scorched as if it had just come from the coals of the forge. The heroes exclaimed again, but some of them said, "Perhaps it is a trick." Then they saw a glow of red surrounding Numukeba's body, and after seeing that they said, "Numukeba, show us no more. We believe that it was about you our filelikela spoke. We will go with you on an expedition against Mpeba."

They began preparations. They repaired their weapons and

ordered bullets and gunpowder to be made. In twenty days they were ready, and the night before their departure the heroes sat on their terrace drinking and boasting of great deeds they would perform and the nobility of their families. One of them recited his lineage and recounted the heroic accomplishment of his father, his grandfather, his great-grandfather and his ancestors back to the beginning. Another boasted that he would bring back Chief Monza's head and the heads of all his counsellors. Another said he would bring such terror to Mpeba that in future days his name would be synonymous with destruction. Another declared that no hole would be large enough to contain the bodies of those he would slay. Another said his achievements would be so terrible that the springs of Mpeba would dry up, the rain would stop falling and the crops would wither. Each of the ten heroes boasted his boast, and only Numukeba was silent.

They said to him, "Numukeba of Naradugu, have you nothing to tell us?" And Numukeba answered quietly, "How can I say what I will do? The deeds I will perform have been written on a page I have never seen. I will behave with honor and valor. I do not compare myself as if I were a bright moon among small stars. If one of my companions is besieged, I will assist him. If we break through the gate of Mpeba, I will not be the last. If one of us falters, I will not taunt him. If it is one hero's destiny or another's to take Chief Monza's head, I will not envy but applaud him. I swear only that no act of mine will bring shame to Wassiri." When the heroes heard Numukeba's modest words they fell silent, and soon they went to their homes and slept.

At dawn they set out, and following them came four hundred fighting men of Wassiri. On the fourth day they sighted the walls of Mpeba and saw that the gate was closed. The army camped on a knoll, and the eleven heroes rode by themselves to the gate. Chief Monza's djeli called to them from the top of the wall, saying, "Welcome, nobles of Wassiri. How are your families? How are your fields? How are your people? How are your cattle?" Numukeba answered for the heroes. He said, "Djeli of Mpeba, we are well. And how are the affairs of your town?" The djeli replied, "Here all goes well also. What is the purpose of your visit?" Numukeba said, "Why, we come to thank you." The djeli said, "What is it you thank us for?" Numukeba said, "We thank you for taking such good care of the chief of our town. We thank you for the hospitality you have shown him. But his wives complain that his house needs him, and therefore we come to bring him home." The djeli answered, "Yes, wait a few moments. I will take your words to Monza."

When he returned, the djeli said, "You men of Wassiri, Monza appreciates your visit. He says that tomorrow when the sun rises your people and our people will meet outside the walls and have their discussion. Meanwhile, when darkness comes we will open our gate so that you eleven nobles may come in and feast with us." Numukeba answered, "Yes, it is the custom. We accept your invitation." This is the way it always was when an army attacked a city, and none of Wassiri's heroes questioned it. So when the sun was nearly down, Wassiri's eleven heroes entered Mpeba. They feasted there and drank wine, and heroes on both sides acted as brothers. When it was late Numukeba said, "Now we must rest. Take us to our sleeping place."

So Mpeba's people took the eleven men to a large guest house with many sleeping mats in it. They said, "It is the custom here for our guests to leave their weapons in this small outbuilding until morning." So the eleven heroes placed their weapons in the outbuilding and went to their sleeping mats. But Numukeba kept his magic garan tucked in his belt. The men had eaten and drunk much, and so they slept heavily, all except Numukeba, who kept one eye open.

In the hours when sleep was heaviest, Monza's soldiers assembled in another part of the town, and they came as silently as they could to the guest house. When the signal was given, they burst through the door, slashing with their cutlasses and thrusting with their spears. Numukeba called out an alarm. The heroes sprang to their feet, but they had no weapons to fend off the attack. One by one they were slaughtered in the guest house, all except Numukeba. He struck one way and another with his magic garan, and whoever felt his blow fell and died. Because it was dark, the soldiers of Monza could not tell who was friend and who was enemy, and in the commotion many of them killed one another. Some fled from the guest house and were slain by the soldiers outside.

Numukeba emerged through the door, a red glow emanating from his body. He struck in all directions. Monza's soldiers scattered, some running toward the chief's house, others into the bush. Numukeba went through the streets, striking at everything with his garan. Houses and trees fell as if a great storm were passing through. When Numukeba arrived at the chief's compound he struck the gate and it fell from its hinges. He called out, "Monza, you Chief of Dishonor, let me see you. Tonight is the night your light fades for you." Monza came out, surrounded by thirty of his personal guards. His chest and arms were covered with talismans and emblems, and in his right hand he held a sword with a golden handle, the symbol of his authority. His djeli said, "Monza says for you to leave Mpeba instantly or die."

Numukeba said, "Tell Monza he owes me eleven debts which he must pay before the sun shows itself over the trees. He owes first for his dishonorable treatment of Wakanai, chief of Wassiri." Monza answered through the mouth of his djeli, saying, "Wakanai was taken in war. I could have killed him. Instead, I made him a slave, which is my right." Numukeba said, "You demeaned him, you made other slaves masters over him and gave him the name Djondjonou, Slave of Slaves." Monza answered, "Very well, I give him back to you. I will send for him." Numukeba said, "Deliver him here, riding on your back." Monza ordered his guards to attack Numukeba, but they pulled back. Seeing the way things were, Monza went into his house and came out carrying Wakanai on his back.

Then Numukeba said, "You now owe me ten more debts, one for each of my companions whom you slaughtered in the darkness." Monza again ordered his guards to attack Numukeba, but instead they ran away to hide in the bush. Monza said, "How shall I pay you?" Numukeba answered, "For my first companion, one thousand goats. For my second companion, one thousand cattle. For my third companion, one thousand slaves. For my fourth companion, all the filelikelas of Mpeba. For my fifth companion, all the blacksmiths of Mpeba. For my sixth companion, all the leatherworkers of Mpeba. For my seventh companion, all the unmarried young women of Mpeba. For my eighth companion, all the cowries in your treasury. For my ninth companion, all the gold in your treasury."

Monza said, "Aaaah, it is too much! How will I live if everything is gone?" Numukeba replied, "You will not need anything. For the loss of my tenth companion you yourself are going to die." Monza fell on the ground and rolled in the dust before Numukeba as a slave would do before a king. Numukeba said, "Stand up, Monza, have you no honor?" But Monza continued to grovel, moaning, "Aaaah! Aaaah!" And so Numukeba struck him with his garan and killed him.

He ordered that the bodies of the ten heroes be carried back to Wassiri. The slaves, the livestock, the gold, and all the other forfeits also were taken to Wassiri. When the army arrived there, bringing the chief home, Wakanai's djeli began to sing a song in Numukeba's honor, but Numukeba ordered him to stop. He said, "You may sing that Wakanai has returned to rule, but let your heart ponder on the ten heroes of Wassiri who died in Monza's treachery. When your heart has weighed everything, compose your song. If it is not the greatest dirge ever heard in Wassiri, abandon your profession and become a simple farmer." The djeli said, "Yes, Numukeba of Naradugu, I pledge it."

Numukeba went to a large tree on the outskirts of the town and sat there thinking of his ten companions, blaming himself for their deaths. He said to himself, "Even a small child would not trust the people of Mpeba, yet it was I who spoke for the heroes, saying, 'Yes, we accept your hospitality.' I brought Wakanai home, but is one chief worth the lives of ten honorable and valiant men? Where are the scales that can measure it?" When night came he remained sitting under the tree. Kamanike, the djeli, came and urged him to return to his sleeping mat, but he refused. The favorite wife of the chief brought him food, but he refused it. Four nights and three days he sat there without eating or sleeping. On the fourth day he came back to the djeli's house to bathe and eat a little cooked millet and goat's milk.

After that he went to the chief's house to announce that he was leaving Wassiri. Wakanai said to him, "Numukeba, you have restored us to health, but we have lost our heroes and we need you here. Stay in Wassiri. I will give you land. Select a favorite wife from among our young women. You will have gold and cowries in abundance. Cattle and slaves will be yours. You will have everything." Numukeba answered, "How could I ever live where I cost ten heroes their lives through stupidity? I thank you for what you offer, but I must leave." The chief said, "No, Numukeba of Naradugu, you did only what was our custom. It has always been this way, that when an expedition arrives at the walls of a town the heroes go inside to feast with the enemy before the battle. The fault was in Monza's treachery. But now he is dead and his town is dead. Consider it again and stay with us."

Numukeba said, "It is not my story to stay in Wassiri." He mounted his horse. When he rode through the town gate, all the people of Wassiri were there to see him pass. He became small in the distance, and in time Wassiri could not see him any more.

7
The Town of the Dead

NUMUKEBA RODE TWENTY-ONE DAYS, STOP-
ping every seventh day to hunt small game.
He came to Bozola, a town of Bozo fishermen. The gates were
open, and he entered. He saw no one, but he heard cries of
mourning at the other end of the town. When he arrived there he
saw the people gathered before the house of the chief. The chief's
djeli approached him and asked, "Stranger, who are you and why
are you here?" Numukeba replied, "I am Numukeba of Naradugu. I am on a journey, and I stopped here to be welcomed as a
traveller." The djeli said, "Our chief, Dengenu, is in his house
and will not come out. He cannot receive you, because Death has
come and taken his favorite wife." Numukeba said, "Aaaah! Then
I will go away." The djeli answered, "No, come and stay in my
house, because I see you are a hero." The djeli led him to his
house. Numukeba dismounted, and the djeli took him inside. The
djeli called on his wives to bring food. Numukeba sat and ate.

Numukeba said, "When I came I did not see any sentries at the
gates. I did not see any fishermen fishing. I did not hear the
sounds of pestles in mortars. I thought, 'Perhaps this is a lifeless
town.' Why has all living come to a halt?" The djeli answered,
"Our chief ordered it to be this way. He said, 'All the town will
share my grief. Let no one cut wood. Let no one build a house.
Let no one cast his nets. Let no one grind any millet. Let the fire
in the forges grow cold. Let the leatherworkers put away their
tools.'" Numukeba said, "Aaaah! Must the town die because of
the chief's favorite wife?" The djeli answered, "His counsellors
have urged him to come out and let life go on. But he says, 'No. I

will stay here. I will not eat. When Death claims me and I am seen no more, then the town may do as it pleases.' "

Numukeba said, "Aaaah! Your chief is a child. He should know that Death holds every person's hand from the day he is born. His wife has gone to the country of the dead. Let him bide his time with patience. He too will go there when his sunset comes. Then he will see her again. Why should he destroy his town? He is its father." The djeli said, "You, hero of Naradugu, go and reason with him." Numukeba answered, "I will finish eating. I will sleep. Tomorrow I will talk to the chief." He finished eating. The djeli's wives brought a mat. Numukeba lay down and slept.

When morning came, the djeli conducted him to the chief's house and called out, "Our Father, Numukeba of Naradugu wants to speak with you. Give him the word to enter." From inside, the chief answered, "Tell him to go away. No one enters here." Then Numukeba said, "When Death came, could you prevent him from entering? I am as powerful as Death. I am coming in." He entered the house. He saw the chief sitting listlessly on his mat half-clothed, his hair in disarray. Numukeba said, "Aaaaah! I thought to see the chief here. Where is your master?" The chief said, "I am the master." Numukeba said, "No, certainly you are not the chief. The chief would be immaculately clothed. His hair would be combed. He would be holding his scepter-sword in his hand. His eyes would not be watery. He would not be bent over. Thus anyone can recognize a chief."

The man looked at Numukeba and saw a red glow surrounding him. He said, "Who are you who speaks in this insolent manner?" Numukeba answered, "I am who I am. But you, who are you? Your father had a wife and she died, but he did not put himself in a calabash and close the lid. Your grandfather had a wife and she died, but he did not put himself in a calabash and close the lid. All wives die, all husbands die, all heroes die, all slaves die. Each one has his time when the light fades. Do not make your town into a corpse. Awaken yourself and come out." The chief said, "I heard your words. You said, 'I am as powerful as Death.' If you did not lie, go then to the Town of the Dead and announce yourself. Say again, 'I am as powerful as Death.' Enter there. Find my favorite wife and bring her here."

Numukeba replied, "Aaaah! No person who has died can return from that place. The Architect has written it." The chief said, "I have never seen the writing. My wife, I want her. Therefore she will come." Numukeba said, "I can descend to the Town of the Dead. I can tell your wife what you want, that is all." The chief said, "Very well, I agree. When she has received the message she will come." Numukeba said, "It is a great journey." The chief answered, "I will reward you with one thousand cattle, one thousand goats, one thousand slaves, one thousand of every-thing." Numukeba said, "What good are such things to me when I travel through the bush? Nevertheless I will accept because you challenge me. And when I have done this you will have to come out of the spider's corner and be a chief once more." The chief answered, "Yes, that is the way it will be."

Numukeba said, "Let us swear it in the bush." The chief re-plied, "Aaah! You do not accept a chief's word?" Numukeba said, "The task you have given me, has it ever been accomplished be-fore? The earth and the sky should be witnesses." The chief arose. He and Numukeba walked out of the town to the edge of the bush. There they squatted, neither sitting nor standing, sus-pended between what was above and what was below. Numu-keba swore, "Let earth and sky witness my pledge. I will go to the Town of the Dead. I will search for the chief's favorite wife. I will urge her to return to the chief's house. Let the chief say what he will do in return." The chief swore, "Let earth and sky witness my pledge. When Numukeba has made his journey and returned I will give him one thousand cattle, one thousand goats and one thousand slaves." Having sworn to what was above and what was below, the two men returned to the town.

Numukeba told the people, "Dig a deep hole in the center of the market." They did so. He said, "No, it is not deep enough." They dug deeper, but he said, "It is not yet deep enough." So they dug again until finally he said, "Now you may stop. I will go down and find the road to the Town of the Dead. Fill the hole after me. In four days if you feel the earth shake you will know I am returning. If you do not feel the earth shake you will know I am not coming. If I do not arrive on the fourth day, then it will be the fifth or the sixth or some other day. If I have not returned by the fourteenth day I will not come at all, and the chief's djeli may sing a dirge for me." He entered the mouth of the earth, and after he disappeared they filled the hole to the top.

On the evening of the fourth day, the people gathered in the market. Only Dengenu, chief of Bozola, remained in his house. The people waited until darkness fell, but the earth did not trem-ble. They said, "Ah, he is not coming," and they returned to their homes. When the chief heard, he said, "As I thought, Numukeba of Naradugu is a false hero. If he ever returns I will punish him for his boasting." But the people of the town did not believe that Numukeba was a false hero. They went every evening to the place in the market where he had entered the earth. And on the fourteenth evening they felt the ground shake under their feet. At first the trembling was gentle, then it grew more violent. They saw the earth move where the hole had been dug. They saw the earth thrust upward. They saw a cutlass pierce into the air. They saw Numukeba emerge, covered with dust. The people cried out,

"Aaaah! Numukeba is returning from the Town of the Dead!"

Numukeba looked around him, saying, "Where is your chief?" They answered, "He remains in his house, calling you a false hero." Numukeba went to the chief's house, the population of the town following him. He called out, "Dengenu, I have been below and I have returned." Dengenu answered from inside, "You, Numukeba, speak false words. You have been nowhere and done nothing. I will have you punished." Numukeba answered, "I have been somewhere and I have done something. Come out and I will show you here, where all the town can be witness." The chief came out. He said, "Where is my wife?" Numukeba answered, "Be patient. I have seen your wife in the place below. I will tell you about it." The chief's slaves brought out a leopard skin and put it on the ground. The chief sat on it.

Numukeba began his narration. He said: "As all the town knows, I went down into the hole in the marketplace. Is it true?" And the people called back, "Yes, it is true. We dug the hole and after you descended we filled it with earth." Numukeba went on: "I descended below, and I found a trail. I followed the trail for one day, until it merged with a wide road. At the crossroads an old woman was sitting, eating cooked millet. She said she needed goat's milk to add to the millet, but could not afford to buy it. I gave her two cowries, saying, 'Grandmother, with these cowries you can buy milk.' She said, 'You, stranger, what are you doing here? For I can see that you are not a dead spirit.' I said, 'I am on an important journey for Chief Dengenu.' She said, 'No living person who comes here ever returns above.' I said, 'I am Numukeba of Naradugu. I am as powerful as Death himself. He cannot prevent me from returning. Where is the town where the dead reside?'

"The old woman answered, 'Follow the road. In time you will come to where the road forks to the left and the right. There is a guard at that place in the form of a ferocious rhinoceros. He will allow you to go to the left, where many monsters wait to kill you and eat your flesh. But he will prevent you from going to the right, which leads to the Town of the Dead. You will have to fight him, and I do not think you can succeed. It is better for you to go back up above from where you came.' I thanked her and went on. I came to the fork in the road, guarded by the monster rhinoceros. He said, 'Pass to the left,' but I said, 'No, I will pass to the right.'

"We fought. I struck him with my spear, but it did not penetrate. I struck him with my cutlass, but it did not penetrate. He attacked me with the long horn on his nose, but it could not pierce my vest of mail. With all our struggling we trampled down the bush in all directions. Dust rose into the air. The birds fell silent. At last I struck him fiercely with my magic garan. He fell to the knees of his forelegs. I struck again and he fell to the knees of his hind legs. I struck again and he rolled over on his back. Then I pierced his belly with my cutlass and he died. I said to myself, 'Chief Dengenu is an obstinate man. Will he believe it?' So I cut off the animal's tail and the horn from his nose. I brought them back with me." Numukeba took the horn and the tail from his knapsack and threw them on the ground before the chief. The people exclaimed, "Aaaah! Yes, they are the horn and the tail of a great rhinoceros!"

Numukeba continued: "I journeyed my journey to the Town of the Dead. Before reaching there I met a party of musicians dancing along the road, beating drums and playing flutes. They surrounded me and danced in a circle. These musicians were not like you and me, for though they had skin they had no flesh beneath and the bones of their skeletons showed through. Their music was like our own, but in their songs they had only three words—'how,' 'when' and 'why.' And they refused to leave me until I answered these three words, which I could not do because I did not understand what they wanted to know. At last they attacked me and I had to fight them. My cutlass scattered bones in every direction and severed many heads, but still the heads went on singing. I said to myself, 'Will Chief Dengenu believe it?' And so I took one of the heads and placed it in my knapsack and brought it with me." Numukeba took a skull from his knapsack and threw it on the ground before the chief. The people exclaimed, "Aaaah! He speaks the truth!"

Numukeba went on, saying: "I arrived at the Town of the Dead. There were people going here and there, doing what people do here up above, but there was no substance to their bodies. Looking at one I could see through him and perceive objects on the farther side. One person could walk through another and neither of them would take any notice, like air passing through air or smoke passing through smoke. I found the house of the chief of the town. He said, 'You who are not dead, why are you here?' I said, 'I have come for the favorite wife of Chief Dengenu. Because she left him he will not come out and govern and be a father to his people.' He said, 'If this is so, Dengenu is not fit to be a chief. As everyone knows, the dead will go on being dead, and the living must go on living. I see a red glow around you, therefore I know you are a blacksmith. Dengenu, who is a noble, did not have the courage to come here. Therefore he lacks nobility. He cries in his house, waiting for someone to do something for him. Tell him his Fula herdsman is more fit to govern than he is. Dengenu's favorite wife can never again go back above. But Dengenu can come here whenever he wants and live with her.' I said, 'Yes, I will tell him. But how will he believe me?' And the chief of the Town of the Dead said, 'Here is the brass emblem that belonged to his grandfather, who resides here in this place. Give it to Dengenu. When he sees it he will believe your words.' " And from his knapsack Numukeba took a small brass emblem and threw it on the ground before Dengenu. The people cried out, "It is true, that is the emblem of the father of Dengenu's father!"

Dengenu answered, "Aaaah! Anyone may bring the horn and tail of a rhinoceros, a skull and a brass emblem. But you are a false hero because you do not mention my wife." Then Numukeba said: "I asked the chief of the town if I could speak with your wife. He sent for her and she came. I said, 'Your husband sent me to bring you back,' and she replied, 'No, I cannot go back.' I said, 'He refuses to come out of his house and govern his people because you are not there.' She answered, 'If he will not come out, that is his destiny.' I said, 'But if you return and live with him again, then he will come out, and that also will be destiny.' She said, 'It is like that among the living, but for those who have already died, death is our final destiny.' I said to her, 'When I tell him what you have said, will he believe me?' She answered, 'I will give you something of mine that he will recognize. Then he will know I have spoken to you.' She took off her waist beads and gave them to me. I have brought them to you.' " Numukeba took the waist beads from his knapsack and placed them before Chief Dengenu. The people exclaimed, "Yes, yes, it is her girdle! No other girdle was like it!"

Dengenu stood up, saying, "You, Numukeba of Naradugu, you are not a hero, only a blacksmith. You have spoken falsely. You swore to bring my wife back. Now you bring me a rhinoceros horn, a tail, a gold emblem, a skull and a beaded girdle. What do I want with these things? Because you have spoken a lie, you will be executed." Numukeba replied, "You, Chief Dengenu of Bozola, it is you who speak falsely. You said, 'Go below to the country of the dead and bring my wife back.' You said, 'If you do this, I will reward you with one thousand cattle, one thousand goats and one thousand slaves.' I did not promise to bring your wife back. I merely promised to make the journey, which I have done. All the people of your town are witnesses." The people of the town called out, "Yes, we are witnesses."

Numukeba continued: "I have told you what the chief of the Town of the Dead has said: 'Dengenu, who is a noble, did not have the courage to come here. Therefore he lacks nobility. Tell him his Fula herdsman is more fit to govern than he is.' "

The people of Bozola acclaimed Numukeba's words. The djeli of the chief spoke, saying: "Since I was a young man I have sung praise songs for Dengenu, for his family was great in every way. But he has forfeited his nobility. He refuses to govern. He does not allow the people to do their work. He does not have compassion. He does not stand by his solemn words. He wishes to take

_____*53*

the head of a hero who made a dangerous journey for him. Therefore I cannot serve Dengenu any longer." People answered, "Aaaah! The djeli speaks truly!" The djeli went on: "Now, the chief of the Town of the Dead said, 'The Fula herdsman is more fit to govern than Dengenu.' Therefore I will become the Fula's djeli and compose songs of praise for him and his family."

The people answered, "Yes, it is true. Dengenu cannot do anything for us. Bozola is a body without a head. Let us take the Fula herdsman for our chief." Hearing the tumult around him growing louder, Dengenu went inside and picked up his knapsack and his spear. He departed from his house in shame. He went into the bush. He did not turn back, but walked without stopping toward the west.

Numukeba slept for four nights and three days, then he arose and came out of the djeli's house. A crowd was standing there to greet him. The djeli said, "Great Numukeba, the people of Bozola have made the Fula herdsman chief of the town. Though he was not a noble, now he is a noble. His first words were, 'Our former chief, Dengenu, swore an oath to this stranger from Naradugu, but he did not fulfill his oath. We will not allow it to be a disgrace to our town. Therefore, we give to Numukeba one thousand of Dengenu's cattle, one thousand of Dengenu's goats, one thousand of Dengenu's slaves and one thousand of anything he asks for. Thus Bozola's honor will be redeemed.' "

Numukeba said to the Fula chief, "Honor is found where it lives. You, Chief of Bozola, I thank you for what you intend to give me. Yet I need nothing and ask nothing. The cattle and goats that belonged to Dengenu, divide them among the people of the town. Give each widow one, and one extra for each of her children. Give every old person one, and an extra one for every son his family has lost in battle. Give the blacksmith five and the leatherworker five. Give the paddler of the canoe ferry five and the maker of nets five. Give the woodcarver five and the djeli five. Give every faithful counsellor to the new chief five, and give five to each of the wives of the former chief. When that is done, the remainder will be given to all the people of Bozola to own in common.

"As for the thousand slaves you speak of, I want no slaves following me. There is not enough game in the bush to feed them. Therefore, I leave them with you. But remember that every slave of the thousand is mine. Do not overburden him. If his load is too heavy, carry it for him. If his ax falters, cut down the tree for him. If he is hungry, feed him. If he is thirsty, bring him a gourd of water. If he is too old to work, sit and listen to him and learn what he has learned through his years of labor. A day will come when I will again pass through Bozola, and I will know whether you have heard my words. Since these thousand slaves are mine, I will be their guardian."

Hearing this, an old slave said, "I wish to take a new name. I will be called Child of the Blacksmith." Another slave said, "I also will be called Child of the Blacksmith." Every one of the thousand slaves took the name Child of the Blacksmith.

Numukeba then put on his vest of mail, took up his weapons and mounted his horse. The djeli played on his ngoni and sang a song of praise for him:

> "Though the forest has a thousand thousand trees,
> The tallest is Numukeba of Naradugu.
> Though the night cradles a thousand thousand stars,
> The brightest is Numukeba of Naradugu.
> Naradugu Numukeba,
> Numukeba of Naradugu.
> When all the stories of the world have been told,
> Numukeba's will be remembered longest.
> Were his grandfather only a leper,
> Still he carried the seed of Numukeba.
> Were the town of Naradugu only a broken house,
> Still would it be great for bringing forth Numukeba.
> Whenever heroes sit on their terrace boasting,
> Let them remember Numukeba and fall silent."

And when the djeli finished his praise song, Numukeba gave him a silver talisman from his breast and rode away from Bozola, the red sun glinting across his shoulders.

8
Ndala of Boromala

THE MARKET OF BOROMALA WAS OUTSIDE THE town, because the chief did not like to hear the sounds of people shouting back and forth, smiths hammering on anvil stones and donkeys braying. When Numukeba approached Boromala he came to the market first, and he paused there to rest. An aged man walking with a staff looked up at him, saying, "Most noble person, if you are searching for something to buy, let me be your guide. I know every woman in the town and how she bargains. I know who trades honorably and who cheats. If I hear a certain man say four cowries I know he will accept two. If I hear another man say three cowries I know he wants no more, no less. Tell me what you are looking for."

Numukeba said, "Grandfather, there is nothing in the world that I want. Tell me, though, what people are these, because I live in a distant place." The old man said, "Why, this is a town of the Bororo people. Our ancestors came here long ago from the north. It has always been a good town, and so other people also came and settled. Traders travel here from as far away as Timbuktu." Numukeba said, "Yes, that is good." The old man said, "Do you need a good sword? We have fine blacksmiths. Do you need work in the mystic sciences? We have good filelikelas. Do you need a wife? I can find you one because I know all the families of Boromala. Do you need a scribe? We have a Muslim learned man here who can write."

Numukeba replied, "No, Grandfather, I need nothing. But explain to me why that young boy over there is being led by a rope around his neck. Is he a slave, and if so do the Bororo always treat their slaves in such a manner?" The old man said, "Why, the man is Namba, and the boy is his son, Ndala." Numukeba said, "Aaaah? A man leads his son with a rope around his neck?" He rode forward and spoke to Namba, saying, "You, owner of the rope, is it truly your son Ndala at the other end?" The man replied, "Noble person, whose name I do not know, yes, this is my son Ndala." Numukeba said, "I have never heard before that a man leads his son in the streets in this manner." And Namba answered, "I am merely teaching him good ways." Numukeba said, "Is this the way to teach virtue? I have always heard that a person teaches good by doing good. Where I come from what you are doing would be unthinkable."

Namba said, "Noble person, if you see it that way it is only because you do not understand the circumstances. I have many sons and all of them except Ndala are good workers. They go into the fields and cut brush. They care for the cattle. They do everything that is expected of them. But Ndala has strange ways. He goes to the fields with his bush knife. He begins to work. He begins to sing and puts his bush knife down. He hears wild birds singing and he sings with them. He makes a small thumb harp out of reeds. He sits and plays on it. He makes up songs to sing about the wind, the trees and the fields. Evening arrives, yet he has not done any work in the bush. He comes home, he eats, but he has not accomplished anything. At night when the others are sleeping he makes an ngoni harp, and when it is finished he plays it. When it is time to go to the fields, he is playing his ngoni. I take the ngoni and put it in the fire. In this life a person's first responsibility is to help the family survive. If all do not work, the family grows lean and withers away. Therefore I lead him this way so people may see with their eyes the boy who does not want to do anything but sing and play the ngoni."

Numukeba said, "You, father of the boy, what you are doing is not right. Take off the rope." Namba took the rope from Ndala's neck. Numukeba put some cowries in the boy's hand, saying, "Go somewhere and buy an ngoni." Ndala went to the leather-worker in the market and bought an ngoni. When he returned, Numukeba said to him, "Sing for me." The boy answered, "Yes, but what shall I sing? I do not know praise songs for great men." Numukeba said, "Sing what your heart tells you to sing." The boy began to pluck the strings of the ngoni, and after a while he sang:

> "Boromala is where we live.
> But what is Boromala?
> Before Boromala it was bushland
> On the edge of the river.
> Was the river always there?

No one in Boromala can tell us.
The Architect created things long ago
When we Bororo were not yet living.
When did the antelope arrive?
No one in Boromala can tell us.
When did the lion arrive?
No one in Boromala can tell us.
We Bororo arrived in our time,
And we lived in Boromala.
But Boromala was not always Boromala.
What was everything like in the beginning?
No one in Boromala can tell us."

While Ndala sang, the sounds of the marketplace gradually ceased. Women stopped calling out what they had to sell. Men playing games on the earth with seeds stopped playing. Even the donkeys stopped braying. Everyone was silent.

The boy's father said to Numukeba, "There, did you hear it? Wherever did he learn such nonsense?" But the people in the marketplace spoke sharply, saying, "You, Namba, it is you who speak nonsense. You have an empty heart." Numukeba said to Namba, "For music like this you lead your son like a bull through the marketplace? The people are right. You have an empty heart." Namba said, "You do not understand. I am teaching him good ways. He must tend cattle, he must cut brush, he must do all the things that make the family strong."

Numukeba answered, "It is said that a man who knows only half knows nothing. It is true that the family must live like a single body. If an arm fails, the family falters. If a leg fails, the family falters. But there is more to understand than that. I will tell you something, and if I am wrong let your old ones correct me. When the Architect created things he first made the bush, the mountains and the lakes. Then he created the creatures of the bush. Then he created people. But he said, 'Something is missing. The world is not complete.' He pondered for forty days, and at last he said, 'What is needed to make the world complete is music.' So he created music, and he taught humans the art of singing. He said, 'Now it is done.' We need the bush so that we can clear it and make our farms. We need the animals of the bush for meat. And music ties all things together. We celebrate the birth of a child with music. We mourn the death of a person with music. We invoke our protective spirits with music. We need music for dancing, and we need songs to encourage us when we are performing hard labor in the fields. Music opens our hearts. It prepares us for battle. Without music, how could our bards recount the history of our families?" The people affirmed what Numukeba said, exclaiming, "Haaah! Yes, that is the way it is."

Numukeba then said, "Namba, I will take the boy under my protection. He will sing for me, and in time he will become a great djeli. For the work he will not do for you in your fields, here is a bag of cowries in exchange. Is it agreed?" Namba said, "Yes, noble person, it is agreed." Numukeba said to the people in the marketplace, "You are my witnesses." And they all called back, "Yes, what was spoken between you and Namba, we have heard every word. If he ever complains that his son was taken away against his will, we will put him down." Numukeba placed the boy behind him on his horse. With one hand the boy held Numukeba's belt, and with the other he held his ngoni. They rode out of the marketplace on the main trail into the town of Boromala.

It happened that in Boromala a rich merchant named Ntini Ndunu was holding a celebration because he had completed a successful trading expedition to Timbuktu. He was sitting in front of his house as if he were a great chief, and numerous djeli who had come from distant places were singing his praise. Whenever a djeli finished singing a praise song, Ntini Ndunu gave him a gift and passed out cowries to the townspeople who were gathered there for the occasion.

One djeli sang:

> "Ndunu of the esteemed family of Ntini,
> Who is more generous than Ndunu?
> He gives feasts for the people of Boromala,
> He gives wine to the people of Boromala,
> He gives cowries and gold to the people of Boromala,
> Whatever the people of Boromala need, he gives it."

Another sang:

> "Who has more cattle than Ntini Dunu?
> Who has more corn than Ntini Dunu?
> Who has more fields than Ntini Dunu?
> Who has more slaves than Ntini Dunu?
> In the Kingdom of Sinsani they know his name.
> In the Kingdom of Kaarta they know his name.
> In the Kingdom of Segu they know his name.
> Where is the place where Ndunu's wealth is not
>   known?"

One by one the bards sang songs to Ntini Ndunu, each receiving a gift of cowries for his praise. Now, Numukeba and the boy, Ndala, sat on the edge of the crowd observing the celebration. When every djeli had sung, Ntini Ndunu was not yet satisfied. He saw Ndala with his ngoni and called him to come forward, saying, "You, boy, does your ngoni have a song in its belly for me?" Ndala answered, "Celebrated person, I am not yet a djeli. I sing with my ngoni, yet I am too young to recite the achievements of great men. I can sing only the words that fly from my ngoni like birds. If I were to sing something now, who knows what my ngoni would tell me to say? Perhaps it would only be a song to the cattle grazing in the bush. It would be very small singing compared to what all these great djeli have given to you."

Ntini Ndunu smiled. He said to Ndala, "Surely in the belly of your ngoni there are a few words of praise in honor of my family? Forget the cattle for a moment and sing something for me. Then you too will receive a gift, like the others." Ndala said, "Important personage, I cannot tell you what will come out of my ngoni. Perhaps it will not be pleasing." Ntini Ndunu said, "Do not be concerned. Everyone will make allowances for your inexperience." Ndala answered, "Very well, since you urge me and promise not to hold it against me."

He struck the strings of his ngoni. He sang:

> "Ntini Ndunu is great in Boromala,
> The djeli of the country proclaim his greatness.
> What is the greatness of Ntini Ndunu?
> His greatness is the land and cowries he owns. . . ."

Ndala broke off his singing. Ntini Ndunu said, "Go on, go on. Are you already at the end?" Ndala answered, "No, I only begin. Yet the words that come from the heart of my ngoni, I do not know what they are until I hear them. My ngoni gives me the words. My ngoni says, 'The words I put in your mouth are true, because I cannot say what is false.' But Ntini Ndunu, you are my elder, the age of my father, and I should be respectful. I am only a boy, and no words that come from my mouth ought to say what offends a great man of Boromala. I do not know what phrases my ngoni will give me to sing. Therefore, I do not want to sing any more."

Ntini Ndunu was intrigued by what he heard from Ndala. He said, "No, you must go on. No song should be left hanging before it starts. I want to hear." People in the crowd also said, "Yes, yes, go on. We want to hear the words the ngoni puts in your mouth." So Ndala began again, listening intently to his ngoni:

> "Ntini Ndunu is great in Boromala,
> The djeli of the country proclaim his greatness.
> What is the greatness of Ntini Ndunu?
> His greatness is in the land and cowries he owns.

Ntini Ndunu was poor before he was rich.
In the beginning he owned nothing at all.
He travelled in the land of the Bororo
Seeking to own something that would be his.
He met an old woman on the road to Kalada
And she said, 'You, who are a Bororo,
Help me with a problem that perplexes me.
I am old and ready to die
And I want to divide my cowries among my children.
I have three children and eight cowries.
And each child should receive the same.
Tell me, stranger, how should the cowries be di-
 vided?' "

Ntini Ndunu interrupted, saying, "Enough of your singing, boy, your ngoni knows nothing of the greatness of my family." But the people liked Ndala's singing, and they also wanted to know how eight cowries could be divided three ways equally, so they said, "No, he must not stop now. Let him go on." Ndala continued:

"Ntini Ndunu said to the old woman,
 'I will divide the cowries for you.'
He took the eight cowries in his hand,
And returned three, keeping five.
He said, 'Old woman, give each child one.
That way the division will be equal.'
He left her there, taking five cowries with him."

Ntini Ndunu spoke sharply, saying, "Bring your noise to an end. If it is you who speaks, you lie. If it is your ngoni that speaks, it lies. Go wherever you were going when you intruded on this celebration." But people called out, "No, let him go on." Ndala's ngoni fed him words, and he continued:

"With his five cowries, Ntini Ndunu bought cloth,
And he traded his cloth for more cowries,
And with his cowries he bought salt,
And he traded his salt for more cowries.
Thus Ntini Ndunu became rich.
But what he owns is not his.
Everything belongs to the old woman's three children."

When the people heard the end of the song they exclaimed, "Aaaah! Aaaah!" Ntini Ndunu shouted loudly for his slaves to seize Ndala and beat him. But when the slaves were about to put their hands on the boy, Numukeba arose and went forward. He said, "Ntini Ndunu, the boy did not ask to sing for you. He said, 'I do not want to offend.' He said, 'The words are not mine, they come from the heart of my ngoni.' You said, 'Go on singing. No song should be left hanging.' Therefore he sang for you. Because you are wealthy you suppose that everyone must flatter you. But truth does not care how many cattle you have. Now, Ntini Ndunu, give this boy his gift in return for his song, as you have done with the djeli who flattered you."

Ntini Ndunu said, "This boy has lied and injured my reputation. The five cowries I took from the woman were a loan, but I have never been able to find her. I am known as an honorable merchant everywhere. If I were a chief I would have the boy taken as a slave and beaten every day." When the people heard Ntini Ndunu admit he had taken the five cowries, they exclaimed, "Aaaah!" Numukeba drew his cutlass from its scabbard and said again, "Give the boy his gift." Ntini Ndunu gave Ndala a handful of cowries. Numukeba said, "You gave each of the djeli two handfuls for flattering you. Is not truth worth more than falsehood? Give the boy three more." Ntini Ndunu gave three more handfuls. After that, Numukeba mounted his horse, placed Ndala behind him, and rode away.

They arrived at a certain town and heard that a great Muslim practitioner of the mystic sciences was stopping there on his way to Timbuktu. His name was Sirabley Karomoko, and because he was a follower of Mohammed he was called a morike. Numukeba took Ndala to the house where Sirabley Karomoko was lodging. He said to Sirabley, "Great morike, though your name is known everywhere, our meeting is only coincidence. Like you, I am on my way from one place to another. But something of significance has occurred, and I would like to consult you."

The morike did not cast kola seeds or sand on the ground to read. Instead, he took up his Koran and held it in his hands. After a few moments he said, "Yes, you want to ask about this boy who carries the ngoni. What do you want to know?" Numukeba said, "I have taken him under my protection because he was mistreated by his father. I feel the boy will become a great djeli when he is grown. But he has a gift, and because of this gift he will always be in danger. If he sings for a person of prestige, his ngoni gives him the words of his song, and the song tells the truth of the person's history no matter what it is. If he should sing for a chief or a king or someone else of influence, perhaps his song will say, 'You are not the son of your father but of a stranger who slept with your mother.' Or perhaps the song will say, 'Your family is not noble. Your grandfather was a fisherman and your grandmother was a girl from the bush.'"

Sirabley Karomoko said to Numukeba, "Yes, I perceive that what you tell me is true. A person who has something to hide should never ask him to sing praise songs for his family. How it happens that Ndala's ngoni gives him truths not known to others, I cannot say." Numukeba said, "Distinguished morike, can you tell me if in Timbuktu there is a school for djeli that can teach Ndala the art of being circumspect as well as honest? Perhaps he can learn the art of parables, and thus say what is true without saying directly. If he is able to do this he will not stir animosity wherever he goes."

The morike pondered a while, then said, "No, the gift of speaking what is true should not be squandered on parables which mean different things to different men. Ndala's gift is Ndala's destiny. He will say many things that people will be glad to hear. What Allah has given this boy is his and his alone, even if it causes cities to fall and chiefs to hang themselves in the bush." Numukeba asked, "Great Sirabley, are you saying that he will cause such things?" Sirabley answered, "The Koran in my hands does not disclose everything. Yet I look at Ndala and perceive a mystery behind his eyes. I know only that he has a gift, and that a song can have a force as powerful as armies or floods. I have no more to tell you." Numukeba paid the morike for his services and went away.

He found a house occupied by two sisters where he could lodge for the night. They were cordial, and placed a fresh mat on the floor for Numukeba. He said to them, "Kind women, I need two mats, one for myself and one for the boy." They answered, "Aaaah, the slave can sleep in the hut in back with the other slaves." Numukeba said, "Kind women, the boy is not my slave. He is my djeli." They exclaimed, saying, "How can it be? He is only a young boy dressed in the rags of a farmer." Numukeba said, "Yes, he is my djeli, and if he were only one year old and naked, still he would be my djeli. Here are some cowries. Buy some fine cloth, and before dawn tomorrow prepare new clothing for my djeli." They agreed. Numukeba and Ndala slept.

When they awoke, Ndala's new clothes were waiting for him. The women brought them a calabash of water so they could bathe, and then gave them food. Numukeba said, "Though I have already paid you cowries for the clothing, I promise you an additional gift because you have given my djeli clothing worthy of him. Though I cannot now tell you when, on a certain day I will send you four cows. But do not get up each morning saying, 'Is it today?' When the time comes, you will know. This is the pledge of Numukeba of Naradugu." They answered, "We thank you."

Now, Numukeba wanted to buy a small horse for Ndala, but he had given away the last of his cowries. So he rode to the house of the chief, whose name was Nianga, and announced his presence in the town. He said to the chief, "My name is Numukeba and I come from Naradugu." The chief said, "Yes, your name is known to me." Numukeba said, "How is it known? For this is the first time I have been in your country." The chief answered, "Men must go slowly from one place to another, attached to the earth, but names have wings. Why are you here?" Numukeba said, "I merely go from one place so that I may reach another. Your town lies astride my trail, therefore today I am standing in the shade of your tree." The chief said, "What do you need from me?" Numukeba answered, "I need a small horse, but I do not want a gift." The chief said, "If you have gold or cowries, you may buy a horse." Numukeba said, "No, I want to trade you a horse for a horse." The chief said, "Where is the horse you want to trade?" Numukeba said, "It has not yet been created. Give me the use of a good forge in your town for three days. On the fourth day I will bring the horse."

The chief instructed one of his slaves to conduct Numukeba to a forge on the edge of the town, and to say that the blacksmith should assist Numukeba in whatever he wanted to do. Numukeba removed his fine clothing and his talismans and began to work. He called for iron and more iron. He forged all night and the next day without stopping. He worked this way three days, and on the evening of the third day his creation was completed. It was an iron horse as tall as a man. On the morning of the fourth day twelve slaves carried the iron horse through the town and set it on its feet in front of the chief's house.

The chief came out. He exclaimed, "Aaaah!" The people of the town gathered. They also exclaimed at the sight. Numukeba said, "This is the horse I want to trade. Give me a small horse for the boy to ride." The chief had a small horse brought for Ndala. He said, "Never before have I seen such a creation made of iron. The king himself does not own anything like this. But I am perplexed. Why should a man work so hard that a small boy can ride?" Numukeba answered, "This boy is my djeli. It is not proper for him to walk behind me when I am riding. He will ride in front, singing the truths that are known to him."

Nianga said, "This child is a djeli? Is it possible?" Numukeba answered, "Would I have said it?" And the chief said, "Let him sing for me." Numukeba said, "Nianga, do not risk it. The boy sings what comes from the heart of his ngoni, and the ngoni does not care whether it pleases or offends. If a man's father is a hyena it does not matter to the ngoni. If his wife sleeps with other men, it does not mater to the ngoni." Nianga said, "Yes, the boy seems even more wonderful than the iron horse. Let him sing. Before my counsellors and the people of the town, I pledge that I will not hurt him whatever words come from his mouth."

So Numukeba said to Ndala, "If your heart is willing, sing for Chief Nianga." Ndala took up his ngoni. He plucked the strings and listened to them. Then he sang:

"Nianga, the lion,
    Son of Kunkotiti, the lion,
    Grandson of Waraba, the lion,
    Great-grandson of Diara, the lion,
    This, your house, is the house of the lion."

The sound of the ngoni continued, but Ndala did not sing any
words. Nianga said, "That is good, but it is only the beginning. Is
there nothing more?" Ndala answered, "Yes, great chief, but my
ngoni says to me, 'When you have called a man a lion, let it rest
there.'" Nianga said, "No, boy, there are deeds and accomplishments to speak of. Where is the story?" So Ndala continued
singing:

"Diara, the first of the lions,
    Rode many horses and had many wives.
    Tchi! He was courageous.
    And when Diara's life faded
    Waraba, his son, became chief.
    Yet Waraba was the child of a concubine,
    He was not Diara's first-born son.
    How did Waraba become chief?
    He went hunting with Diara's first-born son,
    The one entitled to the chiefdom.
    The two of them killed an elephant.
    They quarrelled over the game,
    Each of them saying, 'This is my elephant.'
    Waraba struck his brother and killed him.
    In the town he said, 'Oh, my brother died,
    Trampled in the bush by an elephant.
    In revenge I killed the elephant with my spear.'
    Diara said, 'Aaaah! Aaaah! My son of sons is dead.
    Because Waraba avenged his death,
    He will rule when my day fades into night.'
    Thus it happened that Waraba ruled.
    And after Waraba came his son, Kunkotiti.
    And when Kunkotiti was father of the people
    A messenger came running from a Bambara town.
    He said, 'A great Fula army is attacking us.
    Here are gold and cowries. Come and defend us.'
    Kunkotiti said, 'Yes, surely I will come at once.'
    He took the gold and cowries.
    He thought, 'What is the Bambara town to me?'
    Kunkotiti never went to help the Bambara town,
    And it fell to the enemy and was destroyed.
    When his time came, Kunkotiti's day became night,
    And then Nianga became chief and ruled.

_____ *65*

Nianga's story is not yet finished.
If the djeli wish to praise him, let them wait.
If the djeli wish to blame him, let them wait.
He will perform a dishonorable deed
That will never be forgotten."

When Ndala finished singing, Nianga said, "Aaaah! Aaaah!" The people of the town were silent. The chief's djeli said, "The boy is mad. He knows nothing at all of Nianga's family. His voice is that of the hyena crying in the night." The chief said, "Take the boy to the edge of the town and whip him until he can no longer cry out." The chief's slaves took hold of Ndala, but Numukeba said, "Chief, what are you doing? You said, 'Let the boy sing.' He did exactly what you instructed him to do." The chief answered, "I did not invite him to accuse me and abuse my ancestors."

Numukeba said, "You pledged before your counsellors and the people of the town that you would not hurt him whatever came from his mouth." The townspeople said, "It is true. Those were the words." Numukeba said, "I do not know if Ndala's song was right. The ngoni gave him the words. When he sang that Nianga, Kunkotiti, Waraba and Diara were lions, you did not complain. Ndala wished to stop there, but you said, 'Go on, go on,' hoping to hear more praise. So now I give you and your town Ndala's proverb: When a man hears himself called a lion he should let the matter rest." People in the crowd said, "Yes, it is a good proverb." The chief ordered Ndala to be released, and after that he went into his house.

Numukeba said to the chief's djeli. "The chief has forgotten to give Ndala his gift." The djeli said, "Is a gift ever given in exchange for insults?" Numukeba answered, "Whenever has an honest chief refused to pay for a song?" The djeli said, "If I ask him he will abuse me." Numukeba said, "If he does not give something, Ndala will go on singing." The djeli went inside, and when he came out he brought a handful of cowries for Ndala. Then Numukeba and Ndala mounted their horses and rode away.

After they were gone, Nianga called the chief of his soldiers, saying, "Bring all your men here, every one with his weapons in his hands." The army assembled. Nianga instructed them, "Go after the man and the boy. Kill them and bring me their heads. If you fail, it is you who will die." One hundred men rode from the town in pursuit of Numukeba and Ndala. Then Nianga called the chief of his slaves, saying, "Take the iron horse. Carry it away and throw it in the bush." The chief's slaves assembled. They tried to lift the iron horse, but they could not raise it from the ground. Ten slaves tried, then twenty, but the iron horse stood as if rooted in the earth. The slaves pulled with ropes and pried with levers, yet the horse would not move. And though it was daylight they began to perceive a reddish glow emanating from the horse. The slaves backed away, fearful of what they saw, and the iron horse remained where it was.

Nianga's one hundred men rode after Numukeba and Ndala. Ndala said, "Master, my ngoni speaks to me. It says Nianga's soldiers are coming behind." Numukeba said, "Let us go to where the ground is high." They reached the top of a knoll from where they could see the dust of many running horses. Numukeba said, "Ndala, I have sworn to protect you, yet our pursuers are numerous. Ride on as fast as your horse can go. I will stand here." Ndala answered, "No, Master, I am your djeli, as you have proclaimed everywhere. The blood of a djeli is the blood of his master. I will stay by your side." Numukeba said, "You are only a boy. You are ignorant of combat. Go and live on, so that you may sing of this event." Ndala replied, "No, my ngoni will remember everything."

Numukeba drew his cutlass from the scabbard across his chest. He gave it to Ndala, saying, "Stay close to me on my right side. Do not let the enemy come between us. Do not fall from your horse. I will face forward, you will face backward, and thus if I see one of the enemy coming behind you I can strike him down. The Architect has given you the gift of music, perhaps he has given you the gift of combat as well. Stay close. Here on this knoll is where our destiny will be tested."

Nianga's one hundred horsemen arrived, shouting war cries and insults. Numukeba sat with his magic garan in his hand and Ndala sat with the cutlass in his hand. As the enemy closed in, Numukeba began to strike with his garan and Ndala began to thrust with the cutlass. Blades aimed at Numukeba were deflected by his vest of mail. Each time he landed a blow with his garan, a man fell from his horse. Again and again he shouted to Ndala, "Stay close! Stay close!" They fought, they fought. Many bodies littered the ground. At last the enemy warriors pulled away to regroup, and they saw that only forty of them were still alive out of the hundred that had come. They also saw a red glow around Numukeba, as if he were reflecting the light of an evening sun. Some of them said, "The man and the boy are jinns. Otherwise how could they kill so many of us?" They attacked once more, and again men fell from their horses. At last those who were left turned and rode from the field.

Numukeba said to Ndala, "Our destiny has been tested," but he heard no answer. He turned and saw Ndala's horse, but Ndala was not in the saddle. He dismounted and found Ndala lying with a fatal spear wound in his back. Numukeba's grief and remorse were great. He cried out, "O Architect, where are you?" He sat on the ground with Ndala's head in his lap. Darkness con-

sumed him. He seemed to hear a voice saying, "Every man lives
and dies according to the story written for him," but Numukeba
was not consoled. He thought he heard Etchuba saying, "There is
no story. The spear wound was chance." Still he was not consoled. Numukeba thought, "Because I considered myself a bene-
factor, I took the boy from his village. Had I left him there he
would now be alive." He was motionless for a long while.

Finally he picked up Ndala's body and mounted. Leading the
boy's horse by a rope, he rode back slowly to the town. When
people saw him coming, they scattered to their houses. He went
directly to the chief's house. He called for Nianga to come out.
Nianga did not come out. Numukeba struck the post of the house
with his garan, and the roof collapsed. He called, "If you do not
come out, Nianga, you will be buried in the rubble of your
walls."

Nianga came out. In his fear he could not speak. Now the
townspeople began to gather. Numukeba said to them, "Did you
hear him say he would not hurt the boy?" They called back,
"Yes, we heard it." Numukeba took the ngoni from Ndala's horse
and placed it on the chief's leopard skin. The people heard a voice
coming from the ngoni. The ngoni was singing. It said:

> "Nianga swore the oath of chiefs,
>   Swearing he would not disgrace the town.
>   He swore the same oath as Kunkotiti, Waraba and
>   Diara.
>   He placed his hand on the drum of his father,
>   He said, 'I will be honorable in all things.'
>   He said, 'I will never be frivolous with my power.
>   I will not persecute the weak in any way.
>   I will never go to war out of vanity.
>   If I speak any words they will be true.
>   If anyone criticizes me I will listen.
>   If anyone praises me I will be modest.
>   I will protect slaves, women and children.
>   If someone offends me I will be generous.'
>   This was the pledge of Chief Nianga,
>   This is what he swore on his father's drum.
>   But he did not like the words he heard from Ndala,
>   The words the ngoni gave Ndala to sing.
>   He sent one hundred horsemen to kill the boy.
>   Every horseman had a spear, a club and a cutlass.
>   One hundred of Nianga's soldiers went to kill Ndala.
>   Each thought, 'I will bring back Ndala's head.'
>   One hundred men rode out without honor
>   Because the chief sent them out without honor.
>   Thus Nianga, the fourth lion, disgraced his town.

One man and one boy fought alone,
They destroyed the army of Chief Nianga.
Disgrace and dishonor belong to Nianga.
This is the song sung by Ndala's ngoni."

When the ngoni was finished singing, the people looked at Nianga, waiting for him to answer, but Nianga was silent, his eyes on the ground. People said, "Is Nianga truly the one we accepted as our father?" They spat on the earth and turned their backs to the chief. The chief's djeli laid his linguist's staff in front of Nianga, signifying that he would never again speak for him.

Numukeba said to the people, "Prepare a funeral for Ndala." They began at once to prepare. Women took Ndala's body into the ceremonial house and made it ready for burial. When night came Numukeba did not sleep. He sat silently in front of the ceremonial house. The next day Ndala was buried. All the people of the town were there. Only Nianga was not present. Someone said, "Go bring the chief so he can see what his dishonor has done." They went for the chief. They returned without him, saying, "Nianga was there but he was not there." People asked, "What did you see?" They answered, "He was lying on his mat. His face was bloated and his eyes were staring. In his right hand was the gourd from which he drank the poison." People said, "We will not bury him. Take the body into the bush and throw it away."

Numukeba did not speak to anyone. He placed the ngoni on Ndala's grave, mounted his horse and departed from the town. When he was alone in the bush he looked toward the sky, saying, "O Architect, you could not have written Ndala's story! What is there to believe?"

9
The Rock
at Torigudu

BECAUSE HE DID NOT WISH TO SEE A HUMAN
face, Numukeba turned from the trail and
rode through the desolation of the bush without stopping to hunt
for food or water. He thought, "Let my thirst and hunger comfort
themselves. It does not matter, for I do not understand the meaning of living." He lost count of the days. It was only when his
horse lay down and would not move that Numukeba's mind
emerged from where it hid. He thought, "Am I the Architect of
horses? Am I writing in golden ink, 'This horse who carries me
everywhere must die in the bush?' It was not he who caused the
death of Ndala." He went searching till he found a water hole. He
carried water back in his skin bag and gave it to his horse. After a
while the horse stood up. Numukeba did not mount again but
walked, leading the horse by its bridle lines.

In time he came to a river. There he drank and slept, and when
he awoke his belly cried for food. He left his horse to graze and
walked along the river searching for something to eat. In the shallows where marsh grass was growing, Numukeba saw a manatee
feeding. He raised his gun but did not fire. The manatee did not
try to flee. He remained where he was, looking at Numukeba.
Numukeba said aloud, "You, manatee, has your story also been
inscribed in the book of golden writings? Or is your destiny
written in the firepower of my gun?" With a movement of its
flipper the manatee threw a large fish on the bank.

Numukeba said, "I am perplexed. I would have killed you, but
you feed me. How is it with you and your people? Do you also go
out to perform charities and brave deeds? If so, where are your

weapons? Where are the talismans that should cover your chest? Where are the slaves? Do you have djeli to praise your accomplishments? Whom do you consult to know the future?" The manatee spoke in the language of its kind, which was unintelligible to men. Numukeba closed his eyes and pondered, and it seemed to him that the manatee had said, "Great deeds are drops of rain that are lost in the river, and destiny is only a sliver of time in an aged world." Numukeba thought, "How did I comprehend his words? I do not know his language."

He picked up the fish and turned to thank the manatee, but the manatee was not there. Instead, a morike, a Muslim holy man, was sitting at the river's edge. Numukeba said, "Aaah! was it you?" The morike did not speak. He held up his hand, palm forward. The hand glowed, and in the palm Numukeba saw a picture of his village. After that another picture appeared, and he saw his former slave, Malike, fighting against Famoli. Then he saw Etchuba, the Owner of the Red Powder, sitting at the edge of the trail. One picture followed another, and Numukeba saw everything he had done and every place he had been since leaving Naradugu. He saw the boy Ndala with his ngoni, and after that the pictures faded.

Numukeba said, "Great morike, you must come from Timbuktu or Jenne where the knowledge of mysteries is unexcelled. Though I have told you nothing, you know everything about me. Tell me then how life goes for my household in Naradugu." The morike held up his hand again, and now Numukeba saw his house and people moving back and forth in the courtyard. But his wife was not among them, and he said, "I do not see her, the one I want to see." The picture changed, and Numukeba saw a funeral taking place and many people mourning. Darkness fell on Numukeba. He said, "Great morike, what I have seen cannot be true. I have not done anything to offend you, so do not play tragic games."

Again the morike held up his hand, and once more Numukeba saw the funeral of his wife. He said, "Aaaah! Aaaah!" Darkness closed him in. He did not hear the sounds of the running river and the birds. He heard nothing. How long he sat there he did not know. Finally the darkness lifted a little and he said to the morike, "The fire of performing heroic deeds has burned out. Let the daylight fade for me. Why should I go anywhere? Why should I look for honor and accomplishments? I have lost the boy Ndala, I have lost my wife. What have I achieved but poverty? Can the praise song of a king's djeli outweigh what has happened to me? I will go no farther. I will sit here on the riverbank until my body has lost the key of life. Let the hyenas and the vultures fight over my bones."

The morike raised his palm toward Numukeba, but Numukeba said, "Show me no more, morike. Whatever else is known to you, store it in the strongbox of your head." Yet Numukeba could not keep his eyes from looking. And this time he saw himself, girded for combat, sitting on his horse before a great rock. He said, "No, morike, do not tell me of the future, because there is no meaning to it. There are merely the things that happen, like thistle seeds blowing in a storm." He closed his eyes to ponder, and when he opened them the morike was no longer there. In the shallows of the river he saw the manatee grazing.

Numukeba returned to where he had left his horse. He spread his camel-hair blanket and sat on it, saying, "This is where I will stay to the end." Night came, then morning, but Numukeba did not feel the light of life fading for him. He arose at last and cooked the fish given to him by the manatee. He felt strength flowing into him from the rays of the sun. He groomed his horse and rewove the ribbon in its tail. He bathed, put on his armor and his amulets, mounted, and rode away toward the south.

He did not count the days that he was in the wilderness of the bush. He rode, hunted, rode again. Sometimes he asked himself, "Why am I here?" And there was only one answer, "Because that is the story of Numukeba of Naradugu."

At last he perceived a trail, and he followed it. He arrived at the outskirts of a town. Seeing a girl carrying firewood, he said, "Where am I, and what town am I approaching?" The girl said, "This is Torigudu." He asked, "Why are there no people visible in the fields?" She answered, "The crops do not grow well in Torigudu and the people are tired." Numukeba said, "In my country when crops do not grow well the people increase their efforts." The girl said, "I am too young to explain it. Talk to the old people and they will give you the answer."

Numukeba went on and rode through the town gate. People were in the streets going from one place to another and women were working at their mortars. Now and then a man greeted him listlessly. He thought, "Yes, it is so, Torigudu is a tired place." He arrived at the chief's compound and dismounted. To the slave who stood at the entrance he said, "I have just arrived. I want to make my presence known to the chief." The slave went away, then returned, saying, "The chief will see you in his reception house." He held the bridle of the horse, and Numukeba dismounted and entered. The chief was sitting on a leopard skin. He said, "I see you have travelled far. Why have you come?" Numukeba answered, "Chief of Torigudu, I come on the wind. In Naradugu no one ever spoke the name of your town. I arrived here only because this is where the trail led me. I ask you, in turn, why is Torigudu here?"

The chief answered, "Aaaah, it is here because it is here. Here is where our ancestors came from the east. Here is where our old ones have been buried. Here is where our houses and fields are. A tree stands in one place because that is where its seed was planted. One does not ask the tree for an explanation. But if a bird comes and sits in its branches one may ask, 'Why are you here?' "

Numukeba said, "Chief, your words are good. I am Numukeba of Naradugu. I travel through the world. I do not know what I am looking for, only that I am living out my story. Give me permission to rest four days, then I will go on." The chief said, "Yes, rest here." Numukeba said, "Chief of Torigudu, I feel that the force of life has ebbed from your town as if your ancestors had disowned you." And the chief answered, "Aaaah, it is because of the hero Dagala. It was he who destroyed the virility of Torigudu." Numukeba said, "How did it happen?" And the chief answered, "We will speak of it another time. Meanwhile, rest and be refreshed."

A slave conducted Numukeba to a small house outside the compound and laid a sleeping mat for him. Women came with a calabash of warm water and helped Numukeba bathe. After that the chief's wives brought food. When he was finished eating, Numukeba slept. In his sleep he heard a voice saying, "Every man has the story that was written for him." Another voice said, "No, there is no story. As the river flows it washes pebbles against one another. A pebble brushes against a pebble. This is how a man finds a wife for his house, or game in the bush, or a friend to confide in, or an enemy to defeat." And a third voice said, "No, there is no river. We simply exist, like a tall mountain. We are only a dream enclosed in a great calabash that we call the world."

When the evening sky covered Torigudu, the chief's senior slave came for Numukeba and led him to the reception house. The chief was sitting on a leopard skin, and next to it was an antelope hide for Numukeba. The chief said, "I can see that you are a hero who has achieved something, therefore I will speak of Dagala. Before Dagala became great, Torigudu was a good and prosperous town. Our people were industrious, our fields were fertile, and traders came here from as far away as Sahel. Dagala's family came from Banamba, therefore he was called Banamba Dagala. He was a person of valor. His name was heard, and his praises were sung in Dioni, Kaorola, Jenne and Timbuktu. Dagala conquered forty courageous men. He subdued twenty cities. He overthrew seven kings. He killed ten jinns. Dagala captured ten thousand cattle, ten thousand sheep, ten thousand goats and ten thousand slaves. He won much gold and many cowries. He had twenty wives.

"A time came when there was no more fighting for him to do. He drank and boasted with other heroes, but that was not enough. He became restless and angry. He insulted the people and provoked them. He stood on the top of his house and challenged the river. He challenged the wind and the sea. He challenged the jinns. At last he fired his gun at the clouds and challenged the Sky People to come down and fight. This is the way things were with Dagala. At last he became mad. He went through the streets naked brandishing his weapons. He killed whomever he wanted. When Dagala was in the streets, people went into their houses and closed their doors.

"At last the elders met and decided that Dagala must be expelled from the town so that life could go on. They called him to their council and said, 'You, Dagala, have been praised by many djeli. Your deeds are known everywhere. What has happened? Now you are only an evil force in Torigudu. No one is safe any more. Our people are in disarray. If you were the former Dagala we would praise and honor you. But now an evil spirit has come into you. The elders say you must go away. Find another home for yourself somewhere in the bush. Begin your journey. We will remember your deeds that were good and try to forget that you have become a demon.' These were the words the elders spoke to Dagala.

"Dagala's eyes became red with anger, as if there were a forge in his belly. He said, 'I will never leave Torigudu. You old men, live on as you wish, yet the light will fade for you and your bodies will go into the earth. But I, Banamba Dagala, will remain behind forever to harass your people, your wives and your cattle.' Those were the very words Dagala spoke, and after that he departed.

"The next morning he rode into the market wielding his long cutlass, and he cut down everyone within reach. He rode through the streets, slaughtering men and women alike. Other heroes of Torigudu came out to confront him, but he slaughtered them also. Then he rode to the great rock at the edge of the grove where we make sacrifices to our ancestors. He called out, 'Great rock, here I will live. I will enter and remain in this place.' The stone did not break or open, yet Dagala rode his horse into it and disappeared. He became one with the rock and could no longer be seen.

"From the interior of that rock Dagala comes out whenever he wishes. He continues to harass and slaughter. So it has been for some time, and many of our people have moved away from Torigudu. Our vitality is gone, and we merely live from day to day."

Numukeba exclaimed, "Aaaaah!" After a while he said, "Have you no heroes to deal with Dagala?" And the chief answered, "Once we had heroes, but now we do not have them any more. Therefore I speak to you about things, Numukeba of Naradugu. I consulted our filelikelas. I consulted our morikes. They have read their kola seeds and divined the future. They say it is Numukeba of Naradugu who will stand against Dagala."

Numukeba said, "Aaaah! Your filelikelas and your morikes are wrong. I am only a stranger here. I did not come to perform great actions, because I no longer understand their meaning. What are valorous deeds? Merely the sound of steel against steel. They give us ashes where once there were cities, widows where once there were wives. Heroes fall and die like kola fruit dropping from trees. The light has faded for a thousand thousand heroes, yet is the world a better place?" And the chief answered, "Who knows the answer? The world is full of good and evil, and always they struggle together. Sometimes evil wins, but good must rise again and fight once more. If this is not true, what is there to tell our children to encourage them?"

Numukeba stood up, saying, "No, it is useless. I do not want to earn any more songs of praise. You allowed me four days to rest in your town. After that I will go." He returned to his sleeping place and slept. The next day he went hunting and brought back an antelope for the chief. The day after that he killed a boar and brought it to the marketplace for the people to divide. That night he did not sleep well, but when he did he saw the morike at the river's edge holding up his glowing hand with the picture of Numukeba on his horse before the rock.

In the opening eye of morning he dressed in his armored vest and his talismans, took up all his weapons, sent a slave for his horse, and rode to the house of the chief. He said to the chief, "Guide me to the rock so that I may see if it is the one written in my story." The chief had his horse prepared. He called on his guards to assemble. He called his counsellors. He sent for his djeli. And they all rode through the town gate to the sacred grove, at the edge of which stood a boulder twice the height of a man. Numukeba thought, "Yes, it is the same. But the morike did not show me the outcome. Perhaps I will die here." He sat on his horse with his eyes half closed, feeling the warmth of the sun penetrate his body. After a while the people saw a red glow surrounding him.

Numukeba said to the chief, "I will confront Dagala only because I am ensnared in a web of events. How it will come out I do not know. If Dagala subdues me, entreat him not to take my head, so that my entire body may be carried back to Naradugu." He rode forward to the great rock, and he struck it a hard blow with his magic garan. The rock gave off a bell-like sound and shuddered. Numukeba called out, "Dagala, killer of women, children and cattle, come out of your hiding place! Numukeba of Naradugu calls you. Dagala, sower of death among the helpless, come out and taste your own death. Dagala, your weapons have lost their honor. Let them regain prestige in combat according to the code of noble heroes. You cannot preserve your life by hiding in a rock. If you do not come out, I will enter and find you."

Numukeba waited, but there was no answer. Again he called, "Dagala, scourge of women, children and old men, the djeli sing of you only in derisive epithets. Once you were great, now you are as lowly as a giver of enemas. Once you conquered cities and gave charities to the poor, but your credits were all consumed by your madness. In the mouths of people your name is not spoken, because it has an evil sound. When they say 'smallpox,' to them the word means Dagala. This is how you have fallen, Dagala. Redeem your name by courage and honorable combat. I am waiting."

There was no answer. Numukeba struck a hard blow with his garan, and the rock shuddered again and gave off a shrill bell-like sound. Numukeba called out, "Dagala, if you are paralyzed by fear, give me a signal and I will ask a woman of Torigudu to take my place. Then perhaps you will have the valor to leave your shelter."

The rock trembled. It shattered into a thousand fragments and dust rose into the air. The sound was like heavy thunder. Dagala emerged, riding his horse. His eyes were red, like coals in a fire. A black scarf covered his nose and mouth. A thousand leather talismans covered his arms and chest. In his left hand he held a musket, in his right hand he held a heavy ball of iron on a chain, in his belt were six knives, and on his chest was a long cutlass that glistened brightly in the sunlight. Dagala's horse also was covered with talismans, and its eyes also were red like burning coals. The people of the town fell back among the trees of the grove to make themselves less visible. They said to one another, "Aaah! it was better with Dagala inside the rock!"

Two heroes sat silently in their saddles for a moment looking at each other. Dagala spoke first, saying, "You whose name is something, you who come from somewhere, why have they sent an uncircumcised boy to meet me? Where is the honor in killing an inconsequential person like you? Yet I will kill you, and after that I will take your head. And when that is done I will destroy the town and everyone in it. Where Torigudu stands there will be only ashes and bones, and after that the spirits of the bush will reclaim it and it will be forgotten for all the times yet to come."

Numukeba answered him, saying, "Dagala, I cannot see your face because of the black cloth that covers it. But your spirit is ugly, as all men can see. Were your own mother here today she would say, 'Dagala was beautiful when he was born, and we welcomed him. But now his spirit is deformed, and we do not want him any more.' Even if you threw your cutlass on the ground and said, 'I concede the battle to you,' still I would have to kill you because you are a curse in the universe of living people. I did not want this contest. I came reluctantly because I have seen enough of death. But now that I am here my cutlass says to me, 'Wield me firmly so that I may pierce the belly of this devil posing as a hero.' Come foward, Dagala! Every hero lives, every hero dies. Because I have insulted you and enticed you from your fortress in the rock, I grant you the first three blows. Strike well, for if you do not kill me at once you are finished."

Dagala charged his musket and fired, but Numukeba waved the bullet aside with his magic garan. Dagala fired again, and again Numukeba deflected the bullet with his garan. Dagala charged his weapon once more, and this time the powder burned but did not explode, so that the bullet remained in the barrel. And now Numukeba put powder in his musket and fired, but Dagala held a silver-covered bone before him and the bullet passed him by. Numukeba fired two more shots, but the silver-covered bone protected Dagala.

Then the two heroes rode their horses at each other, Dagala twirling his iron ball and Numukeba slashing with his cutlass. The iron ball struck Numukeba and knocked him from his horse. But when Dagala came riding back, Numukeba's cutlass severed Dagala's bridle lines so that he could not guide his horse. Dagala dismounted, and the two heroes fought on foot. As they moved back and forth in the grove they stirred up dust, which hung in the sky like a dark grey cloud. Trees fell all around them, as if a great storm were passing through. The noise of the battle was heard in open fields far beyond the town.

The sun rose high in the sky and began its descent toward the west. Still they fought. The cloud of dust turned red as the afternoon grew old. Now Dagala fought only with his iron ball and chain, and Numukeba fought only with his cutlass. Dagala pressed Numukeba backward and was about to strike a finishing blow, but Numukeba's cutlass cut off the hand that held the weapon. Yet Dagala did not falter. He picked up the iron ball with his other hand and continued the battle, shattering Numukeba's cutlass. Then Numukeba took up his garan and struck a mighty blow. Dagala fell and lay lifeless on the earth.

The people came out of their hiding places in the grove, shouting, "Take the head, take the head!" But Numukeba did not take the head. He said, "No, I do not want it. For today Dagala behaved with valor and honor. But for his evil deeds and ugly spirit, take the body and throw it somewhere where it will never be found. Take the hand if you wish, and keep it. It is the valorous hand that held Dagala's weapons. And if travellers ask, tell them that Dagala's body was severed from the valorous hand and thrown in the wilderness."

He mounted his horse and rode back to the town. He entered

his house and lay on his mat. He remained in the house for four days. The people brought him food and water, but he neither ate nor drank. Musicians arrived with drums and ngonis and there was a festival, yet Numukeba did not appear. On the fifth day he came out. The chief's djeli began to sing a song of praise, but Numukeba said, "Do not sing." The djeli answered, "Numukeba of Naradugu, great events do not occur every day, but when they do I must sing of them. The past and the present are tied together by the songs of the djeli. Therefore I will recite what happened so that our children and grandchildren will remember." Numukeba said, "Sing then, djeli. But it has no meaning."

He sent a slave for his horse. He mounted. He went out of the town called Torigudu. People said, "Where he is riding, there is only lifeless bush." The chief said, "Did he not come from the bush? Now he returns, that is all."

10

Conflict in Massina

NUMUKEBA JOURNEYED DEEP INTO THE WIL-
derness. For two days he saw no life. On the
third day he saw an old rhinoceros grazing alone in the plain. He
rode forward without swerving until the two of them came face to
face. Numukeba said, "You, old warrior, are you going to challenge me?" The rhinoceros did not move one way or another.
Numukeba said, "Let it be. I do not want to fight you. You are
the age of my grandfather. I respect you. How are your children
and your grandchildren?" The rhinoceros continued to watch
Numukeba with tired eyes. It did not point its horn. Numukeba
said, "I can see that you are a hero like myself. Your armor is
scarred by battles, and your horn is chipped. Where are your
wives and slaves, and where is the djeli who should be singing
praises for your accomplishments? When you left your people
behind and went out to seek honor, did you say to them, 'He
whom you see coming will be alive, he whom you do not see
coming will be dead'? Why are you here, old man? What did you
find here that was not there?"

Numukeba dismounted and sat on the earth. He said, "Have
you discovered honor in this wilderness? If so, tell me what it
looks like. If it is invisible, where do you hide it? Does it live in
your heart? And when you die and the vultures claim your heart,
where will your honor be then?" As Numukeba went on talking,
the rhinoceros dropped to his foreknees and then lay on the earth,
watching and listening. Numukeba said, "You have lived a long
life, fought many battles and learned the meaning of things. Give
me something to add to my knowledge. Though you do not

_____79

speak, I will understand the language of your eyes." But the rhinoceros did not speak, and the meanings within its eyes did not convey themselves to Numukeba. At last Numukeba said, "Very well, let it be. Perhaps your knowledge is unfathomable."

He made his camp. He built a small shelter of branches and leaves. He built a fire and fanned it to a glow, and he sat beside it remembering his departure from Naradugu. He retreated into his mind. His fire burned into red embers and slowly faded into the blackness of the night. His stomach did not ask for food or water. A cold wind swept across the bush, but he did not feel it. Stars crept across the sky, but he did not see them. Calls of the night birds merged with pictures of his village and the sound of swift-moving rivers. His thoughts flowed out into the darkness and were lost.

And in the place from which his thoughts had departed he heard a voice saying, "I had many wives. We grazed in succulent grass. I guarded my people. I led them from one place to another. I showed them where the water holes were hidden, because I was the one who had been given the gift. I showed the young bulls how to give their horns strength and force by piercing them into the sand of a certain river. I defended the people from intruders. I protected the wells. In time I thought, 'This is not enough. I will grow old, and who will remember my name?' I went into the bush looking for the thing that would make my name immortal. I fought others of my kind and killed them, thinking, 'Now my name will be remembered.' I uprooted great trees and left them lying on the earth, thinking, 'Whoever sees these trees will know of me.' And now where I came from is hard to remember. I stored my achievements in my heart, but my heart is tired. I speak of these things to you, Numukeba of Naradugu, because you understand me."

Numukeba saw the sun rising behind a large cottonwood tree whose long shadow fell across the grey ashes of his dead fire. A butterfly landed on his hand, then flew away in search of nectar. He thought, "Here on this terrace of heroes I have sat all night with my companion without sleeping." He stood up. The rhinoceros lay where it had been the night before, but its eyes were closed and the life spirit had gone out of its body. Numukeba said, "Aaaah, my friend, did you have to go? Do not be concerned that the achievements stored in your heart will be eaten by vultures." And though such a thing had never before been done by his people, Numukeba gathered many heavy stones and covered the body of the rhinoceros with them so that it would be safe from wild creatures seeking carrion.

At last hunger came into his belly. He went hunting. He found an antelope and killed it. He cooked a little of the meat and ate. He placed the rest of the carcass over the haunches of his horse and went on riding. In time he came to a water hole where a young girl was filling her calabash. He asked her, "Where is this place?" The girl answered in surprise, "Why, the place is here." He said, "No doubt there is a town nearby. What is its name?" She answered, "No, there is no town, only the house where I live with my parents." Numukeba said, "I see a trail, does it go someplace that has a name?" She answered, "It goes to the house where the filelikela of Dioni lives. His name is Djoba." Numukeba said, "Do so many people go to his place that they have made a trail on the earth?" The girl said, "Yes, they come and they go." He said, "I have never heard of the filelikela of Dioni." The girl said nothing. She placed her water calabash on her head and went away.

Numukeba drank at the water hole. He thought, "Shall I follow the trail? What is the purpose in it? Trails cover the universe. All go somewhere and nowhere." While he was ruminating he saw an aged blind man coming, feeling his way along the trail with his staff. When the man arrived, Numukeba said, "Aaaah! It is you, Etchuba of the Red Powder." Etchuba answered as if he were greeting an old friend. He said, "Yes, Numukeba of Naradugu, it is I. You are far from home. Have you been dealing great blows to the universe? Have you set the world right and created justice out of injustice? Have you taken chaos apart and assembled order out of it?"

Numukeba answered, "Grandfather, I have done whatever honor and chivalry instructed me to do." Etchuba laughed, saying, "Why, then you are a slave, doing whatever your master orders: 'Numukeba, do this. Numukeba, do that.' How you have fallen, man of Naradugu. Once you were a respected blacksmith. You had a wife, fields, cattle and cowries. Now you wander the bush like a vagrant buffalo cast out by its people. You have grown lean and tattered. What you are looking for is not here."

Numukeba said, "Well, then, Grandfather, I have a riddle for you: Is it better to seek something or to seek nothing?" Etchuba replied, "It is no riddle at all. There is nothing to seek. The forces of the universe are outside of us. A trail takes you where it will. You are a downy feather in a storm." Numukeba answered, "Honor, respect and valor come from the inner heart of a man. If a person is alive he has within him the story written for him by the Architect. The sun does not rise by chance. The seasons do not change by chance. The river does not flow downstream by chance. Their stories are written." Etchuba said, "You speak of great forces in the universe, but are human beings one of them? No, and in that truth lies the folly of a man saying, 'I will begin at this end of the road and travel to the far end.' A flood comes and washes away his road. Or a cottonwood tree falls on him while he is sleeping. Or brigands kill him and take his cowries. Or he is captured by the king's soldiers and made a slave. And if he lives to think about something that prevented him from reaching his destination, the man says in surprise, 'Why, I did not foresee it.' The road is created straight, but accident twists it."

Numukeba said, "Etchuba, when the Architect creates a story he creates a certainty." Etchuba said, "I know of no Architect. There is no such thing as certainty. All things are wafted, beaten upon and scattered about without reason, for there is no reason." Numukeba replied, "You of the red powder, your purpose in life is only to rebel against what is true. You are like the angry son of a lenient father. The father has an orderly household. His fields are well kept, and his crops feed everyone. He tells his children what is good conduct. He tells them the secrets of survival. He shows them how to cultivate the earth. He shows them how to select good seeds and how to plant. He shows them how to build a good house. He teaches respect for those who are elderly. In teaching them all such things, the father shows that there is order in life.

"But the angry son thinks, 'Who is this bearded person who tells me how everything is done? He intrudes himself on me. I am not a slave.' The son says, 'This person says that if corn is planted in a certain way it will grow. But I have the power to prevent it.' The son goes to the field. He kicks the grains out of the earth. The corn does not grow. He says, 'With one foot I have proved that what people planted with their hands ends up in nothing.' So it is with you, Etchuba. With your red powder you make a man take the wrong fork of the road. You make a girl's calabash leak so that when she returns home there is no water in it. You cause an old woman's firewood to become wet so that it will not burn."

Etchuba pondered a while. Then he said, "Numukeba, do not compare me with an angry son. What happens in the world is only a struggle between elements. There are the light of the sun and the dark of night, the drive of wind, the wetness of water, the heat of fire and the force of chance." Numukeba answered, "No, it is not so. There are our ties with our ancestors. There are friendship and generosity. There are courage, honor between adversaries, and valorous deeds. There are feelings between a man and his wife. There is knowledge. We sense what is true and what is false. We create weapons and tools from ore dug out of the hillside. These are the elements of living." Etchuba laughed. He said, "I tell you again, Numukeba of Naradugu: There are only light, darkness, wind, water, heat and chance. And of them all chance is the greatest."

Numukeba was silent for a while, his eyes fixed on the trail leading from the water hole. At last he said, "Let us submit to a judgment. There is a filelikela living nearby. His name is Djoba, and he comes from Dioni." Etchuba said, "Aaaah! the filelikela of

Dioni. Before he was born my beard was already grey. Does the water bird go to the land bird to learn how to fish? What does the Oracle of Dioni know? There is no point to it." Numukeba said, "Have you forgotten the proverb that tells us: 'When the king's pronouncements are challenged, he may submit to the counselling of a slave'?" Etchuba again exclaimed, "Aaaah!" After a moment he said, "Very well. Let us hear the wisdom of Djoba, though his knowledge is feeble."

So the two of them went together along the trail, and in time they came to the house of the filelikela of Dioni, surrounded by a fence of brush. An old man came to the gate to greet them. They said, "We are travellers going from one place to another. We have a dispute. We want your master to judge." The old man asked them to wait. He entered the house. He returned, saying, "Yes, he will see you." They entered. The filelikela was seated on a cowhide. They sat on a mat that had been placed on the ground for them, and Numukeba answered, "I have the meat of an antelope outside. Have your slave take it." Etchuba said, "Here are twenty cowries," and he laid the cowries out before him.

Numukeba said, "Filelikela of Dioni, I contend that when a person is born into the world he has within him a story written by the Architect. If he is rich or poor, if he has five wives or none, if his crops flourish or wither, if he is a slave or a hero, that is his destiny. My companion denies it." Etchuba said, "Djoba of Dioni, though you are practiced in the mystic arts, I was here long before you. I knew your father and your grandfather. My companion does not accept what I tell him, that there is no fate, only accident in the universe. His mind does not grasp that what a man does in his life is determined by the chances that beset him on the road from birth to death."

The filelikela took out his kolas. He dropped them on the earth and studied the patterns they formed. After that he took out a long silver chain and threw it down, studying its configurations. In time he spoke, saying, "Etchuba—for I know your name—your argument has no proof. Your red powder causes people to do this and that, but perhaps what they do is only part of the Architect's story." To Numukeba he said, "Blacksmith of Naradugu—for I know your name—your argument has no proof. Who has ever seen the Architect writing a person's story? Your thoughts make you perform a certain deed, but who can prove that your thoughts are not merely grains of chance blown into your mind by the wind?"

He paused for a while, then continued: "Only one thing can be said to be true. Time is everything. It goes back to the beginning and extends to the end. We live and struggle in the Sea of Time. Why does a man struggle to perform great deeds? For the Sea of Time swallows him and his deeds. Even the wind is made still and fire extinguished in the Sea of Time. We speak of our grand-fathers, and of their grandfathers, but who came before them and what were their achievements? We do not know, because they have all merged again into the great Sea of Time."

He became silent, and when it was clear that the filelikela of Dioni was finished, Numukeba and Etchuba thanked him and left the house. Etchuba said to Numukeba, "You see? He is an idiot." And he took red powder from his pouch and threw it on Numu-keba, saying, "Blacksmith of Naradugu, if a day comes when you want to tell your story, remember that the story was not written by an architect in the sky but by the red powder of Etchuba." Then, feeling the ground with his staff, he began walking slowly to the east. Numukeba said, "Oh, Twister of Roads, envy of order in the universe has driven you mad. It is not your eyes that are sightless but your spirit. You yourself are living out a destiny written for you by the Architect. Your understanding of the uni-verse is crippled." Etchuba called back, "Oh, Blacksmith of Naradugu, try to perceive things as they are. There is no uni-verse, you merely wander in a cloud of dreams contained in a great calabash."

Numukeba rode to the west. When he saw the sun sliding to its rest he camped. He sat on his camel-hair blanket watching the light fade. He thought, "The truth is mysterious. Perhaps there is no universe. Perhaps there is no Architect. Perhaps the cloud of dreams is itself a dream. Perhaps everything is random. Perhaps the only certainty is death. Perhaps my achievements are merely writings in the air that can never be read. Still, they are the writ-ings of Numukeba of Naradugu. I am Numukeba. I am here." And thinking these thoughts, he fell into a deep sleep which no sounds could penetrate.

He was awakened by rough hands pulling at his clothing. It was daylight, and he was surrounded by a crowd of noisy Fula warriors. They already had taken possession of his weapons and now they were stripping him of his amulets. They forced his arms behind him and tied his wrists together. They called him insulting names and kicked at his body. Then they began to argue as to whether they should kill him or take him as a slave. One said, "Why should we dispute about it? Let the Bambara decide." And he shouted at Numukeba, "What will it be? Shall you be a slave or shall we take your head?" And Numukeba answered, "Take my head. I will never be a slave to the Fula." Some of the Fula waved their cutlasses threateningly as if to comply at once, but others restrained them, saying, "Wait. We can have his head any time we wish. Let us take him back to Massina. We can sell him or give him to the king."

So they put a rope around Numukeba's neck to lead him with, and the other end was tied to a horse. They mounted and rode,

Numukeba following on foot behind. They rode all day, not stopping to eat until evening. They made fires and cooked their meat, talking noisily about an expedition they had made against a Bambara village. Someone threw a piece of meat to Numukeba, but because his hands were tied behind him he could not put it to his mouth. A warrior said, "Bambara, why do you sit without eating anything?" Another said, "He cannot pick up the food." Another said, "Why, it lies on the ground in front of him. Let him bend down and eat it where it is. All Bambara eat that way."

Numukeba answered quietly, "You men of Massina, I do not want to share your food. If you were true heroes, you would not behave in such a manner." They laughed, saying, "Bambara, do you claim to be a hero?" Numukeba said, "When you seized me while I slept you did not ask me my name. Now, therefore, I have nothing to tell you. Let us hurry to Massina so that you can tell the king of your heroic victory over a sleeping man." They answered angrily, "You, Bambara, are nothing to us whether you are alive or dead. Whatever you were before, now you are a slave, so speak as a slave should or do not speak at all." Numukeba said, "Let it be that way. I will not speak as a slave, and so I will not speak."

They travelled five days, the Fula riding and Numukeba, a rope around his neck, walking behind. He drank at the water holes but refused to eat. They arrived at Massina, and Numukeba was placed in a house in the slave quarter of the city with an old man and his wife. The woman gave Numukeba food, which he ate silently. The old man asked him, "How are your people and your fields?" And Numukeba answered, "My city is Naradugu. It is a long time since I left that place. I do not know if I still have people. I do not know if my fields are green or withered away." The woman said, "I also am Bambara. I come from Kaarta." The old man said, "My people were Soninke. I was taken while I was still a young man. Now I build, clear brush, herd cattle, whatever I am told to do. You, man of Naradugu, surely you were a noble. Did they capture you in war?" Numukeba said, "Aaaah! They did not observe the rules of honor. They came upon me when I was sleeping in the bush. They seized my weapons. They did not offer me honorable combat, to which I was entitled. Therefore I despise them." Night came. They slept.

When the sun rose they ate bassi. There was the sound of a horn blowing in the distance. The old man picked up his bush knife. He said, "Now I must go to clear brush. Wait here, man of Naradugu. They will come for you." In time the Fula warriors came riding to the house. They put a rope around Numukeba's neck again and led him through the city to the king's compound. To the guard at the gate they said, "We have a gift for the king." The guard said, "The king is judging cases under his tree." He took them to the place where the king was judging. They waited until the king's djeli addressed them, saying, "You citizens of Massina, what do you wish to say?" Their leader answered, "We have captured a Bambara. We are here to give him as a slave to the king." The djeli spoke to the king, then he said, "The king accepts. How did you capture him?"

The leader of the warriors said, "Aaaah! He was riding a tall horse. He wore a vest of mail, and his chest and arms were covered with talismans. He brandished his weapons, saying, 'You Fula, slaves of slaves, stand aside for me to pass.' We said, 'You Bambara, son of an unknown father, your words are crude. We claim you as property for the king of Massina. If you are a hero, defend yourself.' He said, 'I have defeated a hundred men in my time, so stand aside.' I went forward and drew my cutlass. He did not answer my challenge, but threw his weapons on the ground. I gave him a rope and ordered him to put it around his neck. He did so. He dismounted. We returned to Massina. He followed on foot. We said amongst ourselves, 'He seems strong. He will make a good slave for the king.' Therefore we brought him to you."

Numukeba addressed the djeli. He said, "If I am to be a slave, that is my destiny. But first I wish to speak words to the king." The djeli said, "As a slave you have no right to speak to the king. But I will ask him." He repeated to the king what Numukeba had said. Then he said to Numukeba, "The king will hear you." Numukeba said, "Great king of Massina, your reputation for honor and justice is known everywhere. I address you not as a slave but as a freeborn person who has earned the title of hero. I am Numukeba of Naradugu. The men who captured me are deceitful. In addition, they are not intelligent. Would not a king prefer to have a slave taken in energetic combat than one who surrendered without a blow? I did not surrender. I was not given the chance to give or receive a challenge. I was sleeping in the bush. These men saw I did not wear any weapons. They seized me and tied my hands behind me. They put a rope around my neck, as you now see it. They did not untie my hands so that I could eat. I walked five days without any food. I thought, 'These men surely cannot be soldiers of the great king of Massina.' Now I offer a challenge to the paramount hero of Massina. I am prepared to fight by the code of valor. You will see by my behavior that the words of these men are lies."

Through the mouth of the djeli the king replied, "Bambara from Naradugu, you are now a slave and do not have the right to challenge anyone." He ordered Numukeba to be taken away and put in the fields to work. Numukeba was taken away.

Afterwards a man in a vest of mail stood up in the assemblage, saying, "Great King of Massina, you know me and my family. My name is Malike. My father rode with your father against the armies from the north. I myself fought many battles for the honor of Massina. On a certain day I fought against the Bambara and was captured. I asked the enemy to take my head, but they refused. I became a slave in the country of the Bambara. I lived on. My master gave me his vest of mail and his personal weapons, and he freed me. I came back to Massina. I have never violated the code of valor. I have been respectful of all who deserved respect. Whenever I won cattle in an expedition I shared them with the old and the poor. I never turned back from a battle, yet I never struck a man who held me in fear. If anyone here contends that I am not noble, let him say it to the assemblage."

No one spoke, and Malike continued, "This man named Numukeba, whom you have just accepted as a slave, is a hero. Had he been allowed to challenge any of those who captured him he would have fought to the end. They would have killed him or he would have killed them. He is the Bambara master who set me free. The vest of mail I wear was his. The cutlass I wear was his. You decreed that Numukeba does not have the right to challenge anyone because he is a slave. These are fair words of a just king. But I, Malike of Massina, have the noble right to challenge anyone for a good cause. Therefore I myself challenge the paramount hero of Massina. Who it is to be I leave to you. But if I defeat him, you must release Numukeba from slavery, return his weapons to him and restore to him all his rights as a freeborn man."

The djeli began to repeat Malike's words to the king, but the king stopped him, saying, "I have heard everything." He said to Malike, "Never before has a combat been held to determine the fate of a slave. But your family's name is respected, and the djeli sing songs to honor your father. Therefore I agree to what you propose. The test will be tomorrow morning outside the city walls."

News of the challenge spread to the king's fields where Numukeba was cutting brush. The old man in whose house he lived came to Numukeba, saying, "A strange thing has occurred. After your challenge was denied, a noble named Malike demanded the right to fight in your place. The king agreed. The battle will be tomorrow." Numukeba said, "Aaaah! Malike! He was once my personal slave and my friend." The old man said, "Yes, that is the way he told it to the king. If Malike wins, your rights as a freeman will be restored. We have never heard of anything like that before."

The next morning the people of Massina gathered and stood on the walls and rooftops to see the contest. The craftsmen, the traders, the king's counsellors, the women and the slaves were present. The king sat outside the gate on a stool placed on a leopard skin. His djeli stood behind him. The king's champion, named Asadoko, came riding a tall black horse. Asadoko's breast was laden with talismans. The stock of his gun was inlaid with brass, gold and silver. Malike came riding a tall white horse. His vest of mail glinted in the sun. His gun hung on his back and his cutlass hung across his chest. Fastened to his left forearm was a short knife in a scabbard made of crocodile hide. Fastened to his right forearm was a short knife in a scabbard made of rhinoceros hide. In his left hand he held a spiked iron ball hung on a chain. In his right hand he held a spear.

The two fighters rode to where the king was sitting. The king's djeli said, "Asadoko, Malike, you are here to contest with one another by the rules of honorable combat. The king of Massina says to you:

> 'Let every blow be strong,
> Yet let every blow be honorable.
> Let no one strike from behind.
> Do not insult your opponent's parents.
> Do not demean one another's courage.
> But if your opponent shows fear,
> Turn away and do not strike him.
> Though you are opponents you are not enemies.
> You are both citizens of Massina.
> You are both nobles.
> You are both servants of the king.
> If one man's saddle rope breaks,
> Let the other wait for it to be repaired.
> If one man's cutlass breaks,
> Let the other throw down his own cutlass.
> Remember that battle is skill against skill,
> But it is also honor against honor
> And generosity against generosity.
> Conduct yourselves with valor
> So that your names will be remembered by the djeli.' "

The djeli continued, "The king pledges that if Malike wins, the slave named Numukeba will be restored to his former rights. But if Asadoko wins, Numukeba will remain the king's slave forever."

Now, Numukeba was on the wall, and when he heard the king's words he ignored those who tried to restrain him and leaped to the ground. He went forward to where the king was sitting and addressed the djeli, saying, "Great djeli, I wish to say something about this contest." The king answered directly. He said, "You, man, are a slave. For a slave to put himself forward by demanding speech with the king is an offense to be punished by loss of his right hand. Go back where you came from."

But Numukeba persisted, saying, "Great king of Massina, if it is my destiny I will lose my hand. But I cannot remain silent. I once had a good wife, fields, cattle, gold and cowries. I made a journey to liberate the hunger in my heart for valor. Let others say what deeds I have done. I will not speak of these things. What I want to tell you is about Etchuba of the Red Powder. It was he who caused me to fall into a sleep so deep that I did not hear your soldiers coming. Therefore they captured me and brought me here and gave me to you. Etchuba is the personage who makes a straight line crooked. His devotion is to deflecting fate and twisting trails. It was Etchuba who sent me here. He wanted to make his evil mark on Massina. Now, because of him, two of your heroes are prepared to fight, and one will die. He who dies will leave widows, children and friends behind. Songs to the victor will say he killed another noble because of a slave. Songs to the loser will say he died because of a slave. Djeli who come in another generation will say the king of Massina caused a noble to die because of a slave. Should a djeli ever again sing a praise song for me he will say that I was the cause of the killing.

"Great king of Massina, when I made my challenge in your court I did not imagine where it would lead. Speak of me as your slave if you must, but my destiny is not to be a slave. I am freeborn, the master blacksmith of Naradugu. Through me the force of the sun passed into weapons, bush knives and hoes. It is said in the world that your great-grandfather who founded Massina, though a noble, was also a master of the forge. Therefore he is an ancestor of mine, for all blacksmiths are related.

"Because my story is already written, a combat between Malike and Asadoko will decide nothing. I beg you to put it aside. Instead, I make a different challenge now. Those men who captured me while I was sleeping maligned me, saying that I threw down my weapons and with my own hands placed a rope around my neck. They are craven men, and they deceived you with their words. A contest between Malike and Asadoko would be nothing more than a wager. But a contest between my captors and myself would be a royal judgment. I will fight them all, singly or together, whatever they choose."

The king was angered to hear Numukeba speak so openly. But he consulted with his djeli, who said, "The Bambara is right. A fight between Malike and Asadoko will not bring honor to Massina. If the cause of the affair was Etchuba of the Red Powder it is he who should be on trial. Whether the Bambara is truly a hero we do not know. However, Malike is a noble and he spoke well of him. We may say among ourselves, 'Who in Massina ever heard of allowing a slave to prove by combat that he is or is not a slave?' Still let us remember the song that says:

'The land belongs to the king.
The cattle belong to the king.

The wine belongs to the king.
The fields belong to the king.
The gold belongs to the king.
The cowries belong to the king.
But the greatest property of the king
Is the administering of justice.'

Therefore, do not be confined by what other kings have done.
Dwell on this matter in your heart."

The king said, "Let it be that way. I will dwell on it." He ordered the combat between Malike and Asadoko to be cancelled.
His slaves came out of the city to carry his stool and leopard skin
back to his house. Women returned to their homes. Craftsmen
returned to their crafts. Slaves returned to clearing brush in the
king's fields.

The king called his counsellors together to discuss Numukeba
of Naradugu. Some said one thing, some said another, until at last
the king said, "Yes, let the Bambara fight against his captors. In
this way I will know who lied." Secretly he thought, "If the
Bambara is killed I will be rid of him. He is a thorn in my foot for
having addressed me as an equal. If he wins, he will be free to go
away, and I will be praised for having administered compassion-
ate justice." He ordered that Numukeba's horse and his weapons
be returned to him for the combat.

The next day at sunrise Numukeba's captors assembled on the
battlefield outside the city wall. There were fifteen men in all.
They began to ask, "Where is the Bambara who wants to throw
his life away?" And again, "Tell the clown from Naradugu to
hurry, for we have other affairs to attend to today." Before long,
Numukeba came riding through the city gate. His horse, its tail
and mane newly braided with colored ribbons, pranced forward.
Numukeba's armored vest glistened, and the scarf around his
neck trailed out behind him. The talismans on his chest undu-
lated with each step of the horse. His back was to the eastern sky,
and his tall shadow reached out toward the Fula warriors. The
Fula said to one another, "What is the reddish light that surrounds him?" Others answered, "It is nothing, only the rays of
the morning sun." But they became uneasy when they saw that
Numukeba's cutlass and spear glowed with the red evanescence
of hot metal just taken from the furnace of the forge.

Numukeba said to them, "You men who claim to be freeborn
heroes, let us not waste time with talk. You sought to achieve
glory by claiming what was false, and you cast doubt on my
honor. Therefore we will fight to the death. All that remains is for
you to decide whether you will fight me one by one or all together." The Fula warriors rode away a little distance and consulted. One said, "The Bambara appears to be a jinn." Another

said, "No, he is only a man." A third said, "Perhaps we should all fight at once and get it over with." A fourth said, "What would the people say, fifteen men against one?" Finally the leader said, "Let us do it this way: I will challenge him first. If all goes well, that will be the end of the matter. Yet if he has great mystic powers and begins to overcome me, then the rest of you will join the battle." Someone said, "Aaaah! The king would not consider it to be honorable combat." The leader said, "Very well, then perhaps you will choose to be first instead of me?" There was silence, and the leader asked, "Or does someone else choose to be first?" No one answered. The leader said, "Then it will be the way I planned it. If things go badly I will call out, 'Hoooo! Massina! Massina!' And when you hear the call you will come to my assistance."

The king was sitting on his stool outside the city gate. He raised his forged iron staff, topped with the hair of a lion's mane, to indicate that the fighting was to begin. The leader of the Fula party rode forward to face Numukeba. He said, "My name is Hamadi, and I come from the family of Ardo which is known everywhere for its achievements and valor. My ancestors were among those who created Massina." Numukeba answered, "You told me everything about yourself when you and your warriors captured me like an animal in a snare, and when you lied to the king about your deed. The family of Ardo was honorable, as is known everywhere. But because you behaved with malice and without honor, you cannot possibly be a descendant of that family. Therefore, you lie again. Your horse has more honor than you because it does not drool falsehoods with every breath. So let us not talk about who you are. Strike the first blows. I will allow you three shots, and after that you must defend yourself."

Because Numukeba's words had been heard by the people watching from the wall and the rooftops, anger replaced uncertainty in Hamadi. He stood up in his stirrups, raised his gun and fired at Numukeba. The musket ball struck Numukeba's armored vest and fell to the ground. Hamadi loaded, stood up in his stirrups and fired again. This time Numukeba waved the ball aside with his magic garan. Once more Hamadi loaded and fired. His powder did not explode but merely fizzled, and the ball fell harmlessly from the barrel.

With his right hand Numukeba drew his cutlass from the scabbard across his chest. In his left hand he held his garan. He rode forward, slowly at first, then as fast as his horse could run. When the two men came together, Numukeba struck Hamadi on the side of the head with the flat of his cutlass to show his contempt. Hamadi struck back, but Numukeba's talismans deflected the blow. The two fighters and their horses merged in the vortex of a dust cloud. They parted and came together again. Numukeba struck Hamadi's cutlass with his garan, breaking the blade. Once more they rode away from each other. Once more they charged. This time Numukeba seized Hamadi around the waist and hurled him to the ground. Hamadi stood up and saw Numukeba looming above him. He called out, "Hoooo! Massina! Massina!" His warriors came riding with loud cries, wielding spears and cutlasses. They surrounded Numukeba and began striking and thrusting with their blades.

Numukeba wheeled his horse one way, then the other, his garan in his left hand and his cutlass in his right. Two Fula heroes fell. Numukeba broke through the wall of horsemen, rode off, then came back striking blows on all sides. Another Fula hero fell and was trampled under the feet of the horses.

While the battle was going on, Malike of Massina rode from the city to the place where the king was sitting. He said, "Great king of Massina, have we forgotten the rules of honorable combat? When armies meet in battle one man may have to fight a brigade. But what is happening here is a dishonor to Massina. I ask your permission to go out and support Numukeba." The king said, "You have already given me much trouble, Malike. Let things be as they are." Malike answered, "King of Massina, in time to come your djeli will not be able to praise you for what you are allowing to happen. As for me, my family is as noble as any other man's, even yours. When my children ask me, 'What did you do when Numukeba was outnumbered fifteen to one in front of Massina's gate,' what shall I tell them? Though Numukeba is Bambara, he is a valorous hero. You are king of Massina, but I am king of myself. Therefore I am joining in the combat." And before the king could answer, Malike galloped into the middle of the fighting.

He brought his horse to Numukeba's side. In his right hand he held his spear, and in his left he held his spiked iron ball suspended on a chain. Numukeba fought and Malike fought. The Fula warriors at first were puzzled, then fearful. A red radiance shone around Numukeba, and a blue radiance shone around Malike. Fula after Fula fell from his horse, until only one remained. He called out, "Enough, I am beaten. Take my head." Numukeba answered, "Not yet. First tell the king that you and your companions lied." They rode to where the king was sitting. The Fula dismounted. He said, "Great king of Massina, the story we told was false. The Bambara was sleeping. He could not reach his weapons. First we tied his hands behind him, then we put a rope around his neck." The king said, "Aaaah! For lying to the king you will die."

Numukeba said, "Great King of Massina, declare now that I am not a slave." The king answered, "Yes, Numukeba of Naradugu is not a slave." Numukeba said, "Tell your djeli to proclaim it from the turret of the city wall. Let him say it three times, and let the people of Massina witness it." The djeli went into the city and climbed to the turret. He called out, "Numukeba of Naradugu is not a slave." The people answered, "We hear you." A second and a third time he called out, "Numukeba of Naradugu is not a slave." A second and third time the people answered, "We hear you." The djeli said, "You have witnessed it three times. It is done."

Later that morning the king held court. He judged disputes and heard petitions. Afterwards he sent for Malike, and he said to him, "Malike of Massina, when you went out to assist Numukeba against his opponents you acted with valor. Still, I had just said, 'Let things be as they are.' You ignored my words, saying, 'You are king of Massina, but I am king of myself.' You have heard the proverb, 'Two male hippopotamuses cannot share the same riverbank.' Two kings cannot live in the same city. Therefore, I expel you from Massina. Go elsewhere. Achieve your achievements. Accumulate honor, but do not return here."

Numukeba asked permission to speak, and the king assented. Numukeba said, "Great King of Massina, it is said everywhere that you are a person of justice. Yet justice cannot be weighed in a gold-dust scale, for it measures things that cannot be seen or heard. It cannot measure secret thoughts in a man's mind, or secret feelings of what is right and wrong. When Malike saw me alone in battle his heart ruled him. He did not debate with himself, saying, 'If I do one thing the king will praise me for it, and if I do another thing he will criticize me.' Honor seized him and he came to join me. This was the story written for Malike and the story written for me. How could I go on living, knowing that because a man risked his life for me he was expelled from his city? Great king, give Malike and me a task to do to earn his pardon. We will go on an expedition for you against the Hausa, the Malinke, the Soninke, the Fasa or the Bororo, whomever you wish." The king listened. And at last he replied through the mouth of his djeli, "I will consider it. Come back in three days and I will give you an answer."

On the third day they returned. The king said, "My senior wife is sick with an ailment that my masters of mystic knowledge are unable to cure. They say that milk from the cows of Walatadu can restore her health. Therefore, go to Walatadu and get the cows. When you have brought them back, the sentence against Malike will be lifted."

Numukeba and Malike replied, "King of Massina, never doubt that we will do it."

II
The Cows
of Walatadu

MALIKE AND NUMUKEBA WENT TOGETHER TO a morike of Massina and informed him of the expedition they were about to begin. They said, "Tell us, master of the mystic sciences, what we have to know so that our enterprise will be successful." He took up his Koran and held it in his hands. He contemplated. For a long time he was silent. Finally he said, "The place to which you are going is dangerous. It is a land of magical forces. I will consult with other morikes of Massina. Come back in three days and I will have something to tell you."

The two heroes went away, and on the third day they returned. The morike said, "We have consulted the Koran. We have consulted our kolas. We have divined with sand. None of us can foretell the outcome of the expedition. You must go to Timbuktu and see the master morike of that city, Mochtar Kadiri. Only he can tell you what you want to know."

Malike and Numukeba prepared for the journey. They repaired their spears and had new saddle ropes made for their horses. They ordered new sandals to be made by a garanke and bought new scarves for their necks. Numukeba said, "Let us delay one more week. I want to make new weapons." He went to a forge. He smelted ore. He shaped iron. He labored day and night. He forged a long heavy gun, too large for a man to handle. He suspended it on one side of his horse, the mouth of the barrel pointing forward. He forged another gun just like it and suspended it on the other side of the horse, the mouth of the barrel pointing backward. He made lead bullets. They were very large. He said, "Now I am ready."

The two men departed from Massina, riding northward along the bank of the river. They travelled one week. They came to Timbuktu. They went to the house of Mochtar Kadiri. Many persons sat in front of the house waiting to speak to the morike. Numukeba said, "Aaaah! We will grow old and our beards will become grey before we can talk to him." Malike said, "No. Let us sit where we are on our horses. He will notice us." Mochtar Kadiri was explaining the meanings of the Koran to some young men, and when he was finished he came out and stood in his doorway. He saw Numukeba and Malike on their horses. He said to them, "Many people are waiting." Numukeba answered, "Yes, we also will wait." Mochtar Kadiri recognized them as heroes. He saw blue light around Malike and red light around Numukeba. He went into his house. After a while he came out and said to them, "Dismount, Numukeba. Dismount, Malike. Come in. My slaves will take care of your horses." They dismounted. They entered the house of Mochtar Kadiri.

They said to him, "It seems that you know our names." He answered, "Yes, who you are was revealed to me by my kolas." They said, "Great morike, it was told to us in Massina that you are the only one who can perceive the beginning, middle and end of our expedition to Walatadu." He divined. He said, "Aaaah! Your enterprise will be dangerous. There will be steel against steel, knowledge against knowledge, skill against skill, and magic against magic. The kolas speak of a hill that breathes." Numukeba asked, "What is the meaning of 'a hill that breathes'?" The morike answered, "The kolas speak only tangently. What the hill is, you will discover in time." Numukeba said, "Great morike, if a story is written, is it not written? Is there nothing more you can tell us?"

Mochtar Kadiri pondered, and after a while he said, "We say that a person's story has been written. That we believe to be so. Yet has the story been written completely? The Writer writes, 'Thus will Numukeba and Malike be born.' He writes, 'Thus will Numukeba and Malike grow into manhood.' He writes, 'Their character will be good, and they will have honor.' Yet can the Writer set down everything? Must he inscribe in golden ink that on such and such a day Malike will eat bassi for breakfast, and Numukeba will find three fleas in his clothing? A person's story is not written in such a manner. There are gaps in the writing which the person must fill in. If he has valor, honor and generosity he will fill them according to his character. If he does not have valor, honor and generosity he will fill them differently. If a man has the protection of mystic forces and if his weapons have mystic power, the outcome of his struggles will be better than if he does not have them. Therefore he asks for the help of a morike. Let us consider. Did the Writer of All Stories die after he had written them? No, he is as he was. And if a time comes when the Writer sees that a person has come to a gap in his story, he says to himself, 'At this point my ink ran dry while I was writing. Now, therefore, I will fill in what was not written. Let the person help me write. Let him be aware. Let him decide things. Let him do something. Let him be thoughtful. Let him draw upon the resources of the universe that surround him.' So the kolas reveal some things and not others. Only when the time comes can a person know his story in all its fullness."

Numukeba felt enclosed in a dark shadow. He said, "Great morike, you speak with wisdom, but you have given a role in the world to Etchuba of the Red Powder. For if the gaps you speak of are there, then he can twist and warp all of us as he pleases, and any amulets you might prepare for us are useless." Mochtar Kadiri reflected. He said, "Who can say that the story of Etchuba himself was not written in golden ink?" There was no more to be said or to be asked. Numukeba and Malike placed cowries on the morike's mat and departed. They went to the heroes' terrace, drank wine, and listened to the boasts of men who had earned honor in combat. When night came they found a house where they could spend the night. They slept.

In the morning when Numukeba awoke, Malike was already dressed. He said, "I arose early. I went here and there making inquiries. There is an unusual slave filelikela in the city by the name of Koloba. He is unusual because he is a child of twelve years. I spoke with some of the heroes of the city. I said, 'If he is only twelve, how can he have any knowledge?' They answered, 'He is in the form of a boy, but he has great knowledge brought from the land of the unborn.' Therefore, let us visit this filelikela."

They went searching for Koloba in the slave quarter of the city. But if they asked a person, "Where is the house of Koloba?" the person would only wave his hand vaguely or say he did not know. Malike said, "It seems they are afraid of Koloba. Therefore he must have great mystic powers." At last an old woman pointed to a decrepit house, saying, "Yes, Koloba lives there. But what would people like you want of him?" Malike said, "Grandmother, do not be concerned." The woman said, "Koloba is my grandchild, therefore I am concerned." Malike said, "Aaaah, you can trust us, because I myself was once a slave. Does Koloba truly have mystic knowledge?" The woman answered, "If you do not believe it, why are you here? His first words were, 'Bring me my shells.' We brought him tiny snail shells from the river. He put them in a box. He shook them and listened to the sound they made. When he was only one year old he performed a divination. He divined, saying, 'The sacred grove to the north of Timbuktu is burning.' People laughed, but they went to see, and found that the grove was burning. When he was only three he divined that the eldest son of the king would die. The king's son died. When he was four he divined that smallpox would come to the city. It came."

Malike said, "Grandmother, we are going on an expedition and we want Koloba to give us help." She said, "If you have a divination present, give it to me and go in." They dismounted, gave her a handful of cowries and entered the house. Koloba was sitting on the earthen floor whittling a stick. Malike said, "Koloba, what is the pointed stick for?" And the boy answered, "To place on the roof of the house to keep the hawk from alighting there. We do not want him." They said, "Grandson, we need help from you and your shells."

He looked at them sternly and said in a young boy's voice, "Do not speak to me elder-to-younger, for I am older than you." Malike said, "Yes, it is true. We will call you filelikela. We come with respect." The boy got up from the floor. He went to a stool in a dark corner of the room and sat down. He lighted an oil lamp, which threw a dim flickering light on his face. He took up a small wood box and shook it. It echoed with the sound of shells. He closed his eyes and chanted words in a strange language. He chanted a long time, and it seemed as if nothing were happening. Then, in the faint light, the heroes saw that Koloba's face was changing. It became the face of an old man. His skin was filled with wrinkles. His hair turned grey. His arms became thin and bony. Numukeba and Malike felt themselves to be in the presence of a mystery.

When Koloba spoke, it was with the high-pitched, cracked voice of an ancient grandfather. Placing his box of shells on the ground, he said, "I know your names, Numukeba and Malike. You are heroes who have performed valiant deeds. You are on a journey to Walatadu. You are going for cows whose milk is wanted by the king. It is a journey with danger. There will be combats. There will be death. What you accomplish will change Walatadu for all time to come. Remember this: If you succeed in getting your cows, take only the white ones. But you need talismans to give your weapons force. I will give you two strings of shells, one for each of the large guns on Numukeba's horse. Tie the shells around the barrels. I will give you two more strings of shells. Tie them around your necks, and if they speak, listen to them. If you do all things well you will return to Massina. Here are the two strings of shells to wear. Here are the two strings for the guns. I have said everything."

Koloba picked up his box again and began shaking it. In the dim light they saw his face changing. The old man's face disappeared, and the face they now saw was youthful. Koloba put down his box and spoke, saying in a boy's voice, "Though you gave my grandmother cowries, they belong to her, so now leave something for me." Numukeba and Malike placed more cowries on the ground. They said, "Filelikela, we know now that you truly have mystic sight. We thank you for what you have done." The boy said, "My knife is no good. I need a knife for whittling." Malike gave him a knife from his belt, and the boy said, "Good, it is a grown-up man's knife." And he said, "I also need a scarf for my neck." Malike offered him his scarf, but the boy said, "No, I do not like blue. Give me a red one." So Numukeba took the red scarf from his neck and gave it to Koloba. Koloba said, "If you see my grandmother outside, tell her I am hungry."

When they left the house they told the old woman, "Koloba says he is hungry." The old woman said, "Young boys are always hungry. Did you find what you were looking for?" They answered, "Yes, Grandmother, we found it." They placed the strings of shells around their necks and on Numukeba's guns. They mounted their horses and departed from the city. They rode along the river awhile and then went north into the bush toward the city of Walatadu.

The journey was long. On the eighth day they saw spires of smoke rising above the city. They rested, and the next morning they rode to the city wall. The gate was closed, and a guard standing on the wall called out, "Who are you, where do you come from and what is your reason for coming?" Malike said, "I am Malike of Massina." Numukeba said, "I am Numukeba of Naradugu." The guard answered, "Why are you here? This is a closed city." Numukeba said, "I see by the way you talk that you are a slave. Were you a noble you would have asked, 'How do your people fare? How are your crops? How are your cattle?' Bring the king's djeli so that we may speak to him equal to equal."

The guard disappeared behind the wall. Time passed. They remained where they were, at the gate. The djeli appeared. He did not greet them with courtesy. He said only, "What do you want in Walatadu?" Malike answered softly, saying, "How is your king? How is his family? Do his cattle and fields thrive?" The djeli said again, "Why are you here?" Numukeba said, "Perhaps we are confused, perhaps we have arrived at the wrong city. We thought that this was Walatadu, governed by the great King Seku Ndome. If this were really Walatadu we would be greeted courteously. You would be saying, 'Enter the gate, rest yourselves from your journey.'" The djeli replied, "Yes, once it was so. But our king was warned by his morikes that two heroes would come riding from the south to make trouble for the city. Therefore the gate was closed and everyone who arrives must be questioned."

Numukeba said, "Yes, perhaps we are the ones the morikes

spoke about. Yet if the king is generous with us we will not cause difficulties." The djeli asked, "What is it you want?" Numukeba answered, "We want nothing except forty white cows from the king's herd. Give them to us and we will go back to Massina and you will not see us again." The djeli exclaimed, "Aaaah! You want a great deal. I will speak to the king tonight. Be here in the morning just as the sun rises." So Numukeba and Malike made their camp in a little grove outside the city. When darkness came they lay on their blankets to sleep. At that moment the shells that Numukeba wore around his neck began to speak. They said, "The djeli talks now to the king. The king becomes angry. He says, 'Numukeba and Malike are presumptuous. Why should I give them forty white cows? I owe them nothing. They insult me. I will give them forty spears, forty guns, forty arrows, and forty cutlasses.' The king sends for the leader of his best battalion. Now he is instructing him. He says, 'Take forty warriors. Let them wait inside the gate. When Numukeba and Malike come at dawn, open the gate and attack. Let no warrior come back into the city until Numukeba and Malike have tasted death.' This is what King Seku Ndome says."

Numukeba and Malike sat up, saying, "Seku Ndome is not a noble. He has no honor." Then Malike's shell necklace began to talk. It said, "Go to the gate at dawn as you agreed. But do not make contact with the enemy there. When they appear, turn and ride away as if you are fleeing. Just to the west of the city you will see two large rocks. A narrow trail goes between them, where one man must ride behind another. Lead the enemy through the rocks and meet them on the other side one at a time."

They slept. They awoke before dawn. They adjusted their vests of mail and their weapons. They mounted their horses and rode to the gate of the city. The sun began to be visible. The gate swung open and forty horsemen charged forward with fierce battle cries. Numukeba and Malike rode to the west. They saw two large rocks and passed between them. They readied their cutlasses and spears. And when Seku Ndome's warriors arrived, one at a time, Numukeba and Malike cut them down. The bodies of the king's warriors fell one on another. Because those who were behind could not see what was happening in front, they continued to come until the last of them lay lifeless on the ground.

Numukeba and Malike rode back to the gate of the city. To the slave standing on the wall they said, "Tell the king's djeli to come now and give us our greeting." The djeli came. Numukeba said, "The king's soldiers lie dead over there to the west. We give the city permission to bring them in and bury them. But as for you, ears and mouth of the king, this is what we say to Seku Ndome: 'King, you are false and treacherous. Even your name is a lie. Therefore we do not like it. It does not tell us whether you are

Bororo, Fasa, Burdama or merely the child of a father who was not his father. You, Seku Ndome, you who sent your dogs after us, perhaps you have courageous young men who want to challenge us. Perhaps you have sons or nephews who would like to retrieve a little honor for your city. If so, send them out. If not, open the gate of Walatadu and we will come in and receive a proper greeting from you.' Repeat these words to Seku Ndome without making them soft."

The djeli went to the king, and he repeated Numukeba's words without making them soft. Seku Ndome pondered. He thought, "The insult is too great." Yet he worried. He called his counsellors together. He said to them, "These heroes have supernatural strength. They have killed forty of my soldiers. Now they challenge me directly. They ask me to greet them in a civil way, yet they demand forty white cows." The counsellors consulted, and they said to the king, "The matter is simple. If you deny them entry they will besiege the city. People will not be able to go to the fields or the wells. Give them a hearing. Agree to what they ask for. Do not speak directly, but artfully, and tell them the cows are theirs for the taking. Let them promise not to return to Walatadu. They are honorable heroes, as one may see from their behavior. They will not return. As for the cows, they are safe, for they are guarded by the Great Reptile. When Malike and Numukeba see him they will turn away, yet because of their obligation to honor they will not be able to come back to the city."

The king said, "Aaaah! A good plan. But I will leave it to my djeli to speak the artful words, because their insults rankle in my belly." The djeli went back to the gate and said to Numukeba and Malike, "The king will greet you in his house, and you will speak to him there about the cows." He ordered the gate to be opened. Numukeba and Malike rode foward. Crowds gathered in the streets to watch them pass. The king's compound was on the far side of the city. When they arrived, they positioned their horses at the entrance and remained sitting in their saddles. The king came out, and a stool was placed for him. He sat down and waited for Numukeba and Malike to dismount, but they did not do so. The king said to his counsellors in a low voice, "They insult me again. They do not get down from their horses." The counsellors replied, "Do not notice it. Merely greet them."

The king said, speaking through his djeli, "Men of Massina and Naradugu, how are your people? How are your fields and your crops? How are the rulers of your cities? The citizens of Walatadu welcome you. If you come in peace, you shall have peace. May Walatadu, Massina and Naradugu have amity between them." Malike said, "Great King of Walatadu, the people of Massina are well and the king is well. The king sends his greetings to you. The nobles of Massina send greetings. The craftsmen, the traders, the women and the slaves send their greetings." Numukeba said, "Great Seku Ndome, thank you for your welcome. As for my people it is a long while since I have seen them. But they surely wish you well. For them I say, 'May you and the citizens of Walatadu flourish. May nothing ever happen to injure the good feelings we have for one another.'"

Then, as if nothing at all had happened, the djeli said, speaking for the king, "Numukeba of Naradugu, Malike of Massina, what can King Seku Ndome do to assist you in your mission, whatever it is?" Numukeba answered, "Great king, what we must have is forty white cows from your herd, so that we may take them back to Massina." And when this answer was relayed to the king, he appeared thoughtful, then said, "Why, it is a strange request. Still, I have thousands of cattle. I am willing for you to have what you need." The djeli, speaking artful words, said, "The king agrees that you may take forty white cows. Go the place where they are grazing. A Fula herdsman will show you the way and herd for you. Beyond a certain hill are the cattle. There is only one condition. You will relax with the heroes of Walatadu. After that you will go for the cows, but you must not come back to the city, for the proverb tells us, 'When you have announced your departure, go forward and do not look back.'" Numukeba said, "Yes, let it be that way." Malike said, "Yes, let it be that way."

The djeli led them to the boasting terrace. There they ate, drank and listened to Walatadu's heroes tell stories of their achievements. After a while one of the men turned to Numukeba and Malike, saying, "You who are silent, tell us what merits you earned that allow you to be sitting here with us." Malike said, "What is there to tell you? When I was a young man I fought for Massina and was captured by the enemy. I became a slave. Of his own free will my master freed me and I returned to Massina." They said to him, "No more than that?" He answered, "Why, only the small events that came between one thing and another." They addressed Numukeba, saying, "Your companion has not done anything worthwhile. What about you? Tell us about your accomplishments." Numukeba answered, "I was a blacksmith. I made iron blades for hoes and spears. I left my city. I journeyed from one place to another. There is nothing marvelous to tell." The heroes looked at the vest of mail that Numukeba wore. They looked at his spear shaft and saw that it was scorched where his hand held it. They looked at the large guns that were suspended at the sides of his horse. They grew angry. They said, "Have you come here to mock us? Any woman could tell a story with more adventure and valor in it. We recite this and that, and you speak as if such things are worthless."

Malike answered them. He said, "Friends, from what you say you are indeed valiant men. We do not mean to detract from it. If you do not hear any great deeds from us, it is not because we mock you, but perhaps because we have travelled far and are weary. We have come to Walatadu only for cows. We do not wander the universe to make our names great. Therefore we have little to tell you. If we fight sometimes it is only because honor compels us. Yet we should not leave your company without bringing you something. Therefore, I give you a song that was created by an ancient djeli in Massina:

'Do not seek too much fame,
But do not seek obscurity.
Be proud
But do not remind the world of your deeds.
Excel when you must,
But do not try to excel the world.
Many heroes are not yet born,
Many heroes have already died.
To be alive to hear this song is victory.' "

Numukeba and Malike arose. They mounted and rode slowly out of the city. The gate closed behind them. Led by a Fula herdsman they went to the east. At a certain place the Fula motioned to them to stop. He said, "Masters, the king has given me to you, therefore he has given you to me. I can see what kind of men you are, because I have the gift of perception. I have to warn you that what you are trying to do is impossible, for the king's herd has mystic qualities, and it is guarded by the ancient reptile that lived here before Walatadu was built. Turn away. The reptile is too great to confront."

Numukeba said, "A reptile in Walatadu is a cousin to a reptile in Naradugu. I have seen many great reptiles. Let us not waste time." The Fula said, "Master, this reptile is not cousin to any other. It could encircle the city of Walatadu. When its belly is on the ground its back is higher than the tower from which the muezzin chants the azan." Numukeba said, "When we see it we will know how large it really is. But if he is even half that large, why does he not eat the king's cows?" The Fula answered, "As I told you, the reptile was living before people came. When Walatadu was founded the reptile threatened to destroy it. It said, 'You humans who want to settle and build a town, the water in the wells flows only because of me. Without water you cannot live. If you bring me one young girl every year, the water will flow. If you fail, I will cause the water to sink into the earth and disappear.' Now, these people who had just arrived had journeyed a long distance and they were tired. They did not want to look for another place. So they said, 'Yes, we will do it, providing that you

will guard our cattle for us and keep them safe from the enemy.'
It has been that way ever since. Thus the reptile does not eat the
cattle, only the girl who is brought as a sacrifice once a year."

Both Numukeba and Malike exclaimed, "Aaaah! And the girl is
truly given?" The Fula said, "Yes, sometimes a slave girl, sometimes the daughter of a noble family." Numukeba said, "Let us
move ahead." They continued on their way until the Fula again
stopped them. He said, "We have arrived." Malike said, "Where
is the reptile? I do not see him." The Fula answered, "There,
across the vale." Numukeba said, "I see only a hill over there,
with some trees on the top. Is the reptile on the hill or below the
hill?" The Fula said, "Master, the reptile is the hill, and the hill is
the reptile. The cattle are beyond."

Numukeba and Malike sat long where they were, in silence.
When at last he spoke, Malike said, "The morike spoke the truth.
The hill breathes." Numukeba said to the Fula, "Tell us about
this monster's habits so that we will know how to deal with him."
The Fula said, "Master, it is said that sometimes it goes deep into
the earth, and afterwards it comes out again to receive the warmth
of the sun. It lies for months at a time where you see it now.
Therefore seeds fall on its back and trees sprout there. But when
it wishes to it can move swiftly. If it is angry it lashes its tail, and
the wind it stirs up causes trees to fall and clouds of sand to sweep
across the fields and houses of Walatadu."

Numukeba said to Malike, "There is no strategy to follow. We
must do what we have to in straightforward combat." So they
went across the vale toward the head of the reptile until they
were close enough to make their voices heard. Numukeba called
out, "Great reptile, grandfather of Walatadu, we need to take
some cattle from the herd. We mean you no harm. Therefore let
us pass." The reptile raised its head, and it seemed as if a small
hill had suddenly appeared next to the large hill. It opened its
mouth and hissed, and the sound was like water rushing down a
cataract. Numukeba hurled his spear. It arched in the air and as it
buried its point in the earth it burst into flame. The reptile did
not fear what it saw. It moved forward and swallowed the fiery
spear. Numukeba rode swiftly ahead and struck the reptile with
his magic garan, but the reptile felt nothing. Malike attacked,
striking rapidly with his cutlass and his spiked iron ball, but the
reptile felt nothing. It lashed with its tail and caused a powerful
wind to rise and sweep across the land. The wind caught up sand,
leaves and brush and carried them to the west, where they rained
down over Walatadu. Numukeba and Malike rode away to a safe
distance to consider what to do next.

While they pondered, the talisman of shells that Numukeba
wore, given to him by the boy filelikela of Timbuktu, said to him,

"The Great Reptile of Walatadu cannot be killed by iron, copper, or lead. Your guns and spears are useless. Only river shells like the ones you wear can destroy it. Therefore, use them as weapons." Numukeba and Malike removed the strings of shells from around their necks and held them in their right hands. Again they attacked, Numukeba against the front of the reptile and Malike against the back. Numukeba struck the head and Malike struck the tail. Suddenly all became still. The reptile lowered its head to the ground, its tail stopped lashing and its eyes closed. The Fula called out, "The hill no longer breathes."

Almost at once water seeped to the surface of the ground where the dead creature lay. The earth became sodden and soft. The reptile began to sink. It went down slowly, embraced by the muddy earth, until it disappeared altogether and there was nothing more to see. Water continued to rise from below. A lake formed. Birds that had been stilled by the combat began to sing again. On the far side of the lake Numukeba and Malike saw the king's vast herd of cattle. They circled the lake. They said to their Fula herder, "This is why we are here. Separate forty of the best white cows from the herd and drive them toward Massina."

Now, in Walatadu the king's scouts reported to him that the reptile was dead and that the two heroes were taking the cattle away. Anger filled Seku Ndome's belly. He called his djeli and his counsellors, saying, "Did I hear from your mouths that the Great Reptile would cause Numukeba and Malike to go home without anything? Let me hear it again. Did you say it?" They answered, "Yes, great Seku Ndome, those were our words. But the two heroes possess mystic powers beyond anything we could imagine."

Seku Ndome said, "Ha! You give my cows away and say it was not your intention. That is not good enough. I want my cattle returned, and I want the heads of Numukeba of Naradugu and Malike of Massina. Listen to my instructions. Ten battalions of fighters will assemble before the next call to prayers. Every fighter will be prepared to be a true hero or die. To the man who brings me the head of Numukeba I will give land, slaves and cowries. To the man who brings me Malike's head I will give land, slaves and cowries. Every man who returns without bleeding or causing blood to be shed will be executed and his family will be banished into the bush. And I will expect every man to speak the names of those among his companions who held back from the fighting. And if I do not see the cattle again, or the heads of Numukeba and Malike, my counsellors who advised me in this matter will be put down from their positions and exiled from Walatadu. These are my words." The message was carried to all corners of the city, and the ten battalions assembled quickly.

They received the king's admonitions. They poured through the city gate, two hundred on horses and two hundred on foot, and they went in pursuit of the two heroes and the cattle.

But the talismans given to Numukeba and Malike by the boy filelikela of Timbuktu spoke to them, telling them what was happening in Walatadu. So Numukeba instructed the Fula herder to take the cattle ahead and hide them. He said to Malike, "At last we know the purpose of the heavy guns I forged before leaving Massina. One points forward, the other to the rear. We will ride ahead as if we are unconcerned. When they are close I will fire the gun pointing to the rear. The enemy will be astonished, and they will be in disarray. Then we will turn and go back to meet them, and I will fire the gun pointing forward." Malike said, "Yes, that is good. The guns have the mystic force given to them by the forge. But let us give them more power still. When you load these formidable weapons, let us also put in the shell talismans given to us in Timbuktu." Numukeba answered, "Yes, that is good." They loaded with powder and bullets, and they added also the shell amulets from around their necks and the barrels of the guns. They rode on.

They heard the king's horsemen approaching, shouting battle cries and insults. When the enemy was close, Numukeba fired the gun pointing to the rear. The explosion was like thunder, and it made a large cloud of black smoke. When the smoke wafted away, Numukeba and Malike saw that a wide swathe of the enemy had been cut down. Horses without riders were galloping in all directions. The horsemen still in their saddles were confused. But they came together and prepared for another attack. Numukeba and Malike turned to face them, and now Numukeba fired the second large gun, the one that pointed forward. Once more there was the sound of thunder, and again a great smoke cloud rose in the air. When the air cleared, it was seen that the survivors among the enemy were riding frantically toward Walatadu. The foot soldiers were just arriving, and when they saw the horsemen fleeing, they also fled. Before reaching the city, however, they stopped and reminded one another of the king's harsh admonitions. So instead of going back to Walatadu they went in another direction to find sanctuary in a distant town where Fula people were living.

Numukeba and Malike began their long return journey to Massina. They passed the city named Gao. They passed Timbuktu. They continued southward along the Joliba River. And when at last they reached the wall of Massina they drove the cattle through the gate and into the streets. They drove them before the house of the king. The cows were lowing. The king came out. Malike said, "Great king, here are the white cows from Walatadu that you asked for, so that your senior wife can be cured of her illness." The king said, "Aaaah, yes, they are fine cattle. But my senior wife has already recovered her health." Malike said, "Your words are like gold, great king. We are grateful that your wife is well. But now that we have brought the cattle you wanted, according to our agreement, I am waiting for you to withdraw your order that would exile me from Massina."

The king answered, "Malike and Numukeba, I realize that you made a long journey in search of these cows. But the reason I needed them no longer exists. Therefore you may keep them for yourselves if you wish. However, it remains true that 'Two male hippopotamuses cannot share the same riverbank.' You, Malike, declared yourself to be a king. For this reason I have to send you away."

When Numukeba saw that the king was not joking, he spoke, saying, "Great king of Massina, perhaps my ears did not hear your words clearly. I thought I heard you say that even if we brought you what you asked for, still Malike must leave. I know you could not have said it, for you are spoken of everywhere as the father who is just. It is true that we went on a long journey. Our quest was dangerous. We fought outside the wall of Walatadu against hundreds of warriors, and we killed many and drove the others away. We forced King Seku Ndome to give us the cattle, but he was treacherous and untrue to his word, unlike Massina's father who is just. We fought the Great Reptile of Walatadu and killed it, though we would not have been able to do it except for powerful medicine given to us by a filelikela of Timbuktu. We brought the cows back to Massina, just as you told us to do in exchange for revoking Malike's exile. So, you see that my ears are clogged with the dust of the long journey, and therefore I misheard your words. Forgive me for this. One should not mishear a king's words. Yet I beg you to repeat them for me, and this time I will hear them correctly."

Now, a large crowd had gathered in the street in front of the king's house. Everyone heard Numukeba's address to the king. The king saw by their faces that they sympathized with what Numukeba had said. He replied, "Why, Numukeba, it is truly a bad thing not to listen carefully to the judgments of the king. But I see that you and Malike are weary from your long expedition, so I do not take any offense. My words were these: Thank you for the cows you brought from Walatadu so that my senior wife might be made well. Fortunately my senior wife has recovered from her illness. But what I pledged, I pledged. My words are like granite. I revoke the order of exile for Malike. I proclaim that as long as I live, and as long as my sons live, Malike and his family will have safety and respect in Massina. When I spoke before, this was my meaning. Let the citizens of Massina be witnesses."

The crowd in the street applauded and praised the king. The

cattle were taken away to the place of grazing. The chief djeli sang heroic songs about the accomplishments of Malike and Numukeba. And recalling the events of that day, the people of Massina composed a saying: "The words of the king are enduring, but it is good if they are spoken more than once."

12

The Fight with the Tuareg

NUMUKEBA RESTED SEVEN DAYS, THEN HE told Malike that he was departing from Massina. Malike asked, "Where will you go?" Numukeba answered, "Why, who can say? Perhaps to Tekrur in the west, perhaps to Fada-n-Gurma in the east, perhaps even to Bornu." Malike said, "The time for you to go back to Naradugu is almost here. Why speak of Fada-n-Gurma and Bornu? What is to be found there that is not everywhere else?" Numukeba said, "What is there, I do not know. But the journey will give knowledge, and knowledge is strength. Challenges are waiting in the bush."

Malike answered, "Numukeba, we have become like a single person. Therefore you are blood of my blood, and I am blood of your blood. Your children and mine will forever be blood brothers and sisters, my house will be your house, and your house will be mine. If I should ever come again to Naradugu we will say I am coming home, and if you should return to Massina we will say you are returning home. Therefore when I speak to you it is merely you yourself speaking in another voice. Listen, then, Numukeba, to what I am going to say." And Numukeba replied, "Yes, I am listening."

Malike went on, "To be a hero is something, yet it is not everything. To find valor is something, yet it is not everything. Do not endlessly seek to see the naked face of destiny. Destiny is always with you like a companion. Too much seeking drives a man mad, and he loses himself and forgets the small things that can make life good. Numukeba, blood of my blood, you have searched the world, and now you ought to go back to your forge in Naradugu and shape the iron on which your town depends. Make hoe blades, make weapons, use the gift that comes to you from the sun. Your accomplishments and good deeds already are part of the history of the world. Go home, heat your forge again and set your house in order."

Numukeba brooded. He said, "I pledged not to come back before four years. The time is not yet used up. But even when it is, what is waiting for me in Naradugu? My wife is dead. Therefore my house is dead." Malike answered, "Aaaah, Numukeba, your house is not dead. Ngoroni and Mamoye, your two sons, are saying to each other, 'Where is our father?' Who teaches them to hunt? Who teaches them to forge? Who teaches them what is just and what is unjust?" Numukeba said, "My friend, speak no more of it. My story is not yet played out. I must go again into the bush, wherever it takes me. I will sleep in your house once more, and when the sun rises again I will leave."

Numukeba slept. He arose, dressed and put on his vest of mail. As he rode to the gate of Massina, all the djeli of the city went ahead of him singing of his achievements. They sang:

> "Numukeba of Naradugu
> Who brought honor to Massina,
> The white cows he brought from Walatadu
> Radiate brightness on the fields.
> Numukeba of Naradugu
> Whose right hand holds a garan,
> Massina agrees to let you depart
> But stands vigil for your return."

Numukeba went through the gate. He rode into the bush. Massina lost sight of him.

Now, although Numukeba put the affair at Walatadu in the deepest part of his mind where old things are stored, Walatadu was not finished with him. For magic dust from the skin of the Great Reptile of Walatadu had left its mark on Numukeba. The skin of the reptile was covered with a fine yellow powder resembling that on the wings of butterflies, but it was a powerful talisman. When Numukeba struck the monster's head with his garan, the powder floated into the air and sifted into Numukeba's eyes. Even though the reptile was dead and absorbed back into the earth, the powder continued to do its work.

Day by day Numukeba's eyes became dimmer. It seemed to him that the sun was a little less bright than before. The stars in the night sky had less glitter. It seemed as if the moon were covered by a mist. When he hunted, he did not perceive his game clearly, and he had to hold his bullets close to his eyes to count them. At first he said to himself, "It will pass," but in time he recognized that his sight was fading. He thought, "I will consult a morike," but there were no morikes in the wilderness. He thought, "I will go to Wagadugu, there are many masters of mystic science there."

So he rode toward Wagadugu, but it lay a great distance ahead and his eyes were dimming rapidly. One morning when he awoke he was wrapped in darkness. He sat on his blanket waiting for the light to come, but it did not come. At last he arose and found his way to his horse, which was grazing nearby. He mounted and rode to the east, guiding himself by the heat of the sun on his face in the morning and on the back of his neck in the afternoon. And when the sun began to go down he dismounted and felt the ground with his hands for a place to sleep. It was then that he realized that he had left his gun behind him at his previous encampment. He thought, "What does it matter? Of what use is a gun if you cannot see?" The next day his water bag went dry. He thought, "Let my horse find water for us both." He dismounted and held the horse by the tail, allowing the horse to go wherever it chose in search of a water hole. The horse found water trickling from between rocks, and they both drank.

Hunger took Numukeba, but he could not hunt. After several days he became weak. And one morning when he called his horse to come back from its grazing it did not come. He thought, "Oh, my faithful friend. Have I not always cared for you? Did I ever abuse you? Have we not journeyed everywhere together? Now you have gone in search of water and forgotten me." He waited a long while, but his horse did not return.

So he went on foot, travelling toward the east, using his cutlass as a staff to warn him of rocks, trees and termite hills. Because he was getting weaker, his vest of mail became heavier, and he discarded it. At a certain place he fell into a dry riverbed, and there he lost his magic garan. One by one he lost each of his weapons. Thorn bushes tore the clothes from his body. He had only one sandal left. He found shade under a towering rock, and there he lay down on the bare earth. He slept. He awoke. He slept again. Sometimes when his eyes were closed he thought, "It is merely a dream. This cannot be the destiny of Numukeba of Naradugu." But when he opened his eyes there still was nothing but darkness surrounding him. He said aloud, "Death wishes to put his cloth over my head. I will not accept it." He arose. He began to walk toward the morning sun. At last he fell next to a termite hill and did not rise again.

A bent old woman was following some honey birds in search of honey. She passed close to the termite hill and saw Numukeba lying there. She exclaimed, "Aaaah! The birds lead not to a bees' nest but to a corpse." Approaching Numukeba, she poked at him with the end of her long staff and saw his eyes flicker. His cracked lips formed words, but no sounds came from his mouth. She saw a single silver talisman hanging from a cord around his neck and took it. She said, "You, wild man of the bush, the Spirit of the Bush has given you to me as a present." She poured a little water in his mouth from her water gourd. Little by little she revived him. Seeing that his eyes enclosed him in darkness, she placed the end of her staff in his hand and led him through the bush. They arrived at her house and she sat him under a nearby tree. She gave him more water and a little raw millet. Then she put a poultice on his eyes and wrapped them with leaves, saying over and over again, "The Spirit of the Bush has given you to me. Now I have a slave to do my hard work."

When Numukeba was able to speak, he said, "Woman, I cannot see, but I thank you for what you have done." She answered, "Yes, I am to be thanked." Numukeba said, "Woman, who are you and why are you here in the bush?" She answered, "The bush is my home. I was not treated well in my village when I was a girl. People abused me. They said, 'That girl Jeneba is a witch. She causes our goats to die. She causes our wells to dry up. She makes our cattle sterile.' A child was born without legs, and the people said, 'This is the end. Let that girl Jeneba go into the bush to live.' They drove me away. They threw stones and cursed me. The bush became my home. Therefore I am here. But I am old now, and I need a slave. The Spirit of the Bush gave me a dying slave when I went searching for honey, but I kept you among the living. Therefore you will hunt game for me, dig roots, bring firewood and pestle my grain."

Numukeba answered, "Woman, you have had a hard life. But I am freeborn. I cannot be anyone's slave." The woman answered, "Whether you were a trader, a hunter or a king makes no difference. You are my slave. I call you Djon. When I say, 'Djon, dig roots,' you will dig them. When I say, 'Djon, make the fire,' you will make it." Numukeba said, "How can a man without sight perform such tasks? He goes searching for firewood, but though firewood is all around him he cannot see it. He goes searching for roots, but though he walks on the leaves of those roots he does not know they are there. He takes a spear and feels his way through the bush, and the antelope laughs at him." The woman said, "The Spirit of the Bush has given me my slave. I will cure your eyes. And after they are cured you will have no excuses."

Every day the woman put fresh poultices on Numukeba's eyes. In time he could perceive light. In time he could perceive Jeneba, and he saw that she was truly an old woman. He could see to find firewood and roots. He had no spear, but he set traps for small game and brought her meat to eat. She did not thank him. She merely said, "Djon, do this" or "Djon, do that." He became strong again. But his feet were bare and his body was clothed in rags. He resembled the lowest of ill-kept slaves. He slept on the ground in the open.

Sometimes when the old woman ordered him to do a task or spoke to him abusively, Numukeba thought, "Why do I remain here? Though she calls me Djon, I am not a slave. Yet this old woman kept me alive and gave me back my sight with her poultices. She owns nothing but what she can find in the bush. She was treated unjustly by her village, for I can see that she does not have malevolent powers. The story that the Architect wrote for her was not good. Or did Etchuba of the Red Powder contrive it all? Now that she is old and cannot straighten her back she has found something, a slave, to make her life seem worthwhile."

So although Numukeba could have walked away and left the old woman behind, he did not do so. He stayed and did the work she wanted him to do. He repaired her roof with grass. He gathered much wood. He captured bush rats in his traps, skinned them and dried their meat over a fire. He found a young tree whose wood was almost as strong as iron. He carved a spear from it, and with the spear he hunted larger game. He killed a bush pig. He killed an antelope. The old woman had plenty of meat. She ordered Numukeba to pestle wild millet in her mortar. He saw that her life was getting more bearable. He said to himself, "I will stay a little longer, for I have a debt to pay."

One day a party of Hausa warriors appeared. They rode to the old woman's house and asked for water. She ordered Numukeba to give it to them, saying, "My slave will bring it." They saw that the old woman was the poorest of the poor, and they wondered that she owned a slave. They said, "Grandmother, how is it that an aged outcast like you owns a slave?" She answered, "The people of the village did not respect me. They drove me away without anything. All my life I did everything for myself. No one ever came to me saying, 'Grandmother, here is a little meat.' No one ever said, 'You have suffered enough, come back to the village to live.' No one ever brought me a small boy to find my firewood, or a girl to pestle my mortar. My name is not remembered in the village. I have no children to support me in my old age. I went into the bush. There was a hollow tree there. I placed my head in the hollow and spoke, saying 'Spirit of the Bush, do something for me to make my life worth living.' I came back. I slept. The next morning I followed the honey birds in search of a bees' nest. I found my slave. He was blind and nearly dead. I brought him home and restored him to health. In this way I earned him, just as if I took him in battle."

One of the Hausa said, "Grandmother, you did indeed earn him. But who knows what is in his mind? Now that he is well, one day he will go away and you will be just as you were before.

We are gathering slaves to sell to a rich merchant. Therefore we will buy your slave from you." She answered, "Why should I sell him? He was given to me in my hand by the Spirit of the Bush." The Hausa said, "Sell him, Grandmother, while you still have him to sell. Perhaps we will pass this way again next year. We will ask, 'Where is the slave that was put in your hand? We will buy him.' And you will say, 'Aaaah! I do not have him any more. He went away in the night.' And so you will have neither slave nor cowries. Take the cowries now. With cowries you can buy grain for your mortar and cloth to cover yourself."

The old woman considered. She said, "Yes, I will take the cowries." They paid her cowries. They tied Numukeba's hands behind his back and put a rope around his neck. Then Numukeba spoke for the first time, saying, "I can see that you are freeborn men and persons of honor. Listen to me. I am not now and have never been a slave. I am Numukeba of Naradugu. It is true that the old woman saved my life and restored me to health. But that does not make me her slave to sell on a whim. If you take me and sell me to someone else, neither does that make me a slave." The Hausa warriors laughed. They said, "Slaves are taken where they are taken. There was a king of Jenne who was captured in war. He said, 'Stop, I am a noble and a king. You cannot make me a slave.' The hero who captured him said, 'If I catch a fish and he is large and has much meat on him, that is good. Should I ask the fish if he is a noble?' "

The Hausa warriors journeyed two days, stopped in a small village to collect more slaves, then went on, travelling to the east. In twelve days they came to a wide river. Warriors, horses and slaves crossed in great canoes manned by Nupe fishermen. In another week they arrived at the city of Katsina. There the slaves gathered by the Hausa were delivered to the rich merchant named Kano Musa, and placed in a stockade with other slaves. Numukeba thought, "I will talk with Kano Musa and reason with him," but Kano Musa did not show himself at the place where the slaves were kept. One night, sitting before the fire with the other slaves, it seemed to Numukeba that the man sitting next to him had the face of Etchuba, and he said, "So it is you again, Person of the Red Powder! I never thought to see you as a slave in Katsina." When the man turned toward him Numukeba saw it was not the face of Etchuba. But he said to himself, "Yet Etchuba is here, for this is not the story that was written for me. Or was it written? Perhaps the Architect has no pen and no ink. Perhaps he sits somewhere on a tall mountain and merely lets his mind wander, and as he thinks a certain thought it happens to some man or woman here on the living earth. Or perhaps the Architect is old and becomes confused, so that events belonging to one person go into the life of another."

He pondered, thinking, "Is there a purpose in anything? Perhaps the stories of the Architect are only an assortment of meaningless objects in a large calabash. Like a benevolent father, he gives this object to one and that object to someone else, just as they happen to come out of the calabash. It must be so, for where is there any meaning in the death of my wife, or of the boy Ndala whom I chose to be my djeli? Where is there meaning in the suffering of any person of good heart, while the universe is full of evil? O Architect, yes, you must be growing old and forgetful. Perhaps your pen flows, but what it writes does not bring order to the universe. Because I had sympathy for the old woman Jeneba, I stayed to help her and was sold to the Hausa, and by the Hausa I was sold to Kano Musa." Darkness closed in on Numukeba's heart, a blackness deeper than that of blind eyes.

One night he dreamed that his wife was speaking to him. She said, "My husband, the story given to a person is a frame on which the weaving is done, but it is the weaver who weaves. Even though it is written that he shall be a hero, he alone says what kind of a hero he will be. Even if he is a slave, he alone says what kind of a slave he will be." Numukeba awoke, saying, "Thank you, my wife, for speaking to me." The darkness lifted from his heart. A slave who was awake in the night perceived a red glow around Numukeba. He awakened others so they could see it. Someone said, "Whoever he is, there is a force within him."

The following day Kano Musa sold Numukeba to Kidal Omar, chief of Gusau. Numukeba went to Gusau with a rope around his neck. When he arrived he was sent to the chief's fields to cut and burn brush. Other slaves asked him, "You, Bambara, what is your name?" He replied, "Why do you ask? Are we not all called Slave?" They asked him, "How did you get here? What were the circumstances?" He answered, "I am here for exchanging charities with an old woman living in the bush." They asked, "Were you captured or were you bought?" He answered, "Yes, both captured and bought. I was not born a slave." They said, "What is the difference? Now you are a slave of Chief Kidal Omar."

The slaves slept in small houses at the edge of the town so they would be out of the chief's sight and close to the fields. Now, one night an old slave was awake when the others were sleeping, and he saw the red light emanating from Numukeba's body. He became fearful, and in the morning he went to Kidal Omar's compound and said to the chief house slave, "The new Bambara whom the chief bought is a demon, for he glows in the dark." The chief house slave told the chief's djeli, and the djeli told the chief himself.

Kidal Omar said, "Aaaah, can I believe it? You, djeli, go down to the slave quarters tonight and see if it is true." The djeli did as he was instructed. He entered the house. He saw the red light glowing. He returned to the chief and said, "Yes, it is true." Kidal Omar said, "Can I believe it, even from your mouth? I will see for myself." The next night Kidal Omar went to the slave quarters. He entered the house. He perceived the red glow. He returned home. He called his paramount diviner and said, "A certain slave glows with a red light in the dark. What does it mean?" His diviner consulted his Koran. He said, "He is someone who died a natural death but refused to stay in the land of the dead. It is not good to have him here." Kidal Omar said, "Yes, I will dispose of him."

So the chief had Numukeba taken to a slave market in Sokoto. Numukeba was sold to Djado, chief of Ansongo. He was taken to Ansongo, and he worked in the chief's fields. It happened that the chief wanted many new weapons made, and he sent for his blacksmith. The blacksmith said, "Master, it is a large task, and ore must be gathered. Let one of your slaves assist me." Chief Djado said, "Yes, take the new Bambara slave, use him until the work is done."

Numukeba went with the blacksmith. They travelled to a place where there was ore. They dug. They made many trips, until there was enough ore for the smelting. They put it in the furnace, smelted and created iron. Numukeba revealed nothing about himself, but merely did what he was told to do. The chief was impatient and came every few days to see if the weapons were finished. He scolded the blacksmith, threatening to send an expedition to Wagadugu to get what he needed.

One night Numukeba said, "I was not always a slave. I understand something about the forge. Let it be this way: You make weapons during the day and I will make weapons at night." The blacksmith said, "What can a ragged field slave know about the forge? It is an art passed down from ancient ancestors." Numukeba said, "Let us do everything quickly, and the chief will be pleased with you. Give me a boy to work the bellows. Tomorrow you will see."

The blacksmith gave him his son to work the bellows. Numukeba forged all night. In the morning there were six new cutlasses. The blacksmith exclaimed, "Aaaah! The jinns must have come to help you." Numukeba said, "Where the power comes from is something I cannot tell you. But let us continue day and night, and four days from now you can deliver to the chief everything he wants. There is one secret condition. If a time comes when I ask you for weapons for myself, you will give them to me. You will not ask, 'What does a slave want with weapons?' If I ask for one thing you will give it. If I ask for another you will give it. Even if I ask for a horse you will provide it." The blacksmith considered it. He said, "Yes, let us forge night and day. I pledge what you ask for, but you, in turn, pledge that you will never reveal that I gave weapons to you, for it is treason to arm a slave." Numukeba said, "I pledge it."

So they forged, and the bellows fed wind to the fire night and day, and on the fourth day all the weapons were completed and the blacksmith took them to the chief. After that Numukeba was sent back into the chief's fields to work with other slaves cutting and burning brush.

One morning one of the chief's scouts came riding into the town, crying out, "A great party of Tuareg is approaching from the north." The Tuareg were known everywhere for their fierce and relentless ways. The chief ordered drums to be beaten, signalling to the people to come in from the fields and prepare for war. The chief's cattle were brought into the town, and the cattle of ordinary people were driven away and hidden in a valley some distance away. Djado sent mounted fighters out to turn the Tuareg back. The soldiers went out, they met the Tuareg, and the Tuareg slaughtered them. Then the chief sent his djeli to negotiate with the Tuareg. The djeli went out, and when he returned he said, "I spoke with them, but they are men without faces, for they wear black veils just below their eyes. I reasoned with them, saying that they could have all our cattle except those of the chief. They laughed. They said, 'It would be a dishonor to take everything from the poor and leave the chief with what he owns. It is the chief's cattle we want.' "

Djado, chief of Ansongo, cried out, "Are there no heroes in my town to challenge the Tuareg? Whoever turns them back will be given a half share of my cattle, and his family will be honored in Ansongo as long as they live, from one generation to another." Word of Djado's offer was carried to some nearby towns, and heroes from those places came quickly to Ansongo. There were forty men, each wearing a hundred amulets, so that they wore four thousand amulets in all. Each man had six knives in his belt, a cutlass across his chest, a gun on his back and a spear in his hand. They said to Djado, "We do not fear the Tuareg. We will persuade them with steel that they have made a mistake." The forty heroes rode out of Ansongo. They met the Tuareg in a valley beyond the second range of hills. There was a fierce battle. One by one the heroes fell and did not rise up from the earth. None of them returned to the town. There were no more heroes who wanted to challenge the Tuareg.

Numukeba went to the blacksmith. He said, "Now it is time to redeem your pledge." The blacksmith said, "What do you want?" Numukeba said, "Give me a vest of mail. Give me a good spear. Give me a sharp cutlass. Give me a gun. Give me a knife for my belt." The blacksmith gave him these things. Numukeba said, "Give me a tall horse." The blacksmith went away and came back with a tall white horse. Numukeba said, "Braid the horse's tail and mane with colored ribbons." The blacksmith did these things. Numukeba said, "Give me a white cloth to cover my face in the manner of the Tuareg." The blacksmith's wife brought a white cloth, and Numukeba covered his face. Numukeba rode to the chief's house. The guard at the door reported that a hero with a white horse and a white veil was waiting to see the chief.

Djado came out. He said, "Who are you and why are you here?" Numukeba replied, "Even if you know a man's name, can you tell what kind of story is written for him? I am here because you asked for help against the Tuareg. You do not have much time left if you want your town to be alive tomorrow. Therefore I wish to hear the pledge you made. Speak plainly so that all of Ansongo understands." The chief said, "Half of my cattle to whoever turns back the Tuareg." Numukeba said to the crowd standing in the street, "Have the people of Ansongo witnessed it?" The people called out, "Yes, we are witnesses."

Numukeba rode through the gate of Ansongo. He rode across the first range of hills. He rode to the crest of the second range of hills and sat there on his horse looking down on the Tuareg encampment. One Tuareg said to another, "A lone rider sits up above. What does he want?" Word travelled around the camp. It reached the ears of the leader of the expedition. He looked up. He saw the lone rider sitting there. He instructed a messenger to find out what the man wanted. The messenger rode to the top of the hill. He said, "My master, Azel Amasdan, would like to know your purpose in being here." Numukeba answered, "Give my greetings to Azel Amasdan. Tell him I hope his people and his flocks are well. Tell him it is Numukeba of Naradugu who inquires. Say that Numukeba would like to sit with him alone, as if on a heroes' terrace. Tell him I am freeborn Bambara. Tell him I have performed many deeds. Tell him his honor will not be diminished by sitting with me, just as my honor will not be diminished by sitting with him."

The messenger rode back to Azel Amasdan. He said, "The person is a Bambara hero by the name of Numukeba. He asks if your family and flocks are well. He says, 'Let Azel Amasdan meet me, and we two will sit alone and talk.'" Azel Amasdan looked at Numukeba on the hill. He said, "Very well, I will go." Some of his warriors said, "Do not go. It may be an ambush." Azel Amasdan replied, "I see by the way he sits in his saddle that he has honor. Bring me my horse and a camel-hair blanket." He mounted. He rode to the top of the hill. He saw that Numukeba wore a white veil on his face. He said, "Since when do Bambara cover their faces?" Numukeba said, "I wear it so that we will be equal in every way, you with your black veil, I with my white veil." Azel Amasdan said, "So be it." He dismounted, spread his blanket on the ground and sat down. Numukeba dismounted and sat facing him on the blanket. They studied each other's eyes. Then Numukeba placed all his weapons on the earth behind him, and Azel Amasdan did the same.

Azel Amasdan said, "What shall we say to each other?" Numukeba answered, "Why, let us say everything. Let us speak of the creation and the nature of man." Azel Amasdan said, "Yes, that is good. The Creator created and begot mankind, then he begot wild creatures, horses, camels and flocks. Some of the creatures he made were made imperfectly, and they became demons. Is it not said that way among your people?" Numukeba answered, "It is said differently, yet much the same. But can you tell me, Azel Amasdan, what it is that decides a man's fate?" Azel Amasdan said, "Why, it is the ghost that lives within him. Thus, when I look into your eyes I search for your ghost, and when you look into my eyes you search for mine. In this manner our ghosts commune and measure one another. If my ghost has courage I have courage, and if my ghost has honor I have honor." Numukeba asked, "Do you never hear of the Architect, the Writer of Stories? It is said among the old people that what a man does is what has been written for him in golden ink." Azel Amasdan said, "I have never heard of it. I think it cannot be so, for if a man does only what is written for him he need not have a ghost at all."

Numukeba said, "Azel Amasdan, what is the nature of a hero?" Azel Amasdan said, "Why, surely you know as well as I. He must have honor, purpose, courage, generosity and charity. Is it not so where you come from?" Numukeba answered, "Yes, it is so. But if a slave has honor, purpose, courage, generosity and charity, is he not also a hero?" Azel Amasdan replied, "No, it cannot be that way. A slave cannot have any purpose, for he can only do what his master tells him to do. He has no need of courage, therefore he does not have it. He has no possessions, therefore he cannot be charitable or generous. He cannot have honor because his words and actions are only to please his master."

Numukeba said, "I do not believe it is that way. How can you know the nature of the ghost that inhabits your slave's body? Have you ever sat with him like this on a blanket and looked into his eyes to see what is there?" Azel Amasdan laughed. He said, "No. A noble may not sit with a slave in this manner." Numukeba said, "How do you know that I am not a slave?" And Azel Amasdan said, "I know it. I knew it before I came up from the encampment. My heart told me, saying, 'He who rides the white horse has a noble ghost.' Therefore I came."

They continued to talk this way, while the sun moved across the sky. And after a while Numukeba said, "You, Azel Amasdan, I like the ghost I see in you, and I like what it says to me. Yet what I have come for is something else. I ask you to turn away and do not make war against the people of Ansongo." Azel

Amasdan said, "Hah! How can I do it? I brought many warriors to this place and promised them the cattle of Chief Djado. If I tell them to go away they will not believe the words that come from my mouth. It is only combat that will end the matter." Numukeba said, "Is honor to be found only in a cutlass then? Where is the honor in making widows out of wives and clogging water holes with corpses?" Azel Amasdan answered, "It has been so ever since the world began."

Numukeba said, "Azel Amasdan, if you will not turn back without combat, I will give you combat. Let us fight in the spirit of honor known to both of us. Let us fight until the end. If I fall and cannot rise again, then the contest is yours and you will do what you must to get your cattle. If you fall and cannot rise, your fighters will go away from Ansongo." Azel Amasdan sat quietly for a while. Then he arose from the blanket and descended to his camp. He returned. He said, "Yes, Numukeba, you can have what you ask for. I have instructed my men. Whatever happens, may this combat be steeped in honor. May the bards sing of it, and may their songs be to the vanquished and the victor alike." They took up their weapons and mounted their horses. They rode apart, one to the east and one to the west. They turned and faced each other.

Azel Amasdan pointed his gun and fired. The bullet grazed Numukeba's arm. Numukeba pointed his gun and fired. The bullet grazed Azel Amasdan's thigh. They drew their cutlasses and urged their horses forward. They came together, steel ringing on steel. They parried, turned and wheeled. Neither could strike a mortal blow. The battle went on. The mouths of their horses foamed. Azel Amasdan cut a deep gash in Numukeba's cheek. Numukeba cut the flesh of Azel Amasdan's chest. Blood flowed, but the fighting went on until Azel Amasdan called out, "Numukeba, let us pause for a moment while our horses rest. Let us sit a while on the blanket."

They dismounted and put their weapons on the ground. They sat on the blanket, each looking into the other's eyes. Azel Amasdan said, "Numukeba, remove the white veil so that I can see your face." Numukeba said, "Yes, remove the black veil from your face also." And when they both had done this, they sat silently, each contemplating his opponent. After a while Numukeba said, "Azel Amasdan, what caused us to meet here in this way? Our trails twisted and turned, going this way and that, and today they came together. Could they not have avoided one another?" Azel Amasdan said, "No, I do not think so, for our ghosts sought each other and bent the trails to meet on this hilltop." Numukeba said, "You do not believe it was chance?" Azel Amasdan said, "No, because it was the purpose of our ghosts to come together." They did not speak for a while, then Azel Amasdan said, "Let us mount and continue before our horses grow cold and stiff."

They mounted and resumed the fighting. Dust rose and hung in the air. As they wheeled and turned, Azel Amasdan struck with his cutlass and laid open Numukeba's arm from shoulder to elbow. Numukeba's cutlass opened a deep gash in Azel Amasdan's belly, so that his intestines protruded and lay on the saddle before him. Azel Amasdan gathered them with his left hand and tucked them under his girdle. They went on fighting. Azel Amasdan's cutlass severed the saddle rope of Numukeba's horse, so that Numukeba fell to the ground. But when Azel Amasdan turned and charged at him, Numukeba seized him and pulled him down. Both were now on foot, but Azel Amasdan was weak and his arms were heavy. He could no longer raise his cutlass. When Numukeba saw how it was, he also lowered his cutlass. But Azel Amasdan said, "No, Numukeba, do not insult me and take away my honor." So Numukeba struck again, averting his eyes as he did so. After that he heard no sound, and when he looked again he saw Azel Amasdan lying dead where he had fallen.

He said, "Azel Amasdan, in the place to which you have gone let them sing praises of your honor and valor. Had both of us lived we would have been friends." He did not take Azel Amasdan's head. Instead, he took only his right forefinger bearing a heavy silver ring. He lifted the body and placed it on the camel-hair blanket. He put grass under its head for a pillow. After that he covered his own bleeding face with the white veil and rode back to the town.

He went to the chief's house. Many people of Ansongo were gathered there. The chief came out. Numukeba said, "I have done what I promised to do. The Tuareg will depart. I fought with their hero of heroes, Azel Amasdan, and killed him. Now the town is safe." The people applauded him, both for his deed and for saving their cattle. But the chief said, "How do we know your words are true?" Numukeba answered, "They are true because I say they are true." The chief asked, "Where is the head of Azel Amasdan?" Numukeba said, "I chose not to take his head. Yet because I knew you would demand proof I took his right forefinger to show you." He held up the severed forefinger bearing the ring. The crowd murmured, "Aaaah, he has shown the proof."

Numukeba said, "Chief of Ansongo, you made a pledge in return for my achievement, half of your cattle. The people of the town witnessed it. I will come back in one week to claim what you promised. Meanwhile, let all the djeli of Ansongo compose praise songs for Azel Amasdan. Let them say in their praises that the courage of Azel Amasdan could fill all the granaries of the land, and that his honor shone like a brilliant star." The chief said, "Yes, I will see that it is done. But you, hero of the white veil, give us your name." Numukeba said, "Not yet. In time I will reveal everything."

Numukeba rode off, going by a roundabout way to the house of the blacksmith. To the blacksmith he said, "Your weapons were good. Now I must rest, because I have many wounds and have lost much blood." The blacksmith brought him into his house and his wife dressed the wounds with tree butter. Numukeba remained there one week, until his wounds began to heal. Then he dressed himself in the slave clothes he had worn before and went to where the chief was listening to complaints and judging disputes. He stood at the edge of the court silently until the chief finished rendering justice. Then he spoke in a loud voice, saying, "Djado, chief of Ansongo, I have come to receive what is owed to me, half of your cattle."

All in the assembly looked at Numukeba in surprise. The chief said, "Are you not my field slave?" Numukeba answered, "Though it appears to you that I am a slave, I am freeborn and a performer of noteworthy deeds. In Naradugu I shared the Cow of Heroes. I am the conqueror of Nkala of Naradugu. I am the conqueror of Chekele of Massiba. I am the conqueror of Massina Da. I put down Chief Bassa of Kassala and forced him to give up his chieftaincy. I put down Chief Dengenu of Bozola and sent him into the bush. I have conquered armies and cities. In Torigudu I conquered Dagala, a great hero who had merged into solid rock. My name is sung in Massina, Walatadu and other cities. Now, single-handed, I have turned the Tuareg away from Ansongo by combat with Azel Amasdan. For this accomplishment you owe me a debt."

The chief said, "Aaaah! But you are only a slave. Azel Amasdan was conquered by a hero with a white veil and a white horse." Numukeba said, "What was his name?" The chief answered, "He did not reveal his name. He said he would do so in time." Numukeba said, "Yes. The time is today. His name is Numukeba of Naradugu. I am Numukeba of Naradugu. You see the wounds on my face and my body. They were the gift of Azel Amasdan. Therefore do not doubt me any longer." The crowd murmured. The chief consulted his counsellors, then he said, "The veiled hero showed us proof. He showed us the ringed finger of Azel Amasdan." Numukeba said, "Is this what you want to see?" And he took Azel Amasdan's finger from his knapsack and held it up. Again the chief consulted his counsellors. At last he said, "Yes, we accept you as Numukeba of Naradugu. The debt will be paid."

Numukeba said, "That is good. Henceforth no person is to call me slave. If a Cow of Heroes is shared in Ansongo, the heart is to be put aside for me. Even if I am not here to claim it, let no other man touch it, but leave it for the hawks and eagles. And the right foreleg of the cow is to be put aside for Azel Amasdan, and it also shall be left for hawks and eagles, so that his ghost will know that we respect him. As for the cattle, I have no need for them. I give them to the people of Ansongo, to be distributed in this way: One cow will be the portion of every family of slaves. One cow will go to every old man and old woman without a family. One cow will go to every woman whose husband died in battle or hunting. One cow will go to every orphan. Four cows will go to the blacksmith for whom I worked, in exchange for weapons he will provide me. Four cows will go to the elder tradesman of Ansongo in exchange for good cloth from which my clothing will be made. Four cows will go to a metalsmith in exchange for a set of silver stirrups. Four cows will go to him who provides me with a horse fit for a hero to ride. Is it agreed?" The chief assented with a motion of his head, and the people who crowded around the court of justice called out, "We have witnessed it."

Numukeba said, "Good. Now let the chief's djeli speak of the hero of the Tuareg, Azel Amasdan." The djeli took up his ngoni. He plucked the strings for a while, setting a new rhythm that the people had not heard before. Then he sang:

> "Ngonis sound for Azel Amasdan.
> Koras sound for Azel Amasdan.
> Drums resonate for Azel Amasdan.
> Bells ring for Azel Amasdan.
> Women's skirts swirl for Azel Amasdan.
> Azel Amasdan, this is your song.
> Who does not know of Azel Amasdan?
> Azel Amasdan, Amasdan Azel.
> If you do not know him, listen.
> He is a lion among the Jedala,
> Lion among the Tuareg,
> Lion among the Burdama,
> Descendent of ancient Lemtuna.
> Honor past honor is his.
> Valor beyond valor is his.
> Azel Amasdan lived his time,
> When his time came he departed.
> But his name will rise again and again
> Like a new moon in the night sky."

The cows were divided, and Numukeba received his weapons, his horse, his silver stirrups and his clothing. He prepared to leave Ansongo. The chief's djeli came to him, saying, "Numukeba, you lack only one thing. The universe is full of dangers, but you do not wear any talismans." Numukeba answered, "The heroes who went against the Tuareg wore four thousand talismans, but they were slaughtered. I went against Azel Amasdan with no talismans at all. I myself am my talisman."

He departed from Ansongo. People inside the town gathered at the gate to see him go. People working in the fields came and lined his trail. The chief's djeli rode a while beside him playing a kora, which until that day had been reserved for praising kings.

13

Ouya Bemba

After leaving Ansongo, Numukeba came to barren land where nothing marked the landscape except rocks and termite hills. Ahead of him he saw a fork in the trail, and briefly he pondered whether he would go to left or right. Then he said to himself, "Does it make any difference?" As he reached the fork he saw a familiar form sitting nearby in the shade of a large boulder. He said, "It is he who blows thistledown randomly in the air! You, Etchuba, are you never tired of pursuing men to make their lives shapeless?" There was no answer. Numukeba rode closer. He saw that it was not a person he was speaking to, but a clay effigy of Etchuba sitting under a canopy of leaves.

He said, "So, Owner of the Red Powder, you are reduced to this! Have you at last lost the key of life? Now you have returned to clay, like ordinary men. The heat of day dries and cracks your skin. Pangolins burrow beneath you as if you were a termite hill. Arrogant dispenser of chance, now I see you in your true form." A voice came from the effigy, saying, "Oh, Blacksmith of Naradugu, do not believe I am nothing. I am still here in the universe. Men seek me out to beg for good fortune. Humans built this shrine so they could appeal to me when they are about to go on long and dangerous journeys." Numukeba answered, "They don't know you, Etchuba. You are merely a hyena feeding on the order of the world as if it were carrion. What have you ever done for anyone that is good? You want only to twist straight roads, to torture truth and to convulse what is placid."

The voice from the clay effigy said, "Numukeba, it used to be a pleasure to sit and talk with you, but the pleasure is gone because you have become brittle. You no longer resemble the great blacksmith from Naradugu. He listened and reflected. He searched for the meaning of things. You, however, are only a denier. Were the sun to die this minute and the world to go black you would deny it, saying, 'It is only a trick of Etchuba.' Though my eyes are sightless, you are more blind than I. You say I am cruel and arrogant, but that is because you do not grasp the true universe around you. Is lightning cruel because it burns down a house? Is a river arrogant because a fisherman drowns in it? Chance is neither good nor evil, it is merely a force of nature. If chance can strike down a hero it can also create a hero. As chance can burn down a city, so it can create a kingdom. If chance may make a journey long, likewise it also may make a journey short."

Numukeba said, "Your words are poisoned honey. I ask again, what have you ever done that is good?" The voice of Etchuba answered, "Chance is neither good nor evil. Everything that happens is only an event in an endless ocean of events. You call something good because you desire it to be that way. You think of yourself as the most living of all living things. Every man thinks himself to be the most living of living things. Yet what is good for one is disaster for another. Speak no more about evil, for you put me to sleep. One thing happens and another thing happens, that is all."

Numukeba answered, "Your words have no meaning." And Etchuba's voice replied, "Does your journey have meaning? Where is the meaning in being a hero? Does a blacksmith have more meaning than a leatherworker? Does a leatherworker have more meaning than a Fula herdsman?" Numukeba said, "There is meaning in the universe. If a man fulfills what is written for him, that has meaning. If he acts with courage and honor, that has meaning. If he faces death without cringing, that has meaning. If he takes care of his family, that has meaning. If he defends his village, that has meaning. If he cares for his corn and cattle, that has meaning. It is only you, Etchuba, that is meaningless. You are no more than a wild dog skulking its way around the refuse dumps of the village."

Numukeba dismounted and drew his cutlass. With one blow he cut off the head of the clay effigy. His second blow was downward, splitting the effigy in two parts. He struck again and again until where the effigy had sat there was only a pile of earthen lumps. As he sheathed his cutlass he heard Etchuba's voice again, saying, "Oh, Great Blacksmith of Naradugu, you have done battle with a pile of dirt. Long will the djeli sing of it. They will say:

'Out of Naradugu came Numukeba.
He crossed the world looking for honor.

He drew his cutlass fearlessly
And pulverized a pile of sunbaked mud.' "

Dust floated above the Etchuba shrine, and a little of it settled on Numukeba. Once more he heard the voice of Etchuba. It said, "Your last words to me were 'wild dog.' Therefore I give you 'wild dog.' " Numukeba mounted his horse and rode away along one of the forking trails.

He went on until the sun was low in the sky, not stopping to eat. He dismounted and lay down in the shelter of a large tree, thinking, "I will eat later." He fell into a deep sleep. When at last his eyes opened his body was confined in a strange form, that of a dog. His horse was grazing nearby, and his weapons and clothing were lying on the ground. He tried to call his horse, but the sound that came from his throat was not human. He sniffed at his weapons, but they were not useful to him. Hunger overtook him. He went running into the bush in search of game. He caught a hare and ate it raw. He thought, "Am I truly a dog, or merely a man enclosed in the skin of a dog?" He wandered in the bush, smelling at the earth as he went. He arrived at a small village and loitered nearby until a group of boys came out and drove him away with stones. When the sun began to go down he found a small cave and went in. He lay with his chin on the earth. He thought, "Is this the place to which all searching leads?" And he said to himself, "Etchuba has failed, for though I have a dog's body I still think like a man. But perhaps all dogs think like men."

And while he was ruminating on his circumstances, another dog appeared at the entrance to the cave. The two of them gazed at one another, and in a way he did not understand, Numukeba was aware that the other dog was a master of mystic sciences. He said, "If this is your house, forgive me. I am a stranger here." The other dog answered, "Yes, your scent tells me so." Numukeba said, "I was only looking for shelter. But fate must have guided me, for I recognize you as a filelikela." The other dog answered, "Yes, it is well known everywhere in the bush. Possibly you meant to say that scent guided you." Numukeba answered, "Perhaps it is so."

The dog-filelikela came into the cave and sat next to a pile of small animal bones. He said to Numukeba, "You are here because you have questions. Did you bring something to recompense me?" Numukeba said, "No, Master, I did not think of it. Before I go away I will bring you something." The dog-filelikela said, "Yes, bring me a hare when we are finished. Now let us begin. What do you want to know?"

Numukeba said, "I am not a dog, but a man in the form of a dog because of the red powder of Etchuba." The dog-filelikela said, "Aaaah, you are a dog that would like to be a man? I have met such dogs before. One wanted to be a buffalo. One wanted to be an antelope and every year performed an antelope dance." Numukeba answered, "No, master of mystic sciences, it is not that I want to be something that I am not. I am already a man, but I have been transformed by powerful magic into my present form. I once performed great deeds, and the djeli sang praise songs for me." The dog-filelikela said, "What great deeds have you done? Have you killed a rhinoceros or a lion by yourself and rolled in its carcass?" Numukeba answered, "No, such deeds are the achievements of dogs, but I am a human hero transformed. I have challenged human warriors and conquered cities."

The dog-filelikela said, "Dog, your mind wanders. You do not perceive reality. If you continue like this you will become a danger to the pack. A dog must know that it is a dog. It must hunt like a dog, mate like a dog, and have canine understanding." Numukeba said, "Master, I agree. Yet because I am transformed, I have a different kind of character. When the Architect wrote my story it was a man's story. I was the paramount blacksmith of Naradugu, and I went on a journey to have my destiny revealed to me. Destiny led me along one road and another from city to city."

The dog-filelikela consulted the animal bones on the ground beside him, and at last he said, "Dog, you do not understand the meaning of destiny. Destiny is not a trail from somewhere to somewhere. It is a fence that surrounds you, and you are contained in the middle. Because the buffalo is formed as a buffalo, he must act accordingly. A tree has the form of a tree, therefore it stretches its roots into the earth and may not go on a journey anywhere. A lion knows only the needs of a lion, and though he may do a rhinoceros dance every year he cannot be a rhinoceros. A man's form is his destiny, and he can never be a rock, a mountain or a river. Thus all creatures are imprisoned within the fence of fate. Your fate was to be born a dog. Therefore, live as a dog and do not let yourself become confused."

Numukeba said, "Great filelikela, is every dog the same dog, or is each dog in some way different from others? One is ill-tempered, one is generous. One is small, one is large. Some go only with the pack, some travel alone. Some are brave, some are cowards. Though they may all live inside the fence of fate, their stories are different. When you tell me, 'live as a dog,' which dog are you speaking of?" The dog-filelikela said, "You who think you are a transformed human, speak no more about it. There is only Dog, the Essence of Dog, and there is no destiny except for him to remain a dog until he is killed by a creature more fierce than himself. The divining bones can tell us nothing more. Therefore, give your divining payment." So Numukeba went out and caught a hare, and he brought it back and left it in front of the cave for the dog-filelikela. After that he prowled for a place of shelter for the night. He found another cave, but it was occupied by a family of dogs and they drove him away. In time he found a hollow fallen tree and crawled inside. The sounds of the bush were muted and he slept.

When Numukeba awoke he lay without moving, reflecting on the events of the previous day. At last he said to himself, "Of course it was all a dream. Now I will hunt for game and continue my journey." But when he moved he saw that he was indeed a dog and that nothing had changed. He called out, "Oh, Architect!" But the sound that came from his throat was only a canine howling. He thought of the proverb that said, "He who lives must strive to remain alive." He went out of the hollow tree and found his way back to the place where he had been transformed. His weapons, his vest of mail and his clothing were still lying there. He placed a foot on the forged blade of his spear, saying in doglike sounds, "Force of the Sun, undo Etchuba's cruel joke! Creator of iron, give me back the form of Numukeba of Naradugu! There is no meaning in what happened to me. It is a distortion of order in the universe." But though he invoked the force of the sun in this way, there was no change in his body. He saw his horse grazing in the distance, but when he tried to approach it, the horse tossed its head and galloped away. Numukeba thought, "If my own horse does not know me, then indeed I am a dog." He went hunting. He caught a small bush rat and ate it. He wandered from one place to another.

The fourth day after his transformation he smelled humans and the smoke of a fire. Cautiously following the scent, he approached the place. From a distance he saw four men sitting together. He lay hugging the earth and watched them. He saw that their shirts were covered with boars' tusks, antelope horns and tufts of lions' hair, which meant that they were a society of master hunters. He moved forward slowly on his belly. He heard them speaking.

One said, "Aaaah! Because of the bush spirit, Ouya Bemba, we are no longer hunters but scavengers. Because we killed his stork when our people were hungry, he has cursed us and made the bush empty of game. Though we said, 'Master, we did not know the stork was yours,' he said, 'From today until the end of time you will never find meat in the bush.' Now we cannot return to our village any more. The djeli would turn away instead of singing our praises. Children would follow our footsteps, chanting, 'No meat, no meat, no meat.'"

Another said, "Are we then to be root diggers like women and children? A hunter without game to pursue has no place in the world."

Another said, "Let us go to Ouya Bemba at the lagoon where he lives and make a case for justice. Perhaps he will relent."

Another, the chief of the hunters, said, "This we have already done. If we plead with him he will despise us. We must now challenge him and preserve our honor. Though he is a jinn we have no choice. Let us remember the saying: 'If a child stands in your path, lift it gently aside. If a woman stands in your path, go gently around her. If a man stands in your path, reason with him. If evil stands in your path, confront it even if you must journey into darkness.' I cannot wander any more in bush country empty of game. I cannot face my village. I cannot face my family. Already I am halfway into darkness. Therefore I will go to Ouya Bemba and challenge him. If I die I will not have lost everything, for people will say 'He lost the light of day but he did not lose honor.' " One by one the other men said, "Master of hunters, I will go with you to confront Ouya Bemba. Though I lose the key of life, still the djeli will have something worthwhile to sing about me, and my name will not be forgotten."

Forgetting that he was a dog, Numukeba stood up and walked forward. In his mind he said, "Hunters, I have heard everything, and I am prepared to go with you on your expedition of honor," but what came out of his mouth were dog sounds. The hunters grasped their spears and jumped to their feet. They said, "Fate has brought us a dog to eat." But the chief of the hunters restrained them, saying, "Hold your spears. It is said, 'We do not kill the honey bird that leads us to the hive.' The dog does not run away. He comes to us in a straightforward manner. Perhaps he is not a wild dog but a hunting dog."

Numukeba stopped for a moment, then went up to the chief of the hunters. He tried again to speak, saying in his mind, "I also am halfway into darkness because of injustice. Therefore I am going with you. Do not be misled by what you see. I am still Numukeba of Naradugu. Though I have the form of a dog, it is only because of the malice of Etchuba who delights in twisting what should be straight." The sounds that came from Numukeba's throat were dog sounds, but the hunter chief saw something more in his eyes. He said to the others, "In the mystic way of the universe, there is more to this dog than we perceive. Therefore let no one harm him. In time we will understand everything."

The hunters prepared for their expedition. They sharpened their spears and knives and cleaned their guns. They began the journey to the lagoon where Ouya Bemba lived. Numukeba, the dog, walked beside the chief of the hunters. When night came they camped, and Numukeba lay down among the hunters as if he were one of them. The chief of the hunters said, "This dog surely is not what he seems." He put down a cheetah skin, and Numukeba accepted it as a sleeping mat. Morning came. They chewed on roots to kill their hunger, then continued their way.

They arrived at the lagoon. The chief of the hunters called out,

"Ouya Bemba, we whom you have maltreated are here! Come out of your hiding place in the water. Bring your weapons and your medicine, for we are ready to send you into the darkness that is blacker than night." The jinn did not appear. The chief of the hunters called again, "Ouya Bemba, do not be modest. We have not come to praise you. We are here to collect the taxes you owe. Your name is an offense to all people. You are a stench befouling the bush. You are the carrion of the universe. Make your appearance now, or the djeli will sing of your cowardice." Still Ouya Bemba did not appear. Then Numukeba spoke in the language of wild dogs, which the four hunters did not understand. He said, "Master of the bush, a child may rob a blind man of his staff, but that does not make him great. You may take game away from hungry hunters, but that does not prove you are worthy or valiant. You are petulant, but do you have any honor? Without honor you are nothing. If you are afraid of four hunters whose livelihood you have destroyed, then I, a dog, will challenge you. Come out of your hiding place. Give back what you have taken or fight according to the rules of noble heroes."

The hunters did not understand Numukeba's howlings, but there was a sudden turbulence in the water and Ouya Bemba emerged and stood on a rock in the center of the lagoon. His head was large and his arms were long. Around his neck hung a collar made of a thousand talismans. His eyes shone like hot coals. His chest was covered with armor made of sea shells. His fingernails were pointed steel blades. After gazing with anger at the hunters for a moment, he said, "You hunters who cannot kill a bush rat, you come to kill me, Ouya Bemba?"

Though the jinn was a fearsome spectacle, the hunters did not flinch. Their chief said, "You have wronged us and made our life a misery. We are here seeking justice. Give us back our game or we will fight you and rid the world of your evil. We have lost so much already that we do not fear death. Choose one of us to begin the battle. If he dies, then you will have to fight the second, then the third, then the fourth. But do not think you will have an easy time. We have mystic powers, and even a jinn is not invulnerable."

Ouya Bemba turned his eyes toward Numukeba. Because he was a jinn he saw what the hunters could not see. He said, "Yes, I accept the challenge. But common hunters are not worthy to fight me. I choose the dog as my adversary." Hearing this, the hunters mocked, "Haaah! Haaah! The great Ouya Bemba chooses to fight with a dog! Long will the djeli of the world remember it." But Ouya Bemba answered, "Your words are ignorant. The dog is the hero Numukeba from Naradugu. He has fought many battles and slain many warriors. He has raided great towns and taken their cattle. He has brought down powerful chiefs and destroyed cities.

Fula, Soninke and Bambara djeli recite his accomplishments. Among all of you, only he has earned the right to fight me. Therefore I accept him as my opponent."

The hunters looked at Numukeba. They said, "He has the form of a dog. How can he hold a weapon?" Ouya Bemba answered, "I will show you his true form." He caused a stream of brilliant blue light to burst from his fingers, and the light crossed the water and touched Numukeba. The dog disappeared, and the hunters saw Numukeba standing naked in his human form. Numukeba said to the hunters, "Give me a shirt to wear." The hunter chief gave Numukeba his own shirt, studded with horns of animals and tufts of lions' hair. Numukeba said, "Give me a loincloth." One of the hunters gave him a cloth. Numukeba said, "Give me a cutlass and a spear." They gave him a cutlass and a spear. He said, "Give me a gun and a knife." They gave him a gun and a knife. And when he was equipped with everything, a red glow surrounded him and he stood in luminescent splendor facing the jinn of the bush.

Numukeba said, "Ouya Bemba, master of the bush, I thank you for undoing the mischief of Etchuba of the Red Powder and restoring my human form. I owe you a larger debt than I know how to pay. Yet I came here in the company of these hunters to help them receive justice. Once they were esteemed because they never returned from the bush without meat for the village. They swore the oath of all good hunters, saying, 'When the people are hungry we will feed them.' When game was scarce they shared everything, contenting themselves with the same small portions that others received. A time came when the game moved to a distant part of the country. They travelled many days in pursuit. They arrived here, near the lagoon, and they found a stork, thinking, 'At last we have something for the village.' They killed the stork. Then you appeared. You berated them, saying, 'The stork was mine. Therefore you will suffer. From this day on all game will elude you.' They took the stork home and fed the people, but they themselves did not eat any of the stork's meat. Since that day, it has been as you wanted it to be. All game has eluded them. In their village they are held in contempt. They are ridiculed by their wives, and the djeli have forgotten their names. Can one stork mean so much to you? Because of the debt I owe you, I speak reasonable words. Why must the death of a stork destroy a village? Give these hunters back their game."

Ouya Bemba answered, "Numukeba of the Red Glow, I hear you. Remember your thoughts when you learned of the death of your wife in Naradugu. Because I am a jinn, do I have no feelings? The game that the hunters killed was not an ordinary animal of the bush, but my son in the form of a stork. Therefore grief and anger turned my blood to poison." Numukeba said,

"Aaaah! They did not know the stork was your son." Ouya Bemba said, "Your people have a proverb: 'My-life–ebbs-out is the child of I-did-not-know-it.' Before they killed my son did they ask, 'Who are you and how are your people?' I will not relent. As for you, Numukeba, give up the fight and go your own way."

Numukeba said, "Great Ouya Bemba, I cannot forget my debt to you. But my debt to the hunters came first. I came into their camp in the form of a dog, and because they were hungry they wanted to kill me for meat. But their chief dissuaded them, saying, 'There is more to this dog than we perceive.' Therefore they did not kill me. And though they did not understand my language, I pledged to go with them in pursuit of justice and honor. They said, 'If we die, we die, yet our valor will live on in the minds of men.' I said, 'Though I am confined in the shape of a dog, I will share your challenge to Ouya Bemba.' I became one of them." Ouya Bemba answered, "Numukeba, they did not comprehend your words, therefore there was no pledge." Numukeba said, "Had my mouth been altogether soundless, still I pledged to myself. I am bound. So I ask again for you to restore the game these hunters must have to keep their village alive. If you will not do it we must struggle, for with your own mouth you said, 'I choose the dog as my adversary.' "

Ouya Bemba said, "Let us stop talking on and on like women washing clothes at the river. Prepare yourself. I am coming." He stepped from the rock. He was buoyant and did not sink. He walked across the surface of the lagoon, his eyes burning like coals. Blue streaks of light flashed from his fingers. As his foot touched the bank, the earth shook. He took his gun from his back and drew his cutlass from the scabbard on his chest. He said to Numukeba, "When this small affair is ended, I will send your head to your village." Numukeba answered, quoting a proverb, "'Do not waken your messenger until you are sure you have a message to send.' First, great Ouya Bemba, let us make our compact with the earth and sky as witnesses. If you conquer me, the hunters will abandon their expedition and you will allow them to return to their village unmolested. If I overcome you, you will cause the game to return to the bush so that the hunters may find meat for their people."

Ouya Bemba said, "Yes, yes, I agree. Let us make our pledges with the earth and sky as witnesses." They came together. They squatted down, not quite sitting on their heels, the earth below and the sky above, and each swore his pledge. Ouya Bemba said, "The earth has heard and the sky has heard. Let us begin." They stood apart and faced each other. Numukeba's body glowed and gave off a reddish light. Ouya Bemba's body glowed and gave off a bluish white light. Numukeba said, "Because I made the first challenge, even in the form of a dog, you may strike first." Ouya Bemba said, "No, because you are only a human and I am a jinn, you may strike first." They argued until Ouya Bemba became impatient. At last he said, "You are indebted to me for giving you back your human form. Strike first, and in this way your debt will be paid."

So Numukeba sighted his gun and fired. When the bullet reached the light surrounding Ouya Bemba it was deflected to one side as if by a vest of mail. Then Ouya Bemba sighted his gun and fired, and when the bullet reached the red glow around Numukeba it shattered. Numukeba poised his spear, moved forward and launched it. Ouya Bemba deflected it with a movement of his right hand. Ouya Bemba launched his spear at Numukeba. Numukeba said, "I myself am my talisman," and he waved the flying spear aside with his left hand. The two opponents, one a hero, one a jinn, grasped the handles of their cutlasses and closed the distance between them. Numukeba's cutlass glowed red and Ouya Bemba's cutlass glowed bluish white. They fought hand to hand. Blood flowed from each of them, but there was no mortal wound. They struggled. Dust rose from the ground and enclosed them like a mist. The earth shook beneath their feet as if from a great herd of running cattle.

The fighters struggled, sometimes on dry land, sometimes in the shallow water of the lagoon. A time came when Ouya Bemba said, "Let us pause and contemplate things." They paused, moved apart and sat on their heels. Ouya Bemba said to Numukeba, "You are indeed a valiant fighter. Even when you have lost your head, the djeli will compose a new song for you." Numukeba answered, "You, Ouya Bemba, even though you are a jinn you fight with noble honor." They rested. They arose and continued the combat. Then, when the day grew old, Ouya Bemba sent a flash of light from his fingers and Numukeba's cutlass disappeared from his hand. Except for the small knife in his belt, Numukeba was disarmed. Ouya Bemba said, "You of Naradugu, you are finished. Give me your head." But Numukeba answered, "Do not trust what you are saying. The end has not yet come."

Ouya Bemba advanced and struck at Numukeba with his cutlass. Numukeba caught the sharp blade with his right hand and held it firmly. He called out, "Force of the sun, let my hand be a forge!" And slowly Ouya Bemba's cutlass became red and then white as if it were being tempered in hot coals. With his left hand, Numukeba grasped the blade and bent it back on itself until it was no longer a weapon but only shapeless steel. Now Ouya Bemba also was weaponless except for a small knife in his belt. They fought with small knives. And just as the sun reached its sleeping mat, Numukeba's knife pierced the navel of the jinn.

Ouya Bemba fell, saying, "Aaaah, Numukeba, you have

wounded the center of my life force!" He lay on his back. He did not move. The blue-white glow around him faded. Ouya Bemba had journeyed into the endless void of the final darkness. And as the hunters stood looking in awe at Numukeba's accomplishment, three deer came to the shore of the lagoon to drink. The hunters said, "Aaaah! The jinn has given us back our game!" They raised their guns to kill the deer, but Numukeba said, "No, not yet. Because Ouya Bemba fought honorably and fulfilled his pledge, these three deer shall go free as our song of praise. Now we shall give him his tomb, and tomorrow we will hunt." They gathered stones and covered the jinn's body with them. When that was done, Numukeba went into the lagoon and washed his wounds.

The night came. They slept. In the morning they saw the tracks of many deer, antelope and other bush creatures. They hunted and killed their game. The chief of the hunters said, "Now you will return with us to our village so the people can thank you with a celebration." Numukeba answered, "No, I must go and find my weapons." They said, "We will dry our meat, then we will go with you." They dried their meat and hung it in a large tree. After that they accompanied Numukeba as he searched for his possessions. Because they were accomplished hunters, they found a dog's footprint on the earth. Numukeba said, "I see nothing." They said, "We see the old footprints you left when you were coming to our camp. Follow us." They travelled. They brought Numukeba to the tree where he had been transformed into a dog. His clothing and his weapons were where he had left them, and his horse was grazing nearby. Numukeba returned the shirt, the cloth and the weapons the hunters had given him. He dressed in his own clothes and put on his vest of mail. He hung his gun on his back and his cutlass across his chest. He groomed his horse with grass, took burrs from its mane and rebraided its tail.

He prepared to mount, but the chief of the hunters said, "Wait. There is one more thing." He took a rhinoceros horn and a tuft of lion's hair from his own shirt and fastened them to Numukeba's vest of mail. Numukeba said, "May your hunting be good." The hunters said, "May your journey bring you to your destination." They parted. The hunters went back to get their dried meat, and Numukeba rode away in search of a trail to follow.

He pondered while he rode. He thought, "Etchuba sent me to the land of the dogs, but he could not keep me there. Before that he sent me to Massiba where I was wrongfully imprisoned, and Massiba could not hold me. He caused me to pursue a wounded bush rat who was really human, yet I made peace with the man and returned from that place beyond the tunnel. He caused me to be robbed of my weapons and talismans, but I went on to conquer King Bassa of Kassala. He caused me to be captured and taken slave by the Fula, but slavery could not hold me. Therefore he is no more than a mosquito on the skin. The diversions he invents are nothing but dreams floating in the universe. The reality is the birth payment given to each person by the Composer." After a while he thought, "Still, when and how will my destiny become visible?"

The trail he followed took him along the bank of a river. When he stopped to rest he saw a large manatee browsing in the shallow water. It seemed to Numukeba that he knew the manatee, that they had met in another place. He said, "Peaceful One, have we not spoken together before?" The manatee answered in the language of manatees, and the sounds did not reveal any meanings to Numukeba. Yet in his mind, Numukeba was certain that the manatee had said, "Do not go forever seeking destiny, for what is at the end is only the falling darkness of death. Destiny is the constant companion within you. If you act honorably or dishonorably, that is destiny; if you love, that is destiny; if you are generous or meanspirited, that is destiny. Do not use up your life searching for what you already have. You have defined yourself by your honor, your generous deeds, your valor and your mistakes. Everything that exists for you in the universe is at your forge as well as in the bush."

And while Numukeba reflected, he saw that the manatee had disappeared from the water and that a morike was sitting on the riverbank. Numukeba said, "Aaaah, it is you." The morike did not answer, but held up his hand palm forward. The hand glowed, and in the palm Numukeba saw a picture of his two sons, Ngoroni and Mamoye, riding in the bush, spears in their hands and cutlasses across their chests. Though the morike did not speak, Numukeba seemed to hear the words, "They are riding the bush in search of their father." Numukeba said, "My sons! You are too young to make an expedition like this!" The morike became invisible, and once again Numukeba saw the manatee grazing in the river among the water plants.

He said to himself, "How will they ever find me? How will I ever find them? The bush is wide. The bush is capricious. The fault is mine. I have been away too long. I thought, 'All revelations wait for me in the bush.' Had I remained in Naradugu, perhaps my wife would now be alive. Had I remained, my sons would not now be risking their lives."

He mounted his horse and turned it northward. He rode. He did not look to the east or the west. When night fell, he travelled by moonlight, thinking, "Does Naradugu really exist? Or is it an old dream that was dreamed?"

14

Bamanake of Dorma

*I*N TIME HE CAME TO THE RIVER CALLED JO-liba, and he followed it until he arrived at the city of Segu, whose king was Da Monzon. He ferried the river in a large canoe manned by Da Monzon's slaves. He went to the market and inquired for a place to sleep. Instantly he was surrounded by women and girls, each trying to lead him to her house for lodging. There was a great commotion. More people gathered and competed to make their voices heard over the others. And while Numukeba was considering ways of escaping the chaos, a man on a white horse rode up and with a few words scattered the people. He said, "I am Ngolo Da, the king's djeli. You appear to be a hero, and therefore I wanted to liberate you from the crowd. Ride with me." They rode out of the marketplace to a quiet part of the city. The djeli said, "Something in your appearance tells me I have seen you before." Numukeba answered, "I am Numukeba of Naradugu." The djeli answered, "Aaaah, Numukeba! Yes, I recognize you now. I saw you once at Massina. But you are older, and the lines of a hard life mark your face. The bards of many cities, even of Segu, sing of your achievements."

Numukeba answered, "For their songs, I thank them. Yet I was not aware that time had altered my appearance." The djeli said, "Yes, just as a stone is weathered by water and sand, a man's face speaks of what he has endured and accomplished. Are you in Segu for a special purpose?" Numukeba said, "I entered Segu only because Segu is in my path. I am searching for my two sons, Ngoroni and Mamoye, who somewhere in the bush are looking for their father." The djeli said, "Numukeba, my house is your house. Ride with me." They went to Ngolo Da's house. The djeli's slaves brought mats for them, and they sat down. The djeli's favorite wife brought food, and they ate.

Ngolo Da said, "Everything you have done is known to us. We sing of the accomplishments of Numukeba of Naradugu on all important occasions. Our heroes emulate you. They say, 'Numukeba did thus-and-thus. We also will do thus-and-thus.' Yet whatever they do, their deeds are only shadows of yours. Sometimes when a young man makes it known to Da Monzon that he is going out on a great expedition, the king laughs and says, 'Ah! Do you think you are Numukeba of Naradugu?' Year after year it has been this way, and the king's words have become a proverb."

Numukeba answered, "Why do you speak as if many years have passed? In Naradugu, before I fought with Nkala, I said, 'Whoever wins our battle shall leave and go from one place to another proving his worth. After four years he may return and speak of his accomplishments.' It was agreed to by all, so that the spirit of vengeance would die and the town remain peaceful. Though I have not counted the seasons, I am ready now to go back to my forge. But first I must find my two sons wherever they are wandering in the bush."

The djeli looked for a while at Numukeba. Finally he said, "Great Blacksmith, you of whom the songs are sung, it was eight years ago when you performed valorous deeds at Massina and Walatadu, eleven in all since you departed from your forge." At first Numukeba could not speak, then he said, "No, it is not possible. The chronicles of the bards are distorted. They confuse me with some hero of a former time." Ngolo Da asked his wife to bring a mirror. When he received it he handed it to Numukeba, saying, "A mirror does not lie. It speaks like a pledge. Look at your face, Numukeba, and consider what the mirror tells you." Numukeba looked. He said, "The light is dim." Ngolo Da raised the oil lamp. When Numukeba put down the mirror he said, "The mirror has a mystic power. I see the face of my father." The djeli answered, "No, my friend, the face is yours." Numukeba said, "It cannot be so. Perhaps it is another prank of Etchuba, or a gift of the jinn Ouya Bemba." The djeli answered, "My friend, it is the gift of the Architect which all men share. Do not doubt it any more. Eleven years have passed since you left Naradugu."

After that, Numukeba did not speak. He sat on into the night. When the sun rose, he was there in the same place as if he were carved in wood. Ngolo Da's wife brought him a gourd of food and placed it next to his mat, but Numukeba did not eat. The djeli came and sat facing him. He said, "Numukeba, there are mysteries all around us. Mystery is in the air we breathe, in the blood in our veins, and on the roads we travel. It is one of the elements of the universe. You will not unravel the mystery by sitting forever without moving, you will only grow older. You must continue your search for your sons. Prepare yourself and go before it is too late."

At last Numukeba moved from his mat. A slave brought a calabash of water, and Numukeba bathed. Ngolo Da's wife washed his clothing and he dressed. In the evening Ngolo Da took him to the king's filelikela. Numukeba said to the filelikela, "Master of mystic science, my two sons are riding in the bush searching for me. Which direction shall I take to find them? Though I have no cowries or livestock with me, when my expedition is finished I will send you a just payment for your help."

The filelikela said, "I know you, Numukeba. Who does not know you? Your presence here is payment. Yet when you return home you may send me whatever you choose. If I do not divine correctly, you may send me empty eggshells, chaff from your grain, and hairs combed from your horse's mane. If I divine correctly, send me a gift from your forge." Numukeba said, "Yes, let it be that way."

The filelikela took out his kolas and spread them on a tray. Numukeba asked, "What do you see?" The filelikela said, "Why, everything in the universe that touches man is here: the writings of the Architect, chance happenings, honor, the force of the sun, mystery, the hardness of iron, the softness of woman, compassion, fertility of the earth, honor, generosity, kinship within families, the creations of the blacksmith and the leatherworker, bravery in war. Also there are malevolence, greed, dishonor, deceit, brutality, hardness of heart and evil medicine. There is life, there is death. These are the secrets of the kolas. Sometimes they speak and reveal, sometimes they tell us nothing."

Numukeba said, "Master, implore the kolas to reveal." The filelikela gathered up the kolas and spread them again on the tray. He studied them and reflected. He gathered and spread them again. At last he said, "Every kola speaks, but what they say does not come together." He put the kolas away and brought out brightly colored river shells which he scattered on the ground. They said nothing with any meaning. He divined with sand, then with braided rope. At last he brought out a forged iron chain. Holding it in his hand he said, to Numukeba, "Touch it with your fingers, perhaps the flow from the forge may help us." Numukeba touched the chain. It began to glow with a red luminescence.

The filelikela threw the chain on the ground and studied its configurations. He threw the chain three times, and after the third time he said, "The chain speaks to us, Numukeba. Your two sons are going westward from Walata toward Djara. Look for them there." The red glow of the chain faded, and the filelikela said, "There is nothing else to be learned. If what I have told you is false, let the djeli sing of it. If what I have said is true, let the djeli sing of it." Numukeba said, "When will I find my sons?" The filelikela answered, "Why, the chain divines only in parables and riddles. It never says, 'on the third day' or 'on the fortieth day.' It says only, 'when the time comes.'" Numukeba said, "Master of mystic sciences, you say 'time,' but I no longer understand the meaning of time. When I went into the bush from Naradugu it was for four years, but eleven years have gone by without my knowing it. Time devours me. Will the life force in my veins continue until I have done everything I still have to do?"

The filelikela answered, "Time is an invisible sea that washes the shore of what has happened and the shore of what is yet to happen. We who are alive are small objects floating in the Sea of Time. I cannot tell you any more." Numukeba said, "Master, I thank you. But for what I have to do now I need strong talismans. I need talismans to help me find my sons. I need talismans so that I do not sink and disappear in the Sea of Time. I need something to counteract the medicine of Etchuba who waits for me everywhere on the highway. Give me these things, and when I have returned to Naradugu I will send you a forging such as no man has ever seen before." The filelikela said, "I will consult with other learned men of mystic science. We will consider what you are asking. Come back in four days."

Numukeba arose and departed, thinking, "Four days? Will each day be a month of my life?" He returned to the house of the djeli, Ngolo Da. He said, "My friend, take me to a good forge. I must prepare myself for what lies ahead." Ngolo Da took him to the best forge in Segu. He gave the blacksmith gold, saying, "Lend Numukeba of Naradugu your forge so he may forge what he needs. Give him your purest iron. Give him slaves to fuel the fire and work the bellows. Whatever he needs, provide it." The blacksmith said, "This is Numukeba of Naradugu? Who has not heard of him? Take back the gold, I do not want it. If the king of Segu came and said, 'do this' or 'do that,' I would accept his gold. But from Numukeba I do not want anything. I give him the forge, the iron, a slave to bring fuel, a slave to work the bellows, and a slave to carry. I ask only that I be allowed to place my mat nearby so that I may observe while he works." Numukeba answered, "Are we not both blacksmiths? All blacksmiths are brothers. We receive our knowledge and power from the same source. Place your mat where you wish."

Numukeba removed all his clothing except his loincloth. Slaves brought fuel and iron. He began to forge. He made a new vest of mail. He made a new cutlass longer than his old one. He made a new blade for his spear. He made a new barrel for his gun. He made bullets and gunpowder. He forged all day and all night. He did not stop until midnight of the third day. Then he said, "I am finished." He went to the home of the djeli and slept, and in the morning he returned to the house of the filelikela.

The filelikela said to him, "Numukeba of Naradugu, eight doctors of mystic science assembled to consider your needs. We consulted each other and we divined, each by the method in which he is most accomplished. Four of us were Bambara filelikelas. One divined by kolas, one by sand, one by strings, and one by shells. Four were Muslim morikes who divined in the pages of the Koran. What we have to tell you is this:

"Though they are not visible, you already have three powerful talismans. You have the birth payment given to you by the Composer when you were born. You have the heart that beats within your breast. And you have the sun power possessed by all masters of the forge. These are great talismans. Without them you would have perished long ago. You will find Ngoroni and Mamoye through much searching, as they will find you through much searching. Your purpose and theirs are the same. We are giving you some amulets that may help. One will turn away arrows, bullets and spears. One will staunch the flow of blood. One will cause wounds to heal. One will sharpen your sight and your hearing. One will protect you from leopards hiding in the limbs of trees." The filelikela went on naming the attributes of the medicine packets.

Then he continued, "As for Etchuba, we have prepared an antidote. Here is a packet of white powder. If he threatens you with mischief, throw white powder on him as he throws red powder on you."

Numukeba said, "Great filelikela, I thank you. But there is still one more thing. I need an amulet to prevent me from the gnawing of time." The filelikela answered, "Who can deal with the mystery of time? An infant is born, it lives a year and dies. Who can say it has not lived a full lifetime in that year? Who can say that it has not achieved knowledge and wisdom equal to that of its father or mother? We cannot see time, we cannot touch it with our fingers, yet it swallows every living thing. My grandfather and his grandfather lived. My ancient grandmother lived and gave birth to children. Otherwise would I be here talking to you now? But where are they? We are not able to see them, though sometimes they may speak to us. Who can fathom it? Explain the meaning of time, describe its features, then perhaps we can give you an amulet to deal with it."

Numukeba said, "Master of the mystic sciences, thank you for what you have provided for my needs. Though I have a hundred years by then, when I reach Naradugu you will hear from me." The filelikela said, "Yes, Numukeba, let it be that way." Numukeba went to the house of Ngolo Da, the djeli. Ngolo Da said,

"Not yet. I spoke of you to the king. He said, 'What, the hero of Naradugu is here? He should have come to my court and announced himself. Bring him at once.' " Numukeba said, "Very well, let us go." They went to the king's house, where he was dispensing justice in the shade of a tall tree. The djeli said, "Great king, here is the hero of Naradugu."

Da Monzon reproached Numukeba, saying, "Aaaah, Numukeba, am I too small for you? Are you too great to sit with Segu's heroes on their terrace? You do not come to me to ask permission to enter the city. You fraternize only with blacksmiths and men of mystic science. Can you truly be Numukeba of Naradugu?" Numukeba said, "Great king, I am the man to whom the name has been given. If honor is good, I have earned it. If valor is good, I have earned it. If my accomplishments put my name in the mouths of djeli, that is good. But now I have only one purpose, to find my two sons so that they do not perish in the wilderness in pursuit of noble achievements."

The king spoke to the djeli, and the djeli spoke for him, saying, "Yes, Numukeba, find your sons, but do not think that you can silence the voices that tell them they must look for valor and honor. You yourself, by your own actions, inspired them on their way. They said, 'Our father's name is engraved on the hearts of men. Let our names also be engraved.' " Numukeba said, "Yes, great king, it is so. But now I must find them and teach them everything I have learned. And when this is done and they are ready, I will send them to you to serve with Segu's famous heroes."

The djeli said, speaking for the king, "Yes, Numukeba, that will be good. In exchange for your promise, Da Monzon offers you a gift to take with you on your journey. Do you need cowries, gold, slaves? Name your gift and it is yours." Numukeba pondered, and at last he said, "Great king, I would like to have your djibedjan, the horse you ride four times a year during important celebrations." Now, the djibedjan was a tall white horse sacred to the king. No one other than the king was allowed to touch it except its groom. On each ceremonial occasion it was brought to the king so that he could ride it through the four quarters of Segu City in all his splendor. The horse's bit was silver, its stirrups were silver, and a silver breastplate hung around its neck. When Da Monzon heard Numukeba's request he did not reply, but turned to speak in a low voice to his counsellors. At last he said, "Numukeba, I offer you my personal gun instead. It has strong medicine given to it by the paramount morike of Timbuktu, so that no talisman can turn its bullets aside. And its polished stock is inlaid with silver and bronze to form the symbol of the house of Da Monzon."

Numukeba answered, "Great King of Segu, I thank you for

your generosity, but I need no gun other than my own, into which I have forged the potent fluid of the sun. It was never in my mind to ask for anything, but you said, 'name your gift,' and therefore I spoke of the djibedjan. I need nothing else." The king conferred again with his counsellors. He offered Numukeba slaves. He offered him cattle. He offered him wives. He offered a brigade of warriors to accompany him on his expedition. Numukeba said, "Great Da Monzon, I do not want any of these things. When you sent for me you spoke kind and thoughtful words of respect. This is generosity enough. If you cannot part with your djibedjan, let us say the matter is finished. I promise I will never speak of it."

But having pledged a gift of Numukeba's choosing, the king was bound by prestige and honor, and so he said at last, "Bring the djibedjan, clothed in all its silver trappings." The groom brought the horse. Numukeba thanked Da Monzon with words of praise. He mounted. He rode away. Behind him rode four of the king's djeli playing their ngonis and singing. They sang:

> "Numukeba of Naradugu.
> Who does not know the trail he followed?
> Numukeba the Bambara.
> Who has not heard the bards sing of Numukeba?
> He is Waraba, the lion,
> He is Diara, the lion,
> He is Kunkotiti, the lion,
> He is Nianga, the lion.
> The lion devoured Chekele of Massiba
> The lion devoured Bassa of Kassala
> The lion devoured Monza of Mpeba,
> The lion devoured Dengenu of Bozola.
> The names of those defeated by Numukeba
> Stretch like a highway from Songhai to Futa.
> The heart of the Cow of Heroes is his.
> The right foreleg of the Cow of Heroes is his.
> All of the Cow of Heroes is his.
> Dagala of Torigudu fell,
> Hamadi of the family of Ardo fell,
> Fourteen Fula heroes of Massina fell,
> Seku Ndome of Walatadu fell
> Five hundred spearmen of Walatadu fell,
> Azel Amasdan of the Tuareg fell,
> Ouya Bemba the jinn of the lagoon fell,
> All fell to the weapons of Numukeba of Naradugu."

At last Numukeba raised his hand to the djeli, saying, "You masters of the ngoni and the kora, you are generous, but now give me the gift of no more singing. It does nothing for my heart. It only reminds me that I stayed in the bush too long. If you can tell me where my journey goes and whether I will ever again see Naradugu, do so. Otherwise, speak your song silently." One of them, his friend Ngolo Da, said, "Numukeba, may your journey be straight and swift. Yet remember these things: If heroes seek achievements, so, also, achievements seek heroes. If the universe is full of mysteries, do not doubt that they were written by the Architect." They parted. The four djeli turned and rode back toward Segu. Numukeba rode northward on King Da Monzon's tall white djibedjan, whose silver trappings sparkled in the sunlight. He wore on his arms the medicine packets given to him by the filelikela of Segu. His gun hung on his back, and his cutlass across his chest. The light of the forge emanated in a red glow around him. He tested his new weapons. With one slash of his cutlass he cut through the trunk of a tree. He shattered a boulder with his spear. He fired his gun at a distant hill and blew away its crest.

He rode on, toward the country of Kaarta. He passed through Kaarta. He passed through Kaniaga and came to Djara, and there he turned east toward Walata.

One evening just as darkness was falling he came to where a beggar was sitting before his fire next to the road. He approached the man, saying, "Traveller, in which direction are you going?" The man answered, "Direction? There is no direction." Numukeba said, "Why, yes, to the contrary. There is the direction toward Djara and the direction toward Walata." The man responded, "No, there is only here. Have you ever been anywhere that you did not call here?" Numukeba said, "You are only playing the game of words." The man replied, "Ah, it is no game. It is the perception of truth that comes from poverty." Numukeba said, "Perhaps that is so, but I cannot perceive it. There are a thousand cities and ten thousand villages, each in a different place, and each place has a name." The man said, "Now it is you who plays the game of words. In every one of those places if you ask even a child where he is, he answers, 'here.' "

Numukeba dismounted. He said, "I hear you. What does it have to do with poverty?" The man answered, "Why, poverty gives a person time to think about the world. Perhaps for nobles like you it seems different. But for me, when I have walked all day begging for a few grains of corn, I sit by the roadside, build my fire and roast the grains I have collected. When darkness comes it encloses me like a wall. There is no direction, no different place. Everything is here. Wherever I go, 'here' goes with me. I contemplate the universe from here." He poked some corn kernels out of the fire with a stick and put them in his mouth one at a time, chewing carefully so that there would be no waste.

Numukeba said, "Did you always live like this?" And the man said, "No. In the beginning I was the son of Niamesi, king of Dorma. As I grew older I realized that I did not know anything. My uncle taught me to fight and hunt, but I said to myself, 'This is hunting, this is fighting, but it is not knowing.' I asked my father, I asked the filelikelas, 'Where is knowing?' They said, 'Knowing is what you are taught by the old ones.' I was not satisfied, for I did not know anything. To kill a deer is not knowing. To kill an enemy is not knowing. Therefore I went into the bush to seek knowing. I lived in poverty, even though I came from the chief family of Dorma." And Numukeba asked, "Have you found what you were looking for?" The man answered, "One thing only, that there is no direction and everything is here."

Numukeba sat near the fire. He said, "I am Numukeba of Naradugu." He gave the man a piece of dried meat. He said, "I also have been seeking in the bush." The beggar asked, "For what?" Numukeba said, "For honor and a good name." The man asked, "Was there no honor in Naradugu?" Numukeba said, "Was there no knowing in your father's city?" And after a while he said, "After I have found my two sons I will return to Naradugu. Why do you continue to live the life of a beggar? Go back to Dorma and be a king's son again. There is no virtue in poverty. Many men have it and they do not want it. Their wives suffer. Their children die young. Perhaps they have gained knowing, but their knowing pierces their hearts."

The man said, "I have thought of returning to Dorma. But I would not be received. People would say, 'Who is this beggar of beggars who claims the king as his father?' They would drive me away. When I left Dorma I was young and good-looking. Now I am old and my features are warped. It would be useless." Numukeba said, "A king's son is a king's son. Perhaps your father has been looking for you. Surely by this time you have gained whatever knowing is to be found through poverty. Knowing is also to be found in Dorma. As you have said, when you have arrived in Dorma you will still be 'here.' "

Numukeba put his blanket down nearby and slept. When morning came, he resumed his way toward Walata. The sun set. He camped and built a fire. When the embers faded, he slept. In the morning while he was preparing to leave, he heard a voice calling him, "Numukeba! Numukeba!" He saw the beggar coming along the road. When the beggar arrived he said, "I have been walking all night to catch up with you. Let us talk." They sat on the ground face to face, and the beggar said, "I listened to your words, 'Go home to Dorma.' I examined them carefully. I said to myself, 'If I return to Dorma alone, they will drive me away or kill me. Therefore I need a hero as a companion.' " Numukeba said, "Aaaah! I cannot help you, for time is wasting me. I am searching for my sons."

The beggar said, "Who knows where your sons are? Dorma is only a few days to the north. After Dorma you can resume your journey to Walata." Numukeba answered, "No, my friend, for me your 'few days' may be a few months. If I go with you or not does not matter, for the outcome is already determined." The beggar answered, "No, nothing is already determined. If it were, why would there be so much struggling in the world?" Numukeba meditated. The beggar said, "The Prophet once addressed his pupils, saying, 'To give something as charity earns a credit. To give what you do not need for yourself earns only a small credit. To give someone what you yourself need earns a large credit. To give what you yourself need to a person who has still greater need of it, that is the most worthy charity of all.'" Numukeba said, "When I went out into the world from Naradugu I earned many credits. I do not want any more. Now I have my own expedition and I cannot turn aside. Let us each go on his separate journey." He mounted his horse and continued toward Walata.

Whenever he passed a village he inquired about Ngoroni and Mamoye, but no one had seen or heard of them. He camped at nightfall, and once more in the morning as he was preparing to resume his way, he heard the beggar calling from the road, "Numukeba! Numukeba!" The beggar arrived. He said, "Numukeba, I have been walking all night. I do not sleep, I do not eat. You do not want to earn any more credits. A man does not want what he does not want. Good. But you owe me a debt, and this you cannot evade." Numukeba answered, "A debt? How can it be?" The man said, "You found me in the bush. I was not going anywhere. I was satisfied to be where I was. I accepted my life. But you intruded on me. You came and sat at my fire. You said, 'Go back to Dorma and be a king's son again.' I said, 'They will drive me away.' You said, 'Perhaps your father is looking for you.' My mind became unsettled. At last I said, 'I will do as Numukeba urged me. I will go back and be a king's son.' It was you, Numukeba, who set this story in motion. Therefore you undertook an obligation to go with me to Dorma. I can see that you have nobility of spirit. Because of honor you will go with me as my champion."

Numukeba thought, "Yes, it is true. I said, 'Go back to Dorma.' Who knows what he will find when he gets there?" And he said, "Very well. Let it be that way. I will accompany you. But time eats my life. Your walking is too slow. We will find something for you to ride." They went from there, Numukeba on his horse and the beggar on foot, until they came to a village. There Numukeba bought a donkey, paying with cowries he took from the trappings of the horse. The beggar mounted the donkey. He said, "Let us take this trail to the north. It will lead us to Dorma."

That night when they camped in a grove by the trail, Numukeba said, "If I am your champion and someone asks, 'For whom are you acting?' what shall I say? I do not know your name." The beggar answered, "My name is Bamanake." Numukeba said, "Good. When you spoke of the Prophet I thought you were Malinke. Now I know you are Bambara like me."

They travelled four days, and on the fifth they came to the cultivated fields around Dorma. Numukeba said, "Now you must ride in front and speak for yourself. I will follow." Bamanake met a party of men on the road. He said to them, "Tell the city to prepare, for I am arriving." The men laughed, and one of them said, "Are you coming to give enemas?" Bamanake said, "Tell the city that Bamanake, the king's son, has come home." Again the men laughed, and one of them said, "Can a wretched beggar on a donkey be the son of a king? Which king do you claim as a father? The old king, Niamesi, is dead and his brother rules Dorma." Bamanake exclaimed, "Aaaah! My father is dead? When did he die?" They answered, "We do not speak of your father, for who knows who your father was? But Niamesi has been dead for two years, and his brother Koloba is now the father of the city. Why does it interest you so much?"

Bamanake answered, "If what you say is true, then I spoke in error. Tell the people that Bamanake, son of Niamesi, is waiting to enter. Let the djeli come out to welcome me with singing. Let the trail be swept clean. Let the musicians play their koras and drums. As for my uncle, let him vacate the king's quarters and return to his own house." The men laughed again, saying, "The beggar is mad. He believes himself to be king of Dorma." They went on to their fields. But a small boy who had been loitering nearby ran to the marketplace of the city and told what he had seen. The news spread from one place to another. Guards in the royal compound told the king's counsellors, and the counsellors told the king. The king said, "Drive the madman away." People went out of the gate to where Bamanake was sitting on his donkey. They threw sticks and stones at him, and his donkey ran first in one direction and then another. At last the people said, "Let him be. He has had enough."

But Bamanake rode back and said to them, "Is this what the citizens of Dorma are like? A stranger comes and no one asks, 'How is your health? How are your cattle?' No one asks, 'Who are you? Where are you from? Where are you going?' " The people were ashamed. They asked, "Yes, who are you, then, and where are you going?" He answered, "As I told you, I am Bamanake, son of Niamesi. I have been in the wilderness tasting poverty. Now I have returned. If my father is truly dead, then you know I should be the ruler of Dorma." The people returned into the city and told what they had heard.

When the story reached the royal compound, the king was troubled. He said, "Whoever the person is, he is merely a wild man of the bush. My brother's son Bamanake is no longer alive. Many years ago he renounced everything and went away in rags to seek poverty in the bush, and the bush devoured him. This man is mad, but he makes mischief. Therefore, take him and put him under guard. I will decide later how to dispose of him." So a party of soldiers went out and took hold of Bamanake, pulling him from his donkey.

Numukeba went forward, his cutlass in his right hand. He said, "Soldiers, what are you doing? Is this man besieging your city? Has he challenged anyone? Has he committed a crime?" They answered, "Why, we do as the king says. The king is just. He has reasons. The squalid beggar says he is Bamanake, son of Niamesi, but Bamanake is dead. The man calls for the djeli to play the kora for him as if he were king of Dorma. That is treason." Numukeba said, "Can any of you say of your own knowledge that he is not Bamanake?" They answered, "What the king tells us is true and just. Who are you to question us?" Numukeba relied, "I am who I am. I am the pledged companion of Bamanake, son of Niamesi. When we met in the bush he said, 'If I go to Dorma, who will listen to me? The people will drive me away as if I were a dog.' I made a pledge to Bamanake between the sky and the earth. I am his champion. If you intend to take him and mistreat him you will have to fight for him."

Numukeba poised his spear in his left hand, and in his right hand he held his cutlass. The soldiers saw his weapons shining in the sunlight. They saw his vest of mail. They saw the fine horse that had been the djibedjan of the king of Segu. They saw its silver bit and silver breastplate. And they saw a red glow in the air. They said to one another, "This man is a great hero from somewhere. Let us not provoke him." Numukeba said, "Before we commit ourselves to a struggle, ask the people of Dorma to come out. Someone will recognize Bamanake." So they sent a messenger into the city, and soon many people came out to look at Bamanake. They crowded around him and peered into his face, but they said, "He is only a beggar from the bush." The soldiers said to Numukeba, "You have heard." They began pulling Bamanake roughly. Numukeba said, "Are there no more people in the city?" They said, "Yes, but it is useless." Numukeba said, "Go get the others." So they sent back again and more people came. Among them was an old slave woman whose eyes were dimmed by cataracts. She put her face close to Bamanake's. She said, "This man is the eldest child of Niamesi. I was there when he was born. I carried water for the midwife. I washed him and wrapped him in a cloth."

The soldiers laughed, saying, "Old woman, you are nearly blind. You cannot see anything." She said, "If you doubt me, look at his left thigh. It has a white blemish shaped like a battle-ax." They examined Bamanake's left thigh and saw the blemish. The soldiers were disturbed. They said to one another, "Someone must inform the king." So a messenger was sent with the information that an old female slave had identified Bamanake. The king called his counsellors together. They discussed everything. One said, "She identified him by the white blemish on his thigh." Another said, "Great affairs of state cannot hang on the words of a blind slave woman." A third said, "A king's son cannot have a blemish."

Still another said, "Great King of Dorma, does it make any difference whether the old slave woman was right or wrong? The matter cannot be left floating in the air. If the man is not Bamanake, he should be killed for his impersonation. If he is Bamanake, still you will have to kill him. Otherwise the kingship would be in question." The king perceived these words to be true. He said, "Yes, take him somewhere, kill him, and cover him with stones and earth so that he will never be found." Someone said, "The man has a protector who appears to be a noble hero." The king said, "Everything is simple. Bring them both here, saying the king wants to greet them. Surround my quarters with guards. When I say, 'Take them,' the guards will cut them down."

The king's djeli went out to where Bamanake and Numukeba were waiting. He said, "You who claims Niamesi as his father, come to the king's court with your protector. Koloba wishes to greet you and give you gifts." Numukeba said, "That is good. But Niamesi's son cannot ride to Koloba's court on a donkey. Bring him a good horse from the king's stable." The djeli answered, "Yes, it will be done." He sent a slave back to the city. When the slave returned leading a horse, Numukeba said, "No, it will not do. The horse is old and weak. Bring a good horse." The slave led the old horse away and came back with another. Numukeba said, "No, it will not do. Its trappings are worn and it does not come from the king's stable." The slave led the horse away. When he returned he led a spirited black horse with a bronze bit and bronze stirrups.

Bamanake mounted. Numukeba said, "Now give him weapons." The djeli ordered weapons to be given to Bamanake. They gave him a cutlass and a spear. Numukeba said, "Give him a knife for his belt." They gave him a knife. Numukeba said, "Give him a gun." They gave him a gun. Numukeba said, "Good. Let us go. But you, djeli of Koloba, ride ahead and sing a praise song for Bamanake." The djeli answered, "Unknown hero, whoever you are,

I cannot do what you ask. Who can sing a praise song for a beggar arriving from the bush? The king would not accept it." Numukeba said, "Do not speak of beggars. There was Niamesi, and he was king of Dorma. Niamesi had a son named Bamanake, which no one disputes. Bamanake left Dorma and went into the wilderness. No one denies it. You may sing of these things. How can the king resent it?"

So the procession to the city began, the djeli in front with Bamanake and Numukeba behind. After them came the soldiers and the people of Dorma. The djeli composed and played his ngoni. He sang:

> "Koloba is our father.
> He is like a full moon in the sky
> Throwing its light over Dorma.
> The city is his and the kingdom is his
> The cattle are his and the goats are his.
> The gold and the cowries of Dorma are his.
> The fields around the city are his
> And the slaves are his.
> Before Koloba became our father
> Our father was Niamesi, and the two were brothers.
> Niamesi's son was Bamanake,
> And Bamanake went searching for mysteries.
> Bamanake went into the wilderness and was lost.
> Niamesi found death, the light faded for him.
> Koloba became our father.
> He is generous and rules justly."

They entered the gate of the city. They rode to the king's quarters and waited under an aged banyan tree. Koloba came out of his house and sat on a stool placed on a leopard skin.

One of the amulets that Numukeba wore around his arm spoke to him, saying, "The king's guards are hiding behind the houses and walls. They plan to come out and slaughter you." Numukeba said to Bamanake, "Do not dismount. Keep silent. I will be your linguist." When the king saw that the two men did not dismount he was affronted. He spoke angrily through the mouth of his djeli. The djeli said, "The king perceives an insult because you do not come down from your horses." Numukeba said, "Bamanake is a noble. He is the son of the royal father of Dorma, Niamesi. He is Koloba's equal. Since Koloba speaks to him only through the mouth of the djeli, Bamanake will speak to Koloba only through me. Bamanake says to Koloba, 'Why are you sitting on the royal stool of my father?' " The djeli passed the question on to Koloba, then answered, "Niamesi was our father until he lost the key of life. Koloba is Niamesi's brother, and therefore he became our father. He was given the right by the elders of Dorma. The festival was held and all the sacrifices were made. Koloba was given the kingship."

Numukeba replied, "It is said that a just kingship is stronger than granite. Bamanake asks Koloba, 'If you are a rightful king, why are you preparing to kill us?'" The djeli said, speaking for Koloba, "Koloba says you are wrong, he merely receives you with honor. But you show disrespect by remaining mounted." Numukeba said, "How may we safely dismount when Koloba has five hundred guards behind the walls with their weapons drawn? Bamanake says, 'When Niamesi died, did anyone go into the bush to look for his son? No, Koloba decreed that Bamanake was dead, and he took the kingship for himself.'"

The djeli whispered to the king and then spoke for him, saying, "The king wishes you no harm. He offers you a guest house in the city with attendants and slaves." Numukeba answered, "No, Bamanake rejects it, for the king would have us murdered in our sleep. Tell Koloba this, that the two men before him are sitting on the horses of kings. I, Numukeba of Naradugu, ride the horse of the king of Segu. Bamanake rides the royal horse of Koloba himself. Ponder on its meaning. We will not stay in the city, but will camp outside the walls. We will receive Koloba's emissary there and discuss what is to be done." At hearing Numukeba's name, many persons in the court exclaimed, "Aaaah! Numukeba of Naradugu!" And though the king was about to give the signal for his guards to attack, the name Numukeba stopped his hand. Numukeba and Bamanake rode out of the gate and camped near the city's main well on top of a high knoll.

They slept there. In the morning many women came for water with their jars and waited at the edge of the well, for no one could draw from the well until the king's slaves had filled their containers. In time, forty slaves approached to get water for Koloba's household, but Numukeba stopped them, saying, "No, you may not fill your jars yet, because Koloba's emissary has not yet arrived." One of the slaves said, "Noble personage, if we do not bring the water quickly we will be punished." A woman of the city also said, "Until Koloba gets his water none of us may fill our jars." Numukeba answered, "Mother, why is that? Are you not all the king's children?" She said, "Yes, so we are told. But if we fill our jars first, the king's water will be muddied."

Numukeba spoke to Bamanake, saying, "How is it going to be?" Bamanake said, "Let the people take their water first. Let the king's slaves return to the city and tell Koloba we are waiting for his emissary." The king's slaves went back to the city, but the women still would not draw their water. They said, "The king will punish us severely." Bamanake said, "People of Dorma, have no fear. He who rules Dorma is not your true king. Your king is here, Bamanake, son of Niamesi. Take your water now. The king does not own the water of Dorma, he holds it in trust for his children." Still they hesitated. Then the old slave woman who had identified Bamanake said, "I know Bamanake when I see him, and Bamanake is truly the son of Niamesi. What he tells me to do, I do." She filled her jar and carried it away, and after that the other women also took their water and carried it back to the city.

When the king's slaves arrived at the royal quarters they told how they had been turned away from the well. Koloba became angry. He said, "Send my soldiers out to cut short the daylight of Bamanake." But his counsellors soothed him, saying, "Great king, do not forget that his companion is Numukeba of Naradugu. Send your djeli to talk with him." Koloba said, "What shall he say? That Koloba of Dorma must drink muddy water?" They advised, "No, offer them gifts of gold and cattle." So the djeli rode to where Bamanake and Numukeba were sitting on the knoll, and he said, "The king sends his greetings. He says he wants you to accept gifts from him before you continue your journey. He offers you a calabash of gold dust and one hundred cattle."

Bamanake answered, "Why, tell Koloba we are not going anywhere. Tell him that his gold comes from the earth, which belongs to all men. Tell him that he holds the cattle in trust for the people of Dorma, and I have not heard them offer their cows to me." The djeli went back and said to Koloba, "He does not accept anything." Koloba's advisors said, "Aaaah! It was not enough. Offer him more." So the djeli returned to the knoll and said, "The king was not pleased. But he wishes to be generous. He says, 'Give Bamanake and his companion two calabashes of gold and two hundred cattle. Also give them cowries to fill their knapsacks and two hundred slaves.'" Bamanake answered, "Yesterday Koloba wanted to kill us. Today he presses gifts on us. He does not understand anything. We are not going on a journey." The djeli spoke to Numukeba, saying, "You, Numukeba, reason with your companion as we have been doing with the king. Bamanake will listen to you."

Numukeba said, "At last you call him by his name, Bamanake. That is good. But the land bird does not tell the sea bird how to fish. From now on, Bamanake speaks for himself. I ride with him only to assure that he receives honorable treatment." The djeli addressed Bamanake again. He said, "I will tell the king you do not accept the gold, the cowries, the cattle and the slaves. But what is it you want?" Bamanake said, "I am Bamanake, son of Niamesi. Therefore I want everything. Let Koloba take his family and go on a journey of his own. I pledge not to molest him or his children or his children's children." The djeli answered, "Aaaah! After this there cannot be any more words." He rode away.

Numukeba said, "Bamanake, remember the proverb: 'To say "fire" does not burn down a city.' Now Koloba has no choice. He will send out his best fighters to put you into darkness. Go to another city and raise an army, then come back and besiege Dorma." Bamanake answered, "No, I have acted in honor, and honor is strength. Therefore everything will go well." Numukeba said, "Everything does not 'go' by itself. Are you willing to fight twenty or fifty men at a time? And if you destroy fifty, another fifty will come."

Bamanake answered, "I have learned something in the bush. When it is time for a seed to fall, it falls. When it is time for a tree to sprout, it sprouts. When it is time for a limb to break, it breaks. When it was time for me to search for knowing, I searched. Now it is time for me to stand and face Koloba of Dorma." Numukeba asked, "Have you ever been tested in a combat like the one that is coming?" Bamanake said, "I learned about war when I was still young. It was Koloba himself who taught me. From my father, Niamesi, I learned the meaning of honor. As Koloba's djeli said, 'Now there cannot be any more words.'" Numukeba said, "It is true. Still we must ponder everything."

They hunted for small game, then they returned to their knoll near the well, built a fire and ate. And while they were sitting there, the old slave woman with the dimmed eyes came and said, "Koloba is planning to send an expedition against you tonight when you are sleeping." They said, "Thank you, Grandmother. You are a good woman. May you have many more years." And Numukeba asked, "Grandmother, is there any way into the king's quarters without passing through the anterooms?" She answered, "Am I not the one to know? There is a place in the back of the wall where the stones are loose." Numukeba asked, "Will you guide us tonight when the moon is down?" She answered, "Meet me on the far side in the grove of silk-cotton trees." She departed. Bamanake asked, "What are we going to do?" Numukeba said, "We will have a private council with Koloba. We will discuss matters of state. We will be his counsellors."

The night became dark. There was no moon in the sky. Numukeba and Bamanake put more wood on the fire to keep it burning. After that they left the knoll and went in a wide circle to the silk-cotton grove behind the city. While they were waiting there, five hundred of the king's guards came out and went silently toward the knoll where the fire was burning. They surrounded the knoll, drew their weapons, and charged at the fire where they supposed Bamanake and Numukeba were sleeping.

Not finding anyone there, they dispersed in all directions shouting battle cries.

The old slave woman came to the silk-cotton grove. She led Bamanake and Numukeba to a place where the wall was cracked and broken. They removed loose stones, entered, and found themselves in the king's inner court. They went into Koloba's sleeping quarters and found him there with one of his wives.

Koloba sat up on his mat, saying, "Who is it?" Numukeba lifted the oil lamp and held it before Bamanake's face, then before his own. Koloba exclaimed, "Aaaah!" Numukeba said, "Do not cry out or I will submerge you in the river of darkness." Koloba said, "Aaaah" again, but weakly. He said, "What is it that you want?" Bamanake said, "Let us talk about Dorma." Koloba said, "What is there to say about Dorma?" Bamanake said, "We have come to act as your counsellors." Koloba looked toward the corner of the room where his weapons were. He could not reach them. He said, "Yes, that is good. What do you advise me?"

Bamanake said, "You are my father's brother. You taught me to hunt and you taught me the art of combat." Koloba said, "Yes, as if you were my own son." Bamanake said, "You spoke of the white mark of the battle ax on my thigh, saying, 'Your victories will be numerous.' " Koloba said, "Yes, I spoke of it." Bamanake said, "When I left Dorma and went into the bush I did not want victories, I wanted to find knowing. I learned secrets of the bush, but I did not understand that a man is the son of his mother and father. Only when Numukeba said, 'Perhaps your father is looking for you' did I think of it. Was my father looking for me?" Koloba answered, "Would I know it?" Bamanake drew his cutlass and rested its point on the king's mat. He asked again, "Was my father looking for me?" And this time Koloba said, "Yes, when he grew sick he said, 'Find my son, Bamanake.' " Bamanake said, "But you did not find him." Koloba said, "No, the bush was too big." Bamanake said, "When you became king, did you say, 'I pledge to be the good father of Dorma,' or did you say, 'I will hold the king's staff in trust until Bamanake returns'?" Koloba answered, "Why, I said only what the elders required me to say—'I pledge to be the good father of Dorma.' "

Bamanake said, "You pledged with cowries that were not yours." Koloba said, "Aaaah, I did not know it." He looked again toward his weapons, but they were out of reach. He said, "Bamanake, I will share my wealth. Take six calabashes of gold, forty calabashes of cowries, five hundred slaves, two thousand cattle, four thousand goats, and a thousand copper bars. Go to another place and establish a new city. Traders will come from Timbuktu and Jenne and your kingdom will become great." Bamanake said, "My uncle, we are here as your counsellors. Do you agree?" Koloba answered, "Yes, I agree." Bamanake said, "Very well. When your court convenes tomorrow, tell the people this: 'When darkness came to my brother Niamesi, I swore to be your good father. But Bamanake has returned. Therefore I relinquish what I accepted and what I pledged. Your new king will be Bamanake.' " Koloba answered quickly, "Yes, I agree." Bamanake said, "Swear it three times, so the spirits of our ancestors may hear." Koloba swore it three times. Then Bamanake and Numukeba went out of the king's private quarters and departed through the break in the wall. They found their horses in the grove and mounted. Bamanake said, "It is done." Numukeba said, "No, it has not even begun. He swore too willingly. We will have to fight."

When the king's guards returned from their searching, they told Koloba, "The two men you sent us to kill, they have fled. They left nothing but their fire." Anger burned in Koloba's belly. He said, "No, they have not fled. They loiter now outside the city walls. While you were searching this way and that, they entered my quarters and abused me with treasonous words. Tomorrow when the sun rises, go out and find them. Bring me their heads. If you fail to do it, every tenth man among you will be executed, his house burned down, his family driven into the bush, and his name cursed before the fetishes of Dorma." The king's guards sharpened their spears and counted their bullets. They said, "We are ready."

Numukeba and Bamanake camped that night on a distant hill. When morning came, they saw Koloba's army passing through the gate of the city, five hundred men, half on horse and half on foot. Numukeba said, "The sun takes away the blanket of night. Now we must ride." They mounted. They departed, leaving their smoking fire burning so their pursuers would know the direction. They rode all day, and all day Koloba's fighters followed them. Night came and they camped. In the morning they rode, again leaving their smoking fire to beckon Koloba's men. Four days they rode, and four days Koloba's army pursued them in the wilderness.

On the fifth morning they saw a large Fula raiding party driving a large herd of cattle before them. Numukeba said, "Fate led us here. Let us speak with the Fula." They went forward, then sat and waited until the Fula warriors arrived. One of the Fula approached them on his horse. He said, "Who are you and what do you want with us?" Numukeba said, "We meet only by chance because our paths are entangled. We are Bambara pursued by the soldiers of Dorma." The Fula said, "You appear to be nobles. Why does Dorma pursue you?" Numukeba said, "In the bush I met my companion, Bamanake. He wanted to return to Dorma, thinking his father was king. I agreed to ride with him so they would not abuse him. We went together. But his father, Niamesi, had lost the light of day, and his brother, Koloba, took the kingship. Now Koloba wants to kill Bamanake. We do not flee, but lead Koloba's warriors on a tour of the bush."

The Fula asked, "And who are you whose horse is decorated with the silver breastplate and stirrups?" Numukeba answered, "I am Numukeba of Naradugu." The Fula sucked his breath. He said, "I have heard of Numukeba of Naradugu." Numukeba asked, "You, leader of the Fula expedition, who are you?" The Fula said, "I am Bororo of Kano." Numukeba replied, "I have heard the djeli praise your accomplishments." Bororo said, "Let us rest and talk."

They dismounted. Bororo put down a camel-hair blanket, and the three of them sat. Bororo's personal slave brought milk for them to drink. Numukeba said, "Your fighters appear to be valiant. You have taken many cattle." Bororo said, "We captured them from the Soninke. There was a battle. We lost many men, but the Soninke lost more, and in the end they gave way and let us have the cattle." Numukeba said, "The king of Dorma also has fine herds." Bororo asked, "Why do you mention it?" Numukeba answered, "Bamanake and I have pledged our honor to drive Koloba from Dorma. Bamanake is the son of Niamesi. He is the rightful heir to the kingship. But five hundred of Koloba's warriors pursue us. We lead them in circles, yet they persist. With fifty valiant heroes we could contend with them. Bamanake would then take the kingship." Bororo said, "You spoke of cattle." Bamanake broke his silence, saying, "Yes, if Koloba has a thousand cattle, I will give up half. If he has two thousand, I will give up one thousand. If he has four thousand, I will give up two thousand."

Bororo closed his eyes and was silent. Then he said, "I have sixty men in my expedition. If I send twelve home with the cattle we have already taken, forty-eight fighters remain." Bamanake said, "With Numukeba and myself there will be fifty." Bororo said, "Each of us will have to contend with ten of Koloba's fighters." Bamanake asked, "Is it too many?" Bororo answered, "No, it is not enough. We are Fula. Yet we cannot help it if they are so few. Let us swear by the earth that we will fulfill our obligations to one another." They placed their hands on the ground and pledged. Bororo said, "Let us pledge to the sky." They raised their hands toward the sky and pledged. Bororo said, "Good, let us begin." He went back to where his men were waiting. He instructed twelve of them to go on with the cattle. The others followed Bororo, riding at a gallop to where Numukeba and Bamanake were waiting. They held their cutlasses aloft and fired their guns into the air. Bororo said, "We are ready. Let us go and have our conversation with Koloba's fighters."

Numukeba, Bamanake and Bororo rode together in the lead.

They turned toward Dorma. In time they saw Koloba's soldiers. They closed the distance between them and met in a wide plain. Guns were fired and smoke drifted in the air. Spears were launched. Horse pressed against horse and the air rang with the sound of steel. Koloba's fighters gave their battle cry, "Dorma!" The Fula gave their battle cry, "Kano!"

At first Numukeba, Bamanake and Bororo fought side by side, but they became separated and drifted to different parts of the field. With his spear Numukeba toppled one after another of the enemy from their horses. With his cutlass he cut a swathe through the warriors of Koloba. Elsewhere, Bamanake fought likewise, and each time he struck a blow he said, "Koloba taught me! Koloba taught me!" Across the plain Bororo slashed and thrust, and if he did not strike one of the enemy he struck another, so densely were they packed. So, also, did the other Fula warriors. Many fighters of each side fell dead or dying on the ground. Dust rose from the earth and hung like a mist around them.

A large hero on a tall horse rode up to Numukeba, pointed his gun and fired. But the medicine packets Numukeba wore protected him. The bullet rolled from the barrel of the gun and fell harmlessly, and Numukeba slew him with one blow. Bororo was struck by many cutlasses, but because of his amulets none of them pierced his skin. Bamanake wore no amulets, but the blemish on his thigh in the shape of a battle ax was his protective medicine. The enemy pressed in on him, because it was his head above all others that Koloba wanted to see. He poised his spear in his right hand, but a slashing cutlass blow severed his wrist and his spear fell to the ground. He raised his cutlass with his left hand and went on fighting. He struck down many of Koloba's soldiers.

The enemy saw their companions littering the ground everywhere. They wavered, and at last, as if by common understanding, they turned and galloped from the field. The foot soldiers could not keep up with them, and the Fula warriors followed on their horses and destroyed them. The Fula came together with Bororo, Bamanake and Numukeba. They counted those of them who were alive. Only thirty-eight of forty-eight remained. Bamanake wrapped the stump of his wrist in a cloth. He said, "Now let us bury our dead, go back to Dorma, and confer with Koloba."

They returned to Dorma. When they entered the gate of the city they found the streets deserted. People had fled beyond the walls or were closed up in their houses. Bamanake, Numukeba and Bororo rode with their fighters to the king's compound. There was no sentry at the entrance. Bamanake called, "Koloba, come out. We are here." Koloba did not come out. Bamanake called again, "Koloba, my uncle, your army is gone and the people of Dorma have turned their faces away from you. Your egg of life is broken. If you do not come out now, I will send my Fula fighters in to get you. Do not be dragged out like a mole from its hole. Honor, you do not have it, but if any valor still lives in your heart, come out and face me."

Koloba came out with his royal staff and stood in front of his door. He said, "Bamanake, what do you want? I wish you no harm. I offered you rich gifts. I am your father's brother." Bamanake answered, "Aaaah, Koloba, the words that come from your own mouth are feeble. Where is your djeli? Let him manipulate your meanings for you so they will sound more eloquent. You yourself cannot convince us of anything. Let your wife speak for you. Let your house slave speak for you." Koloba was silent, and, Bamanake went on, "You pledged three times to renounce the kingship. You said three times, 'I agree, I agree, I agree.' Our ancestors heard you. The spirits of the bush heard you. The spirits of the water heard you. The Architect heard you. My companion, Numukeba, was right when he said, 'Koloba lied, he spoke too willingly.' You sent your fighters after us to take our heads. But now your story is finished."

Koloba said, "Bamanake, it was a misunderstanding. You and your companions are noble heroes. Be generous. When I accepted the kingship I thought that surely you were dead. I swore to be a just father over Dorma. When there was a drought, I gave the people part of my crops. When raiders came to loot our city, I protected everyone. When I presided over litigations, I judged fairly. I brought craftsmen to Dorma from other cities. I collected taxes gently. When my fighters pursued you into the bush, they misunderstood my intentions, and for this they will all be punished. Listen to me, Bamanake. We will divide Dorma into two parts, and each of us will rule half. There will be Dorma Bamanake and Dorma Koloba. We will become greater than Segu or Jenne. Timbuktu and Walata will envy us."

Bamanake answered, "Koloba, when I went into the bush long ago in search of knowing, I did not foresee the consequences. Now that I have returned, I will rule Dorma in honor as my father ruled. As for you, do not give us any more words. I offer you a choice. Take your family and leave Dorma before dawn tomorrow, or go into your private quarters and never emerge. Whatever you decide, you will be forgotten and your words will be forgotten, and in this way Dorma will purify itself."

Bamanake, Numukeba and Bororo turned their horses and rode away. People began to emerge from their houses. They fed all the heroes and gave them rooms in which to sleep. In the morning, Bamanake, Numukeba and Bororo went back to the king's compound. They waited. All was silent, and nothing in the king's grounds moved. They sent a Fula warrior inside. When he came out he said, "Koloba is there but he is not there." They dismounted and entered. They found Koloba hanging from the rafters.

Because Koloba had taken his own life, he was deprived of a funeral ceremony. They took his body into the bush and left it there to be eaten by jackals and hyenas. Koloba's cattle were rounded up in the fields, two thousand of them, and one thousand were given to Bororo and his Fula heroes. Bamanake claimed the kingship, and a time was set for him to receive the symbols of authority and pledge himself to the people. Bororo departed for Kano, and Numukeba prepared to continue his search for his sons, but Bamanake urged him to stay until after the celebration was over. Numukeba said, "Very well, but if I stay I must have a forge where I can do my work."

Bamanake gave Numukeba a forge. Numukeba said, "Good. Now I need raw gold for what I am going to do." Bamanake provided Numukeba with gold. Numukeba worked the gold for fourteen days, and out of it he shaped a golden right hand. On the fifteenth day he brought it to Bamanake, saying, "Let this hand replace the one you lost in battle." The hand had a collar made of leather, and it fitted over Bamanake's wrist. Bamanake said, "Numukeba, I will wear it whenever I appear before the people. With this hand I will hold my staff or my ceremonial ax. Whenever I wear it I will think, 'Numukeba is with me.'"

The day came for the swearing of the oath. There was feasting and dancing in Dorma. Cattle were sacrificed. Bamanake made his pledge:

> "I will be a good father in Dorma.
> I will not abuse those who are helpless.
> I will not demand more taxes than a man can pay.
> I will not send out agents to spy on the people.
> I will not complain if a djeli does not compare me to the sun.
> I will never say I do not need the advice of counsellors.
> I will listen to the complaints of slaves as if they were nobles.
> I will never judge in favor of a person because I like him.
> I will never judge against a person because I do not like him.
> I will never claim straying cattle as my own.
> I will never make war for trivial reasons.
> If a hero of Dorma dies, I will take care of his family.
> If famine comes I will share the corn of my granaries.

I will preserve the honor of Dorma.
If I do not speak the truth, let my corpse be thrown in
the bush."

Four of Dorma's greatest djeli faced Bamanake with their koras
and sang for him. Each of them sang a djouba, which was only
performed for a king twice, at the time of his pledging and at the
time of his funeral. They recited Bamanake's lineage, his father's
great deeds, and his own achievements against Koloba. When
they were finished, they took up their ngonis to sing praise songs
to Numukeba, but Bamanake made them put their ngonis down.
He said, "Whenever my djeli recite the accomplishments of Numukeba of Naradugu, they will use the kora and not the ngoni."
They took up their koras again and sang about Numukeba.

The celebrations lasted four days, and after that Numukeba
prepared to leave. Bamanake offered him gold, cowries, cattle and
slaves to take with him, but Numukeba refused everything. He
said, "Divide these presents among the people of Dorma. Now I
want only one thing, to find my sons, Ngoroni and Mamoye, before they are devoured by the wilderness." He rode out of
Dorma. The king's musicians rode behind him, and people lined
the road from the city gate to far into the bush country.

15

The Conflict
at Futa

UMUKEBA RODE SOUTH TO THE ROAD THAT
led to Walata. At the crossroads he saw the
bent figure of an aged man sitting before a fire. Though the man
did not turn to show his face, Numukeba knew it was Etchuba.
He dismounted and approached. He kicked the hot embers of the
fire, scattering them in all directions. He said, "You, old man,
why do you not till a field or do something else that is useful in
the world?" Etchuba said, "Aaaah, Numukeba of Naradugu."
Numukeba said, "Yes, as you have known from the beginning.
Otherwise why would you be here waiting?" Etchuba answered,
"You are vain, Numukeba. Do you think you are the only living
person who concerns me? My friend, you are an elder now, for I
see grey hairs in your beard." Numukeba said, "Etchuba the ma-
licious, are you the cause of it? Is it you who stole the substance
of my youth?"

Etchuba answered, "No, fellow traveller, a mystery greater
than myself is responsible. Turn your eyes to the sky. The great
blue calabash under which we all live contains mysteries too large
to understand. The fault is there." Numukeba said, "Aaaah, you
acknowledge something greater than yourself?" Etchuba answered, "Have I ever denied it? Yet each living thing contains its
own mysteries. Therefore the great blue calabash does not di-
minish my significance." Numukeba said, "Do not call it significance, old man, but mischief. And if time consumes ordinary men
it consumes you as well." Etchuba answered, "No, that is one of
the mysteries, for I am always here." Numukeba said, "Were you
born old and infirm? No one is born old. Before you were an old

man you were a young man, and before that you were a child. Therefore as the years pass, you will become older still, and one day you will lose the key of life." Etchuba replied, "No, I will never lose the key. As long as there are people who insist that nothing can deter or deflect them from destiny, I will be here." Numukeba said, "It is your arrogance, not knowledge, that speaks." Etchuba said, "Have you never heard the story of Certainty and Chance?" Numukeba said, "Must I hear it? For everything you tell me is falsehood."

Etchuba began: "In ancient times there were two brothers. They went hunting in the bush. They tracked an elephant. The first brother, whose name was Certainty, shot an elephant but did not kill it. The elephant fled. The second brother whose name was Chance, ran on ahead, and through the power of his medicine he created the appearance of a mountain. When the elephant saw what appeared to be a mountain, he turned back, and then Certainty shot him again and killed him. Certainty said, 'My brother, the elephant is mine, because I shot him twice and you did not shoot at all.' Chance answered, 'No, my brother, for I created the illusion of a mountain and turned the elephant back. Therefore the elephant is mine.' They argued. Anger stirred in their bellies. They wrestled. First Certainty threw Chance to the ground, then Chance arose and threw Certainty to the ground. They became enemies. They parted, one to the east and one to the west. They went their ways. Yet they met again, and Certainty said, 'It was my bullet that killed the elephant.' Chance said, 'No, it was the illusion of the mountain that killed the elephant.' They wrestled. Chance threw Certainty to the ground. Certainty arose and threw Chance to the ground. They continued fighting. After a while they parted, still in anger. Time and time again they met, wrestled, and went their own ways. Sometimes one of them won, sometimes the other. This is the way it has always been since the day of the elephant hunt."

Numukeba answered, "No, Etchuba, Certainty wins. Your child's story does not change the universe. The sun moves from the eastern rim to the western rim and nothing can alter it." Etchuba said, "The sun is a divine element. If you are indeed divine, why did you have to leave Naradugu in the first place to prove your honor and create a name for yourself?" Numukeba answered, "When I was conceived, the Architect created my form in his mind, and he touched it with his finger and gave me my birth payment. The Architect gave me my character, therefore I am not merely dust blowing in the wind."

Etchuba clicked his tongue. He said, "Numukeba, though your beard is streaked with grey, you still do not grasp things the way they are. When you left Naradugu you went out in the bush only to challenge accident and chance, even though you mumbled to yourself about fate. Without chance, fate has no meaning. Struggle on then, Numukeba, but there is no honor for you if you do not understand the struggle. Honor comes only with understanding. Let the bards sing of how you once battled with an earthen effigy of Etchuba, but it will all be a parody and wise men will mock your name."

Etchuba opened his pouch and threw red powder on Numukeba, saying, "The white hairs in your beard are few and lonely. Therefore I give them companions and you a new name, Numukeba of the White Beard. Let your sons, Ngoroni and Mamoye, recognize you if they can." Numukeba drew out the packet of white powder given to him by the filelikela of Segu. He threw powder on Etchuba, saying, "For the many gifts of adversity that you have given me, I now repay you, warper of human lives."

When the powder fell on Etchuba he sat quietly without speaking. Numukeba asked, "Do you have nothing more to tell me?" Etchuba did not answer. He began to be transformed. His face changed, his body shrank, and the grey films disappeared from his eyes. Slowly, slowly, the figure of the blind old man turned into that of an infant child. It sat playing with pebbles on the ground and making gurgling noises in its small mouth.

Numukeba looked in wonder at what the white powder had accomplished. And while he contemplated the transformation, a woman traveller came along the road. Seeing the baby sitting there she said to Numukeba, "Is the small child yours?" Numukeba answered, "No, he is not mine." The woman said, "Where is his mother?" Numukeba said, "She is not here." The woman asked, "Does he belong to anyone?" Numukeba replied, "No one owns him." The woman said, "He cannot be left here in the bush. I will take him." Numukeba said, "Yes, take him. You are a good woman. Yet do you know what he will be when he grows up? Who knows what his birth payment was?" The woman answered, "When the Architect gives a child, who can ask such questions?" Numukeba said, "What if he was an evil force in his previous life?" The woman answered, "Though you appear to be a noble, you speak like a person with a brittle mind." She picked up the infant Etchuba and placed him in a cradle cloth on her back. After that she resumed her journey.

Numukeba sat on a rock and reflected on what had occurred. He thought, "Is Etchuba disposed of, or has he merely been deflected? Can the form of an infant wipe out his malevolence? An infant grows into a child and then an adult. The powder should have turned him into a stone. Still, he has been entangled in the net of time." It was late, and so Numukeba put down his blanket and slept. When the eye of day opened, he prepared to continue his journey. But just as he was mounting his horse he saw the woman returning with the infant Etchuba. When she arrived she said, "This child is a jinn. I do not want him. He grows heavy on my back as if he were a load of stones. We came to a place where a man was leading a cow, and I bought a little milk. But the child swallowed it down and cried for more. I bought more milk, and again he swallowed it and cried for more. I bought all the milk the cow could give, and still he was not satisfied. I bought an ember and made a fire for the night, but he spat on the fire and extinguished it. He picked up a stick and shattered a termite hill. A boy came driving a herd of goats, and the child pushed a tree and uprooted it. It fell on the goats and killed them all. Take the child back. I want nothing to do with him."

Numukeba said, "Woman, how can I take him back? I do not own him. Place him where you found him. No one will ever reproach you. If he is not a jinn, he is worse than a jinn. What he is you cannot tell from his appearance." The woman placed Etchuba on the ground where she had first seen him. She hurried away. Numukeba mounted his horse. Looking down at the infant, he said, "Oh, Etchuba, you are perverse. The woman offered to love and care for you, and you repaid her with malefactions. You can never win the game you are playing because you lack human feelings." He departed, riding toward Walata. He came to a water hole. He dismounted and leaned over it to drink. His reflection looked back at him from the surface of the water, and he saw that his beard and the hair on his head were pure white. He said aloud, "Aaaah! When I find my sons, will they recognize me?" Night came and he camped. He slept. In his dream he saw a tall man with a white beard standing before him. He heard himself speaking, saying, "I am Numukeba of Naradugu. Is this a road to somewhere, or is it a place without any meaning?" The man answered, "I am the Great Caster. If you are alive, every place has meaning. If you are dead, no place has meaning." Numukeba said, "Great Caster, you are the one who gave me the gift of forging. Explain to me about destiny. Am I on the right trail or am I merely wandering from one place to another? I have seen things happen that could not have been part of my birth payment."

The man answered, "Some call me the Architect. Some call me the Composer. Some call me the Conceiver. Yet above all I am the Great Caster, for I cast everyone's life in brass. There is the answer to your question." Numukeba said, "If destiny is cast in brass it is indestructible." The Great Caster answered, "Yes, but it is not so simple. I model destiny in wax, and the model is perfect. I enclose it in clay and bake a mould. When the wax is gone I fill the cavity with molten brass. The mould is opened, and there stands in brass what once was wax. But it is not quite the same. There are small holes and defects, and where the wax was smooth the brass may be marred and rough. Chance has entered. Wherever there are small defects a person's road may become strange

and uncertain." Numukeba said, "Aaaah, Great Caster, can it be
believed that you, who are perfect, can create an imperfect
thing?" The Great Caster answered, "Oh, Numukeba! Have I
ever stood on the roof of my house and claimed to be perfect?"

The dream faded and Numukeba awoke. It was daylight. He
resumed his journey, pondering the words of the Great Caster.
He seemed to understand now what had eluded him, that the
faults were in the brass itself. And he said silently, as though he
were still in dialogue with the figure he had seen in his dream,
"Aaaah, but if you are the father of all craftsmen, why is it you
did not take time to smooth and braze the flaws in the casting and
make them invisible?" But in the inner vault of his mind no one
answered.

Before the sun was high in the sky, Numukeba saw a stream of
people moving toward him on the road. He stopped a woman and
asked, "Where are the people going?" She answered, "Who
knows where they are going? They come from the town of Futa,
where there is going to be a battle. The Malinke are camping on a
hill outside the walls, and they are preparing to attack." Numukeba asked, "Can Futa defend itself?" She answered, "The Malinke are numerous and violent. They swore that if Futa does not
surrender, they will turn the town to ashes and leave no one
alive." Numukeba asked, "Has the town no heroes to defend it?"
The woman said, "Yes, but only a few. We are Soninke people.
All we know is simple farming and trading." Numukeba asked,
"What does your chief say?" The woman answered, "Our old
chief died, and his son is on a visit to Timbuktu. Because we are
helpless, we are going wherever we can to find relatives." Numukeba asked, "How far is your town from here?" She answered,
"Not far. We started out just before dawn."

Numukeba rode on, passing many fleeing townspeople. Beyond a bend in the road he saw Futa in the distance, and on the
far side a high hill where the Malinke were encamped. Arriving at
the town gate, he found it closed and bolted from within. He
called out, "People of Futa, open for me." Men appeared on top of
the wall, brandishing their spears. He called to them, "Do not
fear me. I am not Malinke, but Bambara. The Malinke are still on
their hill." After a while he heard the bolts sliding, and the gate
opened wide enough for him to enter. Inside the walls he was im-
mediately surrounded. The fighting men of Futa were indecisive.
Some wanted to launch their spears at Numukeba, while others
restrained them.

He said, "Since you have no chief to receive me, I will speak
with his mother." They said, "His mother is dead." He said,
"Then I will speak with his djeli." They answered, "His djeli has
gone with him to Timbuktu." Numukeba said, "Very well, I will
speak to his counsellors." They answered, "His counsellors?

Haaah! They have disappeared from the town and are halfway to Walata." Numukeba asked, "Who is the captain of your battalion?" They said, "What do we know of battalions? We are farmers." Numukeba said, "What then can you expect from life? You are a body without a head." But one of the men protested, saying, "Nevertheless, we will defend our walls." Numukeba said, "You will never survive without meeting the Malinke before they get to your walls." The man said, "Yes, if the two young men return we will do it."

Numukeba said, "Who are the two young men?" The man replied, "Why, we do not really know, but they are Bambara like yourself. They came only yesterday, and when they saw how things were with us they rode away to get help, saying they would return." Numukeba exclaimed, "Aaaah, Bambara like myself! What were their names?" The man answered, "We do not know. They did not tell us. But it was clear that they were heroes. They rode fine stallions. They wore vests of mail. They carried spears, cutlasses, guns and battle-axes, and they wore many talismans on their arms." Numukeba said, "Perhaps, like the chief's counsellors, they are halfway to Walata." The man responded, "I do not believe it. These young men are heroes." After that he fell silent.

Numukeba said, "Take me to the chief's house. I will wait for them there." They took him to the chief's house, even though some men still wanted to launch spears at him. He sat under the fig tree where the chief held his councils. And when the sun had moved high in the sky, there was a hubbub at the town gate. Numukeba remained where he was, waiting. He heard horses coming. Suddenly they burst into view, forty Bambara warriors pointing their guns upward as if to challenge the Sky People. Leading them were two young men. When the party arrived at the chief's council place, the two young men dismounted and approached Numukeba. One of them said, "You who are here, if you are Bambara as they say, join us and we will be forty-one." Numukeba said, "I am Bambara. You have been on a hard journey gathering fighters. Let us exchange thoughts."

One of them said, "You seem to be a person of valor. We do not know you, but if you are Bambara, that is enough." Numukeba replied, "You, also, appear to be valorous men. You could have ridden away and abandoned Futa to the Malinke." They said, "We pledged to come back." Now though the two young men were no longer boys as he remembered them, Numukeba recognized them to be his sons, Ngoroni and Mamoye, and he felt a great wind blowing in his heart. He said, "Many pledges are made in the world, though many die before they are fulfilled." One of the young men, whom he recognized as his elder son, Ngoroni, answered, "Some men must pledge three times for the world to believe them. We need pledge only once, for we are the sons of a great hero from Naradugu."

Mamoye, the younger, said, "Surely you have heard of Numukeba? He is known everywhere." Numukeba answered, "Why, I have heard men speak of him." Mamoye said, "The greatest djeli in the country recite his accomplishments." Numukeba said, "And you, have you found valor and honor in your journeys?" Ngoroni said, "Everything we have done, we have done well. We have accomplished something. But we are travelling in search of our father, whom we want to bring back to Naradugu." Numukeba said, "Yet you stop in the bush to help defend Futa, a town few people have heard of?" They answered, "Yes, because that is the way of honor." Ngoroni asked, "You, Uncle, though your beard is white we can see that you are strong and valorous. What is your name that we may address you properly?"

Numukeba answered, "You two young men have not mentioned your own names. Let it be this way. I will ride with you against the Malinke. When our achievement is completed, then we will reveal ourselves. Do you agree?" Ngoroni answered, "Very well, let it be that way. Meanwhile, you are our senior. If you have advice to give us in battle, we will listen, because we perceive you to be an experienced fighter, and the whiteness of your beard tells us that you have survived many battles. Remember, however, that we also have fought before and cut men to the ground. We will refuse to hear only one thing from your mouth. If you say, 'Ride away, take refuge somewhere, the Malinke are too much for us,' our ears will hear nothing. It will be as if your lips were moving silently in the dark of night."

Numukeba said, "Why do you imagine you might ever hear such words from my mouth? If I do not fight courageously, remind me. If my blows lack force, speak of it. If I falter while facing the Malinke, I owe you my left hand. If I turn away from their furious charge, I owe you my right hand. If I ever abandon you in the battle, I owe you my head as if I were one of the enemy, and you may throw my body in the bush to be eaten by hyenas." The young men were abashed. Ngoroni said, "Uncle, I lacked respect. My words were not good." And Numukeba answered, "Speak no more of the matter. All men boast when they are going to war. Now let us repair our weapons and consider what we are going to do."

They sat together and honed their spears. Ngoroni said, "Let us go out soon and strike them." Mamoye said, "Yes, let us drive them from their hill." Numukeba looked into their faces. He saw them as boys and as men. He said, "If you are searching for your father, why will you waste time fighting the Malinke at Futa?" Ngoroni answered, "It is the way of honor. We ask ourselves, 'What would our father have done?' And we know he would not have passed Futa by. Therefore we do not pass it by. Even though we are searching for Numukeba, fate has put Futa in our path. The people of Futa have not offended anyone, but the Malinke wish to subdue them. We have no choice but to stand against the Malinke." Numukeba said, "The battle will be bloody. Women will become widows, and children will become fatherless. If you lose the light of life, how then will you find what you are looking for?" Mamoye said, "If it happens that way, it will be because the Composer has written it." When Numukeba finally answered, he said, "Who can tell what the Composer has written? It is too much to understand. But what you say of the way of honor is true. I also am obliged to stand against the Malinke. Therefore we are related in honor, as if we were a single family. Our horses will be shoulder to shoulder and flank to flank, and we will fight as if we were one hero with six arms."

Now, it was the custom of the Malinke to make their attacks at dawn, and much of the day had already slipped away. Numukeba said, "They will not begin until tomorrow. We will send them an emissary to let them know we will be ready. The emissary will tell them this: 'The people of Futa have never injured you. Why are you assaulting them? They do not want anything but to farm and harvest their crops. Futa has never taken slaves from you. Futa has never insulted you. Futa has never stolen your game from the bush. Futa has never taken your cattle. Futa has never conspired with your enemies. Futa has never befouled your wells. Futa has no hoard of wealth. Therefore, go away in peace and no blood will have to flow from your bodies and ours. Though you may be great in war, your battle will not be easy. Futa is prepared to defend itself. Though you have many spears, guns and talismans, Futa also has spears, guns and talismans. If you kill all the men, women and children of Futa, where is the honor in it for you? And if you fail to do what you now intend to do, how will the djeli of Walata, Timbuktu and Segu sing of it? Whatever happens tomorrow will be remembered in the songs of bards.'"

An emissary was chosen. He mounted his horse and rode out of Futa. He went to the hill where the Malinke were camping. And when he returned to where Numukeba, Ngoroni and Mamoye were waiting, he said, "I delivered the greetings from Futa. I inquired about the welfare of their families, their cattle and their crops. Then I gave them your message." Numukeba asked, "And what did they answer?"

The emissary said, "First they greeted Futa in the usual manner. Afterwards they said: 'Futa offends us in every way. It offends us because it is there. Its name is offensive to our ears. The people offend us because they would rather grow a stalk of millet than prove their courage. Most of all, they offend us because they are unbelievers. Is there a single mosque in Futa? No. Do the people acknowledge the Prophet? No. What is in Futa that is worthy of preserving? Only the cattle. Therefore we will take the cattle, we will take slaves, we will take women of our choice. Futa will be burned and the bush will reclaim it.' These were the words the Malinke gave me to bring back."

Numukeba asked, "How many Malinke are in the camp?" The emissary said, "Five hundred horsemen." Numukeba said, "We must devise a plan." He went to the doorway of the chief's house and sat there, thinking alone. When at last he returned he said to Ngoroni and Mamoye, "Tonight, when all is dark, let men and boys of Futa go out in the bush and build fires at different places on all sides of the Malinke encampment. Let there be many fires, so the enemy believe themselves to be surrounded by war parties. Let the fires be tended all night. The Malinke will not know the direction from which we are coming. We will attack at dawn, before they take up their positions in the valley. We Bambara will strike the encampment, and the Futa warriors will surround the hill down below." They said, "Yes, that is good."

Night came, and the men and boys of Futa went out and made campfires in the bush. Ngoroni, Mamoye and their Bambara company put down blankets and slept. Numukeba did not sleep. He felt no fatigue, only the wind blowing in his heart because he had found his sons. He thought, "This surely cannot be the end of our stories. O Great Caster, let there be no flaws in your brass tomorrow." He watched the stars move in a wide arc overhead. And when a certain star touched the horizon, he awakened Ngoroni and Mamoye, saying, "It is time." They arose and put on their armored vests. They took up their weapons and aroused their company of Bambara fighters. They aroused the fighting men of Futa.

Numukeba, Ngoroni and Mamoye went out of the town first, and the others followed. The Bambara made a wide circle and approached the encampment from the far side, while the men of Futa went to their positions at the base of the hill. Numukeba rode with Ngoroni on his right and Mamoye on his left. When they were nearly at the crest they could see grey light of the eastern horizon. Numukeba said, "From this moment the road behind us is closed and the road ahead is open. We can go only one way, and the coming battle can be fought only once. Those who survive will thread their way home through a litter of corpses, and those who fall will nourish the earth. Let the Malinke bleed, let them feel fear, let their families mourn their dead. If the time ahead is long, let it be long. If the time is short, let it be short. All men live out the time that is given to them."

Firing their guns and calling out their battle cries, the Bambara rode into the encampment of the Malinke. The Malinke ran this way and that, snatching up their weapons and looking for their horses. For a while they were in confusion, not knowing the direction from which the Bambara were coming. Many Malinke fell, but soon others were fighting back. The Bambara were compressed in the center of the battle, with the Malinke all around. When guns had been fired there was no time to reload, and men fought with spears, cutlasses and battle-axes. Numukeba went wherever the fighting was heaviest, and with him rode Ngoroni and Mamoye. Their horses were shoulder to shoulder and flank to flank, and they struck down one Malinke after another.

The sun rose. The dust from the horses' hooves drifted in the air, and the sun shone through it with a pale light. The fighting went on. Now it was late morning. The Malinke moved down the hillside, followed by the Bambara. When the Malinke reached the valley they were attacked by the fighters from Futa. The struggle went on in the valley, and the sound of cutlasses against shields and steel carried through the bush. The sun was halfway up in the sky. The fighting went on. The sun arrived overhead. The fighting went on. The sun moved down toward the west. The fighting went on. The weapons of the Bambara and of the Malinke were brothers, all born at the forge, and they cut down many heroes on both sides.

Though the Malinke outnumbered the Bambara and Futa warriors many times over, they were hard pressed. They withdrew to a grove of trees and regrouped. They returned firing their guns and launching spears. Puffs of gunpowder smoke floated in the air. Then once again it was horse against horse, man against man, cutlass against cutlass. Numukeba, Ngoroni and Mamoye found themselves separated from the other Bambara. A Malinke war-club struck Ngoroni to the ground. Numukeba leaned over and with his right hand lifted Ngoroni and put him in his saddle. A glancing battle-ax knocked Mamoye from his horse. Numukeba leaned over and with his left hand lifted him from the earth and placed him in his saddle. Fighting as if they were a single body with six hands, the three of them, the father and his sons, cut a wide swathe through the horde of Malinke. Then they turned back and cut another swathe. Malinke fell and were trampled by the foaming horses. More Malinke came to fill the gaps.

Numukeba stood up in his stirrups. In his left hand he held his spear, in his right hand he held his cutlass. His weapons began to glow as if they had just come from the fire of the forge. A red light emanated from his body. Seeing Numukeba standing, Ngoroni and Mamoye also stood in their stirrups. Their weapons too began to glow, and red light emanated from their bodies also. When the Malinke saw these things they faltered and began to fall back. Numukeba, Ngoroni and Mamoye rode forward, striking to the front, to the side, and behind. The ranks of the Malinke broke. They turned and rode away swiftly, and when other Malinke saw them leaving the field, they also turned and left the field. This time they did not stop at the grove to regroup. They departed from the hill and the valley and disappeared into the bush, going toward Walata. The battle of Futa was over.

Of five hundred Malinke, more than three hundred lay dead or dying. Of forty-one Bambara, twenty-eight lay dead or dying. Of one hundred men of Futa, only forty remained alive. One Bambara cried out, "We own the field." Numukeba answered, "No, death owns the field." They gathered up their dead companions and carried them back to the town. There was mourning in Futa. The women of the town washed the corpses and prepared them for burial. The next morning there were ceremonies for the dead and the corpses were buried. The ceremonies went on for four days. The Bambara who had come to serve with Ngoroni and Mamoye went to the battlefield and stripped the Malinke dead of their weapons and everything else of value. The townspeople gave them gifts of goats and cattle, and after that the Bambara departed.

Now, when Numukeba, Ngoroni and Mamoye came back from the field they went to the chief's house. People put down mats for them in the first antechamber. They rested. Women came and bathed their wounds and put ointment on them. They sat silently for a long while. At last Numukeba said to his sons, "You young men have earned honor for all time." They said, "And you, uncle, showed valor beyond the praises of djeli. Until today we did not know the true meaning of the word 'hero.'" Numukeba answered, "Ngoroni and Mamoye, you were my right hand and my left hand." They looked at him in wonder, saying, "How do you know our names? We did not tell you." Numukeba said, "I knew your names when I first saw you. Am I not Numukeba of Naradugu?" They stared at him. Ngoroni said, "Are you truly my father?" And Mamoye said, "Are you truly my father?" Numukeba answered, "If Numukeba, the master blacksmith of Naradugu, was your father when you were born, then I am your father now."

Tears welled up Ngoroni's eyes, and also in Mamoye's eyes. In shame, they wiped them away. Numukeba said, "Aaaah, it does not matter. They are from your heart. Only tears on the battlefield are shameful, and I did not see any there." Ngoroni said, "My father, I felt something drawing us together, but I did not expect you to have a white beard and white hair." Numukeba said, "My time in the bush was hard on me." Mamoye said, "My father, now we will return to Naradugu together. This was the purpose of our journey. Some people said to us, 'It is pointless to search. Too many years have passed. When he left, Numukeba said, "On the last day of the fourth year, stand on the roof of the house and look toward the bush. He whom you see coming will be alive. He whom you do not see coming will be dead." Therefore Numukeba has been lost in the bush forever.' But we did not believe these words. We began our search. And in one place and another we heard the djeli singing of the accomplishments of Numukeba of Naradugu. Therefore we continued searching." The wind blowing in Numukeba's heart was too much, and he turned his face away. At last he said, "Yes, my sons, we will go to Naradugu together."

16
Lokosa Dugu

THEY WERE ON THE ROAD THAT WOULD BRING them, in time, to Naradugu. As they travelled, Numukeba asked his sons about affairs in the town and the people he knew. They said, "So-and-so departed from the light of day. He was buried. So-and-so has grown old, he cannot cultivate his fields any longer. So-and-so has become wealthy, he has built a new wall around his house as if he were a great chief." Numukeba asked, "How are the heroes of Naradugu?" They said, "The heroes go here and there, they join in wars or they have single combats. Some went away and never returned; we do not know what happened to them. Some of their wives remain widows and their houses are in disrepair. Some of their wives have new husbands." Numukeba asked, "Are the granaries of Naradugu full?" The sons answered, "There have been good years and bad years, good crops and poor crops. If the rains come, all goes well. If they do not come, the granaries have empty bellies." Numukeba asked, "How are the blacksmiths and leatherworkers?" They said, "Things go on. Yet since you left, Naradugu is no longer famous for forging, and traders go to other towns to get their ironwork."

Numukeba struggled with the words, but at last they came, and he asked, "Your mother, Baniaba, how was the light taken from her?" Ngoroni, the elder son, said, "It happened on the road to Bassaba. In Bassaba is a cave inhabited by a hermit filelikela. Every month our mother went to this filelikela with a goat or a chicken and asked him to divine for her. She asked him, 'What can you divine about my husband, Numukeba? Is he alive? Is he well?' And the filelikela divined for her with kolas, saying, 'Yes, your husband is well. He has survived magical forces, he has survived battles, he has survived dangers of many kinds. His struggles have been great, his valor is spoken about in many cities, and he has earned honor after honor. This is what the kolas tell us.' But sometimes the filelikela said, 'Numukeba is in jeopardy, for he struggles against things that are larger and fiercer than humans, yet the kolas tell us that he has a force within him that will bring him victory.' Sometimes our mother returned home from Bassaba with a troubled heart, but she always said to us, 'Do not fear for your father. In time he will have no more obligations to fulfill, and then he will return to his house and be the centerpost of our life again.' It went on this way. Not one month passed without her going on a journey to the filelikela at Bassaba."

"Then," Ngoroni continued, "one day she was coming home from that place. She was tired from the journey, and she stopped to rest in a grove at the edge of the road. She sat in the shade of a lokosa tree. The spirit of the lokosa claimed her. He caused the roots of the lokosa to snap, and it fell on her. Thus our mother lost the light of life. When the news came to Naradugu, all her family went to get her. Twelve brothers, sisters and cousins went. Mamoye and I also went. We found her, we brought her home, we made sacrifices, we buried her."

Numukeba rode silently. Darkness filled him. He thought, "The knowledge is too much for me. She died because of her concern for my welfare. Had she not made the journey to Bassaba she would now be alive." He did not ask his sons any more questions. He did not speak. Though the sun was overhead, a blanket of blackness enveloped him.

They came to one village and another, sometimes stopping to eat and sleep, sometimes passing by. They hunted and killed an antelope. They dried the meat. They went on. Numukeba hardly spoke. His sons said, "He is too silent. A jackal gnaws in his belly." In time they arrived at a roadside market where women were selling chickens, corn, beans and peppers. Numukeba asked, "What is the name of the village we are approaching?" They answered, "Djurudu." He asked, "What kind of people live there?" They said, "Many kinds— Bambara, Malinke, Hausa." He asked, "Who is your chief?" An old woman answered, "We have no chief." Numukeba said, "Who governs? A village without a chief is a body without a head." The old woman said, "Yes, we are a body without a head, but we survive." Numukeba said to his sons, "Let us buy something." They dismounted. They bought millet cakes from the old woman.

While they were eating, she said to Numukeba, "I see that you are heroes." He said, "Aaaah, everyone is something." She said, "Where are you going?" He said, "We follow the road that leads us." She said, "My husband also was a hero. A long time ago he went to the wars in search of honor. Since then his name has never been heard again." Numukeba said, "Yes, Mother, sometimes it is that way." She said, "Perhaps honor is very heavy, and therefore he must ride slowly on his way home." And after a moment she asked, "I know the form of a yam, I know the shape of a goat, but what does honor look like?" Numukeba said, "It has no shape. It is perceived by the heart. It is outwardly invisible." She said, "Can it fill an empty belly or quench thirst? If not, then what good is it in this hard world?"

Numukeba reflected on the woman's difficult life. He said, "Mother, do not be impatient with your lost husband. One day he will come back with a great name, and the djeli will sing about his achievements. Perhaps he will have won many cattle and slaves in the wars. Perhaps he will bring gold and cowries." The old woman laughed, saying, "Ah, you men playing war all sing the same song. When he left my house I was young, and now I am old. What do I need with him now? If he is still alive, he also is old. He will not be able to work in the fields because his bones will protest. He will find other old men who have come back from somewhere, and they will sit in a special place, drink palm wine and boast, and after that they will divide a cow.

"When Ngoloma left my house he said he was going to Walata to fight in a battle against the Hausa and win for me a herd of cattle whose milk was superior to all other milk. Why did I need milk superior to all other milk? What he won at Walata I cannot say, but he went from there to Timbuktu, and from Timbuktu to Wagadugu, and from Wagadugu to Jenne. After that the bush swallowed him up." Numukeba answered, "Mother, perhaps he died in his struggle to achieve valor." She said, "Oh, valor. I have heard of it. Is it also invisible? One day I passed where a battle between heroes had taken place. I saw skeletons on the ground. Two skeletons lay facing each other. I looked at them and could not tell which was the more valorous or more honorable. I could not tell if they were Bambara or Wolof or Susu or Malinke."

Numukeba answered, "Yes, Mother, I also have pondered such things. When the two heroes you speak of met in the field they lost the key of life, but if they fought with courage and generosity they created something that cannot die." The old woman said, "What they created were wives without husbands and children without fathers. Perhaps my husband's name is sung by a djeli somewhere. Perhaps the djeli sings, 'Ngoloma of Djurudu is great, when the enemy saw him coming they quailed.' But what has greatness done for us? The enemy quailed and the house of Ngoloma lost its centerpost." She put another millet cake in Numukeba's hand, saying, "You, distinguished hero with the white beard, do you have a wife somewhere who makes millet cakes to sell to travellers at the roadside?"

Numukeba thought, "Aaaah, old woman, your spear pierces me!" He took a bag of cowries from its hiding place under his shirt and gave it to her. He said, "Mother, I did not know Ngoloma by name, though perhaps I saw him at Massina, or Kassala, or Boromala or some other place. If so, we may have fought on the same side or on opposite sides. It does not matter. We followed trails across the bush, we hunted to eat, we slept on rocky earth. Who knows, perhaps my horse nuzzled his in some town or village. We belong to the same brotherhood. Therefore I give you these cowries, not as charity but as a just gift from Ngoloma and his brothers. Do not say any more that something did not come back to you from the wilderness."

The old woman held the bag of cowries in her cupped hands. Words could not find their way from her mouth. Other market women gathered around her, asking questions. And as Numukeba, Ngoroni and Mamoye rode away they heard her say, "My husband, Ngoloma, sent me this gift from the bush."

As the sun slid down beyond the western rim of the world they came to the house of a Fula cattle herder. The herder was away in the bush with the cows, and his wife offered Numukeba, Ngoroni and Mamoye mats for the night in the room where her husband usually slept. She gave them bassi, made of millet flour, to eat. Ngoroni and Mamoye lay down and slept, but Numukeba sat enveloped in the dark mist that came from within him. He saw the woman sitting in the doorway to the adjoining room. He said, "Generous woman, because you have given us a place to rest does not mean that you should not sleep." She answered, "Noble guest, it is said that a woman should not sleep until her husband sleeps. With a guest it is the same. If you need anything, I will be here." Numukeba felt warm breezes blowing in his heart to hear a woman speaking in this way. He answered, "Yes, we Bambara say the same: 'A good wife never lets her husband find her sleeping.' Yet I may sit here until sunrise. So forget me."

The woman brought Numukeba a gourd of millet wine mixed with milk, and again she sat in the doorway. When, after a while, she saw that he would not sleep, she found household duties to perform. She put dried cattle dung on the fire and sterilized a butter bowl in its smoke. Numukeba thought, "So it was in Naradugu in the old days." At last he said to her, "Your husband has been treated well by the Architect." She answered, "Yes, he has many good cattle." He said, "I was not speaking of his cattle, but of his household." The woman put the bowl aside and went back to sit in the doorway.

For a while there was silence, then Numukeba asked, "Is there a good filelikela nearby?" She said, "Yes, at the edge of the hill near Soala there is a Muslim morike called Alef Ali." He asked, "Do people speak well of him?" She answered, "I have never consulted him. It is my husband who deals with the mystic sciences." Numukeba said, "Surely you know something." She said, "I know that he is a dwarf, and dwarfs have special powers." Numukeba said, "Aaaah." She went on, "I know that he is an albino, and albinos have special powers." Numukeba exclaimed again. She said, "I know that he comes from Timbuktu, where he studied the mysteries of the Koran. He divines in a hundred and one ways. He uses kolas, but they are albino kolas. He divines with a golden chain. He divines with shells, sand, water, knotted cords, smoke, air and fire. I have heard it said in the market that he sometimes mystically talks in the dark of night with other morikes in Timbuktu or Jenne." When he finished with the millet wine, Numukeba slept.

In the morning, the woman gave them bassi again. Numukeba had no cowries left, so he gave the woman a silver chain from around his neck. She refused, saying, "It is too much for small hospitality," but he pressed it on her. Then Numukeba and his sons departed, Ngoroni riding at his right side and Mamoye at his left. They approached the town of Soala, and when Numukeba saw the hill the Fula woman had spoken of, they turned off the road. They came to a house at the base of the hill. It was surrounded by a fence of thorny brush. The gate was closed, and Numukeba called out, "Master of mystic sciences, Alef Ali, we three are Numukeba, Ngoroni and Mamoye of Naradugu. I come for a divining. May we enter?"

Alef Ali came to the door of his house. His body was thick but he was no taller than a small child, and his skin was pinkish white. His chest was covered with a hundred leather talismans, small leather boxes containing sayings from the Koran. He wore a band of bells above each knee and the edge of his shirt was fringed with red threads. He emerged through the doorway carrying double cymbals made of brass, one part in each hand. Each half was composed of two large brass plates connected by a stick, and he struck the halves together rhythmically, creating piercing metallic sounds. He danced from one end of his courtyard to the other. When he stopped, the ringing of the metal continued to vibrate in the air.

He said, "You, Numukeba of Naradugu, enter. Your sons, as I perceive them to be, let them wait in the courtyard." They all dismounted, and Numukeba passed through the gate and entered the house. Alef Ali sat on a low stool and motioned Numukeba to sit on the bare earthen floor. He said, "The price of the divining is two black female goats and two hens." Numukeba said, "Master, I did not bring these things, but I will send my sons for them." He went to the door and instructed Ngoroni and Mamoye to go to the market and obtain what was required. Then he returned to his place. He said, "Master of the mystic sciences, I have been told of your great reputation. I am going on an expedition, and I need to know whatever you can tell me." The morike said, "Is it Timbuktu or beyond?" Numukeba answered, "Far beyond, though I do not know the direction." The morike asked, "What is the name of the place?" And Numukeba answered, "Lokosa Dugu, the city of all those who died under a falling lokosa tree."

The morike picked up a shell that slid up and down seemingly of its own will on a taut cord. He studied the risings and fallings of the shell. Then he said, "Yes, the sliding shell affirms it. Someone close to you has gone to Lokosa Dugu. But if you go there, nothing is certain. You may find her or not, and if you find her you may not recognize her, because everything is different in Lokosa Dugu. Even if you reach Lokosa Dugu, you might not be able to return to the outer world, because there are many dangers. What they are is not revealed. No living person has ever gone to that place and come back. That is what the sliding shell tells us." He arose from his stool and danced around the room with his clanging cymbals. After that he sat down again.

Numukeba said, "Master, I need to know more." Alef Ali scattered his white kolas on the floor and studied them. Numukeba asked, "What do they tell us?" The morike answered, "They say, 'The answer is to be found in smoke.'" Numukeba said, "I do not understand it." The morike unwrapped a long brass smoking pipe from a cloth covering. He put tobacco in the bowl and lighted it with an ember from the fireplace. He puffed until the tobacco was burning brightly. He began to draw on the pipe deeply, filling his lungs. He drew many times, taking in great quantities of smoke. His eyes closed. His body shuddered. He fell backwards and lay as if in a coma. Numukeba waited silently. Time passed. Still he waited. And when the sun had moved from one place to another in the sky, the morike sat up. He said, "The smoke speaks of a fertilized egg, no more."

He called to his wife to bring a fertilized egg. He received it and placed it on the ground, saying, "Now we must wait." They waited. They heard the sound of a chick pecking its way out of the shell. The chick appeared. For a moment it stood where it was, then it ran quickly to the wall and disappeared into a small hole. Numukeba asked, "Have we learned something?" The morike again danced around the room with his cymbals. And when the noise subsided, he said, "Yes, the egg tells us something. You will go eastward across the bush. You will find an ancient lokosa tree. In its side is an opening. Enter there. The mystic forces tell us nothing more. So now you may give them their payment." Numukeba said, "Thank you, Master, for what you have told me."

Ngoroni and Mamoye returned with the two black goats and the two white hens, and Numukeba gave them to the morike.

Then the three rode away, Ngoroni and Mamoye following their father eastward. The sons said, "Father, this is not the way to Naradugu." Numukeba said, "A river bends, but it reaches its destination." They asked, "Where are we going?" He answered, "To Lokosa Dugu." They said, "We have never heard of it." Numukeba said, "It is the city ruled by the lokosa spirit. Every lokosa that grows from the earth is one of his fingers. He is malevolent. If an innocent person tries to shade himself under the leaves of a lokosa, the finger closes and the person is lost. In this way your mother was taken from the daylight. Before we return to Naradugu I want to see her. Perhaps I can bring her back."

The sons answered, "Father, how can you bring her back? She no longer belongs to the living." Numukeba said, "Who knows about it? Has anyone made the effort?" They said, "Father, there is a saying: 'Do not move things that are lying still.' You have earned honors beyond those of ordinary men. Every djeli knows your name and sings your accomplishments. The credits you have earned would fill all the granaries of the kingdom of Segu."

Numukeba said, "My sons, I am not looking for honors or credits. What I am going to do is for myself. I left Baniaba behind, thinking, 'I will go out and find fields of honor and then I will come back to Naradugu and our lives will go on.' I thought, 'When I return, I will teach my sons everything to be known about smelting and forging. I will teach them to be valiant. I will teach them the arts of hunting. I will make them masters of iron and all other metals.' It seemed to me that it would be this way. I found fields of honor. I made journeys below the river and the earth. I contended with Etchuba of the Red Powder. But while I was confronting these things, time slipped invisibly through my hands and I lost Baniaba, your mother. I took many lives in great battles, but I would give all my victories back if I knew that she was still waiting for me in Naradugu. My achievements do nothing to make my heart feel good, and when the djeli sing praise songs to me their words are bitter to my ears."

Ngoroni said, "My father, nothing you can do will ever wipe from the universe your valorous achievements. The djeli do not tell only of your valorous accomplishments, but also of your generosity. They speak of wrongs made right, of gifts of freedom you made to slaves, and of ten thousand cattle you distributed among the people. The lokosa tree took our mother out of jealousy. We miss her, but everyone dies and people mourn for them. Do not add to our mourning by going to Lokosa Dugu, from where you may never return. We would have neither mother nor father, and all our searching would have been useless."

Ngoroni's plea sounded eloquent in Numukeba's heart. He said, "My sons, I must try. If I come back safely, you will see me. If you do not see me coming, then you will go on and be heroes in your turn. Whatever happens, it was written long ago by the Great Composer. I do not expect to go to Lokosa Dugu and remain there. But I need one special weapon to take with me. Therefore let us find a village with a forge." They rode on, and in time they found such a village. Numukeba went to the blacksmith and said, "Master of iron, lend me the use of your fire and anvil stone, for there is something I have to make. Because I have no gold or cowries with me, I will give you a day of forging in exchange." The blacksmith, who was old and tired, said, "Yes, forge for me. I need twenty hoes and twenty bush knives."

Numukeba forged. He made twenty hoes and twenty bush knives before the sun went down. The old blacksmith could not believe what he saw. He said, "Honorable personage, I did not believe you would finish in five days. It is clear that you are a master of masters in the kingdom of iron. Take whatever you need from the forging shed. Everything is yours. Do what you want." Numukeba slept, and in the morning he began his work. He forged a bar of iron in the shape of a cow's leg bone. Over that he laid another layer of iron. And over the second layer he laid another. He melted his horse's silver breast shield and made a silver layer to cover his iron bar. He burnished the silver and attached to the bar three talismans from his right arm. He hung the strange weapon from his waistband, saying, "It is done."

They went riding again, still to the east, and Numukeba scanned the landscape on every side looking for an ancient lokosa tree. They found one lokosa and then another, but none of them was the one he sought. On the fifth day he found it standing in a grove of acacias. It was very tall and very thick. On one side was a rotted opening barely large enough to admit the body of a man. Numukeba said to his sons, "Here is where I will enter. Where it will take me I cannot tell you. Hunt and feed yourselves. Camp here by the tree. Wait four days. If I do not come back on the fourth day, say to yourselves, 'It appears that our father is not coming.' If I do not return on the fifth day, say to yourselves, 'It is more certain that our father is not coming.' If I do not return on the sixth day, mount your horses and ride to Segu. Tell the king you are my sons, and that I have sent you to serve in his court."

Numukeba dismounted. With his spear, his gun, his cutlass and the new silver-covered weapon he had made, he squeezed through the opening in the tree. When his eyes became accustomed to the dim light he saw that he was in a room like the anteroom of a chief's house. There was a door. He opened it and passed through. Outside it was like the bush in the world from which he had come. There was a trail, which he followed. Up above, a sun shone as in the world of the living, but its light was pale and cast no shadows.

He journeyed. From time to time he glanced at the sun to

measure the advancing of the day, but he saw that the sun was fixed in the sky and did not move. He thought, "I promised Ngoroni and Mamoye I would return in four days, or five or six, but if the sun remains motionless here, how will I know when the time has come?" He went on. He arrived at the bank of a river, but the water did not run one way or another, it remained still. He found a raftsman sleeping by his raft. He wakened him, saying, "Take me across. I am going to Lokosa Dugu." The raftsman said, "Aaaah, another kinsman has arrived. I will take you over, but the payment is ten cowries." Numukeba said, "I have no cowries." The raftsman said, "Very well, I will take your hunting talismans." Numukeba gave him the talismans. The raftsman began to pole his raft. Numukeba asked, "Uncle, why did you call me your kinsman?" The man answered, "Why all those taken by the lokosa spirit are related." Numukeba said, "No, I was not taken by the lokosa spirit. I come because I choose to." The raftsman exclaimed. He said, "That is not possible. Who would come of his own choice?" Numukeba answered, "I am one who comes from the kingdom of the living." The man ceased poling. He said, "Only a madman would do such a thing." Numukeba said, "Then I am mad. Keep poling."

Again the raft began to move. The man said, "In what way do you think Lokosa Dugu is a better place than the kingdom of the living that you would make such a journey?" Numukeba answered, "I do not think it better. I want to find my wife who was killed by a lokosa tree." The man said, "It is a worthless journey. How will you find her? And if you do, will you recognize her? She is not the same as when you knew her in the other world. Still, I see that you are a hero, and a hero may do what other men do not consider possible. But Lokosa Dugu is not merely on the further bank of the river. The trail goes on and on, and it is full of dangers for anyone who does not have a right to be here." Numukeba asked, "What dangers are there exceeding those of the other world?" The man answered, "Why, there are giant buffalo, giant rhino and fierce hawks. There are warriors in the form of lokosa trees and quicksand across the trail. There are monsters such as never seen by the living." Numukeba said, "Pole on, raftsman, so that I may get to the other side."

When the raft touched the further bank, Numukeba stepped ashore. The raftsman said, "One moment, you hero from the outer world. Because you had no cowries you gave me your hunting talismans. You will need the talismans, therefore I give them back to you." Numukeba answered, "Raftsman, I thank you. Because of your generosity I know now that there are not only monsters here but human virtues also. When I come back, give me a message for your family, wherever they are, and I will deliver it."

He resumed walking. He came to a still stream. The water was not running either way. He prepared to drink, but a huge rhino appeared from behind a large termite hill and confronted him. The rhino spoke threateningly, saying, "You, alien, why are you here and what do you want?" Numukeba said, "I am Numukeba of Naradugu. I do not wish to harm you, so stand away while I drink and move on." The rhino said, "You are not a lokosa person. Go back before I kill you." Numukeba said, "You of the fine nose horns, surely you are a noble hero of your own kind. Does a hero kill without honorable reasons?" The rhino answered, "I see a rhino horn on your vest of mail. That is my honorable reason. Therefore I will kill you and wear your skull around my neck."

The rhino charged, but Numukeba sprang to one side. The rhino wheeled swiftly and charged again. Once more Numukeba sprang aside, but the rhino's shoulder brushed against him and knocked him to the ground. He arose and took the gun from his back. He said, "You of the fine two horns, you of the three strong toes, you of the smooth grey hide, you of the small red eyes, great though you are in the bush, you are no match for man the hunter. Where are your talismans? Where are your magic weapons? Let things be. I will pass. If you try to prevent me I will kill you and take your tail for my trophy." While he was talking to the rhino, Numukeba loaded his gun with powder and bullets. The rhino pawed the earth and put his head down. He charged once more. Numukeba fired into the rhino's breast and sprang aside. The rhino passed him. This time it did not wheel about, but went running at a high speed into the bush. It stopped. It stood uncertainly, then fell to the ground. Numukeba went to where it was lying and cut off its tail with his cutlass. He drank at the stream and continued his way.

Farther along the trail a gigantic buffalo came out of a grove and stood in his path. It said, "Alien, I am guardian of the path to Lokosa Dugu. No one goes this way except lokosa people. Turn back or die." Numukeba said, "You of the wide fierce horns, I do not mean to harm you. Therefore allow me to pass without a battle. My gun is already loaded with mystic powder and ball." The buffalo said, "I see you are a hero. I see the rhino tail you carry. I also am a hero. Can one hero stand aside when another confronts him?" Numukeba said, "Heroes can show valor, but they can also reason together. There is no purpose in our fighting. Therefore look the other way and I will go where I have to go." The buffalo said, "Your words have no meaning," and he charged at Numukeba with his great horns. Numukeba killed him and took his tail. He continued on the trail with two tails hanging from his waist.

The trail led to a bog that would not sustain his weight. He threw a stone ahead of him. It sank instantly. He threw a tree branch. It disappeared at once. He threw a feather. It went down like the others. Numukeba sat at the edge of the bog and pondered. And after a long while he drew his cutlass. Holding it with both hands, he pointed it across the bog. He closed his eyes and called on the force of the sun and the forge to help him. His cutlass became red as if it were in the blacksmith's fire. It became blue, then white, then red again. A stream of light shot out from its point and crossed the bog. The bog began to steam. It became dry and hard. When the red light faded, Numukeba sheathed his cutlass and walked across solid earth. He reached the other side. He went on. Fierce hawks attacked him and he cut them down.

He came to a plain where one hundred lokosa trees barred his way. He said, "You who guard the way to the city, you cannot prevent me from entering. I am Numukeba of Naradugu. I have killed the rhino, the buffalo and the hawks, and I walked across the deadly bog. I do not come to hurt you. Spread yourselves a little so that I may pass through." The lokosas answered, "No one passes here." Numukeba said, "I hear that Lokosa Dugu has people from many places. I hear that there are Malinke, Bambara, Hausa, and many others. Why do you object if one more comes?" A lokosa said, "No one comes to this place except those already chosen." Numukeba said, "My wife Baniaba from Naradugu, is one of the chosen. I come only to speak with her." The lokosa answered, "Such things are impossible. Go back quickly the way you came." Numukeba said, "In the words from your own mouth, it is impossible." The lokosa said, "Then you must die on the spot and become a lokosa person."

The trees drew long bush knives from scabbards across their chests. They moved toward Numukeba, having no roots in the earth. They surrounded him, and suddenly it seemed as if he was in a dense forest. He fired his gun, but it accomplished nothing. He threw his spear, but it accomplished nothing. They crowded him closely, and he slashed with his cutlass, but it accomplished nothing. They leaned over him, shutting out the dim light of the sky, and made creaking sounds like bending trees. Numukeba grasped the new weapon he had forged and struck the trunk of the nearest lokosa. The tree groaned and shattered, falling to the earth in splinters. He struck again and another tree splintered, falling in small pieces as though it were kindling. As the trees threw themselves at him, Numukeba struck swiftly in all directions, and one after another they died. He killed twenty, he killed forty, he killed eighty, he killed one hundred. The place where it happened became a great hill of shattered wood.

Numukeba took up his gun and loaded it. He hung his silver-coated battle weapon at his waist along with the tails of the rhino and the buffalo. He followed the trail into Lokosa Dugu. It was a walled city that looked much like Massina or Naradugu. People were moving back and forth in the streets. The sound of pestles and mortars came from the houseyards. He smelled untanned hides in the yards of leatherworkers, and the metallic smoke from a blacksmith's forge. Chickens pecked for grain along the fences, and dogs lay sleeping. The only thing that seemed different was that no person or object cast a shadow.

He approached a woman with a load of firewood on her head, saying, "Mother, why does nothing have a shadow in this place?" She answered, "Can shadows have shadows?" He said, "I am a stranger here. Explain things to me. Are you saying that everything I see is a shadow?" She answered, "Yes, except for you. Obviously you are from the other side, for your shadow follows you." He said, "Mother, where can I find the house of the chief of Lokosa Dugu?" She said, "At the far end of the city, in the walled compound." He went to the gate of the compound. The guard looked at Numukeba's shadow. He said, "Who are you? How did you get here? What do you want?" Numukeba answered, "Tell your chief that Numukeba of Naradugu wants to speak with him." The guard went in, then returned. He said, "The chief is sitting in his courtyard. You may go in."

Numukeba entered. The chief was sitting on his stool beneath the branches of a lokosa tree as if it provided shade, holding a brass staff in his hand. Many strands of beads hung around his neck, and on his fingers and toes were large brass rings. His djeli stood at his side. The djeli questioned Numukeba sharply, asking, "Who are you? Where do you come from? How did you find your way here? What do you want in Lokosa Dugu? Why do you wish to consult with the chief?" Numukeba said, "Chief of Lokosa Dugu, I am Numukeba of Naradugu. The nobles of Naradugu greet you. The farmers of Naradugu greet you. The women of Naradugu greet you. The slaves of Naradugu greet you. From my name, you know I am a blacksmith, but I have spent many years in the bush seeking honor and proving my valor. And while I was away, all the while believing my family was safe, your finger clasped my wife and took her away from the land of the living." The chief answered, through the mouth of his djeli, "Yes, this is the way of all life. The finger flexes, unflexes and flexes again."

Numukeba said, "Great chief, how did my wife Baniaba offend you that you took her?" The chief answered, "Why, she did not offend me in any way. She merely sat under the lokosa tree." Numukeba said, "She was young, she was beautiful, she had small children whom she had to leave behind. Do such things matter to you in any way?" The chief answered, "Why should they matter? All things are born to die. Babies die on their mother's backs. Hunters die in the hunt. Heroes die on the battlefield. Women die in childbirth. Farmers in the field are struck by lightning. People die of hunger, thirst or disease. In the world from which you come, floods kill, poison kills, spears kill, magic and mystery kill. Soninke kill Fula, Fula kill Bambara, Bambara kill Malinke, Malinke kill Hausa, Hausa kill Nupe. All is a sameness, except in the manner of death. If your wife died of smallpox, would you go someplace seeking her? If she died in a burning grove, would you go someplace seeking her? If she died at the claws of a leopard, would you go someplace seeking her? There is only one certainty in the universe, death. Do not make an issue of it."

Numukeba said, "Aaaah, great chief, I hear you, but death is only the end of life, not the meaning of life. The Great Composer writes the destiny of all people. Whether he writes perfectly or imperfectly, it is certain that he draws a road for every person to follow. If only a person's death is important, the Composer is merely playing a useless game. I cannot accept it." The chief answered, "Why, yes, there is the Composer. Some call him the Architect, some call him the Caster. But here, in Lokosa Dugu, we know him as the Moulder. The place where he works has many baskets filled with clay, and each basket is marked 'drowning,' or 'smallpox,' or 'lightning,' or 'fire,' or 'leprosy,' or 'thirst,' or 'starvation,' or 'lokosa,' or something else. The Moulder is very hurried. And when he must conceive a destiny he takes a little clay from one basket or another and moulds it and puts it aside to dry. Thus the Moulder endows people with some manner of death. If it turns out to be a falling lokosa tree, why should anyone complain?"

Numukeba said, "No, great chief, in this matter you are wrong. Man comes from darkness and goes again to darkness, and if it were not for the brief light between the beginning and the end, the universe would be nothing but an everlasting darkness without a moon, a sun, or meaning. It is what happens from birth to death that counts. Therefore people have families and care for them. Therefore people have friends and value them. Therefore men go to fight as heroes in honorable causes and give luster to their names. What you tell me, I cannot accept it. Your words are as false as those of Etchuba of the Red Powder."

The chief said, "Aaaah, do not provoke me any further. Your wife Baniaba lost the key of life. She will always remain here. Go back to the place from which you came and be patient. You yourself will die of one thing or another, according to the basket from which your clay was taken." Numukeba said, "Let me see my wife. I want to speak with her." The chief pushed his djeli aside. Angry words came from his mouth. He said, "You, small man, you affront me. You come from a place that is only a granary of living things that must die. Yet you speak as if you command. Are you somehow greater than the king of Segu? Even the king of Segu will disappear into darkness. Are you greater than the men

of mystic sciences in Timbuktu? Even they will fall into the well
that has no bottom. Tell me no more what to do. Go back to the
other side where you came from and wait your turn. In time we
will meet again."

Numukeba said, "I came with a purpose. I killed the rhino, the
buffalo, the hawks, and your warrior trees, and I crossed your
impassable bog." He threw the buffalo and rhino tails on the
ground. He went on, "You who sit on the chief's stool, you are
not a true chief. You are not a true noble. You are only a collector
of bodies. You have power over helpless people, but a true chief
has valor, honor and compassion. You talk, but your words speak
only to each other and not to reasonable men. What purpose do
you serve in the world? The Architect designed the universe, but
the Architect is not perfect. He slept for a moment, his mind
wandered, and thus, somehow, you came into being. You sit with
imperious dignity in human form. Become yourself. I, Numukeba of Naradugu, the only being in Lokosa Dugu with a shadow,
challenge you. If I live, I live. If I die, I die. But I will lance this
cyst that you call your city. Let my wife Baniaba hear me. The
mystery of time captured me in a net, and the mischief of Etchuba of the Red Powder twisted my road. But you, ruler of Lokosa Dugu, are the worst predator of all. Therefore take up your
weapons. Let us struggle."

The chief of Lokosa Dugu exclaimed, "Aaaah! Aaaah!" He
arose slowly from his stool. He grew in size until he became as
tall as his house. His features changed. His hair turned to tree
thorns. Long dangling roots emerged from his arms and legs.
Though a moment before he had two eyes, now he had eyes all
around his head. With his right hand he grasped a spiked war
club, and with his left hand he grasped a long bush knife. He
towered in the air, standing high above Numukeba. He said,
"Numukeba, once you were a hero in that other place on the
other side. Now you will feel terror. Now you will grovel. Now
you will cry out in pain. Here all things are different." Numukeba answered, "You are only a tree who imagines himself to be a
man. Fight or be silent."

The monster came forward. Numukeba fired his gun, but it
accomplished nothing. He launched his spear, but it accomplished nothing. He struck with his cutlass, but it shattered. He
grasped his burnished weapon made of three layers of steel and
one of silver. The monster struck with his bush knife, but Numukeba fended off the blow. Then Numukeba struck with his
burnished weapon. The monster shuddered but did not fall. Numukeba struck again, and again the monster shuddered but did
not fall. They exchanged mighty blows and the sound of metal on
metal vibrated from one end of the city to the other. They grap-
pled. The lokosa monster seized Numukeba and threw him

down, making a deep depression in the hard earth. Numukeba arose. He seized the lokosa monster and threw him down, making a deeper depression in the earth. The monster arose. Dust hovered above them like the smoke of a great brush fire. They went on fighting. Numukeba felt the strength of his legs slowly seeping away. His weapon became heavier and heavier in his hand.

Now, at the ancient lokosa tree where Numukeba had left the living world, Ngoroni and Mamoye were waiting. It was the fourth day, though Numukeba perceived it as less than a single day in Lokosa Dugu. Ngoroni said, "When our father left us he said, 'If I do not return on the fourth day, say to yourselves, "It appears that our father is not coming."' I do not see him. Therefore things must be difficult for him." Mamoye said, "Still, he said to wait a fifth day and a sixth." Ngoroni said, "The sixth day may be too late. The fifth day may be too late. Let us follow him. He may need us." Mamoye said, "Yes, let us follow him."

They entered the hollow tree and saw they were in a room with a door. They passed through the door and followed the trail. They came to the river that did not flow in any direction. The raftsman was there with his raft, and they asked, "Did Numukeba of Naradugu come this way?" The raftsman answered, "A noble hero with a vest of mail crossed the river four days ago. I warned him of great dangers, but he did not listen. For payment he gave me his hunter's talismans, but I would not accept them." They said, "Raftsman, take us across." He poled them to the other side. They offered him something for payment, but he refused to take anything. He said, "You young men resemble the hero with the white beard." They answered, "Yes, he is our father."

They followed the trail. They found the carcass of the great rhino and saw that its tail had been severed. They said, "Our father passed this way." They found the carcass of the great buffalo and saw that its tail had been severed. They said, "Our father passed this way." They found the carcasses of many fierce hawks. They said, "Our father passed this way." They crossed the dangerous bog, which now was dry. They came to the gate of Lokosa Dugu, and they heard the sound of a great battle inside. They entered. They saw people running back and forth in the streets. They stopped a boy and asked him, "What is happening?" He answered, "A stranger with a shadow is fighting the owner of the city." They went on, and came to the chief's compound. They saw their father, with blood running from many wounds, in combat with the monster. Each son said to himself, "When before has anyone seen anything like this? The monster is tall as a house. He has roots growing from his legs and arms. He has eyes all around his head. Our father, who is large, seems very small. Now I understand the meaning of being a hero." To each other they said,

"Let us go to our father's side." They drew their weapons and went forward. Ngoroni stood at Numukeba's right hand, Mamoye stood at Numukeba's left. They fought.

When Numukeba saw Ngoroni and Mamoye, his ebbing strength returned. He thought, "These, my sons, must survive." He fought harder than before. His sons thought, "Let us not shame our father." They fought fiercely and received many wounds. The lokosa monster weakened. His blows became sluggish. He breathed heavily. His eyes were red. Finally he stood still, his arms hanging limply at his sides. Then a strange thing happened. A bird came flying from the sky and alighted on the lokosa monster's head. The weight was too much for him, and he fell to the ground. He lay without moving. People said, "He has gone into the well without a bottom. Now his son will become chief."

Numukeba said, "I want to see my wife, Baniaba of Naradugu." People answered, "Yes, we will find her. Meanwhile, come and rest in the guest house." They escorted Numukeba and his sons to the rest house. They put down fresh mats for them, and while the three men lay and rested, Numukeba looked at his son Ngoroni, saying, "You have earned honor beyond honor. When my right hand became tired, you became my right hand." He looked at his son Mamoye, saying, "You have earned honor beyond honor. When my left hand became tired you became my left hand." They said, "Father, we have heard of valorous heroes, but when we saw you fighting alone against the lokosa monster we learned the true meaning of valor."

They became quiet, for their injuries were many. They only spoke within themselves, each saying, "The pain is nothing. If my blood stains the mat, let it stain." Then a woman came to the door. It was Baniaba. She brought water in a calabash and washed their wounds. She treated their wounds with tree butter and bound them up. She went out and returned with food and palm wine, which she placed before them. She sat on the earthen floor near Numukeba. He watched her without speaking, until at last he said, "Aaaah, Baniaba, is it really you?" She answered, "Yes, my husband." He said, "Baniaba, Baniaba! I never expected to see you again. Now we will return to Naradugu together. Every morning I awoke from my sleep thinking, 'If I ever return home, will my life be worth living without Baniaba? It would be better to lose my key of life in the bush.' I went from one place to another. I found honor upon honor, but all the honor together did not weigh as much as the name Baniaba."

Numukeba went on, "When my sons told me how you died, I said, 'I will go to Lokosa Dugu to find Baniaba. If the dangers are too great and I die in that place, that will be better than not having her.' Therefore I came. And my good sons, Ngoroni and Mamoye, followed me and kept me from going into darkness. The

Architect has written well for me. Prepare yourself for the journey, Baniaba. When our wounds have healed a little, we will go."

Baniaba answered, "My husband, I would go anywhere with you if I could. But I can never leave Lokosa Dugu. Those who die cannot return again among the living." Numukeba said, "Whatever the Architect has written, surely he did not write, 'Baniaba may never live again in the house from which she was stolen.' Let us prepare ourselves. In four days we will leave." Baniaba looked silently at the ground. Then she said, "If my husband asks, I will try to do even what is impossible. I will prepare for the journey."

Numukeba, Ngoroni and Mamoye rested three days. Baniaba tended their wounds and prepared their food. She sat with them in the guest house and talked. On the fourth day they departed from the city. They came to the place where Numukeba had fought the warrior trees. They came to the place where he had fought the hawks. They came to the place of the fight with the great buffalo. They came to the place of the fight with the great rhino. At last they arrived at the river which did not flow one way or another. Numukeba called to the raftsman, saying, "We are here. Take us across." The raftsman brought his raft. He said, "Great heroes, if I were a djeli I would compose a song celebrating your accomplishment. But I am only a simple man and I cannot play the ngoni. All I can do is pole my raft from one bank to the other." He saw that Baniaba had no shadow. He said, "I will take you across, but I know that the woman will not be able to go with you."

Numukeba said, "Yes, she is coming with us. Here are the hunting talismans that you would not accept when I first arrived. Take them, they are yours. I also pledged to carry a message to your family. Tell me who they are and what I am to say." The raftsman said, "I am Sako of the family of Agada which lives in the village of Silla. I came here long ago, and now only my grandchildren and great-grandchildren are alive. Tell them I send greetings from Lokosa Dugu. Remind them that but for me they would not have come into the world. Tell them to spill a little wine on the earth and put a bowl of food aside for me during every harvest festival. In this way I will know that my name has not vanished from their minds." Numukeba said, "Raftsman, Sako Agada of Silla, I will bring them the message."

The raftsman began to pole across the river. Ngoroni said, "Father, it seems that our mother is growing dim." Numukeba looked at Baniaba and saw that she was growing dim. Halfway across the river, Mamoye said, "Father, indeed our mother is fading." Numukeba saw that Baniaba was fading. When the raft came to the far bank, Baniaba was not there at all. The raftsman said to Numukeba, "It is not your fault. Those without shadows cannot cross over."

Numukeba sat on the ground. Darkness closed him in. He did not move. He did not speak. Ngoroni and Mamoye respected his privacy. They sat nearby in silence. But at last Ngoroni said, "Father, let us continue our journey." Numukeba answered, "My sons, go on without me. I will stay here and grow roots in the earth. Everything has been for nothing. The universe is merely an empty space." Ngoroni said, "We have seen our mother, you have seen your wife. It is something to remember. But we ourselves are alive. Let us go on living. You have two sons who were given to you by our mother, Baniaba. We will try to help you make life worth something to you."

Numukeba was ashamed. He stood up, saying, "My son, I hear you. Let us go." They went along the trail and arrived at the room contained in the ancient lokosa tree. They entered, then emerged through the hole in the tree into the outer world. The bright sunlight warmed Numukeba. He felt whole again. He said, "Let us find our horses." They searched, following hoofmarks on the ground. They found their horses grazing together in a small valley between two hills. They mounted. They rode toward Naradugu.

17
Diero of
Kaurula

THEY JOURNEYED, THE WHITE-BEARDED NU-
mukeba and his sons Ngoroni and Mamoye.
They followed roads and trails, they made new trails across the
bush, they crossed rivers, they rode relentlessly toward Naradugu, yet their reputation rode on ahead of them. In every town
through which they passed, bards took up their ngonis and composed praise songs for them. Every village blacksmith held out a
hammer to Numukeba, saying, "Master of blacksmiths, strike my
anvil three times so I may tell my children you once labored
here."

They came within sight of Naradugu. Ngoroni and Mamoye
said, "Father, wait for a brief moment. We want to go and announce that you are returning." Ngoroni and Mamoye went into
the center of the town, calling out, "Numukeba is coming, the
one you believed to have been devoured by the bush!" Women
stopped pounding their pestles. Leatherworkers put down their
hides. Farmers came in from the fields. People went up to their
housetops and looked across the walls of Naradugu. When they
saw Numukeba sitting on his horse, they trilled their voices, and
the trilling hovered like a cloud of music over the town. Drummers went out drumming a welcome. Trumpeters played their
war horns. Heroes galloped out on their horses firing guns in the
air. The bards of Naradugu went out with their ngonis and koras.
The paramount djeli sang:

"Who is the master of the forge?
He is Numukeba of Naradugu.

What has he forged to be remembered?
He has forged iron, valor and honor.
He went into the world alone,
From Boromala to Walata,
From Jenne to Massina,
From Torigudu to Segu,
From Futa to Lokosa Dugu.
His deeds make Naradugu immortal.
The lands outside the walls are his.
Every house within the town is his.
All the wine is his and all the cowries are his.
Whatever Numukeba wants is his.
Who are the sons of the master of the forge?
Ngoroni the elder and Mamoye the younger.
They are Numukeba's right hand and his left hand.
Thus we call Ngoroni the Cutlass Hand.
Thus we call Mamoye the Spear Hand.
May the house of Numukeba stand forever,
May his descendents populate the land."

The bards and heroes formed a procession to lead Numukeba into the town. As he entered the gate, he saw Etchuba sitting there, not in the form of an infant but in the familiar form of an old blind man. Numukeba called out, "You, Owner of the Red Powder, you are too late. My long journey is finished." Etchuba answered, "Aaaah, Numukeba, I have already forgotten you. Are there not other people in the world?"

Numukeba rode to his house and dismounted. His servants and slaves greeted him, saying, "Master, we knew you would return. Therefore we watched from the housetop every day." Numukeba answered, "I thank you. It was your watching that guided me home." He went first to his forging shed. People who accompanied him said to one another, "Are my eyes lying? It seems that the cold forge is beginning to glow." Numukeba stood in the shed for a while, looking at his tongs, his hammer, his bellows, his pile of smelting sand and the stack of wood that would fuel the forge. Each thing was in its proper place. He said to his slaves, "Because you have taken care of my forging shed, I know that you truly expected me to come back." They said, "Yes, Master, we knew it."

Numukeba said, "I no longer consider you to be my slaves, but good friends. Just as I gave Malike his freedom in the early days of my journey, I now give you your freedom to do as you choose and go where you want. If you wish to stay with me, live on in your houses. If you perform services for me, I will buy them with livestock or cowries." They answered, "Master, we are your family. Do not send us away." He said, "I do not send you anywhere.

The choice is yours. I give you fields from my land, I give you cows, I give you goats. Take these things and flourish. Henceforth if any man calls you slave, defend yourself. Tell him, 'Every noble is part slave, and every slave is part noble. Whoever challenges these words, let him bring his complaints to Numukeba who spoke them.' "

He went into his house. There, also, everything was in its place. He went into Baniaba's room. He said to himself, "Baniaba was my good wife, but she no longer casts a shadow. I will find a new good wife and live on." His servants brought him a calabash of water and helped him bathe. He put on fresh clothing. He lay on his mat and rested. Ngoroni and Mamoye also bathed and rested, lying on mats next to Numukeba's. All through the day, until the sun went down, people of Naradugu stood outside Numukeba's house clapping their hands and singing praise songs. They spoke of Numukeba's deeds and the deeds of Ngoroni and Mamoye. They sang:

> "Who is the lion of lions?
> He is Numukeba of Naradugu.
> Who are the young lions?
> They are Ngoroni and Mamoye.
> They asked, 'Where is our father?'
> People said, 'Aaaah, he was born to die in the bush.'
> They asked the djeli, 'Where is our father?'
> He said, 'Aaaah, he was born to die in the bush.'
> They asked the morike, 'Where is our father?'
> He said, 'Aaaah, he was born to die in the bush.'
> They asked the filelikela, 'Where is our father?'
> He said, 'Aaaah, he was born to die in the bush.'
> They said, 'No, your words are worthless.
> We will go into the world and find him.'
> The young lions journeyed.
> They found evil in the world, they found good in the
>   world.
> They found their father, the lion of lions.
> They earned honor together.
> They came home together."

When morning dawned, Numukeba went to his forging shed. He lighted the fire. He heated iron bars. He began to forge. People said, "Numukeba, come to the marketplace so people can see you." He answered, "Not now. I must forge." Heroes said, "Numukeba, come to the terrace. We are dividing the Cow of Heroes." He answered, "Not now. I must forge." A messenger from the chief said, "Numukeba, come to the chief's court. He wants to greet you." Numukeba answered, "Not now. I must forge." He forged all day and into the night, calling out to his helpers, "Bring more wood, put more wind in the fire." They brought more wood and they worked the bellows without stopping. The next day was the same, and the third day and the fourth. Then he was finished.

The forging was not crude, as if it were a hoe. It was finer than the forging of a cutlass. It was more delicate than the forging of a king's staff. What Numukeba had made was the figure of an antelope with two heads, one facing forward and one turned toward the rear. People came and stood outside the shed, admiring the antelope. They said to Numukeba, "It is a beautiful antelope. Never before have we seen an iron antelope with such perfect form. But the two heads, what do they mean?" Numukeba answered, "One head faces the road that must be travelled, meaning, 'I do not know what awaits me, but I will not hesitate.' The other looks backward at the road that has been travelled, meaning, 'I will never forget where I have been and what I have learned.'" They said, "Aaaah, it is a proverb forged in iron." As darkness fell, the iron antelope glowed red, and the luminescence filled the forging shed.

In the morning, Numukeba sent for eight carriers. He instructed them, "Carry this forging to the city of Segu. Bring it to the house of the king's filelikela. Say to him, 'Numukeba of Naradugu greets you. This is the thing he pledged when you divined for him. He promised you a forging such as no man has ever seen before.' Say that Numukeba thanks him for helping to find his sons, Ngoroni and Mamoye." The carriers wrapped the iron antelope in straw. They suspended it with ropes from two long poles, and four men to a pole they lifted it and began the long journey to Segu.

Numukeba bathed and dressed. He put on his vest of mail and his talismans. He hung his gun on his back and his cutlass across his chest. He took up his spear and mounted his horse, the djibedjan given to him by the king of Segu, and rode to the compound of the chief. The chief received him, saying, "Numukeba, you have been slow in coming." Numukeba answered, "Forgive me. I have been slow in coming only because my journey was not finished until I had made a forging for the paramount filelikela of Segu. I pledged it. It was he who told me where I could find my sons."

The chief said, "You have been to many places and done great deeds. All the djeli speak of it. Contemplate on things. Perhaps you are now too large in the minds of men to fit within the walls of Naradugu. You are a bright star in the sky, but a star is invisible when the sun shines, and at night no star is bright as the moon." Numukeba answered, "Chief of Naradugu, do not think of it any more. I am not too large to fit within my house and forging shed. You are the one who casts light over the town. As you cast light for others, you cast light for me. Had I wanted to rule a town, I would have done so and I would not be here now."

The chief said, "I hear you, Numukeba. When the key of life is lost for me, one of my sons will become the father of Naradugu. Pledge that you will support him." Numukeba answered, "Chief, I pledge it." The chief said, "That is good. If you forge for the king of Segu, that is good. If you forge for the king of Kaarta, that is good. But you will always forge for me and my family, and you will cast our gold, silver and brass." Numukeba said, "Yes, I pledge it."

He went then to the place where the heroes drank wine and made their boasts. When they saw Numukeba coming, they rose to greet him. They said, "Numukeba, because you could not come, we postponed the sharing of the Cow of Heroes." They called a slave to bring the cow, and he did so. They said, "Numukeba, we are not going to kill this cow, because we relinquish our shares to you. The head is yours, the breast is yours, the right foreleg is yours, the left foreleg is yours, the right hind quarter is yours, the left hind quarter is yours. Every part of this cow belongs to you because of everything you have done." To the slave they said, "Take the cow to Numukeba's place and leave it there." Numukeba said, "I thank you, but you applaud me too much, because all of us here are equal."

They sat together and gave Numukeba a cup of wine. He looked from face to face but did not see any face he knew. None of those assembled on the terrace was his own age, and some were scarcely older than his sons. He asked, "Where is Madiminko?" They answered, "He went away. He fought valiantly at Massina, and there he lost the key of life." He asked, "Where is Toto?" They said, "He went out and displayed his valor everywhere, but the night came for him when he fought against the heroes of Gao." He asked, "Where is Tiekele?" They answered, "He went out. He left a trail of victories in many places, but he did not come back." He asked, "Where is Bakore?" They said, "He performed great deeds in the country of the Mossi, he performed great deeds in the country of the Hausa, he performed great deeds in the country of the Songhai, but there he went down into the sea of darkness." Numukeba asked no more about the heroes he had known.

The men said, "Numukeba, you are paramount among the living heroes of Naradugu. Tell us about your victories." Numukeba said, "When the time comes, I will speak of such things, but now I will listen to you." The young men took turns describing battles against towns and cities, victories over enemy warriors, and the capture of cattle. Sometimes a man would stand up, his wine cup in his hand, and depict the thrusting of a spear, the stroke of a battle-ax, or the slashing of a cutlass.

When they had drunk many cups of wine, their boasts became the dreams of storytellers. A man who had fought somewhere against a hero as valiant as himself now remembered battling twenty at a time, and before the rendition was ended the number was a hundred or a thousand. Another who had met his opponent in the middle of a brook recalled the brook as a wide river, and remembered that they had fought submerged beneath the water. And they also projected their thoughts into the future, one saying that single-handed he would conquer the city of Kaarta, another responding that he would subdue the Seven Cities of the Soninke, another saying that if his name were to be mentioned in Segu, the king and his counsellors would take refuge in their houses.

At last they turned to Numukeba. They said to him, "You, about whom all the songs are sung, if you are not ready to speak of your many accomplishments, give us at least some hints and fragments." Numukeba replied, "Young men, I do not doubt your courage and performance. Naradugu is fortunate to have brave men like you to protect it from its enemies. But because I was born before you, and you after me, you have not yet had time to experience everything that I have. If I tell you one thing or another you will not believe it." They answered, "Yes, Numukeba, yes, we will believe."

Numukeba said, "Then listen. I, whom the djeli speak of as the lion, one day I was captured by an old woman who made me her slave. She made me dig roots for her and tend her fire. And after a while she sold me to the Hausa, and I became their slave. In Katsina I was sold to a merchant named Kano Musa, and after that I was sold to the chief of Gusau, and after that to the chief of Ansongo." The heroes exclaimed together, "Aaaah!" Numukeba went on, "But even before that time, I was captured by Fula and thrown into a prison in Massina, and there also I was forced to be a slave." They exclaimed, "Aaaah!" Numukeba continued, "If you wish to hear more, listen. Once I was transformed into a wild dog, and I lived as wild dogs live. If I came to a village, the children drove me away with stones, and I slept in a hollow tree."

The men protested, saying, "Numukeba, you mock us. Have we treated you with any disrespect that you should tell such tales? These are not the deeds of great heroes. These are not the deeds that djeli speak of in their praise songs. What you tell us diminishes what we confided to one another here on the heroes' terrace."

Numukeba said, "I do not intend to make sport of anything I heard from you. I am speaking as if I were alone in my house, talking to myself. Yes, I have done one thing and another which the djeli have put in their songs. But whatever I have done, I have done, and when it was done I was finished with it because the story was finished. A thing that has been accomplished takes on a life of its own as if another man had done it. If I speak of it with my own mouth, it becomes smaller. Let good comrades speak of it if they are still among the living. Let the djeli make their songs about it if they wish. But a courageous deed that is performed is meaningful only when it is being done, because that is the moment when destiny, honor, courage, the power of talismans, the dust of accident, and all the invisible elements of the surrounding universe come together."

He paused. The heroes were silent. He continued, "Did I achieve a certain victory because of my virtue? Or because it was written by the Architect? Because of the force of the sun in my steel? Because of the talismans given to me by a morike or filelikela? Or perhaps because there was a fault in the character of my opponent? Who am I, then, to say, 'I alone, Numukeba of Naradugu, created such-and-such a heroic story'? I did not bring cattle herds, cowries, gold or slaves back from my long wanderings. I brought only questions, and here on the heroes' terrace I give them to you." Still the heroes were silent. Numukeba looked across the landscape, the questions showing in his eyes. He set down his wine cup, arose and mounted his horse. As he rode away, a young man said, "His beard is too white. The great Numukeba is growing old." Another said, "No, it cannot be so. When we boast of killing a thousand men or fighting under water, those boasts come out of our wine cups. A great hero who has done something notable does not have to dwell on it. Have we not all heard the proverb?

> 'The dog that chased the chickens barks loudly of his valor.
> The bull buffalo that impaled the leopard grazes quietly.' "

In the days that followed, Numukeba worked long hours at his forge. First he made the figure of a man sitting on a raft, his head bowed and his eyes closed. When it was finished he gave a messenger instructions to take it to the village of Silla for the family of Agado Sako, the raftsman who had ferried him across the river in his journey to Lokosa Dugu. He said, "Tell them that Numukeba of Naradugu sends it. Tell them that Numukeba brings a message from their ancestor, Sako. Repeat to them Sako's words: 'Remember me at every harvest festival, because if it were not for me you would not have come into the world.' " Numukeba brought out from the vault of his mind the names of other men and women in distant places who had been generous to him and to whom he had made pledges. To some he sent the work of his forge, to some, cattle, to some, cowries.

When all these things were done, he made weapons and hoes, handles for tools, and woodcarvings for the chief. He made stirrups and breastplates for horses, and brass paraphernalia for the earth and sky priests. Traders came again from far-off places to acquire Numukeba's metalwork. It was not then the custom of craftsmen to put their signatures on the things they crafted, but people began to notice that every object made by Numukeba's hand had a certain mark forged into it. They said among themselves, "It must be a mystic force, a talisman. Perhaps it is what gives Numukeba's iron its great strength and power." They asked him about it one day, and he said, "Does it not resemble an ngoni?" They said, "Yes, now that you mention the word, it looks like an ngoni." Numukeba said, "It is the mark of Ndala." And they asked, "Who, then, is Ndala that he should be immortalized in your forgings?"

Numukeba answered, "Ndala of Boromala. He was only a small boy, but he was a master of the ngoni. I have heard the bards of chiefs and kings, but never did I hear anyone who excelled Ndala. The music in his ngoni came from the stars, the clouds and the wind, for he had no teacher. And the words that came from his mouth were not mere praisings of one person or another, but truths that grown men did not dare to speak. In Boromala I took him and made him my djeli. But a treacherous chief named Nianga ordered his soldiers to kill us. We defended ourselves, Ndala, a small boy, fighting like a seasoned hero of Segu. I survived because it was my fate to live on, but Ndala fell. He was my djeli. Now I am his djeli. My hammer is my ngoni. Each time I make this mark on my forgings I am singing a praise song to Ndala." People exclaimed, "Aaaah! Ndala of Boromala. His name will be remembered!"

Numukeba hardly left his forge except to eat and sleep. He sent his assistants to the bush to dig smelting sand. He sent them out for wood for his fire. One man would work the bellows until he was tired, then another would replace him. While one forging was cooling, Numukeba forged another. And although his metalwork was distinguished in former days, now it was finer than ever before. If a hero saw a certain weapon in far off Walata or Massina he would recognize it as the creation of Numukeba and envy its owner. But Numukeba's friends said to him, "Do not work so hard. There is no need for it. You have cattle enough. You have cowries enough. You have gold enough. Rest a little and share in some of the pleasures around you."

He answered, "Nearly twelve years I was away from my forge. Though I am not yet an old man, my beard and my hair are already white. The art of the forge was my birth payment, therefore I bring iron into being out of the sands of the earth. My years were not lost years, for I gained knowledge, which now gives my forgings greater vitality than they had before."

His friends said to him, "Numukeba, what could you have learned while fighting battles that would make your iron better?" And he replied, "Why, it is too much to explain to you. I learned the suffering of being blind. I learned the suffering of being a slave. I learned that victory over a good man does not bring lasting pleasure to the heart, and that hearing the djeli sing of it can bring pain. I learned that going on one expedition after another makes a hero a slave to the filelikelas who must always be consulted. I learned that no matter how many talismans a man wears, he is his own most certain talisman. I learned that a kind deed by a poor woman in a nameless village weighs as much in the universe as a hero giving away a thousand cattle he has taken in war."

His friends answered, "Your learnings are great, Numukeba. Yet how do they help to forge perfect iron?" He said, "I cannot tell you, only to say that my eyes perceive what they did not perceive in former days, and that my fingers sense the forces that flow beneath the outer skin of iron." They said, "That is good, Numukeba. Still, you are lacking something. When you go to your mat at night, does your forge caress you? Does your forge bring you warm water and help you bathe? Does your forge bring you bassi to eat in the morning? Does it bring you guibara to drink when you are thirsty? When you cannot sleep, does your forge sing to you in a sweet voice? When you have something in your heart that you cannot speak of even to friends, do you confide in your forge in the silence of the night?"

Numukeba said, "My good friends, you speak well because you wish me well. When I returned from the bush, I said to myself, 'Baniaba is gone and she can never return. Therefore I will find another good wife and go on living.' But in the darkness I still saw her face, and in my dreams I heard her voice. I was not ready, therefore I did nothing. But now I am ready. There is a young woman of the family of Diabi. I will communicate with her people. If they agree, I will have her for my wife." His friends said, "That is good. Let the chief's djeli speak for you, because his wife also comes from the Diabi family."

So Numukeba approached the djeli with his request. He said, "In the Soninke city of Kaurula is a branch of the Diabi family which has a daughter named Diero. I want this young woman for my wife. Go to Kaurula, speak for me to her parents. If they are willing, discuss the settlement in all its details so that there will be no misunderstanding. For your services I will be generous whether you succeed or not." The djeli answered, "Yes, I will do it for you." The djeli made ready for his journey and departed. The distance to Kaurula was great. It was six weeks before he returned.

He went to Numukeba's house in the evening, and they sat and drank honey water together. He said, "I went to Kaurula. I found the people of the Diabi family. I saw their daughter, Diero. She is a beautiful young woman. Her skin glistens in the sunlight like brass. She is graceful in every way. Her family listened carefully to what I told them. I said, 'Numukeba of Naradugu, the hero whose name you know, sent me to ask for Diero.' Though they knew your name, they asked, 'What is there to commend him?' I said, 'Surely you do not need to ask. His reputation is great in Segu, in Kaarta, in Timbuktu, in Gao, in Katsina, in Jenne and Massina. His trail in search of great accomplishments led him through the country of the Bambara, the Malinke, the Bozo, the Hausa, the Fula and the Wolof. Everywhere he has been he has performed deeds to be remembered.' They said, 'Aaaah,' as if they were hearing it for the first time. They wanted more. I said, 'There is no place between the desert and the sea where djeli do not recite his history. And even had he never wielded a weapon, still he would be famous for the craft of his forge. If you know a hero here in Kaurula, ask him what he would give for a weapon made by Numukeba of Naradugu.' "

The djeli went on: "They listened, but they wanted to hear more. I said, 'Numukeba is not a person who has become poor while pursuing his achievements. He has lands, he has cattle, and his granaries are always full. Everyone respects him.' They asked, 'Does Numukeba have other wives?' I assured them that Diero would be your senior wife even if you should ever take others. They asked, 'Will his marriage settlement be generous?' I replied that you are generous in every way. They said, 'Let us consider it a little.' I returned in three days. They said, 'We acknowledge Numukeba to be a person of great achievements. We have never heard anything said against him. Still, he belongs to the numu caste and is not a noble. Our family discussed everything, and they decided that Diero ought to have a noble for a husband.'

"I said, 'Aaaah, you people! Are you not able to see that Numukeba is as noble as anyone in the Diabi family? You pride yourselves too much because you are related to chiefs and kings. A person can wander in rags and own nothing and still be called a noble. A person can be cruel and ungenerous and still be called a noble. A person can be without honor or valor and still be called a noble. A person can swear oaths and break them and still be called a noble. Though Numukeba is a blacksmith by birth, no noble has ever questioned his right to a place among the highest of the freeborn, and his name is a caste in itself.' I told them what you are willing to give as a marriage settlement. They did not answer, but I looked at Diero and saw that she had no hesitation. I left it there. I returned home. Let us wait a little. The matter is not ended." Numukeba said to the djeli, "You did well. Let us wait."

On the fourth day following the djeli's return, a boy came to Numukeba's shed to tell him a four-man canoe had arrived with a young woman named Diero, who was waiting for him at the river. Numukeba bathed hurriedly and dressed. He went to the riverbank. He saw Diero standing with her personal servant girl near the edge of the water. He said to her, "Aaaah, Diero, I did not think you would be coming like this. I did not know whether your family agreed." Diero said, "No, my family did not agree. I protested, saying I wanted to have Numukeba for my husband. My father and his brothers exchanged loud words which filled the air like feathers. My father said to me, 'My daughter, tell us you object to marrying Numukeba and then the discussion will come to an end.'

"I spoke softly to my father and mother. I said, 'Numerous young men came and asked for me, but you did not want them because of one thing or another. Of one you said, 'His family is not highly regarded.' Of another you said, 'He is a trader. We do not want a trader for a son-in-law.' Of another you said, 'He comes from the leatherworker caste.' Of another you said, 'What has he ever done that makes him distinguished?' And I asked my father and mother why they did not want me to have a husband. They said, 'We want you to have a husband from the Traore family.' I said, 'Who of the Traore family has asked for me?' They said, 'Be patient, he will come.'

"I said to them, 'I do not wish to wait for him.' They said, 'A husband from the Traore family will have great standing in the world, and your children will be under the protection of the king of Segu himself. You will have many slaves. You will have your own cattle. You will be respected.' I said to them, 'I know the history of Numukeba. Who has not heard it from the mouths of the djeli? He does not lack anything that would not mean good for my life. If he is rich he is rich, but if he is poor I will not complain. If he is descended from great families it will be that way, but if he is not, I will not complain. I accept Numukeba as my husband.' My father's words became loud and angry. He said, 'Since what day has a young girl's decisions prevailed over her father's?' He sent me away.

"In the night I went to my mother. I said, 'Help me.' She arranged everything. She hired paddlers and a canoe. She prepared provisions for the journey. She prepared clothing for me. In the morning I carried gourds and calabashes to the river as if to wash them. I left them in the rushes. I found the canoe and entered it. The paddlers brought me here."

Numukeba watched her lips all the time she was speaking. He listened to her as if he were hearing a young woman's voice for the first time. He said, "Thank you for coming, even though you stood against your father. If the Diabi family should raise twenty thousand horsemen and come to get you, I will not give you up. You will be my wife even if the great blue calabash of the sky should crack and fall upon my head." He took her to his house. He gave her a room for herself.

There was a ceremony. Diero became his wife. They lay together on his mat and she became a woman. She soothed his forehead with caresses of her hand. She sang softly to him until he slept. When day arrived she brought him warm water to bathe. She made bassi for him to eat. Numukeba said, "My life is worth living."

Even though Diero's family had rejected him, Numukeba assembled a marriage payment to send them. He sent many fine cows, many fine goats, many bars of copper and iron, and many baskets of grain. In Kaurula, Diero's parents received the marriage payment. They did not speak of an expedition against Numukeba. They said, "Who can doubt it? Our son-in-law is a worthy man." They sent for the djeli of the Diabi family. He stood in front of their house with his ngoni and sang of great and heroic feats accomplished by their son-in-law, Numukeba of Naradugu.

18
The Message
from Gao

DIERO CONCEIVED A CHILD. AND AFTER IT WAS made known to Numukeba, he sent for his sons, Ngoroni and Mamoye. They sat together around a fire, and Numukeba said, to them: "When I was in the bush I thought of you as small children waiting for your father to return. And though I meant to come home in four years, as I had pledged to the heroes of Naradugu, there were mysteries in the bush which multiplied each year by three, and so it was nearly twelve years before I saw you again. But the eleventh year was a generous gift from the bush spirits, because you were looking for me and I was looking for you and we met on the road to Walata.

"When I saw that my beard had turned from black to white I hurried and tried not to let anything turn me aside. I thought 'My two sons are my posterity, and through them the life within me will pass on from one generation to the next. Yet I have neglected them, and they grow into manhood without my being there to counsel them. I have not yet explained to them the mysteries of the forge. The forge is more than it appears, and while some men learn to understand the force that flows within iron, others can only stand and watch with their mouths open.'

"And I thought, 'I have neglected to reveal to my sons the art of the hunt. Though others may show them how to follow the tracks of game and throw a spear, only I can make them aware of the living substance of the bush. Whether a feather floats upward or downward has its meaning. Whether there is dust on one leaf and not another has its meaning. Whether the wind blows or is quiet has its meaning. Whether one bird calls or another calls has its meaning. The bush speaks to us. Who will reveal these things to my sons?'

"I thought, 'Here in the wilderness I have learned that a man's mind may penetrate the largest tree, and the living spirit of the hardest rock may penetrate the mind of man. Each thing lying at random has its life force. Therefore one should not disturb everything he sees. The forces within things communicate with one another, and in this way there comes a unity in the universe. I must return home, for my sons are four years older, and there is still time to share with them the knowledge I have gained.' Yet those years were multiplied by three, and now that we are together again you are no longer boys but men.

"What then is left for me to give you? Land is here, cattle are here, and you can have them. But you have already reached beyond land and cattle. Already in your youthful manhood you have gone into the wilderness, performed acts of honor and courage, and begun to perceive how one thing contends against another. You will become restless here. You have brought me home with you, and now you think, 'What we have done is done. What is next for us?' But it will not be enough to wander in the wilderness, merely looking for things that happen. Everything should have purpose and order.

"When I was in Segu, King Da Monzon welcomed me, and as a gift he gave me his djibedjan. We spoke of you, for whom I was searching. I told him that when you were ready I would send you to serve him alongside the other heroes of his court. And Da Monzon said, 'Yes, send them, I will welcome them with honor.' However, you are men, and though you are my sons I can no longer say, 'Do this' or 'Do that.' If you prefer fields and cattle, I give them to you. If you prefer to serve with the king of Segu, doing whatever courageous deeds he needs you to do, make yourselves ready." His son Ngoroni answered, "Father, I want to serve with the heroes of Segu." Mamoye answered, "Father, I too want to serve with the heroes of Segu." Numukeba said, "Yes, in my heart I knew you would say it that way."

He paused, looking into the fire. He said, "In your pursuit of valor, let it not be merely the striking of steel on steel and the vanquishing of enemies. The struggle is also to comprehend the universe. Each of you received his birth payment, a gift given to you by the Architect when you were born. Each of you has a destiny, and though you had the same father and mother, your destinies are not the same. What your destiny is you will know only with the passage of time. Yet why do I speak of time? I do not truly understand its mystery. For me, four years became nearly twelve, though how it happened I cannot explain.

"Your destiny is your road, the beginning and the end of your journey, and the forces within you will take you from one event to another. What lies between the beginning and the end is full of mysteries. The road itself sometimes seems to disappear, though you will find it again. Sometimes the person you believe yourself to be is transformed into a different kind of person, perhaps into an animal of the bush, or even into a rock or tree. Is it the mischief-maker Etchuba in his eternal feud against the Architect, or is it a flaw in the words the Architect has written? Perhaps you will never know. Whatever happens, remember who you are. If by chance you become a buffalo, remind yourself, 'I may have the form of a buffalo but I am forever Ngoroni' or 'I am forever Mamoye.' And while you have the form of a buffalo, learn what the heart of the buffalo feels, make it a part of your understanding of the universe. And remember that to win at war you must have good weapons, good talismans, skill, intelligence and the knowledge that the Architect gave you a place in the world.

"If Etchuba of the Red Powder cajoles you to believe that things in the universe are merely dust and thistledown riding randomly on the wind, deny him. The gift given by the Architect contains everything that matters, like a deep well of fresh water. My sons, each of you must draw on his own well. Be honorable in confrontations with other heroes. Be confident of yourselves even in the presence of kings. Be generous with those who are poorer or weaker than yourselves. Be strong and valiant against those who are stronger than you. Do not sing your own praise songs, for you will be depriving the djeli of their vocation. I have said enough. The night is not long enough to tell you more. So prepare yourselves for your journey."

Ngoroni and Mamoye prepared themselves. They refurbished their weapons. They braided colored ribbons in their horses' manes and tails. They went to a filelikela and had talismans made to wear on their arms and around their necks. They put on new clothing. With their cutlasses across their chests, their guns hanging on their backs, and their spears in their hands, they departed from Naradugu riding toward the city of Segu. Numukeba watched from his rooftop until they became small in the distance and disappeared across the line where the bush met the sky. After that he went to his forging shed to smelt sand into iron and shape iron into steel.

Sunrise followed sunrise, and the seasons came one after another. Numukeba rebuilt his house, supervised the cultivation of his fields, and presided over the Festival of Hoes and the circumcision of boys becoming men. Blacksmiths came from distant towns and cities to consult him and watch him work.

One morning a djeli named Seku Mori arrived from Gao. He asked at the town gate where he could find the hero Numukeba, and he was led to Numukeba's house by a group of shouting boys, each seeking to be recognized as the paramount guide. The djeli introduced himself, saying "All of Gao sends greetings to the Lion of Naradugu." Numukeba answered, "The days of the lion are past. I am a blacksmith now, as I was in the beginning. Come into the house and rest." They entered, they sat on fresh mats, and Diero brought them a drink of warm milk and honey. They talked for a while of Seku Mori's journey, and at last Numukeba asked, "Why have you come?"

The djeli answered, "The people of Gao sent me to ask you to help them. Gao is in danger." Numukeba said, "Aaaah, what is happening?" The djeli said, "A great expedition from Tekrur is on its way to destroy the city." Numukeba asked, "Why is it coming? What does Tekrur have in its heart against Gao?" The djeli said, "Who can tell? Tekrur says that Gao is not respectful enough of the Prophet of the Koran. It says that the nobles of Gao do not know who their fathers are. It says that the traders of Gao have cheated the people of Tekrur out of their gold and cowries. It says that Gao is too arrogant. It says the wives of the king of Gao are loathsome. It says that Gao obstructs the passage of canoes on the river and robs the canoemen by heavy taxes. It says that Gao conspires against other cities. It says all such things, so who can tell what its reasons are?"

Numukeba answered, "Gao has allies. It will surely defend itself." The djeli said, "The people are preparing for war. They will not give in to threats. But the army that is coming is vast. There are ten thousand Fula horsemen and ten thousand on foot, and they have been joined by five thousand Malinke sworn to avenge insults to the Prophet. The Fula are also assembling a fleet of one thousand canoes to attack the city from the river. The people of Gao have constructed moats, and two thousand fighters have come in from the villages. Every spear has been sharpened, every gun has been primed, and every cutlass has been given an edge. Yet the Fula expedition is so large that it leaves the countryside barren wherever it passes. Without more help Gao cannot survive."

Numukeba said, "The city should not wait for the invaders to arrive. It should go out and meet the expedition from Tekrur." The djeli answered, "Yes, it is so. We have consulted our best practitioners of the mystic sciences. They have divined with kolas, chains, sand and colored threads. Our morikes went into seclusion for four days, after which they told us this: 'Gao's forces must be divided into four separate armies, each under the command of a renowned hero. The armies must go out and strike the invaders from different directions before they reach the bend of the river. In this way the attack can be turned, and only in this way can Gao be preserved from destruction and pillage.' The king and the nobles of Gao have agreed on it."

Numukeba said, "Yes, it is a good plan. So why have you been sent to communicate with me?" Seku Mori replied, "We have four armies, but we have only three renowned heroes to lead them. We have a hero for the second army, a hero for the third, and a hero for the fourth. But we need you to lead the first army, which will attack the main body of the Fula." Numukeba exclaimed, "Aaaah! Aaaah! The days of the lion are over. I have already spent my time in the bush. I have had my expeditions. I have met my dangers. I have had my combats. I have suffered my wounds. Before I left Naradugu no one ever came to me saying, 'Numukeba, we need you to help save a city.' Now I have come back to Naradugu, and it is the same as it was in the beginning. I am a master blacksmith. That is the birth payment given to me by the Architect. My weapons are stored away in the thatch of my roof, and I will not take them down again. Good djeli, you must go elsewhere to find what you are looking for."

Seku Mori said, "Yes, I understand. I will rest a little and then return to Gao. Perhaps somewhere a renowned hero can be found." They sat silently, drinking from their gourds, until Numukeba asked, "The three heroes you have already found, what are their names?" And the djeli said, "They are Diallo of Gao, Dembo of Jenne, and Malike of Massina." Numukeba exclaimed, "Aaaah! Did I hear you say Malike of Massina?" The djeli answered, "Yes, those are the three." Numukeba did not speak again. He brooded. He arose and went out of the house. He walked through the town but did not see it. He walked in the open fields but did not see them. The sun was sliding down in the west, but he did not see it. When it was dark he returned to his house. Diero had lighted a lamp, and Seku Mori was still sitting on the mat.

Numukeba said, "For the sake of Gao I would not do it. For all of Kaarta I would not do it. For all of Segu I would not do it. But Malike is larger than Gao, Kaarta and Segu. He challenged the prestige of a king to defend me, fought by my side against men who wanted to destroy me, and delivered me from slavery. We are brothers beyond brothers. Therefore I will go back with you to Gao. As Malike pledged himself, I also pledge myself. Malike's fate, whether it is good or bad, is my fate. I will do what I expected never to do again. If I return to my forge, I return. If I do not return, how does it matter to the universe? Let us prepare. We will begin the journey in the morning."

Seku Mori slept, but Numukeba did not. He took his weapons from the thatch of his house. He honed the blades of his cutlass and spear. He cleaned his gun and refurbished his vest of mail. And after those things were done, he groomed his horse and braided colored ribbons into its hair. When daylight came, Diero brought them bassi to eat. Numukeba said to her, "I never thought to be away from you. But the kolas have been cast for me." He mounted his djibedjan. Seku Mori mounted. The two of them rode through the town. As they passed through the gate, Numukeba saw Etchuba sitting at the side of the road. Numukeba said to him, "Etchuba, do you never tire?" And Etchuba answered, "No, Numukeba, I am tireless."

Numukeba and the djeli of Gao rode into the bush, and they went across the line in the distance, where earth and sky meet, beyond which they could no longer be seen from the walls of Naradugu.

19
The Song of
Seku Mori

SEVEN WEEKS PASSED. ON THE MARKET DAY OF
the eighth week, a girl called out from her
rooftop, "Someone is coming." A guard went to the wall and
looked across the landscape. He shielded his eyes with his hand to
see better through the shimmering heat vapor of the early morning. He said, "Yes, slowly, slowly, a rider comes leading a riderless horse." The rider reached the gate and entered. He was Seku
Mori, the djeli of Gao, and the riderless horse was Numukeba's
djibedjan.

As Seku Mori went through the streets of Naradugu, people
put down whatever they were doing and followed him. He rode
to the house of the chief and dismounted. A crowd gathered behind him. The chief came out and sat under his tree, and all his
counsellors assembled and stood nearby.

Seku Mori took his kora from his back and tuned the strings.
He closed his eyes and began to play a wolosekoro, the poetic
form reserved for praise of great heroes and kings. And when the
tones of his kora became full and resonant, he began to sing:

"Djeli Seku Mori of Gao gives you this narration.
Do not think he merely uses old praises from other
    songs.
The voice you hear is his, but he did not create the
    poem.
It is a chronicle preserved in the heart of the kora
    itself.

The kora says, 'My heart is filled with what I saw,
Help me, Seku Mori, to bring forth my story.'

The great events happened beyond the bend of the
    river.
Five thousand men from Gao met the Fula invaders
    there.
The Fula from Tekrur came across the plain like
    locusts,
Ten thousand mounted and ten thousand on foot.
The sun reflecting from their cutlasses blinded Gao's
    horses.
The pounding hoofs of Fula horses made the earth
    tremble.
Gao's five thousand melted into Tekrur's twenty
    thousand
Like a rushing river melting into the sea.
Numukeba, the white-haired lion, led the heroes of
    Gao.
His weapons glowed, and he sent many Fula into
    darkness.
Fula heroes jostled trying to reach him with their
    spears,
Each wanted to be the one to strike Numukeba down.
Numukeba said, 'It is good if they come to me like
    this,
It spares my horse from pursuing them across the
    field.'
He struck with his cutlass to one side and the other,
And the enemy felt the steel Numukeba himself had
    forged.
The fighters of Tekrur were numerous and full of
    valor,
But death could not tell who was Fula and who was
    Gao.
Light faded for many men, and many horses lost their
    riders,
And the sun itself was shrouded by swirling dust.

Djeli Seku Mori of Gao gives you this story from his
    kora.
It is the kora's story, from the kora's heart it comes.
If there is a man who doubts what the kora tells us
Let him go to that place beyond the river's bend,
Let him cross the trampled bloody field and perceive it
    all,
For the bodies and broken weapons lie there still.

One for one and ten for ten the Gao and the Fula died,
And heroes rode back and forth seeking adversaries.
Then a breeze swept the dust cloud from the field,
And the Fula saw all the Gao gone but Numukeba.
A red glow surrounded him like a reflection from the
 forge.
In his right hand Numukeba gripped a broken cutlass.
In his left hand Numukeba gripped a spear without a
 blade.
The shafts of many arrows protruded from his breast,
The shafts of spears protruded from his sides,
Yet Numukeba sat erect and fierce on his djibedjan.
The Fula looked in wonder and withheld their
 weapons.
Upright in his saddle, Numukeba rode slowly forward.
The enemy parted and opened a path for him to ride.
He turned neither to the right nor left, went straight
 ahead.
He did not pause to pull the spearshafts from his body.
And when he had passed through the Fula horde he
 stopped.
His djibedjan stood proudly without moving.
Then the Fula from Tekrur raised their weapons above
 their heads.
They called out, 'Numukeba of Naradugu! Numukeba
 of Naradugu!'
The name Numukeba swept like a wave across the
 battlefield.
The Fula heroes now pressed close to where he sat,
Saying to him, 'Numukeba of Naradugu, lion of lions!'
Yet Numukeba did not acknowledge their greetings.
He merely sat on his horse gripping his broken
 weapons.
And then they saw he could not reply, for Numukeba
 was dead.

This song you have heard in the voice of Seku Mori
Is a wolosekoro composed by the kora itself.
It is not made of phrases sung in praise to other men.
It is the true story of Numukeba against heroes of
 Tekrur.
Numukeba was born, he lived out his life, he died.
May the song of my kora, like Numukeba's name, live
 on."